Audrey I

THE EXTRAORDINARY EDUCATION
OF NICHOLAS BENEDICT

by TRENTON LEE STEWART
illustrated by DIANA SUDYKA

Megan Tingley Books
LITTLE, BROWN AND COMPANY
New York   Boston

Little, Brown and Company

Hachette Book Group
237 Park Avenue, New York, NY 10017
Visit our website at www.lb-kids.com

Little, Brown and Company is a division of Hachette Book Group, Inc.
The Little, Brown name and logo are trademarks of Hachette Book Group, Inc.

The publisher is not responsible for websites (or their content)
that are not owned by the publisher.

First Edition: April 2012

Library of Congress Cataloging-in-Publication Data

Stewart, Trenton Lee.
The extraordinary education of Nicholas Benedict / by Trenton Lee
Stewart ; illustrated by Diana Sudyka. — 1st ed.
    p. cm.
"Megan Tingley Books."
Summary: Nine-year-old Nicholas Benedict, an orphan afflicted with an
unfortunate nose and with narcolepsy, is sent to a new orphanage where he
encounters vicious bullies, selfish adults, strange circumstances, and
a mystery that could change his life forever.
ISBN 978-0-316-17619-4
[1. Adventure and adventurers—Fiction. 2. Orphanages—Fiction.
3. Orphans—Fiction. 4. Narcolepsy—Fiction. 5. Bullies—Fiction.
6. Genius—Fiction. 7. Mystery and detective stories.] I. Sudyka,
Diana, ill. II. Title.
PZ7.S8513Ext 2012
[Fic]—dc23

                                                            2011031690

10 9 8 7 6 5 4 3 2 1

RRD-C

Printed in the United States of America

For Ben and Sam Hudson

Contents

A BEGINNING AT THE END

The train station at Pebbleton, dark and sooty though it was, glistened in the mist. Electric lamps above the platform cast their light upon a thousand reflecting surfaces: the puddles along the tracks, the streaked windows of the station house, the umbrellas hoisted over huddled, indistinct figures on the platform. To a person of whimsical mind, the scene might resemble something from a tale, a magical gathering in a dark wood, the umbrellas looming like toadstools over fairy folk.

There was, in fact, such a person watching from the

window of the approaching train, a boy of whimsical mind, to be sure (though whimsy was not the half of it, nor even the beginning), and the fairy-tale qualities of the scene occurred to him at once. So too did a great many other things, including the sentence "*It glistened in the mist; the train hissed, and I listened,*" a poetic train of thought that sounded rather like a train itself, which pleased him. But foremost in the boy's mind was the awareness that Pebbleton station was his stop—the end of his train journey, the beginning of a new unknown.

He turned to his chaperone, a plump old woman with spectacles so large the brim of her hat rested upon their frames. "What shall we call this, Mrs. Ferrier—an arrival or a departure?"

Mrs. Ferrier was putting away her knitting needles. "I suppose both, Nicholas. Or however you like." She clasped her bag and peered out the grimy window. "It's a miserable night for either."

"Shall I tell you what I'm thinking, Mrs. Ferrier?"

"Heavens no, Nicholas! That would take hours, and we have only moments. There, we've stopped."

The old woman turned from the window to appraise his appearance, despite having already done so before they boarded the train. Nicholas doubted he had changed much in the course of their half day's journey, and his reflection, easily seen in Mrs. Ferrier's enormous spectacles, proved him right: He was still a skinny, towheaded nine-year-old with threadbare clothes and an unfortunate nose. Indeed, his nose was so long and lumpy that it drew attention away from his one good feature—his bright and impish green eyes—though Mrs. Ferrier had often remarked that someday, should Nicholas come to require spectacles, his nose would do an admirable job holding them in place. It was always best to be positive, she told him.

"Well?" he asked as she studied him. "Do you think they'll take me? Or will they send me back and keep the money for their trouble?"

Mrs. Ferrier pursed her lips. "Please don't be saucy, Nicholas. I say this for your sake. It's nothing to *me* now, is it? Remember your manners, and make yourself useful around the orphanage. Start off on the right foot, and you'll be happier for it."

Nicholas feigned surprise. "Oh! You want me to be happy, Mrs. Ferrier?"

"Of course I do," puffed the old woman as she struggled to her feet. "I want everyone to be happy, don't I? Now follow me, and mind you don't step on the backs of my shoes."

Mrs. Ferrier and Nicholas were the only passengers to disembark the train. Several were boarding, however, and they crowded the aisles most inconveniently as they closed their umbrellas and removed their overcoats. By the time the old woman and her charge managed to descend the steps, the platform was empty save for one man in a somber gray suit and hat, standing rigidly beneath his umbrella. At the sight of them, he strode forward to shield Mrs. Ferrier with it. He was so tall that when he stood over Nicholas his face appeared mostly as a sharp, jutting chin and cavernous nostrils. His suit carried a faintly pleasant odor of pipe tobacco, which Nicholas liked, and the boy's initial impression was neutral until Mr. Collum, which was the man's name, introduced himself to Mrs. Ferrier and told Nicholas to run and fetch his trunk.

"There's no trunk to fetch, sir," said Nicholas, blinking in the mist (for he stood outside the umbrella's protection). "Only this suitcase. I'm Nicholas, sir. Nicholas Benedict." He held out his hand.

"No trunk?" said Mr. Collum, frowning. "Well, I daresay that's common enough, though I hadn't expected it. I haven't met a child at the station before, you see." He was speaking directly to Mrs. Ferrier and appeared not to have noticed Nicholas's outstretched hand. "I assumed directorship of the Manor only this spring, as I'm sure Mr. Cuckieu told you."

"The Manor?" said Mrs. Ferrier with a confused look.

"Forgive me," Mr. Collum said. "You must know the orphanage as Rothschild's End—or 'Child's End, as it is often abbreviated. In these parts, however, it is quite common to shorten the name still further, for ease of speaking, and to refer to the place simply as the Manor. The residence at 'Child's End is the only manor in the area, you see, so this leads to no confusion."

Nicholas began to ask a question, but though he spoke clearly and politely enough, Mr. Collum continued speaking to Mrs. Ferrier as if Nicholas hadn't uttered a word.

"Now, madam," Mr. Collum said, "allow me to accompany you inside the station house, where you can wait out of the damp. I would invite you to the Manor for refreshment, but I'm afraid it's quite a long ride from Pebbleton. Our kettle would hardly have begun to whistle before your train does—it's due to arrive at nine."

Nicholas and Mrs. Ferrier, who was trying not to look shattered at the prospect of waiting in the station house for two hours, followed Mr. Collum into a dim, drafty room with sawdust on the floor and benches along the walls. Near the ticket counter, the stationmaster was telling the train conductor about a wicked egg thief who had visited his barn the night before. The conductor, seeing that Mrs. Ferrier and Nicholas had disembarked at last, gestured at the clock, and the stationmaster accompanied him back out to the train, hurrying to finish his story. The newcomers were left alone with a red-haired man who sat on one of the benches, absorbed in a rain-spotted newspaper.

"May I just have a brief word with you, Mr. Collum?" asked Mrs. Ferrier. "A private word?"

"Of course," said Mr. Collum, who had yet to look directly at Nicholas but did seem aware of him, for he held up a finger to indicate that the boy should stay put. He drew Mrs. Ferrier over to the ticket counter, where they stood with their backs to the room and spoke in hushed voices.

Nicholas strained his ears but could not make out a word of their conversation, so he turned his attention to the red-haired newspaper reader. The man appeared to be of late middle age, perhaps a decade older than Mr. Collum. His tanned, rough hands suggested a different sort of labor from that which occupied the orphanage director (whose own pale fingers were carefully manicured and, excepting one inky smear, as clean as soap could make them). A faint impression in the man's hair suggested he'd been wearing a hat, though Nicholas saw none on the bench, nor any on the hat rack nearby. With some difficulty the man turned to a different section in his newspaper (the damp pages clung together) and resumed his reading, mouthing the words to himself. Nicholas, watching his lips, followed along for a tedious ten seconds

("...*impact on the price of wheat since the war's conclusion*...") before losing patience and interest.

He glanced at the schedule above the ticket counter. Mrs. Ferrier's nine o'clock train was just the fifth one of the day; it was also the last. Pebbleton, it seemed, was not quite on the way to anywhere. Nicholas stepped to the nearest window facing the street. At the curb sat an aged Studebaker with mud on its tires and steam rising from its hood. Beyond it Nicholas could see most of Pebbleton without moving his head. A handful of shops, a few market stalls closed down for the day, an occasional parked automobile. In the gloomy distance, a grain silo put Nicholas in mind of a lighthouse seen through fog. A glary smudge over the trees to the west was all the sunset the evening could muster.

Behind the station house, the train sounded its whistle. Nicholas perked up his ears, hoping the adults would raise their voices. Naturally he was curious to know what they were saying about him. But the clamor of the departing train was so overwhelming that Nicholas couldn't have heard them if they shouted. The windows rattled; the plank floors trembled. Then a ghostly reflection appeared in the window behind his own, and Nicholas turned to discover Mrs. Ferrier looking down on him with grave finality. Mr. Collum lingered at the ticket counter, checking his pocket watch against the station house clock.

For what would be the last time, the old woman and young boy regarded each other. They were compelled to wait for the train to finish leaving the station before attempting to speak, however, which gave Nicholas ample time to reflect upon the occasion. He had wondered what sort of expression

Mrs. Ferrier would put on for their parting, and now that the moment was at hand, he found it to be rather what he had expected: polite, businesslike, and almost comically serious. She was serious for his sake, he knew, in case he was afraid or sad. She was not much attached to Nicholas, perhaps because of his habitual impertinence—she thought him too saucy by far—but Mrs. Ferrier believed there was a way of doing things, and because she took comfort in this belief, she always made an effort.

She need not have bothered, at least not for Nicholas's sake. He was anything but sad. The last orphanage had been the worst yet, and he was glad to leave it. In fact, his time there had been so awful that before his departure he had secretly deposited sardines in many a tormentor's pillowcase, and had clicked his heels as he went out the door. No, he was far from sad, and though certainly nervous, he was not afraid, either. Or not *very* afraid, anyway. The Manor could hardly be worse than the last place, and there was always the chance it would be better.

The train's caboose had not yet cleared the station when the redheaded man rose, stretched, rearranged his newspaper, and exited the station house. Mr. Collum, meanwhile, had finished adjusting his watch and tucked it away. He went to the open door and paused. Glancing at Mrs. Ferrier, he touched his hat in what appeared to be a courteous farewell—though he might simply have been lowering its brim against the weather—and stepped outside with his umbrella. All of this had occurred as if in pantomime, with the train's rumbling, screeching, and clattering crowding out all other sound. When at last something like silence returned to the station house, Mrs. Ferrier laid a hand on the boy's shoulder.

"Nicholas, you know what you must do," she said.

"Oh yes, Mrs. Ferrier! I'm to carry my suitcase out to that Studebaker, and never mind the drizzle. I imagine I'll sit in the back while Mr. Collum rides in front with the driver."

Mrs. Ferrier blinked. "The driver?"

"Why, sure," said Nicholas with a shrug. "That red-haired man with the new hat."

"The red-haired man…" Straightening, Mrs. Ferrier looked out the window behind him. Her eyebrows rose in surprise. "Well, yes, you're correct, though it isn't at all what I was going to say. I was going to say…" She noticed the boy staring at her expectantly, the corners of his lips twitching as if he was suppressing a smile, and she sighed. "Oh, very well, Nicholas. Tell me how you knew all that. This will be my last opportunity to hear one of your exhausting explanations."

Nicholas grinned, raised his chin like a songbird preparing to sing, and throwing his arms out for emphasis, burst forth with an astonishing flurry of words: "Well, the hat *must* be new, don't you think? Otherwise he wouldn't have left it in the Studebaker to spare it getting wet. Which is a funny thing, in my opinion, since hats are meant to protect their owners and not the other way around. But I've known quite a lot of people who go to amazing trouble on behalf of their hats, haven't you, Mrs. Ferrier? I wonder what happened to his umbrella, though? Perhaps he lost it. Anyway, I do wish he'd left a section of the newspaper for me — to cover my head with, you know, as he did, to keep it dry."

"I'm sure he meant to," said the old woman after a

confused pause, "but only forgot." (This was the sort of thing Mrs. Ferrier always said in such cases, as part of her effort to be positive.) "But how did you know he was Mr. Collum's driver?"

Nicholas laughed. It was a squeaky, stuttering laugh, rather like the nickering of a pony. "I certainly doubt he's a passenger! The next train doesn't arrive for two hours, so it's not likely he was waiting for that, is it? Besides, he left when Mr. Collum did, and where else would he be going in this weather if not to that old Studebaker at the curb? It obviously just got here from somewhere out in the country—its engine is still hot and there's mud on the tires—and Mr. Collum said it's a long ride to the Manor. He did say *ride* rather than *drive*, you know, so I got the feeling he didn't intend to sit behind the wheel himself. Now, if there had been horses outside, especially a horse with an umbrella stand attached to it"—here Nicholas nickered again—"I might have come to a different..."

Mrs. Ferrier was shaking her head, a common enough response to everything Nicholas said that he would have continued his speech unabated had she not held up a hand to check him. He'd been about to explain half a dozen other reasons he'd come to this conclusion about the red-haired man, as well as several he hadn't consciously thought of yet but which were sure to occur to him as he spoke. But Nicholas was used to being shushed by Mrs. Ferrier, and at any rate he knew that delaying Mr. Collum would not serve him well. So he let the explanations go with a shrug, and waited for Mrs. Ferrier to proceed.

"Thank you, Nicholas. That will be more than enough to

make my poor head ache for the next two hours." Mrs. Ferrier cleared her throat. "And now this is goodbye. When I said that you know what you must do, I only meant to remind you to hold your tongue in check, and to make yourself useful. There, that's the last I'll say." She lifted his chin with her finger and looked once more into his eyes—a little wonderingly at first, as if she saw some mystery there she could never hope to fathom, and then with a different sort of expression Nicholas hadn't seen in her eyes before, something between sadness and exhaustion. She said, "I wish you better luck, child. Better luck than you've had. Now go on. Don't keep Mr. Collum waiting."

"*Au revoir* and *adios*, Mrs. Ferrier!" said Nicholas spryly, offering her an exaggerated military salute.

Mrs. Ferrier flinched and rubbed her temples, for Nicholas truly had given her a headache. Not for the first time she wondered how the boy could seem to know so much and yet so little. Here, at their final parting, he couldn't think of more suitable things to say? No best wishes, nor even a word of thanks? No, he only spun on his heels, grabbed his suitcase, and marched out into the next chapter of his life, a brash young soldier headed into a battle he felt certain of winning. He never even looked back.

Unlike her former young charge—now kicking the door closed behind him with a shocking bang—poor Mrs. Ferrier could *not* have thought of more suitable words for the occasion. Nicholas Benedict did have an exceptional gift for knowing things (more exceptional, in fact, than most adults would have thought possible), and yet not even he could know that this next chapter was to be the most unusual—and most important—of his entire childhood. Indeed, the strange days that lay ahead would change him forever, though for now they had less substance than the mist through which he ran.

Misery and joy. Discovery and danger. Mystery and treasure. For now, all were secrets waiting to be revealed.

For now, Nicholas Benedict was just a remarkable young orphan with secrets of his own, hastening to the Studebaker, where Mr. Collum sat in the front passenger seat looking impatient, and the red-haired driver was adjusting the rearview mirror, the better to admire his new hat.

Ledgers and Lies

The driver, Mr. Pileus, was a taciturn man. He spoke only when spoken to, and only if he absolutely must. He steered the old Studebaker with a focused, silent intensity, checking the mirrors so often he seemed afraid they might sneak away. Eventually Nicholas would learn that Mr. Pileus was not just the driver but the Manor's handyman, carpenter, and mechanic as well. He would learn this from others, though—certainly not from Mr. Pileus or Mr. Collum. At the moment, neither man seemed in any hurry to inform Nicholas about anything.

Mr. Collum, for his part, was busy paging through a

business ledger, evidently preoccupied with urgent matters of income and expenses. From time to time he would press a magnifying loupe against his left eye—not a monocle but an actual loupe, the powerful sort used by jewelers and clock-makers to show them the imperceptible flaws in a diamond or the tiny workings of a watch. Nicholas supposed he must be almost blind in that eye. Each time, after studying the page for several seconds, Mr. Collum would remove the loupe with a bemused grunt. This was the only sound he made, however.

Nicholas watched the dusky countryside glide past, miles of rolling farmland and forested hills, until it was too dark to see anything but fence posts. He climbed onto his knees to see into the front, where the Studebaker's illuminated dials and gauges drew his attention. He was instantly curious about their functions and inner workings; he'd always been drawn to devices and contraptions of any kind, though he was never allowed to touch them. He wondered if Mr. Collum would resent being asked to turn on the radio; or rather, he tried to convince himself that Mr. Collum would not, when he knew positively that Mr. Collum would.

It had grown too dark for Mr. Collum to study his ledger, and yet he had remained silent, apparently deep in thought, his eyes resting on a page it was no longer possible for him to read. Finally, however, he sighed, put away his ledger and loupe, and began to speak. He didn't turn in his seat but simply lifted his head so that his voice would carry. "Are you awake, Nicholas?"

"Wide awake, Mr. Collum! And I'm eager to—"

"Very good," said the orphanage director. "I was wondering, of course, because of your condition. I would not wish to waste time speaking if my words were not being attended. Tell me, Nicholas, how often do you sail off to sleep? Tomorrow the boys begin metalworking—during the summer we have a different skills activity each week—and naturally it would not do for you to fall asleep with some sharp implement in hand."

The silent Mr. Pileus shuddered, evidently horrified at the thought, and cast a fleeting, reproachful glance at Nicholas in the rearview mirror, as if Nicholas had already wounded himself, and furthermore had done so on purpose.

"That *would* be unfortunate, sir," said Nicholas, "but it's easy enough to avoid. When I have a drowsy spell—which is only every few hours or so—I can feel it coming on in time to lie down. And usually I wake up in a matter of minutes."

"Is that all?" Mr. Collum asked. "I got the impression from your Mr. Cuckieu that you often dropped off without warning—just fell to the floor as though your string had been clipped."

"Oh no, sir!" Nicholas protested. "Well, I suppose I did have a few spells like that when the symptoms were first setting in, but that was over a year ago. It never happens anymore."

"I am heartily glad to hear it," said Mr. Collum, and he did sound relieved. "Every member of our small staff has multiple duties, you see. The less bandaging and stitching our nurse is compelled to do, the more she is able to attend to other tasks. I'm sure you understand that. In fact"—here Mr. Collum turned in his seat to look back at Nicholas—"your chaperone, Mrs. Ferrier, seemed eager to convince me that there is little you do *not* understand. She thought I might find a boy of unusual intelligence to be especially useful at the Manor. Do you consider yourself unusually intelligent, Nicholas?"

Mr. Collum was studying him with narrowed eyes, clearly ready to judge his reply. Nicholas thought fast. A truthful answer would make him sound conceited. Also, Mr. Collum seemed irritated with Mrs. Ferrier, and Nicholas realized it would be wise to distance himself from her. "I'm sure I'm not the best judge of that, Mr. Collum, though I've been told that I'm bright."

"By Mrs. Ferrier, no doubt," said Mr. Collum with a slight shake of his head. "My own impression, Nicholas, was that she wished to give you an advantage. Under such circumstances, crafty matrons like Mrs. Ferrier will make all kinds of unsupported claims. They cannot be blamed, I'm sure, though it does try one's patience."

"I'm sure it must, sir," said Nicholas with an uncomfortable flutter in his belly, as if the Studebaker had just topped a hill at high speed. They were moving along a flat stretch of road, though, and quite slowly at that.

"However…" Mr. Collum scratched his sharp chin. "She was most adamant, your Mrs. Ferrier. She insisted you were the most intelligent person—*by far*—whom she had ever known in her many long years of life. 'More intelligent than yourself, madam?' I asked her, and I'm sorry to say, Nicholas, that she readily confirmed this, which did nothing to add credibility to her claim. I mean to say that if Mrs. Ferrier truly believes that a nine-year-old boy is more intelligent than she is, perhaps that is indeed the case. But if it *is* the case, you can see why I'm disinclined to trust Mrs. Ferrier's general opinion about intelligence. Do you follow my reasoning, Nicholas?"

"I think so, sir," Nicholas replied quietly.

"You think so," said Mr. Collum in a satisfied tone, as if Nicholas's reply had offered some proof of his suspicions. He turned to face forward again. "Exactly."

In the brief silence that followed, as Nicholas struggled to master his disappointment, the uncomfortable flutter in his belly worsened to a disagreeable churning, as if he had been forced to swallow something repulsive. His disappointment was awfully bitter. Nicholas had hoped to impress this new director—to amaze him, even, and win his favor. Though it had never exactly worked out that way before, this time Nicholas was older and had intended to benefit from his experience. He had never counted on Mrs. Ferrier trying to look out for him, if indeed that was what she'd been doing. Now Mr. Collum had formed his opinion and would resent having it changed. Nicholas had seen that happen before, with unpleasant results.

How should he proceed, then? He had plotted any number of different strategies (plotting strategies was the sort of thing Nicholas did when other children were playing jacks or Old Maid), but none seemed right under the circumstances, and he felt beset by uncertainties.

Only one thing was certain. No matter what, Nicholas would guard his secret—the awful secret, the one he had lied to Mr. Collum about—with every measure of wit he possessed: those unpredictable sleeping episodes, the attacks that struck without warning, dropping him from consciousness like a trapdoor into a black dungeon—oh no, Nicholas would never let on about *those*. For if ever word got out that strong emotions could do such a thing to him, that all it took to topple him was a too-hot flash of anger, a too-boisterous peal of laughter... well, after that there would be no end to the persecution.

Nicholas knew this from experience, unfortunately. At Littleview his condition had tempted even the mildest, most good-natured children to make sport of him, to make a regular game of upsetting him or getting him to laugh. (And those pranks, though horrible enough, were nothing compared to what the more vicious children had done.) Having endured such torments, he would have to be a fool to reveal his greatest weakness to anyone at 'Child's End—and Nicholas Benedict was no fool.

You only have to pretend to be one for Mr. Collum, he thought grimly. *And keep your emotions in check.*

"I understand you've lived in several different orphanages, Nicholas," said Mr. Collum, breaking the silence. He turned his head slightly, so that Nicholas saw the director's face in dark profile. So pronounced and angular were his features—the heavy brow, the straight nose, the jutting chin—they might have been chiseled from stone. "I assume you're accustomed to chores, therefore, but you must be prepared for an extra share at the Manor. In difficult times, we must all of us pull our own weight and then some."

"Absolutely, Mr. Collum. Are these difficult times, then?"

Mr. Collum snorted violently. Or perhaps he sneezed. Nicholas wasn't entirely sure. At any rate, he made a loud, abrupt sound with his nose. "My predecessor, Nicholas—the previous, so-called *director* of Rothschild's End—took a respectable institution and single-handedly dragged it into disrepute. Spent it to the brink of ruin! Reckless, criminal, indecent behavior! And now the task has fallen to me to raise it up again. Oh, these are indeed difficult times at the Manor, young man. I can vouchsafe you that. But we must rise to the challenge! Do you hear me, Nicholas? Are you awake back there?"

"Yes, sir! 'We must rise to the challenge,' sir!" Nicholas repeated.

"That is correct," Mr. Collum said. "And to do so, every staff member and every child must dutifully carry out his several responsibilities. You will get on well if only you remember this, Nicholas: Perform your duties and be mindful of the rules."

Nicholas was about to assure Mr. Collum that no child was more dutiful or mindful of rules than he was, when the Studebaker stopped at a deserted intersection. Stretching his neck, Nicholas peered left and right. As far as he could tell, they were still in the middle of empty farmland—the middle of nowhere—and the intersection was nothing more than a country crossroads.

Mr. Collum groaned. "Must you, Mr. Pileus? It's quite late, you know."

Mr. Pileus set his hat carefully on the dashboard and climbed out of the automobile. In the beam of the Studebaker's headlamps, he edged closer to the crossroads, where he stood in an attitude of attention, shielding his eyes from the mist, looking down the road to the left. Then he turned and looked right.

Mr. Collum gave a hiss of exasperation. "What does the man expect to see?"

When at last Mr. Pileus was satisfied that no automobiles were hurtling along the road without headlamps—at least not in the immediate vicinity—he hurried back to the Studebaker, jumped in, and roared forward to get through the intersection before the traffic circumstances changed.

"Mr. Pileus!" said Mr. Collum, speaking up to be heard over the horn, which Mr. Pileus was vigorously sounding as they crossed. "I appreciate your caution, truly I do, but have you ever seen any other automobile on this road at night?"

Mr. Pileus let off the horn—they had made it safely across—and mumbled something about poor visibility.

Mr. Collum sighed heavily through his nose and turned halfway toward Nicholas again. "As I was saying, Nicholas, you shall get on well enough at the Manor if only you observe the rules. And if you are conscientious—I truly hope you are conscientious, Nicholas; otherwise you shall have a tough time of it with me—if you are conscientious, I say, the rules should present no problem to you. They are few and simple. First, you must—"

Just then Nicholas felt his eyelids grow heavy.

Oh no! he thought. *Oh no, oh no!* And though he knew better, he rubbed his eyes desperately, as if he could press down the sleepiness, bottle it up with his fists. Hadn't Mr. Collum already been annoyed? And now this? Falling asleep during his speech about the rules? Oh, he would positively *resent* Nicholas for this! But it could not be avoided. No matter how he rubbed at them, his eyelids only grew heavier; they might as well have been sandbags.

"Pardon me, sir," Nicholas said, interrupting while he still could speak. "Mr. Collum? I'm extremely sorry, but I'm afraid I'm about to drop off...."

At this, Mr. Collum turned fully around in his seat, the right side of his scowling face weirdly lit by the glow from the dashboard instruments. In unmistakable annoyance he sputtered, "What do you mean, you're about to—? But this is very bad timing, young man! Was I not—? And we are almost to the Manor! Are you entirely sure?"

But Nicholas did not—indeed, *could* not—reply. He scarcely even noticed that Mr. Collum had spoken. It was so strange, he thought dreamily, the way one side of Mr. Collum's face was lit. In that glow his skin seemed greenish, like a goblin's. *Was* he a goblin? Nicholas shivered at the thought. His eyelids drooped to a close, opened for an instant, closed again. Mr. Collum was asking him something, and this time Nicholas tried to answer, but it was too late, too late. He was off and dreaming.

When Nicholas awoke, he listened a while before opening his eyes, to determine whether his circumstances had changed. Doing so was an established habit with him and had often served him well. On this occasion, he could tell he was still slumped in the back seat of the Studebaker, though the automobile was no longer moving. He could hear the *tick* and *ping* of its cooling engine, the faint whisper of windblown drizzle against the windows. Somehow he knew he was alone in the automobile, but he felt sure he'd sensed another presence. Had his sleeping ears detected a shuffling of feet in the grass outside? A cough or murmur?

Nicholas opened one eye. Through the window he saw an older boy leaning against the Studebaker, his elbows on the hood, gazing off into the distance. The men must have gone ahead with their evening, he realized, and this unlucky orphan had been dispatched to show him inside. With a twinge of dread, Nicholas wondered how long the boy had been waiting in the damp and whether he was missing some enjoyable activity.

Opening his other eye, Nicholas followed the older boy's gaze. To his surprise, he saw that the boy was looking across a wide lawn toward—well, toward nothing, really. Toward a lane, and the trees along either side of it, and general darkness. Nicholas turned his head. Here was the Manor, a two-story gray stone mansion that stretched out impressively in both directions. In a city it would have occupied half a block. There were enough windows to keep a glass factory in business for years. A few of them betrayed the faint, flickering reflections of interior candlelight. Most were dark.

The Studebaker was parked just at the bottom of the Manor's stone porch steps. Why was the boy not waiting up on the porch, where it was dry? Nicholas leaned forward to get a better look at him. The many droplets of water on the windshield distorted the boy's features somewhat, but he appeared to be about twelve, with an oval, freckled face and a dark brown crew cut. As Nicholas watched, the boy absently ran a hand over his bristly hair; a fine spray of water rose from it. He must have been out there awhile—getting wet on Nicholas's account. Swell. Taking a deep breath, Nicholas opened the door, hauling his suitcase after him.

The boy quickly stepped over and extended his hand. "Nicholas, right? I'm John."

John didn't look happy, exactly, but neither did he seem resentful. Relieved, Nicholas was about to shake his hand when something made him hesitate. Now that he could see John's face up close, he realized that what he'd thought were freckles were actually numerous pitted scars. It occurred to him that the other boy might have some contagious disease.

Evidently, John could tell what Nicholas was thinking. "They're only old chicken pox scars," he said. "I'm not contagious anymore—it's been over a year. They just didn't go away like they usually do."

Nicholas could have kicked himself. If John hadn't felt resentful before, he had reason to now. With an apologetic smile, Nicholas shook his hand. John had a strong grip— strong enough to make Nicholas wonder whether he was squeezing extra hard on purpose. But his expression was perfectly civil, and when Nicholas asked if he'd been waiting long, John shrugged good-naturedly and said it was no trouble.

"Mr. Collum sent me out a few minutes ago," he said, gesturing for Nicholas to follow him up the porch steps. "He told me to show you inside when you woke up."

Nicholas lugged his suitcase up the steps, at the top of which, on either side, towering gray columns rose into darkness, supporting a porch roof so high its features could scarcely be seen. The porch itself was almost as large as the cramped dormitory at Littleview that had been his home for more than a year. "Why weren't you waiting up here, where it's dry?" he asked.

"Oh, I don't know." John glanced around as if he, too, were seeing the porch for the first time. "I checked on you, and then I just stayed down there. The hood was warm and the mist was cool, and—well, I guess it felt more interesting. Also, I..." He paused, looking at Nicholas sidelong, then went on. "I heard about your condition. You might as well know that right off. Everyone says that's why you're getting a room to yourself. They say you have horrible nightmares, that you scream in your sleep. You weren't screaming just now, though."

"The naps aren't so bad," Nicholas said. "It's at night that things get really fun. The director at Littleview couldn't bear it anymore—I kept everyone awake and terrified the toddlers—so he worked it out with Mr. Collum that I could come here, since here I can sleep apart from everyone else. At Littleview there was no room for that."

"Will you grow out of it?"

"*No known cure*," Nicholas intoned in a deliberately gloomy voice. Then he grinned and waved a hand to dismiss the subject. "It's fine, really; it just makes some people nervous. But what does this have to do with why you stayed down there?"

"What?" John looked surprised, perhaps even embarrassed. "Oh, I just thought that if you screamed or thrashed around, I ought to wake you right away. It seemed the decent thing."

Nicholas glanced down at the Studebaker. From up here, its interior was almost impossible to see in the murky night. Had John really gone down to keep a closer eye on him—to wake him if he had a nightmare? It seemed unlikely. They didn't even know each other. Then again, Nicholas could always tell when someone was lying, and John had sounded sincere. Nicholas turned back to study John's face for a clue, but the other boy was already moving away.

"Like I said, it was more interesting, anyway," John was saying, as if he didn't want Nicholas to think him overly decent. "Come on, I'll take you to your room." He walked to the front entrance—a huge double oak door with a black iron latch—only to pause, twist his lips as if considering something, and move along without opening it.

At the end of the porch, John jumped down behind a row of azalea bushes that lined the front of the Manor. Nicholas climbed cautiously down after him, fearing for his shoes. He had been beaten once for tracking mud into an orphanage and did not care to repeat the experience. Fortunately, the narrow path was kept dry, more or less, by the azalea bushes and the Manor's protruding eaves.

"Are we taking a shortcut?" Nicholas asked.

"Not really," said John, creeping along the path. "But it occurred to me that the Spiders will be looking for you, so we're going to take the old servants' stairs. The side door should be open—that one's rarely locked."

Nicholas had stopped walking, a too-familiar dread rising in him. "Did you say the *spiders* are looking for me?"

Seeing that Nicholas had stopped, John turned and came back. "Right, I should explain. I didn't mean actual spiders, of course, but a gang of bullies. A few of the older boys, quite nasty."

Nicholas stood silently, weighing John's tone. Was it possible he'd been joking? No, it was the truth, and Nicholas knew it. He had known it the moment John spoke. It was the truth, and no amount of wishing would make it otherwise.

"I see," Nicholas said. And then he laughed. He couldn't help it. His dread was raging at full force now, but at the same time how could he not laugh at this astonishingly quick arrival of misfortune, this instantaneous destruction of his hopes—hopes that had been so modest to begin with? It was far too absurd not to be funny. A horrible gang of bullies was already looking for him? Of course! Why not!

"That's the spirit," said John with an approving look. "They're ridiculous, all right. The trick is avoiding them, and I can give you a few tips, as far as that goes. You just— Nicholas? Say, are you—?" He cried out in surprise, for Nicholas, who had abruptly stopped laughing (to listen, John had thought), now just as abruptly closed his eyes, dropped his suitcase, and pitched sideways into an azalea.

John managed to catch him under the shoulders and tried to help him upright. Nicholas was deadweight in his arms, however, and only with great effort did John keep both of them from toppling. Nicholas's head lolled on his neck, his eyes remained closed, and for a terrible moment John thought that the poor boy had died. Then, with dawning amazement, he realized a less terrible but equally remarkable fact: Nicholas Benedict had fallen asleep, right in the middle of a laugh.

Shadows and Spiders

The first sensation Nicholas experienced when he awoke was discomfort in his knee. He seemed to be lying on the ground with one leg bent beneath him. He felt an azalea twig poking into his ear, and soft earth under his fingertips. His shoulder blade pressed into a stone. And—as he came to realize what had happened—he felt a rising heat in his cheeks.

It was not unfamiliar, this shame that arrived after collapsing, helpless, in the presence of others. Nicholas had never gotten used to it, had never been able to quash it. Worse, this time it was instantly followed by an electric surge of dismay. His secret was already in jeopardy, and he had only just arrived!

Nicholas steadied his breathing, trying to calm himself and think what to do. Unfortunately, John must have been watching him closely, for though the change in his breathing was subtle, the older boy immediately whispered, "Hey! Are you awake? Can you hear me?"

Nicholas opened one eye. John's concerned face hovered over him. "Don't you have better things to do than watch over the new kid?" he asked, as casually as he might have asked the time.

John did not smile—he had yet to do so even once—but he did seem relieved. Shrugging his shoulders every bit as casually, he replied, "It isn't every day I get to watch someone sleep in the shrubberies."

"Is that so?" Nicholas said breezily. "Where I come from it's quite common." He straightened out his tingling leg and sat up.

"So, does this always happen when you get excited?" John asked, and it was all Nicholas could do not to let the surprise—surprise and panic—show on his face. He knew his eyes had widened, and quickly he rubbed at them as if he were still just trying to wake up properly. Meanwhile John continued. "You went down right in the middle of a laugh. I've never seen anything like it. You have a funny laugh, by the way. Sounds like someone tapping out Morse code. No offense. I mean, it's a fine laugh. I've just never heard one like it before."

Nicholas cleared his throat, trying to gather his wits. John was clearly sharper than most. "Sorry, I'm still a bit groggy.

The fact is, I don't think I've really heard anything you've been saying."

"Oh!" John reached down and helped Nicholas to his feet. "I only asked whether laughing always does that to you."

"Laughing?" said Nicholas. He brushed off his pants, his mind racing. Even if John accepted a made-up explanation, he might still tell others about his original suspicion. How long would it be until someone tested that theory to see if he'd been right?

"Yes, laughing," John said, somewhat insistently now. "You were standing there laughing, and I was trying to tell you something, and then you just closed your eyes and fell over. Has that never happened before?"

There was no help for it, Nicholas thought. His best chance was to gamble on the truth, or at least some version of it. "Well, I believe it *has* happened once or twice. But say, John, I don't suppose we could keep this between us? I can find some way to pay you back. Whatever you like."

John's eyebrows rose in surprise, then just as quickly drew together into a frown. He was quiet for several seconds. He seemed to be working something out in his mind. Nicholas worried he was calculating a particularly hefty bribe.

"Tell me something," John said finally, looking Nicholas in the eye. "You understood what I was saying right away, didn't you? You only pretended not to. Why did you do that?"

Nicholas sighed and ran a hand through his hair. "I've had some bad experiences."

John studied him for some time, considering this. Then he shoved his hands into his pockets, and his gaze drifted upward, as if now he were studying the eaves. At length he muttered, as if to himself, "I'll bet. I hadn't even thought of that." He looked back at Nicholas. "All right, Nick—can I call you Nick?—your secret's safe with me. And forget that business about paying me back. I'm not a creep, you know."

Once again Nicholas was slow to reply. He was grateful, but also confused. He'd had precious little experience with generous behavior. "Sure," he said after an awkward pause, then hurriedly added, "I mean 'sure, you can call me Nick,' not 'sure, you're not a creep.' Because I'm sure you aren't. A creep, I mean."

John narrowed his eyes. "I'm glad, I think. All set, then? Ready to sneak in?"

Nicholas picked up his suitcase. "All set."

John started off again toward the corner of the Manor. "The thing about this place, Nick, is that you're fine as long as there's a grownup around. Really. The staff don't put up with any nonsense, and they give out harsh punishments. So the Spiders won't try anything unless they get you away from the adults. You can usually avoid that if you're careful, but tonight they know I'm supposed to take you upstairs, so they might be lying in wait for you somewhere on the way— somewhere out of sight of the staff."

"What do they want with me, anyway?" Nicholas asked. "They don't even know me."

"They want to 'initiate' you. It isn't personal. They initiated me, too, when I got here last year. They say it's a tradition, but that's just an excuse. People like the Spiders don't need traditions to do what they do."

Nicholas was about to ask what the initiation involved, when they reached the corner. John put a finger to his lips and peered around. He beckoned Nicholas to follow him. They tiptoed into a side yard, where in the prevailing gloom Nicholas made out the shapes of a well, a small raised garden, and a shed. Beyond these he saw nothing but darkness. For such an impressive mansion, the Manor sorely lacked for good lighting. Only a single, second-story window on this side offered the faintest glimmer of candlelight.

John led him through the side door and eased it closed behind them. They stood in a dim passage, the sole source of illumination being a band of light shining from beneath a door to their left. ("Mr. Pileus's bedroom," John whispered.) Voices sounded in other parts of the Manor, drifting down passageways and over transoms. Agitated conversations, occasional spurts of laughter, flurries of footsteps.

John whispered for Nicholas to tread softly and step only where he stepped. Presumably this was to avoid creaking floorboards, though with all the exaggerated caution they were taking, Nicholas could not help but imagine trip wires and land mines. He took his first stealthy step, all his senses on high alert—and in this way, skulking like a thief, Nicholas entered his new home.

At the end of the passage, the boys slipped through a door to the old servants' stairs. The stairway was cramped and dusty, and it was pitch black until John turned the key in a wall lamp, illuminating the wooden steps and a closed door at the top. "Got it?" he whispered. He switched the light off again, and in darkness they began to climb.

"Free time will be over soon," John said, still speaking softly. "Everyone will have to report to the dormitories for bed, so you just need to steer clear of the Spiders until then. I suppose you could hide behind the boxes in your room if it came to that."

"There are boxes in my room?"

"Don't get your hopes up," John cautioned. "They aren't presents or anything. In the old days your room was a guest room, but it's used for storage now. You have a cot, though — you don't have to actually *sleep* in a box. That's something, right?"

At the top of the stairs, Nicholas spied a tiny circle of dim light that seemed to hover in the blackness. He knew this was the keyhole in the door, and when it disappeared, he knew John had put his eye to it. John opened the door a crack and listened, then opened it further and looked out. "I don't see anyone," he whispered, "but we'll keep quiet all the same."

The boys crept out into a short and terribly gloomy passage. Nicholas's eye was drawn to the only discernible light; some paces to the left, where this passage ended at the intersection of another one, a sickly yellow candle burned in a wall sconce. Beneath the sconce stood an antique wooden bureau, atop which a bowl had been set to catch the steady trickle of leaking melted wax. In the dim candlelight, Nicholas took in his surroundings: the faded pattern in the carpet running along the wooden floor; the electric light fixture, missing its bulbs, that hung directly overhead; and the door, just opposite the servants' stairs, that John was attempting to open — the door, Nicholas realized in horror, to his room.

"Couldn't they have picked a spookier place?" he whispered. "If I didn't have nightmares already, I'm fairly certain this atmosphere would induce them."

John gave Nicholas a quizzical look. "How old did you say you were, Nick? You seem, I don't know, kind of *wordy* for a kid your size."

"I'm nine," Nicholas replied, and to be comical he drew himself up to full height, as if his height were most impressive. In fact, as he well knew, he was on the small side even for a nine-year-old.

"Nine," John repeated, and he shook his head. "You don't sound it. I'm twelve, you know, and I'm 'fairly certain' I've never heard a kid use the word 'induce.'" (He said all this in a teasing tone, not harsh at all, but Nicholas nonetheless reminded himself to be careful; others could be less forgiving.) "Anyway, this door's locked. I'll have to go and find Mr. Collum. You'd better stay here. There might be Spiders posted along the way."

Nicholas tried not to appear alarmed. "But if they see you, won't they realize I'm up here?"

"The Spiders aren't especially good at realizing things," John said wryly. "But if they see me, I'll tell them I was just checking on your room—Mr. Collum often has me do errands like that—and that you're still outside asleep. They won't risk sneaking outside. Too many things could go wrong."

Nicholas also saw too many things that could go wrong with John's plan, but he decided not to mention them. He didn't want to appear frightened to wait up here by himself (even though he was). Besides, he wanted to give John the benefit of the doubt. "Perfect, I'll wait here, then." He set down his suitcase, put his hands on his hips, and made a show of glancing around with a look of satisfaction. "I like it here, anyway. It's homey."

"I'll be as quick as I can," John said. "You just sit tight and keep your ears open. If you hear someone coming, better duck into the stairway until you know who it is. It can't hurt to be careful." He was already hurrying away.

"Wait!" Nicholas called, whispering as loudly as he dared. John stopped and looked back. "I...I wanted to thank you. You're going to a lot of trouble for someone you don't know."

Perhaps it was the candlelight striking him from a new angle, but at these words John's face seemed to change—his features seemed almost contorted—and when he spoke, his voice sounded tight and forced, as if he were upset. "Don't thank me, Nick." He made a broad, vague, irritated gesture. "This—all this business—it shouldn't be like this. It shouldn't..." He sighed, and his expression appeared to relax. "Forget it. Just don't thank me, Nick. All right? There's no need to thank me."

"Sir, yes, sir!" said Nicholas. He straightened like a soldier and saluted. "No thanks, then, Captain. No thanks it is!"

John's eyes narrowed. For a moment he looked as if he might smile. "You're a fresh one, Nick," he said at last.

After John had gone, Nicholas surveyed the area near his room. Several paces to the right of the stairway door, the passage ended at a curtainless window overlooking the side yard. Not that Nicholas could actually *see* the yard (the glass reflected his tense face and the candlelit passage behind him, and outside all was blackness), but it was easy enough for him to deduce. He didn't have to think about it. Nicholas was the sort of person who could wander blindfolded for hours and never lose his direction. The side yard lay to the east of the

Manor, and Nicholas knew he was facing east, so this had to be the faintly glimmering window he had seen from below.

Nicholas turned and tiptoed to the intersection (*the candle corner*, was how he thought of it), where the wax dripping into the bowl made a ticking sound as regular as a clock. Indeed, he had been automatically keeping track of the drips since John left. One hundred eighty-seven and counting—approximately three minutes. Nicholas peered to the left, in the direction John had taken. This south-running passage extended past a few closed doors toward the front of the house, where it turned to the right, or west.

Nicholas swiveled his eyes (he was trying to keep quiet by not moving very much) to peer along the passage to the north. It ran a great deal farther in that direction, perhaps even to the very back of the Manor, though it was altogether too dark to tell. In the near distance Nicholas could make out another candle corner, with an identical bowl set upon an identical bureau, but the sconce there was empty.

From what Nicholas could see—or, more to the point, *not* see—the upstairs seemed a horribly gloomy place. He tiptoed back to the door of his room, not a little gloomy himself. Was there really to be no one on this entire abandoned floor but him? He bent to peer through the keyhole. Nothing but darkness. He wondered what sort of bed he had. At Littleview he had slept on blankets on the floor. That had been a fortunate arrangement, actually; though his terrifying dreams had often made him flail and thrash, they could never send him tumbling out of bed. He'd probably been spared many nasty bruises.

Nicholas did not want to imagine how it would be to

awaken from a nightmare in this dark and isolated corner, with the feeling—that much-too-familiar feeling—that some hideous creature crouched in the shadows of his room, so instead he turned his attention to the candle in the sconce, which had just made a sputtering sound. He looked up in time to see its flame tilt sideways, then straighten again.

As if it had been caught in a draft, he thought.

Nicholas was instantly on guard. What had caused that draft? Was it simply a gust of wind slipping through cracks in the old stone walls, or had someone opened a door nearby? He heard no voices or footsteps, but this was not reassuring. If John knew where to step to avoid creaking floorboards, the Spiders might know as well. Quickly he slipped onto the servants' stairs and eased the door closed.

A long minute passed, during which all Nicholas heard was his heartbeat. In his haste he had left his suitcase behind—a mistake, but he couldn't risk retrieving it now. He pictured that tilted candle flame. There might have been other causes, he knew; his mind flashed over several. Still, he felt uneasy. He could no longer hear the dripping of the candle wax, but in the back of his mind he had kept up the count. Two minutes passed, then three.

Nicholas had almost decided it was a false alarm, when he heard whispers in the passage. They were startlingly close to where he crouched on the dark stairs. Indeed, if the door had not been there, he could have reached out and grabbed the whisperers. Or vice versa. Through the key-hole he caught a glimpse of a leather belt cinched carelessly about its owner's waist—two frayed denim loops had been missed entirely—and then a large, scuffed metal belt buckle rotated into view. The person had turned toward the door. A hand passed slowly across the keyhole view, reaching for the doorknob.

There was nothing for it—he could hardly leap away—and so Nicholas swung the door open and sprang out of the stairway with a grin. "There you are!" he cried, beaming at three startled boys in the passage. They were giants compared to Nicholas—eleven or twelve years old, and all of them big for their age. All had crew cuts like John's. The one with the belt buckle, who was also the tallest, had jumped back to avoid being struck by the opening door. He was holding Nicholas's suitcase.

"I heard you were looking for me," Nicholas said, grinning. "You *are* the Spiders, aren't you? I've heard great things about you already! Great things!"

The belt buckle boy was evidently the leader, for the other two were looking back and forth between him and Nicholas, wondering what would come next. But the belt buckle boy was staring at Nicholas in astonishment, as if this newcomer had just claimed to be a talking squirrel and shown his tail to prove it. The boy licked his lips, which were quite chapped, and after a long, considered pause, he said, "What?"

"I'm excited about initiation," Nicholas said, lowering his voice confidentially, as if they might be overheard. "I love secrets! But I'm worried Mr. Collum will stop us. What should we do?"

"Do?" said the belt buckle boy. He glanced around at the others, who were clearly confused. One of them—a pale, lanky boy with a pinched expression, as if he'd just eaten something bitter—was mumbling the words that Nicholas had spoken. He seemed to be trying to get at their meaning by saying them himself.

"Yes, do!" Nicholas said, clasping his hands together. "I've never had an initiation before. It's a kind of welcoming party, right? I don't want to miss it, but Mr. Collum will be here any second!"

"So *you* think..." said the belt buckle boy, with a slowly spreading grin that showed he understood the situation now—or thought he did, anyway. He chuckled, then tried to mask it with a cough. "Well, little buddy, that won't be a problem, see, because we're headed to the bathroom. That's where we do it. Come on, we'll show you. It's just around the corner." He winked at the other boys, who were now exchanging knowing looks. They both spoke up in false-friendly tones, encouraging Nicholas to join them.

Nicholas was surprised by their winks and insincere manner—even a toddler would have been suspicious, he thought—but of course he pretended he hadn't noticed. "The bathroom? But Mr. Collum is *in* the bathroom—that's where he's coming from!"

Once again the Spiders looked stunned.

The pale, lanky boy said, "The bathroom around the corner? Are you sure?"

"But we just saw him in his office talking to John Cole!" put in the third boy, a handsome, muscular brute who seemed already to have a mustache, or at least the shadowy beginnings of one. "How did he get up here so fast? We're fixed good if he catches us, Moray!" He looked anxiously to the belt buckle boy.

"Shut up, both of you, and let me think!" Moray hissed,

and the features of his face—round cheeks, dark, round eyes, a smallish snub nose—all bunched together into a circle of concentration so tiny that a coffee cup might have covered them entirely. He licked his chapped lips again. "I don't see how old Collum could have got past us—"

"He came up these stairs," Nicholas interjected, "and then he told me to go back down and turn off the light while he paid a visit to the bathroom. He seemed to be in an awful hurry—I think it was an emergency."

"*These* stairs?" Moray said. Nicholas watched him working it out in his mind. "The servants' stairs?"

"That sounds like Collum, all right," said the handsome, muscular boy. "Turning off the light, I mean."

"So he really could be here any second?" said the lanky boy. His tone was worried now, but he still looked simply peevish, as if he had mothballs in his mouth.

"That's what he said, isn't it?" whispered the muscular one, shooting the peevish one a contemptuous look. The two of them fell at once into a heated, whispered argument, during which Nicholas learned that the muscular boy was called Breaker, and the other was called Iggy.

Pretending to be alarmed, Nicholas urgently laid his finger against his lips, signaling them to be quiet. With a start, they remembered why they were arguing, and fell silent, glancing apprehensively toward the candle corner. Moray, meanwhile, had screwed his face up tight again, presumably trying extra hard to think.

"I know!" Nicholas said, softly snapping his fingers. "You can sneak down these stairs, and we'll do the initiation tomorrow. Should I bring cookies? I was given some when I left the last place. They're right in here!" He took the suit-case from Moray, who released it without thinking (no doubt he was unused to having things snatched from him), and stepped aside to let them pass. "Don't worry, I won't say a word to Mr. Collum. Just tell me where to meet you!"

Moray hesitated, perhaps wondering what kind of cookies Nicholas had. Then he nodded. "Bathroom around the cor-ner. Right after breakfast. We'll be waiting for you."

"Swell!" Nicholas said, flashing an eager grin. "Oh, that's swell of you, Moray! Thank you!"

Moray regarded him with affection, rather as a weasel might look upon an unguarded chicken. "Don't mention it. Oh, and don't mention it to anyone *else*, either. Not a word about initiation to anyone, got it? You don't want to ruin the surprise."

Nicholas looked horrified. "Oh no! That's the last thing I'd do!"

"Good man," Moray said, patting Nicholas's shoulder. "And be sure to bring those cookies."

Nicholas put his hand over his heart. "I will, Moray! You can count on me! Good night, Moray! Good night, fellows!"

Moray smirked and hurried down the stairs, followed by the other Spiders, looking equally smug. "Did you see the honker on that kid?" whispered Breaker when they were only halfway down the stairs.

Nicholas heard him quite plainly, along with Iggy's snick-ering reply: "How could I have missed *that*? It looked like something out of a root cellar!"

All three were chuckling when Nicholas abruptly closed the door, shutting them into blackness. He heard them stumbling and cursing, which gave him some small satisfaction. He opened the door a crack and whispered down into the darkness, "Sorry! I heard someone coming!" then quickly closed it again. Moments later he heard the downstairs door rattle open and bang shut. The Spiders were much less cautious now that they weren't sneaking up on him.

Nicholas sank to the floor, his heart hammering like a woodpecker against his rib cage. It seemed a miracle that he hadn't gone to sleep and fallen at the bullies' feet. That was something, anyway. And he had managed not to get his head dunked in a toilet (he was sure that was what initiation involved), so all in all it was a successful escape—perhaps even one of his best.

But Nicholas had made things far worse for himself in the long run, and he knew it. There is no fury greater than one born of humiliation, and when Nicholas didn't show up the next morning, the Spiders would realize that he had indeed humiliated them. A nine-year-old duping them so easily? With no warning, no preparation at all? Oh yes, he had made the Spiders look like fools, and they would understand that all too soon. If it hadn't been personal before, it most certainly would be now. The bullies would do everything in their power to get him back. They would do their worst—and from the look of them, their worst would be terrible indeed.

Yet what else could Nicholas have done? Let *them* humiliate *him*? No, that never had been an option. Nicholas simply didn't have it in him to give in to bullies. He never had. If they wanted to humiliate him, they were going to have to work for it.

With a groan, Nicholas leaned back against the stairway door. This whole situation felt sadly familiar. But the Spiders were much bigger than any bullies he'd ever known, and this place was so large that there had to be countless shadowy corners in which to trap unsuspecting victims. *Like actual spiders*, he thought. He drew up his knees and rested his chin on them. Had he really been thinking, back at the train station, that this new place could hardly be worse than the last?

So much for that.

The Spiders had not been gone long (seventy-one drips of wax) when the candle flame sputtered violently and leaned sideways again. Nicholas sprang to his feet and put his hand on the doorknob. Perhaps they were coming back—perhaps they had already realized they'd been suckered. Then came the distant creak of a floorboard, followed by brisk, purposeful, heavy footsteps on carpet—a man's footsteps—and Nicholas knew it was Mr. Collum.

Nicholas also sensed that Mr. Collum was alone, a fact confirmed when the director rounded the candle corner. He looked slightly less official than before, having removed his suit coat, necktie, and hat, but he still had his ledger and still stood straight as a post. Absent his hat, Mr. Collum's hair proved to be black, oiled, and meticulously combed, with a severe part down the middle that made Nicholas think of a path through a thicket. He was carrying a small lantern, its flame turned so low it was scarcely visible.

"So you are still awake," said Mr. Collum snappishly. "After what happened on our way here, I worried I would make the climb only to find you slumbering again."

42

Nicholas bowed. "Perfectly awake, Mr. Collum, and happy not to have inconvenienced you again." He kept every trace of sarcasm out of his tone, but Mr. Collum searched his face nonetheless. Nicholas returned the gaze with a look of blank sincerity.

"As for that," Mr. Collum said, "it's inconvenient enough with you awake." Tucking the ledger under his arm, he reached into a trouser pocket and drew out a length of black ribbon tied to an antique-looking key. It would seem a simple enough procedure; yet he almost dropped the ledger, and then the lantern, and then was obliged to take the key ribbon in his teeth as he got them both resituated (he seemed unwilling to set anything down or to ask Nicholas for help), and in general gave the impression of a man needing more hands than he possessed.

"I had intended to finish explaining the rules," Mr. Collum said, speaking through his clenched teeth as he shifted his things, "but that will have to wait. It's bedtime now, and you must follow your routine, the same as everyone. Here we are," he said, unlocking the door at last.

Mr. Collum turned up the flame in his lantern, revealing a room that would have been comfortably spacious had it not been full of boxes. To the right, against the east wall, was a narrow strip of space in which a cot had been placed. Overhead dangled an ornate light fixture without bulbs. There appeared to be no windows, either, which seemed odd for a former guest room in a mansion. Then Nicholas detected a square patch of stone, just above the cot, that was a slightly different shade of gray from the rest of the wall. A window there would have looked onto the side yard.

"I had Mr. Pileus close that in this afternoon," said Mr. Collum when Nicholas walked over to inspect the square patch. "Do not touch it. The mortar may be damp yet."

Nicholas stared wistfully at the wall. To think he had almost had a window! "But what was the matter with it?"

"With the window?" Mr. Collum said. "Nothing at all. It was an ordinary window. But your peculiar sleeping arrangements call for unusual measures, Nicholas. Naturally, we cannot leave you unsupervised without taking precautions. A boy your age is much tempted to mischief. Thus it occurred to me this morning that we must remove the window. We can't have you sneaking out at night, perhaps falling and breaking your neck in the process. And obviously we shall keep your door locked."

"Locked?" Nicholas spun to face him, aghast. "I'm to be locked into this room, alone, every night?"

"There's no help for it," Mr. Collum said briskly. "Assigning you a personal chaperone would be impossible—we simply haven't the staff. Come now!" he said when Nicholas began taking deep breaths to calm himself. "Buck up! It isn't as bad as all that." He gestured into the corner, where a once-elegant braided cloth rope hung from the ceiling. "If you have an emergency—I mean a true emergency, Nicholas, not just a nightmare or a little thirst—you may tug on that rope. A bell will sound below in the old butler's room, where Mr. Pileus sleeps, and he will come up to check on you."

"I see, sir," Nicholas said, recovering enough to sound polite. "I do hate to bother Mr. Pileus, though. Perhaps we could try it awhile with the door unlocked? I'm not the least bit interested in mischief, I can promise you." He rounded his eyes, dipped his chin, and otherwise did his best to look unmischievous.

Mr. Collum sighed. "Out of the question, I'm afraid, Nicholas. One must always start strictly. In time I might consider easing restrictions, but this will depend upon your behavior. If you were John Cole, for instance, I would probably grant your request. In fact, you would do well to model yourself after John—makes himself useful, excellent deportment, never a nuisance. Indeed, much of the time one would not even know he's here." Mr. Collum said this last part with special emphasis, as if there were no greater virtue in a child than appearing to be absent.

Nicholas lowered his eyes. He could see it was pointless to argue further. *You have to find another way to fix this*, he told himself, and his mind went probing frantically in every direction, searching for a solution.

"You may keep your suitcase beneath the cot," Mr. Collum was saying. "Come along now and wash up in the bathroom. Do you have pajamas? A toothbrush and paste?"

"Yes, sir," Nicholas replied. He knelt to his suitcase, his mind still racing. "Will I have a lamp, Mr. Collum?"

Mr. Collum seemed not to have considered this. He was slow to reply, and when he did so, his tone was reluctant. "You may have a candle. Take one from that box," he said, pointing, "and I shall light it before I leave you."

Nicholas hurried to the box in relief. He rifled through the candles inside, looking for the biggest one. And all the time his mind was working, working.

Out in the passage again, Mr. Collum repeated his awkward ritual, rearranging the things in his hands and under his arms in order to bring out his key and lock the door.

Nicholas wondered at this. "Aren't we coming right back, Mr. Collum?"

Mr. Collum's cheeks flushed, and he looked at Nicholas disapprovingly. "You ask far too many questions, young man. Yes, we're coming back. But I keep things properly secured. My predecessor was a scoundrel. I am a responsible business-man. Your bedroom also happens to be a storage room, and as such it is kept locked at all times. Now follow me, and no more questions. It has been an insufferably long day, and I am much too weary. Tomorrow you will be shown about and told all you need to know."

Mr. Collum did seem weary. In fact, Nicholas suspected that he was so tired he had locked the door without think-ing, then covered up his mistake with that business about keeping things secured. All the briskness had gone out of him — even his reprimand had lacked force — and he yawned several times as he led the way to the bathroom.

They turned left at the candle corner, then right at the end of the south-running passage. In the distance a half-open doorway revealed a sort of gallery, a lofty space in which Nicholas spied the upper railing of a grand staircase, its pol-ished wood reflecting the light of an unseen candle. But they stopped well short of the gallery, and Mr. Collum gestured with his ledger to a door on the right.

"Be quick," said Mr. Collum through a yawn. He did not offer the use of his lantern.

Nicholas hurried into the bathroom, wondering what he was to do about light. As it happened, the bathroom had a wall lamp with an actual bulb in it. He turned it on (half expecting Mr. Collum to scold him), then closed the door and bent to the keyhole. He watched Mr. Collum lean back against the wall and shut his eyes.

Nicholas stared at Mr. Collum, not out of anger or bitterness but because he was concentrating. Now that he was alone, he could turn his full attention to his problem. His mind began reeling in its many strands of thought like so many fishing lines, checking each hook for solutions. He stared at the trouser pocket in which Mr. Collum carried the key to his room. Then he straightened and stared intently at the keyhole in the bathroom door. Then he closed his eyes and stared at every detail his mind had registered since he arrived.

And then he had his answer.

Hiding his toothbrush and toothpaste inside his shirt, Nicholas swung the door open again, talking fast: "I'm so sorry, Mr. Collum, but I seem to have left my toothbrush and toothpaste in the bedroom! I must have set them down when I took the candle from the box, and forgot to pick them up again!"

Mr. Collum opened his eyes, looking bewildered. "You didn't—but didn't I see—why, what on earth were you thinking, Nicholas? This is a bad start," he said, his voice growing angrier, "a very bad start indeed!"

"I really am sorry, Mr. Collum!" Nicholas said, and pressed on quickly. "I'll just dash back for them! You needn't budge! I'll be quick as a wink!" He held out his hand for the key, as urgently as he could without seeming demanding, and composed his face into an expression of anxious embarrassment.

Mr. Collum scowled and began shifting his things. "Forty-five seconds," he said. "One second longer and you'll regret it. Do you understand me, Nicholas?" He held out the key on its black ribbon.

"Absolutely, sir!" Nicholas cried, snatching the key. "Forty-five seconds it is!"

He flew back the way they had come, but he did not go straight to his room. Instead, he ran past the first candle corner and on to the one he'd spotted farther down, the dark one with the empty sconce and the unused bowl. Grabbing that bowl, he ran back to the first candle corner and switched it with the other bowl—the one containing a fresh layer of warm, soft wax. This one he carried to his room. He was perspiring now, his fingers clammy against the key as he shoved it into the lock.

In the privacy of his room, Nicholas knelt over the bowl. He pressed the key into the cooling wax. Slowly and carefully, he tugged it out again by the ribbon, then buffed it with his shirt. He tucked the key into his pocket, hid the bowl behind a stack of boxes, and hurried out again.

"Forty-three seconds," Mr. Collum said when Nicholas came running up. He put away his pocket watch almost regretfully, but at least he hadn't lied. (Nicholas knew the time was accurate, for he'd been counting the seconds in his head.)

"Thanks for your patience, Mr. Collum," said Nicholas, and he handed over the key.

Soon afterward Nicholas stood in his bedroom alone, listening, as the same key locked him in for the night. Mr. Collum had left him with his solitary flickering candle, along with a warning to use it safely, and had informed Nicholas that Mrs. Brindle, the housekeeper, would be up early in the morning to fetch him. Mr. Collum had neglected to leave any matches should the candle need to be lit again later, but Nicholas had chosen not to mention this. Instead, he had hurriedly expressed his gratitude, promised to go to sleep at once, and bidden the director a good night.

Nicholas put his ear against the door and listened to Mr. Collum tramp away. Then he reached inside his pajama top and took out the lightbulb he'd removed from the bathroom lamp. It was still warm to the touch. Nicholas smiled and tossed it onto his cot. Later he would climb a stack of boxes and screw the bulb into the light fixture. For now, he eagerly carried his candle over to where he had hidden the bowl, and with a rush of relief and delight, he inspected the result of his efforts: The key had left a perfect impression in the wax. So he had his mold, and tomorrow, according to Mr. Collum, he had metalwork.

By tomorrow night, then, Nicholas would have his own key.

WHAT'S WHAT and WHAT ISN'T, and WHAT ONCE WAS

The orphanage housekeeper, a widow named Mrs. Brindle, had a variety of minor ailments that troubled her. Chief among them was an itchy eye, at which she was always rubbing furiously with one knuckle, but she also suffered from aches and pains that migrated, unpredictably, from one part of her body to another. No sooner would she learn to favor one elbow or knee—adjusting her movements, applying hot-water bottles and ointments—than its pain would disappear and pop up elsewhere. And so she would cry out or groan whenever she moved, not because the pain was unbearable but because it always surprised her. This morning, for instance, it had been her shoulder that bothered her when she rose from bed; yet when she dropped her ring of keys trying to unlock Nicholas's door and bent to retrieve it, the pain sneaked down to her back.

"You slippery devil!" Mrs. Brindle snarled. (Over the years she had come to think of this traveling pain as an impish spirit, like a poltergeist that haunted muscles and bones rather than cupboards and closets.) "Can you not sit still for one morning? Why not move along to someone else entirely? A larger body! Wouldn't that be nice? You'd have more room to work your mischief, you wicked little beast!" And she said more things along this line, which had long been her habit, as she unlocked the door and pushed it open.

Nicholas, however, being unfamiliar with Mrs. Brindle's angry speeches, had retreated to the far side of the pitch-black room and was in a fair state of alarm. He'd been fully dressed for hours, just in case, but had been awake for only a minute. It had been a long night, and what little sleep he had gotten had been haunted, as it so frequently was, by hideous nightmares, terrible visions so powerful and vivid they seemed not just real but *more* than real, the way things often do when a person is frightened. Sometimes, in fact, they were even worse than nightmares—sometimes they were hallucinations. And the worst of these, which had visited Nicholas many a night, was a horrifying female creature who threatened to smother him.

"Why, whatever is the matter with you?" Mrs. Brindle demanded when she saw Nicholas cowering in the corner. She turned up the flame in her lamp and held it forward, the better to see him.

The increased light made Mrs. Brindle easier to see as well, and Nicholas quickly regained his composure. She was not the awful creature from his hallucination but a stooped woman with wiry gray hair and a runny eye. Through the door she had sounded furious, but in person she seemed merely exasperated. And at any rate, Nicholas could tell now that he was truly awake. It was morning. The horrors had passed.

"Nothing at all is the matter, ma'am!" Nicholas exclaimed, and he offered Mrs. Brindle a sweeping bow. "I was only startled by your sudden entrance. Nicholas Benedict, ma'am. Very pleased to meet you."

"What?" said Mrs. Brindle, rubbing her eye. "How old are you? I was told you were nine."

"Indeed I am, ma'am!" Nicholas said. "I apologize if I'm speaking too quickly. I suppose I'm excited."

Mrs. Brindle stared at him. "Well, you shall have to do your best to hold it in. I'm too weary this morning. Run along to the bathroom now and wash up. I'm to show you around before breakfast."

Nicholas grabbed a few things from beneath his cot and hurried into the passage, which was gloomy but navigable in the gray light filtering through the window. It was just after dawn. He made his way to the bathroom, took the lightbulb from under his shirt, and screwed it back into the lamp. Then he braced himself and set to work scrubbing his hands in the sink.

The harsh soap and cold water stung Nicholas's raw fingertips like nettles. He had no choice but to scrub them, though, for he had worked feverishly last night to scrape out all the damp mortar in his wall, and some of it had dried on his fingers. That was all right. He might be wincing and grimacing now, but the success of his project made up for it. The knowledge that he could remove the stones from his "window" if he pleased—that he could breathe fresh air and look up at the stars—was worth far more to Nicholas than a few skinned knuckles and a few lost hours of sleep. He hadn't wanted to sleep, anyway. He never did.

Once his hands were clean and he had changed out of his pajamas, Nicholas dampened his comb and parted his hair, perhaps for the last time. All the other boys had been given crew cuts, and he presumed the same fate lay in store for him. He took a moment to gaze into the mirror. "Well, Nicholas, it's going to be another tricky morning," he said to his reflection. "Best be on your toes." He stood on his tiptoes and offered himself an encouraging smile.

Turning to the lamp, Nicholas unscrewed the good lightbulb and replaced it with a dead one he had found among the boxes in his room. If the Spiders were going to wait for him here, they might as well do so in darkness. Later Nicholas would report the dead lightbulb to Mr. Collum and request a new one. Then he could keep the extra bulb hidden away, to use whenever he wished.

This dead lightbulb was one of several useful items Nicholas had found in his room. His other nighttime project had been to go through all the boxes and make a mental list of their contents. (He had no need of writing the list down, for he had a prodigious memory—perhaps even a perfect one. As far as he knew, anyway, he'd never forgotten a thing.) Most of the boxes contained threadbare, moth-eaten bedsheets and other linens, but there was also a broken lantern, a broken alarm clock, a half-empty matchbox, a bundle of flour sacks, and a pair of dilapidated old work boots. With the exception of the matchbox, which was a prize find by any standard, all these things might have seemed useless to someone else. But Nicholas could find a purpose for almost anything, including the boxes themselves (that scraped-out mortar needed to be hidden somewhere, after all), and he had been pleased with his discoveries.

When Nicholas returned to his room, he found Mrs. Brindle holding up her lamp and peering at the discolored patch of gray wall over his cot. "Used to be a window here," she said as he put his things away. "Mr. Pileus filled it in yesterday." She gave a little cluck of disapproval. "But it looks cockeyed, somehow. Saggy. Not his best work, I should say. I suppose he felt rushed. Did you feel a draft at all?"

"Not a bit," Nicholas said. "I couldn't have been more comfortable."

Mrs. Brindle shrugged. "Then I suppose it's well enough. Oh!" she cried suddenly. "You beast! You wicked, wicked beast! It's the wrist now, is it?" She sucked in her breath and changed the lamp to the other hand.

"Is anything the matter, ma'am?" asked Nicholas.

"What do you think?" said Mrs. Brindle, shuffling slowly from the room. "Please don't plague me with your questions. I shall tell you all you need to know. Now come along, I have to lock this door."

"Certainly," said Nicholas, darting into the passage ahead of her. "I can't wait to look around. I haven't even been down-stairs yet!"

Mrs. Brindle gave him a weary look. "You needn't plague me with your comments, either."

"Oh, of course, of course," Nicholas said. "I shall do my best not to plague you by any means." And he pretended to lock his mouth with an invisible key.

Mrs. Brindle sighed. Then she locked his door (wincing and muttering as she did so), dropped her key ring into the pocket of her work apron, and instructed Nicholas to keep beside her as she "took him down to where it's civilized" and told him "what's what and what isn't."

Nicholas obliged, walking at a fraction of his normal pace so as not to leave Mrs. Brindle far behind, and was rewarded with a most informative tour. Indeed, because the old house-keeper moved so slowly and talked so incessantly, Nicholas learned quite a lot before they had even made it downstairs. Some things he learned directly, from her occasional plain statements; others he learned by filling in the large gaps in her rambling speech. Mrs. Brindle was clearly interested more in recounting her many burdensome tasks and duties than in telling Nicholas about the history of the Manor, or about any of its practices that did not pertain to cleaning. But there was so much to clean in the Manor, and so many systems and routines dedicated to its upkeep, that Nicholas gleaned a great deal of information simply from her descriptions of chores.

In no time, for instance, he had ascertained that the Manor was composed of three main parts, which Mrs. Brindle referred to as the West Wing, the East Wing, and the Middle Wing. (By "Middle Wing," Nicholas realized that she must have meant the central part of the mansion, since really there could be no such thing as a "middle wing.") He also deduced that the boys' dormitory, which once upon a time had been a sort of parlor, was situated in the East Wing, as were his own room and the rooms of all the male staff. The girls' much larger dormitory, formerly a ballroom, lay in the West Wing. (Mrs. Brindle had referred to it simply as "the ballroom," but Nicholas had gathered that the place was full of cots and that, being a boy, he was forbidden to enter it.) Nor was it hard for Nicholas to determine that the rooms of Mrs. Brindle and the nurse, whom Mrs. Brindle sneeringly called "Miss Pretty Pills," were likewise located in the West Wing.

All this Nicholas learned before they had reached the bathroom, where Mrs. Brindle paused to dampen a cloth and pat her brow while Nicholas held her lamp. During these few minutes she said nothing—only gasped and panted—and the sudden, relative silence was almost unnerving, like the eye of a storm. But then she took back the lamp, groaned, and resumed her endless speech about the endless chores.

Having covered laundry, windows, and floors, Mrs. Brindle moved on to larder and kitchen duties. From her breathless recitations, Nicholas came to understand not only that there was a small farm on the property from which the Manor received much of its food, but that she and the Manor's cook, a widower named Mr. Griese, were very likely in love and didn't know it. Nicholas arrived at this last conclusion because he had once read a novel in which the situation was exactly like that of Mrs. Brindle and Mr. Griese. Admittedly, it had been a very dull novel—he'd finished it only because it was one of the few books available to him, and because it took him only ten minutes—but he found the similarities too strong to ignore, especially the way Mrs. Brindle grew more lively as she spoke about the cook, and went on at length about him without seeming to realize it.

She was still speaking of Mr. Griese when they reached the gallery—the broad, open area at the top of the Manor's grand staircase. Nicholas took in the faded tapestries on the walls, the beautiful, old wooden chairs in the corners, the enormous chandelier that hung over the entranceway below—and still Mrs. Brindle went on about Mr. Griese. "That poor man," she was saying, "in among the pots and the heat all day, yet always so polite, always a gentleman, never a cross word even for those who deserve it...."

Nicholas went to the railing and looked down into the entranceway, hoping to catch a glimpse of another person. It was simple curiosity—naturally, he wondered about the Manor's other inhabitants—but no one appeared.

Mrs. Brindle, meanwhile, had stopped walking, as if she meant to tell him something about the gallery, and yet her speech gave no sign of changing course. Finally Nicholas couldn't help himself. His real life, he thought, was becoming as dull as that novel. "What a chandelier!" he interjected as if he'd only just noticed it, and the better to engage Mrs. Brindle's interest he added, "It must be ever so hard to clean!"

Mrs. Brindle flinched at the sound of his voice. She had become so distracted that she seemed surprised to find herself standing there with him. Putting a hand to her neck (which had begun hurting when she flinched), she snapped, "What's that? The chandelier? Well, yes, of course it's hard to clean! What do you expect? Everything here is difficult to keep clean, isn't it? Sure, it might not have been when the Rothschilds lived here, but *their* housekeeper would've had a *proper* staff, wouldn't she?"

"The Rothschilds?" said Nicholas to keep her going. "Who were they, exactly?"

Mrs. Brindle scowled. "Why, the Rothschilds! The *Rothschilds!*" she repeated in a louder voice. "Is it your brain or your ear that's not working, child? Do you not know where you are? Rothschild's End! Who did you think the place was named for—the Birminghams?"

Nicholas mildly explained that no one had told him anything about the Rothschilds. He assumed they were connected to the famously rich Rothschild family, but beyond that he knew nothing.

"Nothing at all?" Mrs. Brindle asked suspiciously, as if Nicholas was trying to trick her. "How can you know nothing about the Rothschilds? They were so rich! Why, look around you! They had everything a person could want!" Here she paused, with a thoughtful look, and then in a softer tone continued: "Well, everything except a family, mind you—they never had that. And people say the lady wanted one ever so much, poor soul. Sure, she was a grand old lady when she died, but she had no children, no children at all. They say it was in her honor Mr. Rothschild had the place turned into an orphanage after he died, which I believe wasn't even a month later, or perhaps two. They say he had it all nicely written out in his will. What would be changed, and who the director and staff would be, and how things should be run just as smart and fine as ever they had been when he and the lady had lived here.

"Oh yes," said Mrs. Brindle, shaking her head admiringly, "things were done right then. A full housekeeping staff! Can you imagine? Why, everything must have gleamed and beamed! And that's not to mention the other sorts of help they had—the cook's helpers and the extra groundskeepers and, oh, who knows what else? But you know it was grand!"

The old housekeeper had grown more and more wistful as she spoke. She was gazing over the railing, down into the gloomy entranceway, as if the Manor's glorious past could be seen quite clearly there if only there were better lighting. After a silence, though, her face grew peevish again. "No such luck for me, of course. Where's my staff? I *am* the staff. No one to help me but a lot of children—and most of them can hardly wipe their own noses, much less handle a mop bucket. You remember that," she said, casting a stern look at Nicholas. "If things don't exactly shine around here, it's because *you* didn't *shine* them."

With that, Mrs. Brindle turned and, with great caution and even greater slowness, began to descend the wide, curving staircase. She took each step with one hand gripping the banister and the other held out for balance, and she had Nicholas hold the lamp low to the steps so that she could be sure of her footing. After a few steps they had established a rhythm, and Mrs. Brindle once again took up her monologue about chores and duties, interrupting herself only to cry out with the occasional pain and then scold it for not sitting still.

By the time they had reached the bottom step, Nicholas felt that he'd received quite a decent education. Though he'd seen almost nothing, he had a knowledge of the Manor's rooms and general layout that would later prove remarkably accurate. Indeed, on the mental map he'd been drawing, only a very few spaces had yet to be accounted for.

"Excuse me, Mrs. Brindle," he said, extending the lamp toward a closed door on the left of the entranceway, "but where does that door lead? Is it an extra parlor, perhaps? I know those double oak doors lead out onto the porch, and that door on the right is Mr. Collum's office, but what about this one on the left?"

But before Mrs. Brindle even had time to absorb his question, Nicholas began to pace and point, turning this way and that, for he was suddenly caught up in the pleasure of solving a problem, and rather forgot that he wasn't alone. "I know it can't be the drawing room. The drawing room lies on the side passage that crosses behind the staircase"—he gestured beyond the staircase, toward the rear of the Manor—"the one that turns off that north-running passage that leads back to the kitchen."

Mrs. Brindle, carefully releasing her grip on the banister's newel post, looked at him as though he'd insulted her. "The drawing room? The kitchen? How could you possibly know where those are? What are you talking about?"

"Oh, you're right, of course," Nicholas said absently. "I don't mean to say I know *exactly* where they are. But my point is, shouldn't there be another room between here and the boys' dormitory"—he pointed down a passage leading eastward from the bottom of the stairs—"and if so"—turning again toward the door in question—"doesn't this door lead to it?"

"I see," said Mrs. Brindle in an icy tone. "You're playing a prank. Mr. Collum's already shown you around, has he? Last night, no doubt, while I was chaperoning the ballroom. Well,

he might have left me a note. *You* might have told me. But no!
You think it's great fun dragging my bones out of bed half an
hour early. You like to pretend—well, I don't know what,
that somehow you've had a vision of the Manor? Is that it?
That you're a little prophet who likes to point out your poor
old housekeeper's lapses before she can even commit them?"

Nicholas realized he had made a mistake. He tried to say
something to defuse Mrs. Brindle's anger, but Mrs. Brindle
would not be interrupted. She silenced him with an irritated
flapping of her hand, which caused her to wince and cry, "Oh!
You beast! It's back to the shoulder, is it? Homesick, were
you?" Then she fixed her furious gaze on Nicholas again. "If
you truly wanted to rattle my cage, you rude boy, you ought
to have just said, 'What about the library, Mrs. Brindle?
Don't you ever clean the library? Don't you *like* shifting book
after book after book—on and on with the books and the
books—so you can dust those interminable shelves?'"

Nicholas gasped. Could it be true? He sprang to the door
and tried the knob. It was unlocked. Ignoring Mrs. Brindle's
sputtering protests, he swung the door open and barged into
the darkness beyond. He held up the lamp—and gasped
again.

Three walls of books. Floor-to-ceiling books. Books in
the thousands.

Nicholas felt his heart flutter, and looked quickly about
for a soft place to fall. *Oh no*, he thought, *and with the lamp, too!*

Luckily, when Mrs. Brindle came storming in after him a
minute later (she was an extremely slow-moving storm), she
found Nicholas not collapsed on the floor amid shattered
glass and a burning rug, but instead sitting in an overstuffed

armchair, with the lamp held firmly in both hands. By some miracle (and several deep breaths) he had not fallen asleep, despite witnessing the most exciting spectacle of his life. He did look strangely affected, however, with his wide-open mouth and his wildly roving eyes, and at the sight of him Mrs. Brindle lost her anger and grew concerned.

"Boy!" she cried, in her alarm quite forgetting his name. She tried to hurry over to him without tripping on the rug. "Are you not well? Can you hear me? Oh, heavens!"

Nicholas heard her plainly enough, but he could not tear his eyes away to look at her. The innumerable books were all bound in leather, with their titles and author names on the spines in gold lettering, and already he had determined that they were divided into categories—history, botany, chemistry, astronomy, mathematics, physics, economics, fiction, poetry, and more—and organized by systems particular to each category. They varied widely in size, from volumes as slim as slate boards to enormous tomes the size of cinder blocks. And to Nicholas they were all beautiful, every one of them.

"Boy!" Mrs. Brindle said again, at last drawing near. She bent to study his face in the lamplight. "Are you unwell? Shall I fetch the nurse?" She looked anxiously at the door. "It will take me some time to rouse her...."

Nicholas pulled himself together. He didn't want Mr. Collum hearing of a nurse's visit on his first morning at the Manor. He leaped up and flashed Mrs. Brindle a winning smile. "Thanks so much, Mrs. Brindle, but please don't trouble yourself on my account. You see, I'm perfectly well!"

"My word!" Mrs. Brindle said, startled by his abrupt recovery. "Gracious!"

"It was just a false alarm," said Nicholas. "You're aware of my condition, I take it? Every so often I have to sleep—it can't be helped—and for a moment I thought a spell was coming on. That's why I hurried in here and sat in a chair, just in case. Apparently I was mistaken. Tell me," he hurried on, "are we allowed to read these books?" He gestured at the bookshelves.

Mrs. Brindle seemed not to have heard his question. "Step aside and let me sit down," she said, shaking her head. "You just stole half my life away." She lowered herself into the armchair, leaned back, and stared up at the ceiling.

"Shall *I* fetch the nurse, Mrs. Brindle?" Nicholas asked.

"That foolish girl couldn't mend a sock," Mrs. Brindle muttered. "Just give me a moment to collect myself. And carry that lamp away—its fumes are troubling my eye."

Nicholas was only too happy to do so. In the far corner of the library, he had spied a beautiful mahogany desk and beside it—to his delight—a gigantic dictionary on a stand. He walked over to the dictionary, glancing eagerly about him as he did. The library's other furniture included a chaise longue, a rocking chair, and several armchairs, each with its own reading table and lamp. Positioned against the far wall was a rolling ladder that could be pushed along narrow tracks in the floor, providing access to the higher bookshelves, which were very high indeed—the top shelf was at least ten feet from the floor. The south wall, the only one not covered with books, seemed mostly made up of windows, and beneath each one was a cushioned, sun-faded window seat. Nicholas grinned at everything his eyes fell upon. In his opinion the library could not have been more perfect.

Gently laying both hands on the dictionary, Nicholas closed his eyes, as if he might absorb the words through his fingers. He felt almost giddy. In the schoolhouse at Littleview, there had also been a dictionary on a stand—a much smaller dictionary on a much more rickety stand, but he had loved it. It was among the few books he'd ever been able to read. Sure, he had read countless newspapers, for newspapers were easy to come by—one could always find them discarded in the street or left upon tables—but actual books were seldom available, perhaps because the orphanage had lacked funds to obtain them, perhaps because no one thought of it or cared. As a result, the only books Nicholas had read were school textbooks, a handful of novels he had swiped from the Littleview staff, a volume of fairy tales, an outdated almanac— and that dictionary in the schoolhouse.

He hadn't been able to read all of the dictionary, unfortunately; perhaps that was why it stood out so prominently in his mind. On the first occasion he had asked permission to use it, Nicholas had lingered at the stand for several minutes. He had found the definition he'd sought right away, but then had continued reading, page after page, the way a normal person might read a story. He had become much too interested to stop. Indeed, he was so absorbed that he didn't notice the teacher frowning at him from behind her desk. He was turning the pages too quickly, standing there too long, and the teacher thought he was avoiding his schoolwork.

"Nicholas," she had snapped. "You no longer have permission to use the dictionary. Return to your seat."

Nicholas's protests had been to no avail. On the contrary, they were much to his detriment, for as punishment he was forbidden to use the dictionary from that day on. What an agony that had been! But now here sat this one in the library, just waiting for him, and thousands of other books besides. The discovery was enough to push away, for the moment, any thought of Spiders or of nightmares in isolated, locked rooms. An entire library! It seemed too much to have hoped for — and indeed Nicholas never had.

"Oh, you monster!" he heard Mrs. Brindle cry. "You couldn't wait, could you? Simply couldn't wait!"

Reluctantly, Nicholas opened his eyes and turned. Mrs. Brindle had risen from the chair and was rubbing at her hip. He felt a ridiculous impulse to hide behind the mahogany desk, as if he might actually remain in the library forever, reading as much as he pleased and sneaking crumbs from the kitchen at night. *Like an elf*, he thought. *The library elf.* But that was the stuff of fairy tales.

"Well, hurry up," Mrs. Brindle called to him impatiently, as if she had been waiting for ages. "I can't very well see without my lamp, can I?"

Nicholas rejoined her, and together they made their way out. Nicholas paused in the doorway to look back. The books sat upon the shelves in heavy shadow now, like hidden objects in a mystery. As if every unread book were not mystery enough, even in the light. Nicholas turned away with a pang in his chest.

"I'll be back," he whispered.

Taps and Glimmers

In the entranceway again, Mrs. Brindle seemed at a loss for how to continue with the tour. By this time others had begun to stir in the Manor. Drifting down the passages came the sounds of shuffling footsteps, doors opening and closing, sleepy conversations—and the distinct rattling of pots and pans. Mrs. Brindle, touching her hair as if to ensure it was still there, peered intently down the passage leading toward the rear of the Manor. Toward the kitchen, as Nicholas knew.

"Is it that late already?" she muttered, apparently to herself. "And I still have to finish this infernal..."

Mrs. Brindle glanced toward the door of Mr. Collum's office. Nicholas thought she was worried about being reprimanded. Then he realized that she'd actually glanced toward an antique mirror that stood beside the door. It was a large, oval-shaped mirror on a rotating base, the sort one normally might find in a dressing room, and Nicholas could not fathom why it was there. But it was easy enough to guess why the housekeeper had glanced at it.

"Mrs. Brindle," he said, "would you mind telling me what that mirror is for? The entranceway seems an odd place for it."

Mrs. Brindle seized upon Nicholas's question with eagerness. Stepping over to the mirror, as if standing in front of the glass would make it easier to explain, she said, "Why, Mr. Collum had it carried down from upstairs so that he might use it during free times, when it's his turn to watch the library."

"I see!" Nicholas said (for he really did), and he started to ask Mrs. Brindle when free times were, and how long they lasted, and whether children were allowed to take books out of the library. But Mrs. Brindle doggedly continued her explanation.

"Naturally, someone has to watch the children," she said, trying to pat her hair into place and inspect her teeth inconspicuously. "You can't have them unsupervised, can you? Now, with both doors open, you see, and the mirror turned just so, Mr. Collum can work at his desk in *here*"—Mrs. Brindle turned her thumb toward the door beside them—"and still keep an eye on you children in *there*." She pointed across the entranceway.

"I see," Nicholas said again, and he wondered how long he would have to stand there saying "I see, I see."

Not long, as it turned out, for already Mrs. Brindle was smoothing her apron, her face wearing an expression of somewhat strained composure. She looked both dissatisfied and hopeful.

"Are we off to the kitchen now, Mrs. Brindle?" Nicholas asked.

Mrs. Brindle looked shocked. "Why, what makes you—"

"I'm eager to see it," Nicholas said, cutting her off. "Shall we go? I can keep carrying the lamp, if you like."

Mrs. Brindle, recovering, agreed that this would be nice.

If Mrs. Brindle had ever had any intention of continuing the tour beyond the kitchen, it vanished like the steam rising from the pots on the stove. For no sooner had she laid eyes on Mr. Griese's shiny red face—whether red from heat or from Mrs. Brindle's appearance was unclear to Nicholas—than she forgot the existence of any world beyond the swinging doors. Nor did she seem aware of Nicholas's presence, but launched at once into a series of questions about Mr. Griese's health; and how he had slept (she knew it had been his turn to chaperone the boys' dormitory); and how he ever managed to make do with such a small supply of eggs, vegetables, and milk; and so on. She asked these questions in a lively, concerned tone—and without once interrupting herself, Nicholas noticed, to direct angry comments at unseen wicked beasts.

Mr. Griese, for his part, was too engaged in his work and in trying to answer Mrs. Brindle's questions to pay Nicholas any attention at all. "Oh, as for that, Mrs. Brindle," he said, trying simultaneously to peer into a cupboard and salt his pots while casting nervous sidelong glances at the house-keeper, "there's actually a plentiful supply of good eggs and milk, you know, and along with my herb garden—"

"Oh, Mr. Griese, you're entirely too modest! Why, in my experience—"

After some minutes of this, Nicholas backed slowly out of the kitchen. He knew he ought to stay, but the smells, sounds, and talk of cooking had greatly intensified his hunger pangs until he could no longer stand it—he'd had nothing to eat since a sandwich on the train. Perhaps he could just look around until breakfast, he thought as he slipped out. After all, no one had specifically forbidden it.

In the passage outside the kitchen, Nicholas paused to let his eyes adjust. He rubbed his bare arms. The kitchen had been well lit and warm, and he no longer had the lamp. Luckily, the weak light of dawn was filtering into the Manor through windows here and there, and it grew stronger by the minute. Nicholas headed back the way he and Mrs. Brindle had come, thinking to take a peek into the drawing room and the main parlor, which, according to the housekeeper, were often used for group activities.

Before he reached the entranceway, Nicholas turned onto the side passage that crossed behind the grand staircase. His footsteps were muffled now by a thick carpet that covered the center part of the floor, and the atmosphere grew quieter as he drew farther away from the kitchen. It also grew darker and creepier. All the candles in the wall sconces were unlit, and the overhead fixtures were predictably missing their bulbs. There was a window at the far end of the passage, but it was half-shrouded by curtains, and quite a distance away. Between Nicholas and the window, everything was cast in deep shadow. Perhaps he ought to explore elsewhere. What was the point of looking if he couldn't see anything?

He was on the verge of turning back when he heard a faint, rhythmic tapping sound. It was very much like a knock on a door, only softer and more repetitive: three gentle taps, followed by silence, then three more. *What can that be?* he thought, his curiosity instantly aroused. The sound seemed to be coming from the drawing room—or what he believed to be the drawing room, anyway—and Nicholas, listening intently, crept closer on his tiptoes. (It never occurred to him not to investigate, but the taps were certainly strange enough to make him cautious.) He heard another three taps, then silence, then three more. And now he stood just outside the door. With a quick glance left and right, Nicholas bent and peered through the keyhole.

At once he could tell that there was a lamp in the room, for an unseen light source, not particularly bright but steadier than a candle, illuminated his view. That view, unfortunately, was limited to the end of a table, a strip of paneled wall beyond it, and the outer stone edge of what appeared to be a fireplace. By a subtle change in the shadows on the floor, however, Nicholas determined that whoever held the lamp was moving slowly and deliberately along that wall. Soon he should be able to see who it was. Meanwhile the tapping had continued—three taps, silence, three more.

Then the lamp appeared in his keyhole view, and by the light of its low flame Nicholas saw Mr. Collum. He was inching along the far wall, tapping on the wood panels with his knuckles, then pressing his ear to the wall and tapping again. If he had not been tapping and listening in places both high and low, Nicholas would have seen only the man's long legs. Fortunately, though, Mr. Collum bent forward to tap and listen at a low spot, and Nicholas could plainly see the intensely inquisitive expression on his face before he straightened and moved on toward the fireplace.

Nicholas scarcely had time to wonder what Mr. Collum was up to before there came an enormous clamor of footsteps and talking from the direction of the East Wing. A distant door had been opened, and all the boys were moving through the Manor, loudly tramping and jostling one another as they headed to the dining hall for breakfast. Nicholas moved away from the keyhole. He had better hurry back to Mrs. Brindle and see what was expected of him. He began to tiptoe down the passage, but he had taken only a few steps when he heard the drawing-room door creak open behind him.

Nicholas felt his heart quicken. There was no time to disappear around the corner, still several paces away. He was going to have to talk his way out of this. He took a deep breath and turned around. Mr. Collum was emerging from the drawing room, a look of deep concentration on his face. He had yet to see Nicholas standing there in the shadows, and Nicholas was uncertain whether he ought to speak, which would startle and possibly anger Mr. Collum, or wait to be seen, which might seem odd enough behavior to be deemed suspicious.

As Nicholas stood trying to decide, Mr. Collum closed the door and then—as if on a sudden whim—tapped on the wall beside it. He listened, then leaned to press his ear against the wall and tap again. As he did so, however, his eyes fell upon Nicholas and grew extraordinarily round and white, like miniature full moons. His mouth dropped open.

Instantly Nicholas cried, "Oh, good morning, Mr. Collum! I *thought* that was you, but I wasn't sure — it's awfully gloomy in this passage, isn't it? And your lamp is hardly turned up at all. You must have eyes like an owl! I'm afraid I took a wrong turn on the way to your office. Mrs. Brindle said... Mr. Collum? Are you all right?"

After his initial shock at seeing Nicholas, Mr. Collum had leaped away from the wall as if it had bitten his ear, and his large nostrils were flaring and contracting impressively. "I'm quite well, thank you!" Mr. Collum replied, though his agitated, angry tone did not suit his words at all. "Only I thought perhaps I heard a mouse in the wall!"

"A mouse?" said Nicholas, glancing at the wall with a feigned look of concern. "Shall I fetch a trap and some cheese?"

"What? Oh... no," said Mr. Collum, recovering. He straightened his waistcoat, adjusted his tie. "Thank you, Nicholas, but I shall deal with it myself. Did you say you were looking for my office?"

"Yes, sir," said Nicholas as Mr. Collum locked the drawing-room door. "Mrs. Brindle thought you might want to tell me the rules."

"Indeed I do," Mr. Collum said brusquely, tucking away his key. With a thrill of surprise, Nicholas saw that it was the same key he'd used the night before — the one with a ribbon tied to it. Did that single key work on every door in the

Manor? Had Nicholas unwittingly made a mold of a *skeleton* key?

"We will speak in my office," Mr. Collum was saying. "Follow me."

Nicholas correctly guessed that he was to take this instruction literally, and so he did not walk beside Mr. Collum but trailed after him. It required a considerable effort to hold back, though. His relief at not getting into trouble had given him such a terrific burst of energy that he could hardly contain it. He walked with light, bouncing steps, half skipping, and this seemed to help.

Back in the Manor's entranceway, Nicholas looked on eagerly as Mr. Collum unlocked the door to his office. Sure enough, he used the same key as before. Mr. Collum, sensing Nicholas's watchful gaze, glanced suspiciously over his shoulder. Nicholas quickly suppressed his smile and averted his eyes.

From where he stood next to the large mirror, he could see all the way down the north-running passage to the swinging kitchen doors at the rear of the Manor, and even as he looked, he saw a frowning Mrs. Brindle poke her head out of the kitchen. (It was rather a slow poke, like a turtle extending its head from its shell.) Evidently she had finally noticed his absence and was looking for him. Nicholas waved and smiled, and Mrs. Brindle stared at him in some confusion. But seeing he was with Mr. Collum, she only shook her head and withdrew it again.

The director's office was tidy and well appointed, with a desk, filing cabinets, and bookshelves. Opening the curtains over his window, Mr. Collum revealed a pleasant view of the front lawn and the trees beyond it. The sky had cleared overnight, and the morning looked to be beautiful, with a brightening blue sky overhead and birds twittering loudly in the shrubs. Mr. Collum blinked in the sudden light, faint though it was, and took his seat in a straight-backed chair behind the desk. Nicholas started to sit in the chair across from him, then thought better of it, for Mr. Collum had not actually invited him to do so.

Mr. Collum opened a drawer, took out the by-now-familiar ledger, and laid it on the desk before him. He considered it a moment without opening it. Then he grunted bemusedly, as if laying it aside in his mind, and looked up at Nicholas. "Here is what you must know, Nicholas. Observe the rules and we shall have no problems; disregard them and we shall have very serious problems indeed. I believe that is clear enough for you. The rules are clear as well: You must be where you are expected to be when you are expected to be there, obey all Manor staff without argument or disrespectful reply, and waste nothing. Can you remember these?"

"Absolutely, sir," Nicholas said. "Though just to be sure I heard you correctly, did you say the last rule was 'waste nothing'?"

Mr. Collum irritably swept a speck of dust from his desktop. "As I've said before, Nicholas, my predecessor was a scoundrel. A scoundrel and a fool. He squandered a fortune, spending the orphanage funds unwisely and stealing a good bit for himself. As the new director, I am tasked with returning the Manor to good standing. Every penny must be accounted for. Every person must do double duty. And nothing must be wasted."

"An admirable rule, sir," Nicholas said. "I take it that's why we're so sparing with the electricity?"

"Yes," said Mr. Collum. "The previous director, Mr. Bottoms, spent vast sums on the procurement of electrical power for the Manor. He did this despite an abundant supply of candles and lantern oil, which he made no effort whatsoever to utilize. Under my own directorship, we shall make careful, thrifty use of what we have, until it is gone. Now then, Nicholas, if you have no more questions—"

"Oh, but I do have one more question, sir," Nicholas said, and noting Mr. Collum's impatient look, he blurted out quickly, "I only wondered if perhaps we were allowed to take books out of the library."

Mr. Collum frowned. "Certainly not. If books were removed from the library, they might be damaged or lost. You may use them only under supervision and only if you show them proper care. Now then, Nicholas—"

"I'm sorry, Mr. Collum," Nicholas hastily interrupted again, "but do you think perhaps that under my special circumstances—being locked in my room at night, you know—do you think perhaps you might make an exception so that I might have something to read at bedtime? I promise I would take excellent care of…of the books, and…" Nicholas slowly stopped speaking, subdued by the force of Mr. Collum's withering glare.

"I am quite sure, Nicholas," the director said, "that you do not wish to be contrary on your first morning here. The Manor is to be your home for some years—barring adoption, of course, which, to be frank, is unlikely in your case. I advise you to think very seriously about how you intend to comport yourself."

Nicholas looked down at his battered shoes and said nothing. He did indeed wish to be contrary—at the moment it was his most earnest wish of all—but somehow he found the presence of mind not to express this feeling. Mr. Collum was right about one thing, anyway. Adoption, in his case, was unlikely. Had he not been in orphanages all his life? He had not been a beautiful baby; he was not a beautiful boy. At the last orphanage, adoptions of any child had been rare, but Nicholas had paid close attention to the process. He had figured out the right things to say, the right way to act, when prospective parents visited. And one time he had actually come close—the young couple liked him; they even spoke about him with Mr. Cuckieu. But when Mr. Cuckieu informed them of Nicholas's condition, they panicked. Nicholas watched them leave with miserable, guilty expressions, not daring even to look in his direction. Afterward, Mr. Cuckieu, in the guise of being helpful, "explained" to Nicholas that it was "hard enough raising a child without throwing in a lot of extra difficulties."

Nicholas had stopped trying to be adopted after that. He knew better than anyone that orphanages were destined to be his home until he was old enough to escape them forever. And if that was the case, he needed to avoid making an enemy of someone like Mr. Collum, who was powerful enough to make his life miserable. More powerful, even, than bullies like the Spiders.

Mr. Collum was clearly waiting for a contrite response. Nicholas forced himself to look up again and meet the director's stern gaze. "I'm sorry, Mr. Collum. I'm sure you're right. I apologize for losing my manners."

"Very well, Nicholas," said Mr. Collum. "And now that you've found them again, I suggest you hold on to them." He rose from his chair, tucking the ledger under his arm. "Let us go to breakfast, and I shall introduce you to the others." With their meeting thus concluded to his satisfaction (if not at all to Nicholas's), Mr. Collum locked up his office and led Nicholas to the kitchen.

Mrs. Brindle had at last gone off about her business, leaving Mr. Griese alone with his, but the cook's face was still shiny and red. His scalp was quite red, too. He was mostly bald, with only a thin line of short gray hair that began above one ear and ran around the back of his head to the other. Overall, his head bore an uncanny resemblance to a damaged tomato with a trail of fuzzy mold growing on it. This was not the most appetizing thing to be reminded of before breakfast, but Nicholas was far too hungry to care.

Breakfast was a large serving of piping-hot oatmeal, which Mr. Griese ladled into Nicholas's bowl, and a boiled egg, which he put directly into Nicholas's free hand. Nicholas's stomach growled fiercely, his mouth watered, and he was tempted to take a bite right then. He resisted, however, for no one likes to be presented to strangers with a mouthful of egg, and Mr. Collum was already leading him out.

The dining hall held two extraordinarily long, elegant tables that would have served well enough for a gathering of royalty. Instead, they were packed with orphaned children. At a glance, Nicholas estimated that there were about thirty girls and twenty boys chattering and slurping their oatmeal and, in some cases, drooping sleepily over their bowls. The dining-hall curtains had been opened to take advantage of the morning sun, and dust motes swirled like tiny galaxies in the shafts of sunlight. To the left of the tables, Mrs. Brindle sat in a rocking chair near a stone fireplace, supposedly supervising the diners, though her half-closed eyes suggested she was dozing. All in all, it was a comfortable enough scene, but Nicholas did not feel comfortable in the least—in fact, he felt quite anxious and peculiar, for it is no easy thing being made to stand before a group of strangers.

"Children!" Mr. Collum announced in a loud voice. "Your attention, please!"

The dining hall fell silent. Fifty gazes swiveled to Mr. Collum's face, then downward to Nicholas's, where they remained. Nicholas felt his own face grow hot. And then, to his dismay, he felt his *fingertips* growing hot, for the scalding oatmeal in his bowl was heating the thin ceramic to a painful degree.

"Allow me to present Nicholas Benedict," said Mr. Collum, laying his hand firmly upon Nicholas's shoulder as if to prevent escape. "He is our newest resident. I know you will all make him welcome."

A few children clapped, thinking they were supposed to, then quickly stopped and ducked their heads in shame when no one else joined in. A ripple of giggles went through the room. Nicholas had already noticed the Spiders seated near the middle of the leftmost table. They were nudging one another, winking, and sharing secret smiles. He had also spotted John sitting as far away from the Spiders as possible — at the far end of the rightmost table, with his back to the windows. There was an empty chair across from him. Nicholas allowed himself to hope that John had saved it.

When the giggles had died down, Mr. Collum spoke briefly about courtesies, considerations, and other matters of comportment. Nicholas knew no one was listening. They were all staring curiously at him, the new orphan, wondering about him. Nicholas could feel the weight of their stares. He was anxious to be released, and not just because he was nervous — his fingers were really getting scorched now. He would have grabbed the hot bowl with his other hand except that the slippery boiled egg made it awkward. He was worried he might drop something.

"I believe some of you are aware," Mr. Collum was saying now, "that Nicholas has a condition called — what is your condition called again, Nicholas?"

"Narcolepsy," said Nicholas in a faltering voice. He frowned, surprised at his own timidity, and said again, more loudly, "Narcolepsy!"

Mr. Collum looked at him askance. "One response is sufficient, Nicholas." A few titters erupted in the room but were quickly silenced by Mr. Collum's forbidding expression. "What this means is that Nicholas must often take short naps. It cannot be helped, and you must all do your best to accommodate it, however inconvenient this might be. Rest assured, however, that Nicholas will pull his weight. He will have the same duties as all of you, and I'm sure he is eager to prove himself capable and responsible. Am I right, Nicholas?"

"Absolutely, Mr. Collum," replied Nicholas, trying to smile even though his fingers would have screamed if they could. They were going to blister if he waited any longer, he

realized. And so as casually as possible—as if there were
nothing unusual about what he was doing—Nicholas dumped
his boiled egg into his oatmeal, grabbed the hot bowl with his
free hand, and thrust his burned fingers into his mouth.

Several children gaped at him in surprise. Not a few
looked disgusted, no doubt wondering who this uncivilized
creature was who liked to plop eggs into his oatmeal and suck
his fingers.

"Very good," said Mr. Collum, who had failed to notice
any of this. "Find an open chair, then, Nicholas. Your neighbors can instruct you in our morning routines." He sent
Nicholas forward with a light push between the shoulder
blades and returned to the kitchen for his own breakfast.

Nicholas went around the front of the table on his right,
headed toward John in the back of the dining hall. He passed
by an empty chair near the front, but he would never have
sat in it, anyway. The front ends of the tables were occupied
by the youngest children, five-year-olds and six-year-olds,
mostly, and most of them with runny noses. They probably
sat there so they could be seen more easily by orphanage
staff, Nicholas thought. Hidden away in the midst of the
older children, they would be more vulnerable to attack.

Nicholas had also seen an empty chair at the other table,
near the Spiders, but he had been pretending not to see it or,
indeed, the Spiders themselves. If he had made eye contact
with them and they had beckoned him over to join them, he
would have refused at his peril. Peril was coming soon
enough; Nicholas preferred to delay it a little longer.

Murmurs and whispers followed him as he strode to the
back, smiling boldly at the children whose chairs he passed.

Some smiled back; most simply stared. He noticed that almost all of the girls looked haggard, with their bows stuck haphazardly in their hair, and dark circles under their eyes. Clearly it had been a bad night in the ballroom. The girls reminded Nicholas of the children at Littleview, the ones kept awake and unnerved by his screaming. They all looked as sleepy and tired as he felt—though far *more* so than he looked, for Nicholas had long since determined never to appear sleepy when he could help it. He had weaknesses enough without putting them on constant display.

"How are the fingers?" John said drily as Nicholas approached.

"Well cooked," Nicholas said. He hastily set his bowl down (for by now his other fingers were also starting to feel well cooked) and dropped into the chair across from John. "They taste terrible, though. I need to do a better job rinsing the soap off them."

John narrowed his eyes, which appeared to be the way he smiled, and reached for a nearby pitcher. Seeing that Nicholas had not been given a glass, he refilled his own and passed it across. Nicholas was just as thirsty as he was hungry, and gratefully he gulped the milk down. John refilled the glass with the last bit of milk from the pitcher. By the time he'd finished pouring, Nicholas had devoured half of his egg and was holding a spoonful of oatmeal at the ready.

"Thanks," he gasped between bites.

John watched him with a sort of amused curiosity. In this better light of morning, the older boy's eyes proved to be a pleasant blue-green color, almost turquoise. He had unusually good posture—so good it prompted Nicholas to sit up straighter himself—and he looked strong, like an athlete or a farm boy. His chicken pox scars, though, were even more prominent in the light. They were sprinkled about his face in such abundance that Nicholas, without intending to, saw patterns in them. *Like a constellation of scars*, he thought, not because it was funny (he didn't think it was) but because his mind was always looking for puns and rhymes, whether he wanted it to or not, just as it always looked for patterns.

Seated next to Nicholas and John were two boys of about John's age, both looking at Nicholas as if he had stepped on their feet. He smiled at them regardless and started to introduce himself, but they only shifted their chairs so that their backs were to him and started up a private conversation.

"What's eating *them*?" muttered John, clearly taken aback by their rudeness.

"It's all right," Nicholas said with a shrug. "They don't like that I'm sitting by them because I'm so much younger. They think I'm presumptuous."

John blinked and looked wonderingly at Nicholas. "I'm sure you're right," he said after a pause. He silently mouthed the word "presumptuous," shook his head, and scooped up the last bite of his oatmeal.

"I hope it's all right with you," Nicholas said. "I noticed the empty chair, and—"

John, chewing, waved him silent with his spoon. He swallowed and said, "Of course it's all right. I saved it for you. I wanted to hear how last night went. Don't worry," he said in a low tone, jerking his head toward the other boys, "they aren't friends of mine or anything. I only sit back here because I like to keep my eyes on the room. I don't like to have anyone behind me."

Nicholas nodded knowingly. He always preferred to sit with his back to a wall, too, or else right next to a staff member.

John shoved his empty bowl aside and leaned forward. "Say, I'm sorry I didn't come back last night. Mr. Collum put me on a last-minute chore before bedtime. How did everything go?"

Nicholas blew on another spoonful of oatmeal. "Oh, reasonably well, I suppose," he said lightly. "I met the Spiders, got locked in my room, had a bunch of nightmares—yes, all in all, I'd say it was a fine night."

"They found you?" said John with a disgusted look. "That's probably my fault, Nick. I ought to have had you come down with me. I guess you got initiated, then."

"Not exactly," Nicholas said, and he related what had happened.

John looked stunned. "You did that? You actually did that? And you don't mean to go meet them after breakfast?"

"I don't mean to give them cookies, either," Nicholas said. "Not that I actually have any to give."

"But this is the worst thing you could possibly do!" John said a little too loudly. He lowered his voice and said gravely, "Listen, Nick, it's better to run away or even fight them than humiliate them like that. Now they'll be your enemies!"

Nicholas sighed. "I know. But I've been through all this before. Believe me, they would have ended up singling me out anyway."

John pointed an accusing finger at Nicholas. "You don't know that! How could you know that?"

Nicholas puckered his brow. John seemed surprisingly worried, even angry. "I know from experience," Nicholas said mildly. "Sure, they'll have it in for me now, but at least this way I get some satisfaction, right?"

John's angry expression slowly changed into a defeated one. He turned his head, staring without focus at the back wall, and muttered, "I wish you hadn't done that, Nick. I really do. This is the last thing I need."

Nicholas raised an eyebrow—or tried to, anyway. He hadn't quite mastered the single-eyebrow raise yet. "It doesn't have anything to do with you, does it?"

John turned back to him. He still looked forlorn. "Forget it," he said gloomily. "What I ought to have done is shake your hand and give you credit. You have a lot of guts, Nick. No one could say you don't." After this he sat quietly, watching Nicholas scrape the last tiny remains of oatmeal from his bowl. Then he looked over at the table where the Spiders had been sitting and said, "They're leaving now."

Nicholas nodded. He knew very well the Spiders were leaving, for after every bite of oatmeal he had lowered his spoon at such an angle as to offer a distorted reflection of the table behind him. He had done this quickly enough, and glanced at the spoon sneakily enough, that John had not noticed.

"Well," John said after a pause, "since you don't plan to keep your appointment, do you want me to fill you in on the routines around here, like Mr. Collum said?"

Nicholas grinned and said that nothing could possibly give him greater pleasure than learning about routines.

And so, after leveling a dubious look at him, John launched

into a lengthy explanation of the various duties that rotated among the orphans and the staff, and how the schedules were managed, and countless other things related to daily life at the Manor. Nicholas listened, although with only part of his attention. A greater part of it was taken up with wondering about John's troubled response to this business with the Spiders, and a still-greater part—indeed the most by far—was focused on Mr. Collum's mysterious behavior in the drawing room before breakfast. What had he been looking for when he thought no one was watching?

"Nick!" John said after he'd been going on awhile. He snapped his fingers in front of Nicholas's face. "You've gone into a trance. Are you falling asleep, or am I telling you too much at once? If you want, I can write the more important stuff down."

"Oh, no, thanks," Nicholas said almost absently. "I think I've got it." And he rattled off everything John had just told him. He spoke so quickly and with such precision, recounting every detail in such perfect order, that John's face could not settle on an expression—he looked surprised, then suspicious, and finally amazed. By the time Nicholas had finished, it was not he but John who appeared to have fallen into a trance.

"Why, I've never...," John murmured, not finishing his thought. Curiosity and wonder shone in his eyes, as if a light had been switched on behind them. Then, for the first time, he smiled. He even chuckled. "Well, well, Nick! Well, *well*!" And this was all he said, yet somehow it expressed such understanding and appreciation that Nicholas felt he'd been paid an elaborate compliment.

Nicholas gave John a sly look. For some time neither of them spoke. They both knew that a secret had just passed between them, and were pausing to appreciate it.

Eventually Nicholas broke the silence. "So if you think that about covers things…"

"I'd say it does!" John said, shaking his head.

"Then I want to ask you about something I saw Mr. Collum doing," Nicholas said, and he told John what he'd seen.

"Really? He was actually doing that?" John glanced around the dining hall. Most of the children were still eating their breakfast. "I can tell you what that's about—but not here. Too many ears. Let's go out to the park."

The boys carried their dishes into the kitchen, where a sleepy girl plunged them into sudsy water without looking up or speaking a word. Then John led Nicholas through an enormous but sparsely stocked butler's pantry (a shortcut, he said, though a rather depressing one if you paid attention to the empty shelves), on into a sort of antechamber hung about with raincoats and tattered straw hats, and finally out the back door.

It was a truly pretty summer morning, with blue skies and a cooling breeze, and the property behind the Manor was just as pretty. "The park," as John called it, appeared to be exactly that—a big, grassy, wooded area with widely spaced, majestic old oak trees and no underbrush to speak of. From the back door, a stone path led across the grass to a quaint old gazebo, where it then veered westward, toward a long wooden building with a fenced lot behind it that resembled a corral. And so it once had been, as John informed Nicholas, for the building used to be a stable. Now it served as the orphanage schoolhouse, and the fenced lot as a sort of playground.

"Everybody calls it 'the lot,'" John said. "We're not much for imagination around here."

The property was a lovely place altogether, but not altogether in good repair. The gazebo was in desperate need of fresh paint, and there was no water spouting from the decorative fountain beyond it. Much of the grass in the park was dead and brown, especially between the back of the Manor and the front of the schoolhouse, where so many children had walked, forgoing the stone path. The flower beds that ran along the rear of the Manor must once have been impressive, but now they were barren, with the exception of a few sparse clusters of daylilies and other perennials that had not required new planting and had, therefore, sprung cheerily into the world only to find themselves alone and neglected. If Nicholas had not already known that the orphanage had fallen on hard times, the sad condition of its property would have told him plainly enough.

John and Nicholas stood near the back door, considering how best to speak in private. They were not the only ones to have ventured outside. A handful of younger boys were playing marbles on a patch of dirt nearby, and over near the gazebo steps sat two exhausted-looking girls with a jump rope, waiting for a third girl to come out and make a game. In the gazebo itself, watching over them all, was a petite blonde woman in a peach-colored gingham dress. She was pacing back and forth with tiny steps, as if her dress were very tight around her ankles, although in fact it did not quite reach her ankles and did not appear tight in the least.

"That's Miss Candace," John said quietly. "The orphanage nurse. I think she's a bit crazy. Whatever you do, don't let her give you drops. I don't even know what they're for, but she loves to give them. Here, let's just walk around awhile."

The boys began strolling in the direction of the schoolhouse, following the track of dead grass. During free time you could go anywhere in the park, John said, as long as you remained in sight of the chaperone on duty. He pointed past the schoolhouse toward a thin line of trees, hickories mostly, that were much younger and smaller than the towering oaks. "The farm's just beyond those trees. When you're on larder duty, you have to go over in the mornings and evenings— there's a path that cuts through."

Nicholas nodded, trying to suppress his impatience. From Mrs. Brindle's speeches and what John had told him over breakfast, he had already deduced where the Manor's farm was situated, just as he had known at once that the woman in the gazebo was the nurse. That had been a simple matter of counting, for there were only five adults on the orphanage staff (not counting the schoolmaster, who would arrive in August), and Nicholas had already met the other four.

Finally, after what felt like ages but was in fact only half a minute, John deemed they were sufficiently out of earshot. "I'll tell you right off, I think it's nonsense," he said, stopping to look back at the Manor. He put his hands on his hips and studied the impressive building. "But obviously Mr. Collum doesn't think so. Obviously he thinks there really is a treasure hidden somewhere in there."

Nicholas's heart skipped. He thought he must not have heard John right. "A treasure? Are you serious?"

"Apparently Mr. Collum is. I thought he sort of half believed it, maybe, but from what you say, it sounds like more than that." John scratched his head thoughtfully and started walking again. "He called me into his office last week to ask if I'd heard any odd rumors. He hasn't been here long, see, and I've been here over a year. He thought I might know some things he didn't. He made it all sound like he was just curious. He wanted to know if any of the children believed in silly things like ghosts and monsters, or mysterious treasures and secret hiding places, and so on. At least that's what he said. But he went on a long time about the treasure and the hiding places, which did make me wonder."

"What kind of treasure?" Nicholas asked. They were walking at an easy pace toward the back of the park, yet he suddenly felt short of breath. "Do you have any idea what he's talking about?"

"It just so happens I do," John said. "For one thing, on his very first day here, Mr. Collum ordered everyone—staff and kids alike—to go looking for every scrap of paperwork they could find. He knew that the last director, Mr. Bottoms, had scattered financial records all around the Manor—in desks and cubbies, lying on top of windowsills, you name it."

"Why on earth would he do that?" Nicholas asked.

"Because he'd found out he was going to be investigated, and he wanted to make it as hard on the inspectors as possible. What he didn't realize was that they already had enough evidence to arrest him. He'd gone to all that trouble for nothing. And he did go to a lot of trouble—the records he left scattered everywhere had all been falsified. Stacks and stacks of notebooks and ledgers, all of it rubbish. It took Mr.

Collum a week to go through it all, and every day he just got more upset."

Nicholas tried to imagine being desperate enough to take such extreme measures. What kind of director let himself get into such a pickle? "Mr. Bottoms sounds like a piece of work," he observed.

"He might *be* one," John said, "but the real trouble was that he never *did* one. He started out foolish and lazy and ended up foolish and crooked. I guess that's the way it is with some people. Not Mr. Collum, though. You have to hand it to him—he's worked hard. He took this job thinking he'd fix all the problems, and he's tried like the dickens. But things were worse than he'd realized. There was almost no money left. He had to cut the staff's pay, so they all quit. He managed to hire new staff, but they aren't exactly crackerjacks. I think mostly they're people who needed a place to stay and would work for pennies."

"How do you know all this?" Nicholas asked.

John shrugged. "Mostly from being here and paying attention, though some of it comes straight from Mr. Collum. He seems to trust me, though I'm not sure why. Maybe because I keep my nose clean. Anyway, a few times when I've been helping file paperwork in his office, he's gotten upset about something Mr. Bottoms did—he'll open a folder, look through it, and then his face will go red and he'll just pop. He'll go on and on about Mr. Bottoms and all the problems here and how much is expected of him and so on. Then he'll go out to the front porch and smoke his pipe, and when he comes back in, he goes right back to work as if he's never said anything."

"And what do you say to him?"

"Are you joking? I don't say a word. He doesn't want to hear anything from a kid, not even a kid he trusts."

The boys had reached the back of the park, where the grass gave way to undergrowth, and the trees grew much more densely. The park was bounded by real woods. The thick trees rose up a high, steep hill, almost a small mountain, whose crest could not be seen from below. Nicholas could hear a woodpecker at work somewhere in the trees far above them, and his mind returned to the image of Mr. Collum in the drawing room, tapping and listening.

"So the orphanage has a terrible money problem," Nicholas said, looking up into the rising woods, "and Mr. Collum would love to find a treasure to solve it. I understand all that. But why does he think there's a treasure to find?"

"Last week," John said in reply, "Gertrude McGillicuddy was looking for sewing supplies in an old bureau in the basement. She dropped a thimble or something, and when she got down to look for it, she discovered a sort of secret drawer under the bureau. And when she looked inside the drawer—"

"She found that ledger!" Nicholas cried, suddenly understanding. "The one Mr. Collum's looking at all the time!"

"You guessed it," John said. "I could tell right away it was something special—or at least that Mr. Collum thought it was. From the moment Gertrude brought it to him, he started behaving differently. Sort of…well, agitated, I suppose, and preoccupied. And it was the day after he got that ledger that he asked me about treasures and hiding places. So I think we can put two and two together." He gestured toward the Manor. "We'd better head back that way. Miss

Candace is getting worried—you can tell by the way she hops on her toes and shakes her head."

Nicholas caught his arm. "But wait! When I asked if you knew what this treasure business was about, you started out saying 'For one thing.' I take it that the ledger is the one thing. So what's the other thing?"

"You really don't miss a beat, do you, Nick?" John said with a wondering look. "Well, I wasn't trying to keep it a secret. Here, let's walk and I'll tell you." They ambled toward the Manor again. Nicholas could see Miss Candace leaning over the gazebo rail peering in their direction with an anxious frown, as if she couldn't see them very well. Perhaps she needed spectacles.

"I used to hear my parents talk about it," John said. "They would see something in the papers that would remind them, and one of them would say, 'Did anyone ever find out about the Rothschild inheritance?' And the other would say, 'Not that I know of. Still a mystery, apparently.' Naturally I asked them about it."

Here John fell silent for several paces, and Nicholas, though he was burning with impatience, knew better than to prompt him. He could tell that John was thinking about his parents. Nicholas had never known his own parents, so he did not know what it felt like to lose them. But he had known plenty of orphans who could remember their parents perfectly well, and he had long since learned to recognize when they were missing them and feeling sad.

When John began speaking again, whatever amusement or good feeling he had accumulated over the course of the morning had clearly evaporated. He was not terse, exactly, nor did he sound particularly gloomy. But Nicholas sensed the difference in his expression and his tone. He was simply quieter and more matter-of-fact. "You know who the Rothschilds were, Nick?"

"Sure, Mrs. Brindle told me about them."

"Well, a long time ago," said John, "shortly after they were married, Mrs. Rothschild inherited some money. Her father had been pretty wealthy, almost as well off as Mr. Rothschild, and she was his only living relative. It was in all the papers, with headlines like 'The Rich Get Richer,' and that sort of thing. As far as anyone knew, she never spent any of that inheritance—she didn't need to—and yet it was never accounted for."

"How do you mean, 'never accounted'?" Nicholas asked.

John shrugged. "After Mr. Rothschild died, there were lots of people keeping track of where his fortune went, and apparently the money didn't add up. Some of it went into starting the orphanage and setting up a fund to keep it running, and a lot of it went to charity. But if you included Mrs. Rothschild's inheritance—which should have become part of Mr. Rothschild's fortune—there ought to have been more money than there was. As far as people can figure it, her inheritance just...disappeared."

"So it's an actual mystery!" Nicholas said, and he laughed. The mere notion of a hidden treasure was enough to put him in a good mood, but the idea that he might actually *find* it had put him in very high spirits indeed. "How much did Mrs. Rothschild inherit, exactly?"

"I can't say exactly," John replied, "but I remember my parents said it was in the millions."

Nicholas stopped in his tracks. *"Millions?"*

"That's what they said. That's why it was such a big deal."

Nicholas's mind started spinning madly. He had suspected that this "treasure" might be some thousands of dollars. After all, that would be enough to solve quite a lot of problems. But millions of dollars? That was a different sort of treasure entirely. With millions of dollars—with even *one* million dollars—a boy like himself could leave orphanages behind forever! No more bullies, no more Mr. Collums, no more sleeping in upstairs dungeons! Why, with millions of dollars and a mind like Nicholas's, anything was possible! Anything!

John had stopped walking, too, and was looking back at Nicholas expectantly. "Well? What do you think?"

"I think I want to get my hands on that ledger," Nicholas breathed.

Nicholas was eager to discuss the treasure more, but no sooner had John told him about the Rothschild inheritance than he felt the heavy, irresistible shade of sleep drawing down on him. Saying more would have to wait.

Early on, Nicholas had come to think of his different kinds of sleeping spells as "naps" and "collapses." This spell in the park, fortunately, was one of his naps. At the first hint of drowsiness, he sat down on the grass. "Sorry," he muttered, and he tried asking John to look out for him, but already he was too sleepy to form words. He lay back. He had a vision of green leaves and blue sky, and then of John's face wearing an expression of something like sympathy (though perhaps it was just contemplation), and then a black curtain was drawn over everything, and he saw nothing more.

Fifteen minutes later he awoke to the sound of distant voices. Sensing that he was alone, he sat up and looked around, frightening a bunny that had ventured out from under the gazebo and was grazing nearby. It bolted back through a hole in the latticework. There was no one in sight. He could tell from the voices, however, that the girls had gathered inside the schoolhouse and the boys were in the side yard. The Crafts and Skills activity must be getting under way. Nicholas brushed off his clothes, steadied himself, and hurried around the corner of the Manor.

The side yard was a stretch of ground, perhaps a hundred paces wide, that occupied the space between the Manor and the bordering woods to the east. In the morning sunlight, Nicholas absorbed all the details of the shapes he'd seen the night before: the garden, which must be Mr. Griese's herb garden, was carefully tended, with bright yellow and orange marigolds planted around it; the crumbling old stone well had a padlocked wooden cover secured over its opening, no doubt to prevent accidental drownings; and the dilapidated wooden structure beyond it, with the spade leaning against its door, was surely Mr. Griese's gardening shed. Nicholas took in these details with a glance. His main focus was the line of boys streaming in and out of the Manor's side door like a colony of ants.

Chattering and fussing as they worked, the boys were carrying out tools and depositing them upon a number of makeshift tables arranged between the side door and the well. Mr. Pileus stood among the tables, attempting to direct traffic, but his reluctance to speak rendered him fairly useless, and there was a great deal of jostling and colliding. Two boys were kneeling in the grass, picking up the tools they had dropped, and Nicholas saw two others sucking on scraped knuckles. Several of the boys saw Nicholas approaching and quickly glanced away again, as if they were afraid to look at him.

John Cole, who had just set down a box of scrap metal, spotted him and called out, "Hey, Nick! We're bringing stuff up from the basement." He lingered at the table, apparently clearing out space for more things. When Nicholas came over, John added under his breath, "Don't go down there. The Spiders are waiting for you." And he went back inside before Nicholas could reply.

Now Nicholas understood why no one else wanted to look at him. They didn't dare. If they gave the trap away, even accidentally, the Spiders would punish them for it. This surely applied to John as well, so Nicholas went straight to work at the tables, sorting the tools from the materials, trying to give the impression he was actually busy in the yard and not just avoiding the basement. He didn't want anyone to guess he'd been warned. Everything had been placed on the tables willy-nilly, so there was plenty of work to be done. Mr. Pileus saw what he was doing and nodded with approval. Nicholas relaxed. For the moment, anyway, he was safe.

He was also beginning to enjoy himself. Nicholas had never seen so many tools, much less been allowed to use any. With such a store of tools, a skilled person could easily cut, grind, fasten, bolt, pin, solder, weld, or smelt anything that came to mind. Nicholas was fascinated. He was hardly a skilled person himself, but with every tool he touched, a vision formed in his mind of what might be accomplished with it. The only trouble would be learning how best to operate man-sized tools with boy-sized hands.

With keen interest, Nicholas considered the scrap metal, the files, the jigsaw. He had a key to make, and he needed to find the best way to do it. In his pocket he had the wax mold, about the size and shape of a small bar of soap. He almost hadn't risked bringing it. He had studied the key's impression so carefully, memorizing its every groove and dimension, he'd thought he might not even need it. But he had tucked it into his pocket just in case. Later he would melt away the evidence.

Nicholas had concerns about other evidence as well—evidence of his "window" project from the night before—and when he felt sure no one was watching, he cast a casual glance up toward the second floor of the Manor. He had used wadded strips of bedsheets to keep the wall stones in position; and to give the appearance of mortar between them, he had used most of his toothpaste, along with a great deal of grit that he'd swept up from the floor. The discolored patch of wall had looked credible enough from inside, but there'd been nothing he could do about the outside. He worried that the narrow gaps between the stones would show.

One glance put his mind at ease. From below, the spaces were impossible to detect. Nicholas smiled inwardly and began stacking some small iron welding plates, taking care not to squash his fingers. Last night's labor had been hard enough on them, not to mention their scalding at breakfast. Making a key would be delicate work. Fresh fingers would have been better. But he felt sure he could pull the job off, regardless. The tricky part—the devilishly tricky part— would be doing everything on the sly.

Nicholas continued pondering his secret plans as the last of the tools were brought out. Then, for a minute or so, all the boys stood around looking tense. The Spiders had not yet emerged from the basement. The bullies had lost their excuse for being down there, however, and eventually, grudgingly, they filed out into the side yard, glowering. They were obviously furious, all three of them clenching and unclenching their fists dramatically. Nicholas thought they looked ridiculous, like toddlers trying to catch phantom fireflies. But the threat they posed was made clear enough by the way the other boys scattered from their path.

As everyone waited for Mr. Pileus to begin (he was puttering wordlessly among the tools, making some last-minute decision), Moray made a show of removing his belt and letting its heavy buckle thump menacingly against the grass. He did this a few times before putting his belt back on and sharing vengeful looks with Iggy and Breaker, who jutted their chins and clenched their fists some more. They all kept trying to mouth threats to Nicholas, like *You'll be sorry* and *We'll get you for this*, but every time they caught his eye, he would turn away just as they got their mouths moving.

It was clearly driving them nuts, especially Moray, who began to make enraged whimpering sounds and stomp his feet each time Nicholas looked away. Nicholas saw John give him a warning look, but he only smiled and winked. As long as Mr. Pileus was here, and as long as Nicholas was alert, there was nothing the Spiders could do.

At last Mr. Pileus cleared his throat and waved everyone over to him, and the metalworking activities officially began. From the handyman's brief, mumbling speech, Nicholas gathered that the main idea was to fashion some new shelving for the basement but that the boys would be allowed to experiment with different projects. With the boys gathered around him, Mr. Pileus dutifully attempted to instruct them in the proper (and properly cautious) use of the tools, while at the same time uttering as few words as possible. He seemed to hope that demonstrating how to use a miter saw, for example, if done slowly and with the proper expression, would provide sufficient instruction even for the sniffling seven-year-olds. The result was a boy named Oliver nearly mitering the tip of his finger, and Mr. Pileus nearly collapsing of a heart attack.

Over the next couple of hours, this sequence was repeated again and again: A boy would do something Mr. Pileus perceived to be dangerous, and the horrified man would leap forward, wresting away the tool or the boy, whichever the occasion required. His gasps and cries of alarm, the minor but frequent injuries, and the other boys' laughter caused such constant commotion that Nicholas, working feverishly and stealthily, managed to make terrific progress on his key. Indeed, by the time a fourth boy had been sent reluctantly off to Miss Candace for treatment, Nicholas believed he had finished the job.

His success came just in time, for no sooner had he slipped the key deep into his pocket than a wave of drowsiness overcame him.

Nicholas knew that if he napped near the tables, one of the Spiders would contrive to step on him or "accidentally" drop something heavy on his head. And so, without hesitation, he took off toward the yard's wooded border, where no one had reason to go. He did not ask Mr. Pileus for permission. He simply started running. And he managed to put twenty paces between him and the others before his run became a stagger and he was forced to slow down, drop to his knees, and fall forward in a sort of controlled topple.

Nicholas came to rest on his belly, with his cheek pressed into the soft, warm grass, and gave himself over to the irresistible force of sleep. It had been only a few hours since his last nap, but he felt as if he'd put in an entire day's work. And why not? he thought drowsily. Had he not been working ever since he arrived at the Manor? So he had. And all of his projects had been successful, and he had successfully avoided the Spiders. He was safely out in the open, where Mr. Pileus could see him, and the sunlight was warm against his back, and the smell of the grass was sweet. Nicholas heaved one final, deep sigh of contentment, and the world faded away.

When he woke later, blinking his eyes blearily without moving his head, Nicholas could tell he'd been asleep longer than usual. The shadows of the nearby trees had shifted, and he could feel the difference in the sunlight and the temperature of the air. Without consciously thinking about it, he knew he had slept half an hour, possibly a bit longer. He was aware of a certain silence, a stillness that suggested the other boys had gone inside. There was only birdsong and a rustling of leaves in the woods. And then an earthy thump, as if perhaps a fat acorn had dropped from the upper branches of one of the giant oaks. Nicholas sat up, rubbing his eyes. He heard another thump, and this time he detected in it a subtle jingling.

Nicholas felt his mouth go dry. He recognized that sound.

Reluctantly he turned to look toward the Manor. Mr. Pileus was nowhere to be seen. John Cole was nowhere to be seen. Nicholas was alone in the side yard.

Alone, except for the Spiders.

Persuasion, Prediction, Punishment

How had this happened? The makeshift tables were still arranged in the side yard, still covered with tools. It was as if everyone had simply fled, abandoning Nicholas to his enemies. The Spiders were gathered near the open side door, where Moray stood thumping his belt buckle on the ground and glaring across the yard toward Nicholas, and both Breaker and Iggy were looking expectantly back into the passageway as if waiting for someone.

Please, Nicholas thought. *Please be Mr. Pileus.*

It was not Mr. Pileus who poked his head out, however,

but a scared younger boy in knickers. "All clear!" the boy said. He tried to withdraw, but Breaker caught his wrist and yanked him out into the yard.

"Don't go back down without carrying something!" Breaker growled.

"Did you not hear what we told you?" Iggy said, spitting contemptuously as the boy darted for the tables. "Little nitwit."

Nicholas scrambled to his feet, but it was too late. The Spiders had already started toward him. They fanned out as they came, cutting off every line of escape except the woods, where he dared not go. If they caught him out there, hidden among the trees, they wouldn't even have to worry about witnesses. And so Nicholas took a deep breath, brushed himself off, and hurried forward to meet them, grinning as if they were old friends.

The Spiders slowed, then stopped near the tables, their faces betraying their confusion. Moray glanced back at the door, and Iggy and Breaker anxiously searched the Manor windows, no doubt expecting to find a grownup watching from some vantage point only Nicholas could see. But with the exception of the terrified younger boy, who was fumblingly gathering an armload of tools, the Spiders were alone with their prey.

"Where'd everyone go?" Nicholas asked cheerfully as he approached the tables.

"Late-morning chores," said Moray with a triumphant leer. He swung his belt around like a propeller and caught the buckle in his meaty hand. "Me and my boys volunteered to help Pileus with the tools. We bring them in, and he puts them away, see? Which means—"

"You need my help!" Nicholas interjected. He slapped his forehead. "Well, of course! Why didn't you say so?" He rushed forward to the nearest table, where the younger boy had just lifted a socket set from behind a stack of welding plates and was turning hurriedly to go. With a squeak of surprise, the boy collided with Nicholas, who had approached at exactly the wrong angle, and both of them were knocked off balance. The younger boy staggered backward, clutching at his armload of tools, while Nicholas stumbled into the table, his flailing hands scattering things left and right.

"Get in there before Pileus wonders where you are!" Moray hissed, shoving the boy toward the door. Then he grabbed Nicholas, still draped awkwardly over the table, and swung him around. Moray's face was hard now. "Cut the act, Benedict! We aren't falling for that Mr. Innocent stuff anymore. You set us up! You made us wait in that bathroom for nothing!"

Iggy and Breaker moved in to stand on either side of Moray, muttering their agreement that they would not be fooled again.

"You should have done what you said you'd do," said Breaker, stroking his wispy mustache. He flexed his arm muscles as he did so, as if stroking one's mustache required enormous physical effort. "You should have kept your word."

"I should have come to the bathroom and let you dunk my head in the toilet?" asked Nicholas, looking puzzled. "Is that what you'd have done?"

"Spiders always keep their word," Iggy said peevishly. "It's our code."

Nicholas looked up at Moray, who still held his arm in a

firm grip. "Is that true? You have a code? So you really would have let yourself get dunked in a toilet?"

"You better believe it," Moray growled. "If the code…" Then he seemed to realize what Nicholas had said. He grimaced. "I mean *no*. No, I wouldn't have, because I wouldn't have said so in the first place, see? It's only if we *say* we'll do something that—oh, forget this business! No more of your wise-guy questions. You lied to us, and now we're going to make you pay for it."

"See, he said it," Breaker said, "so now you know we're going to do it."

"You bet we are," said Iggy. He tried to crack his knuckles in a menacing way but couldn't get them to pop. He looked even more peevish now.

Nicholas sighed. "You really don't want to hit me with that belt buckle, Moray."

"Wrong," said Moray, swinging the buckle back and forth like a pendulum. "I actually want to do it real bad."

"But it will leave an obvious mark," said Nicholas in his most reasonable tone. "When Mr. Pileus sees it, he'll know what you've done, and you'll be punished."

Moray glared at him. "Don't you worry. We'll just tell him you fell."

"Yeah!" Breaker said with a laugh. "You were so sleepy you fell against a table!"

"Yeah, we'll all swear to it!" said Iggy.

Nicholas looked doubtful. "Sure, but the problem is that *I'll* tell the *truth*. It will be your word against mine, and I'm much more convincing. Remember last night, when I convinced you I wanted to be initiated? Believe me, I won't have any trouble convincing Mr. Pileus where I got such a nasty mark. For that matter, I wouldn't hit me with your fist, either. A black eye or a bloody nose will be even easier to explain."

Moray bent his face close to Nicholas's. His breath smelled like dog breath. "You won't rat on us, because if you do, we'll get you for it, and next time will be even worse than *this* time. I promise you that. I give you my word."

"Yeah!" Iggy said. "We *all* do. How do you like that?"

Nicholas shrugged. "I'll rat on you anyway, though. Believe me, I will most certainly rat."

"'Most certainly rat'?" Moray repeated, looking around at Iggy and Breaker. "Are you hearing this guy?"

"I'm hearing him," Breaker said. "'Most certainly rat.' Get a load of him!"

"He *talks* like a rat!" Iggy said, then laughed really hard to convince everyone it was funny.

"It's up to you," Nicholas said, speaking up to be heard over Iggy's laughter. "You'll have to decide if it's worth getting punished for."

Moray licked his lips and screwed up his face, considering this. Meanwhile, another young boy scurried out from the side door, fetched a tool, and scurried back inside the Manor without a word, like a frightened mouse snatching a bit of cheese. He scarcely even glanced at Nicholas and the Spiders, perhaps for fear of seeing violence in action.

Suddenly Moray brightened. "I have a better idea," he said, putting his belt back on and glancing around at his friends. "I'm going to sock you in the *belly*. How about that, Benedict? No marks!" He was so pleased with himself, he laughed out loud.

Nicholas looked apologetic, as if he hated dashing Moray's hopes. "If I were you, I wouldn't do that, either."

"Oh yeah?" Moray said. He tried to make it come out like a taunt, but he sounded worried. "And why's that?"

"Because you'll hurt your hand," Nicholas said.

Moray and the other Spiders had another good laugh at this. Then Moray punched Nicholas as hard as he could in the belly.

There was a clanking sound, and the next moment Moray was rolling on the grass, clutching his fist and howling. As Breaker and Iggy gaped in astonishment, Nicholas withdrew the metal welding plate from beneath his shirt—it was to slip that plate under his shirt that he had contrived to stumble against the tool table earlier—and heaved it into the air above their heads. They instinctively leaped back before it could crack one of their skulls, and as they did, Nicholas ducked under the table, popped up on the other side, and vanished through the side door into the Manor.

꒰·꒱

In the passageway, Nicholas came upon the younger boy in knickers. He had just emerged from the doorway to the basement stairs, panting with effort, and at the sight of Nicholas he ducked his head. He was no doubt used to being severely teased—few boys wore knickers anymore, not even very young ones—and from his manner Nicholas judged he was often pushed around, too. He was a meek little boy, freckle-faced, with ears that stuck out like pitcher handles. Nicholas had overheard Iggy taunting him during metalworking.

("Hey, Buford," Iggy had whispered, waving a mallet. "Want me to hammer those ears down for you?" And Buford had made a squeaking sound and whispered, "No, thank you, sir.")

"See you later, Buford," Nicholas said, brushing past him. He could still hear the Spiders outside, cursing and arguing about which one had let him get away. Evidently, they didn't intend to follow him.

"How—how did you know my name?" Buford said, turning.

Nicholas had a flash of inspiration. He crooked his finger, indicating that Buford should come closer. "Because I knew this was going to happen," he whispered. "Because I *saw* it."

"You...saw it?"

Nicholas nodded mysteriously. "Yes, and listen, Buford, I need you to give a message to the Spiders for me."

Buford drew back in alarm. "A message? But if they don't like it, they'll clean my clock!"

"Your clock will be fine, Buford," Nicholas assured him. "Now here's the message. I want you to tell the Spiders that I can predict the future."

"The future?"

"Exactly," said Nicholas. "Tell them that's how I always know what they're going to do. Trying to initiate me, trying to ambush me in the basement, socking me in the belly—I saw all of those things before they happened. It's part of my special condition. So if they know what's good for them, they'll leave me alone. If they try to get me again, it's just going to backfire again, because *I'll* know what they're up to even before *they* do. Can you remember all that, Buford?"

"I don't know!" said Buford, wringing his hands. He looked as though he might cry. "It's an awful lot!"

"Just do your best," Nicholas said reassuringly. "You're going to do fine. I can see it."

With that, he turned and ran off, leaving Buford with the unhappy task of telling the Spiders something they would not want to hear. The younger boy felt he had no choice, however, for if Nicholas was telling the truth, then failing to deliver the message might somehow disrupt the *future*. Buford had no idea what would happen if a person disrupted the future, but it might be terrible indeed, and he did not care to be responsible for it. And so without delay he ran outside to deliver the message.

Just like he predicted I would, Buford thought, and he shivered.

"Ah, so you're awake, Nicholas," said Mr. Collum when Nicholas appeared in his study doorway. He was seated at his desk, poring over the precious ledger through his jeweler's loupe. John stood at the filing cabinet behind him with a handful of papers. Mr. Collum removed the loupe from his eye and gave Nicholas an assessing look. "John was just suggesting that I check on you. He said you dozed off during metalworking. I assured him that this was simply part of your condition and that you would be fine. Obviously, I was correct."

John was looking at Nicholas with raised eyebrows. No doubt he had expected Nicholas to have a black eye or bloody lip. "Glad to see you're all right, Nick."

"Thanks," Nicholas said, stepping closer to Mr. Collum's desk. He tried to catch a glimpse of the writing in the ledger, but Mr. Collum closed it and covered it with a schedule of daily tasks.

Mr. Collum made a pencil mark next to one of the items. "I've assigned you to lunchtime kitchen duty for the rest of this week, Nicholas. You'll help prepare lunch and wash dishes afterward. Please report to Mr. Griese now."

Nicholas opened his mouth to speak, but Mr. Collum held up a hand to check him.

"Do not test me, Nicholas," Mr. Collum said sternly. "Every child helps with the chores. Run along now. You're dismissed."

Nicholas saluted, turned on his heel, and with a private roll of his eyes (he had only been about to say "Yes, sir"), he strode from the office and headed for the kitchen. Just as he was about to push through the swinging doors, though, he heard what sounded like a scuffle on the other side. A banging, a whimper, and then the unmistakable sound of Moray's sneering voice, followed by snorts and chuckles.

Nicholas glanced about the passage. The door to the butler's pantry was ajar, and he quickly ducked through it. (Just in time, too, for even as he eased the door closed behind him, he heard the Spiders burst out of the kitchen and hurry away down the passage.) He could not easily duck out again, though. To his dismay, he had unwittingly barged in upon a crew of boys and girls sweeping and dusting the cavernous pantry—a crew being supervised by Miss Candace, whose face positively lit up at the sight of him.

"Nicholas!" she exclaimed. All the children stopped working to stare.

Miss Candace teetered over to him, laying her hands on

many a child's shoulder as she walked (whether from affection or a need for balance, it was impossible to say). She had a bland, flat-looking face with a mottled complexion, and she wore a great quantity of sweet perfume. Patting Nicholas hard on top of the head—he could both feel and hear the painful rapping of her rings against his skull—she bent over him and said, "We haven't properly met! I'm Miss Candace! Now let me have a look at you. I'm a nurse, you know, so you needn't be frightened."

On the contrary, Nicholas was very frightened indeed, for Miss Candace, forcibly turning his head to the side, had thrust her face so close to his that her nose pressed into his cheekbone. Her almond-shaped, searching blue eyes loomed in his peripheral vision as she spread his left eyelids uncomfortably wide with her fingers. Nicholas felt his eyeball drying out. Then Miss Candace wrenched his head the other way to examine his other eye. At length she made a worried, clucking sound.

"I believe you may need drops," she murmured, straightening, and Nicholas heard the other children suck in their breath. "How is your appetite? Are you eating well?"

"Oh, very well!" Nicholas replied hastily, and with a little jump he moved out of her reach. "Thank you so much, Miss Candace! I actually feel terrific! And it really is swell to meet you, but I have to run and help Mr. Griese in the kitchen right away—Mr. Collum said so!" And he dashed out the door again before she could call him back.

In the kitchen, Nicholas found that Mr. Griese had also just arrived and was in the process of removing young Buford from a trash can. The poor boy was covered in potato peels and bits of wilted lettuce, but his tearstained face bore a stub-born expression, and no matter how much the cook pressed him to reveal who had stuffed him into the trash can, Buford stuck to his claim that he had fallen in by accident. He would not look at Nicholas.

"Well, you can't help me like this," Mr. Griese said in dis-gust. "You'll need to go change and wash up. And you," he said, turning to Nicholas, "put on an apron. We're going to have to work double-quick now, so pay attention. I was count-ing on Buford to help me until you learned the ropes."

Nicholas hurriedly donned an apron.

"You might have warned me they were going to do that," Buford whispered resentfully to Nicholas as he left. "You and your crystal ball." He stuck his tongue out and pushed through the swinging doors before Nicholas could reply.

Nicholas set to work. He was quite comfortable in the kitchen, actually—he must have peeled a thousand potatoes in his days at Littleview, to say nothing of the vegetables he'd chopped and the bread dough he'd rolled—and he threw himself into his tasks with gusto. He performed so skillfully, in fact, that Mr. Griese soon stopped prompting him, and they worked together in silence. Nicholas enjoyed figuring out the cook's system of organization and manner of doing things. Through observation and guesswork, he quickly learned where all the implements were stored, and what sort of menu was planned, and how Mr. Griese was going about preparing it. In no time he was handing pepper to Mr. Griese just before he asked for it, and cubing the potatoes even though Mr. Griese hadn't said he wanted them cubed. (He did want them cubed, though, and he grunted in surprised approval when he saw Nicholas doing it.)

When Buford returned, scrubbed and sullen, Mr. Griese said gruffly, "You take the pitchers and bread baskets out to the tables. We've got it covered in here."

Indeed, they had it so well covered that Nicholas found time to peruse the kitchen-duty schedule, tacked to the inside of a cabinet door. It was divided up by names and age-groups, for when the five-year-olds and six-year-olds were on duty, they had to be accompanied by an older child. Nicholas detected this pattern without thinking about it, just as he memorized all the children's names without trying. His real goal was to make note of when the Spiders were scheduled to be on duty. He wanted to be extra careful on those days, as it was easy to imagine them putting bugs in his hash, or soap on his spoon, if they got the opportunity.

When everything was ready, all the orphanage children began filing in through one set of swinging doors to have their plates filled, then filing out through the other doors into the dining hall. Nicholas had to help Mr. Griese ladle the food onto the plates, and he was dreading the appearance of the Spiders. But then the children filed through so rapidly, and he was pressed so hard to keep up, that he could scarcely make eye contact with anyone. It was simply plate after plate after plate, a constant stream of plates. He did recognize the Spiders' oversized hands (Moray's right hand had swollen knuckles); and when he saw John's hands (he could not say how he recognized them), he quickly looked up, but John was already moving on. That was all right—he could talk with John when he'd finished in the kitchen.

The doors into the dining hall were constantly swinging open and closed, and the laughter and conversation from the tables was loud one moment and muffled the next. *The throbbing mob*, Nicholas thought. Most of the children had been served now; he would soon be joining that mob in the dining hall. A whole roomful of strangers and already a few enemies. Nicholas felt another pang of nervousness, which annoyed him, but there was no help for it. He had changed orphanages often enough to know that, for a while at least, he would keep getting nervous in these situations. In the meantime, there was nothing to do but exist and persist.

When the last child went out into the dining hall, Nicholas noticed that the tables out there had fallen completely silent. He heard a familiar voice—Moray's again—beginning to speak in a raised, forceful tone, as if he were making an announcement. Then the doors swung closed, muffling the words so that Nicholas couldn't make them out. What was that about? Were the Spiders making all the others hand over their corn bread? And where was Mrs. Brindle? According to the schedule, she was supposed to be the lunchtime chaperone today.

Just then, as if Nicholas had conjured her with his thoughts, Mrs. Brindle entered the kitchen smelling strongly of perfume. Mr. Griese flushed a slightly deeper red than he already was. "Oh!" he said, glancing at Mrs. Brindle's shoes, then at the spoon in his hand, and then at the ceiling. "Are you on lunch duty today, Mrs. Brindle?"

The housekeeper seemed uncertain whether to smile or frown. Her face settled into a fixed expression of unease. "Why, yes, Mr. Griese. Or have I misread the schedule?"

"No, no!" Mr. Griese protested. "I'm sure you haven't! I only—" He coughed. "Forgive me, I'm a bit disoriented. New help today, you know." He gestured vaguely at Nicholas, who took this as a cue to speak.

"May I be excused to eat lunch, sir?" he asked, already filling his own plate.

"By all means, young—Nicholas, is it? By all means, do," Mr. Griese said, nervously wiping his hands on his apron.

Nicholas backed out the swinging door, leaving the two flustered grownups alone with their confusion.

The instant he entered the dining hall, he knew something was wrong. A perfect silence hung in the room. Two long tables of faces stared at him. What was going on? He spotted John in the back of the room, sitting in the same place as this morning, and Nicholas was about to make a beeline for the chair across from him when he realized, with a terrible plummeting in his belly, that there were no empty chairs anywhere near John. In fact, there were no empty chairs anywhere except at the very front of the leftmost table. Nicholas saw at once that this had been planned. The seating had been arranged so that the only place for him to sit was with the five-year-olds and six-year-olds, all of whom were staring up at him with huge, frightened eyes.

Nicholas cast another quick glance toward John—he was looking back at Nicholas with a somber, unreadable expression—and then looked for the Spiders. They were sitting, as before, near the middle of the leftmost table, all three sneering at him with enormous satisfaction.

They didn't have to touch him to torture him, after all.

Nicholas felt his face burning; his heart was skipping

double-time. He knew he was dangerously close to becoming too upset. He took a slow, deep breath and drew himself up. In the most superior tone he could manage, he said, "You're all being so quiet! I hope it isn't on my account! I assure you, I don't require silence in my presence. Please, everyone, feel free to continue eating—as you were, as you were." He grinned, made a little bow, and dropped into the nearest chair just as Mrs. Brindle remembered her duties and came out through the swinging doors.

The sounds of conversation started up again, with murmurs and snickers up and down both tables. Nicholas winked at the younger children sitting by him. The two seated nearest him were watching him with fearful eyes, their mouths hanging open to reveal the half-chewed contents. They looked as though they thought themselves the two unluckiest children in the world.

"Thanks for saving my seat!" Nicholas said, startling their mouths closed. He leaned toward them and whispered, "You don't have to be afraid of me, you know."

One of the two children, a red-haired girl with pigtails, cut her eyes down the table and back to Nicholas. "Oh, but it isn't you we're afraid of!" she whispered. Then she clapped her hands over her mouth and stared at her plate in distress.

"I'm very glad to hear it," Nicholas said. "I suppose you're afraid of the Spiders, is that it? Because of the announcement Moray made before I came into the room? I don't blame you. Those Spiders can be very scary if you don't know how to handle them."

The children were looking at one another, clearly shocked

that Nicholas knew about the announcement. Farther down, a few children who had overheard him whispered to their neighbors, who then whispered to their other neighbors, and so on down the table. But the children next to Nicholas were speechless.

"Don't worry," Nicholas said. "I understand you can't speak to me without getting into trouble with Moray. But that doesn't mean we can't still be friends. We'll just be the kind of friends who don't speak to each other." He waited until this strange pronouncement got whispered down the table, then said, "What do you say to that, Caroline?"

A skinny girl sitting two chairs down from him nearly dropped her spoon. She goggled her eyes at Nicholas as the other children looked back and forth between her and Nicholas in astonishment. *So that's Caroline*, Nicholas thought, and looking straight at the girl, he said, "Don't answer, Caroline! I was only joking. Of course you can't say anything. Isn't that right, Bobby?"

This time it was a moon-eyed boy whose mouth fell open, and looking directly at him, Nicholas said, "You realize I'm just teasing you, don't you, Bobby? I know that none of you can answer me."

In this way, and by process of elimination, Nicholas had soon identified every one of the younger children by name. The whispers spread like wildfire throughout the dining hall. "Settle down," he said to his neighbors, who were growing agitated and trying to speak to each other without appearing to speak to Nicholas. At his word, they instantly fell silent.

"I can answer your question," Nicholas said. "Oh yes, I know what you're thinking. You're wondering how I knew your names. It's simple. I can *see* things. Ask Buford. Ask the Spiders. They'll tell you. It's part of my special condition."

This announcement was repeated in whispers down the table, until it reached the Spiders, who looked angry (Nicholas noticed with a sidelong glance) but also gratifyingly disconcerted.

As the report of Nicholas Benedict's gift made its way to every set of ears, the gifted boy in question dug in to his food, chewing with obvious relish, as if he'd never had a better meal in his life.

The truth was that it was one of his worst. Nicholas had never felt so lonely. But nobody in this wretched orphanage was going to know that. Not if he could help it. And as soon as he possibly could, he would be leaving them all behind forever.

Starting tonight.

THE RULES WITH RABBIT

After lunch, Nicholas washed the pots and pans—and the seemingly endless dishes—as if his life depended on finishing. Free time had already begun for the other children (with the exception of Buford, who was likewise doomed to kitchen work), and Nicholas was almost in agony as the seconds slipped away. He wanted to go to the library and read a book. Several books, in fact, if time allowed—and perhaps it would, for free time after lunch lasted a whole two hours, and he was a blazingly fast reader. Right now nothing sounded better to him than forgetting his miseries and burying himself in words.

And so Nicholas scrubbed like a fiend. He washed so fast that Buford, drying, struggled to keep up and complained to Mr. Griese. (No doubt he still resented Nicholas for having made him deliver that message.) But his complaints only got him scolded, and he went back to flailing with his towel, glaring all the while.

When at last the sparkling dishes were dried, stacked, and put away, Nicholas flew from the kitchen like a bird from its cage. He still had over an hour of free time left! But just as he was darting across the entranceway, Mr. Collum appeared in his office doorway and called out to him.

Nicholas cringed. He looked at Mr. Collum with a feeling of doom.

Mr. Collum beckoned him over. "It's time for you to receive your haircut, Nicholas. No, do not argue," he warned when he saw Nicholas's look of distress. "Every boy receives a crew cut on his first day. Now run over to the farm and introduce yourself to Mr. Furrow. He'll cut your hair and explain the basic larder duties to you."

Nicholas glanced achingly toward the library door. "Yes, sir," he mumbled, and turned and hurried back the way he had come. Perhaps it wouldn't take long at the farm. He might yet have a few minutes to read.

He took the shortcut John had shown him, cutting through the butler's pantry, the little anteroom beyond it, and out the back door into a hot and hazy afternoon. His eyes swept the park, alert to any dangers. (He also half hoped that John would change his mind and approach him, wanting to be friends again. But John was nowhere to be seen.) Most of the boys were reluctantly involved in a game of Simon Says, led by Iggy, who was making them roll around on the ground and bark like dogs as Moray and Breaker looked on and snickered. The few boys who had managed to escape this miserable game were playing marbles in a patch of hardpacked dirt where flowers once had grown. Perhaps, Nicholas thought, they had won the Spiders' favor by giving over their lunches. The girls, meanwhile, had all sought shady places near the gazebo to doze. Standing on duty inside the gazebo was Miss Candace, carefully watching the boys to ensure no one was injured. She seemed to be under the impression that they were all having fun.

Nicholas hurried off toward the farm.

The short path through the hickory trees was pleasantly serene, its shade offering some relief from the glare and the heat, and at the end of it lay an equally serene little farm: a modest farmhouse, a well-built old barn, a few acres of food crops (with appealingly tidy rows of beans, corn, potatoes, lettuces, squashes, and other vegetables), and an expanse of deep green pasture. Shading his eyes, Nicholas spotted a group of cows grazing at the foot of some wooded hills to the west. There was not a person in sight. A heavy, acrid scent of cigar smoke hung in the air, however, and Nicholas (a very keen smeller) followed its invisible trail into the barn.

Sure enough, inside the barn he found Mr. Furrow tending to some sheep and goats in a pen. Chickens strutted about, wandering in and out of their coop and pecking in the dirt and straw. They were all taking care not to draw too near a huge black mule that stood dozing in the back. It was as if the mule were surrounded by invisible chicken wire. Nicholas felt instinctively wary of the animal.

Mr. Furrow noticed Nicholas and waved him over. He was a wiry, aged man with few teeth and a deep reddish tan, his bristly white hair clipped as short as Nicholas's hair was about to be. His cigar had been extinguished, but the stump of it protruded from his lips like a swollen black tongue.

"You the new boy?" Mr. Furrow asked. "The sleeper? Come for your haircut?" Rubbing his gray-stubbled chin in a considering manner, he studied Nicholas's hair as if he intended to take the utmost care with it, to shape it according to the latest fashion. He had Nicholas turn this way and that. Then, with a grunt and a nod, he reached into a bin and took out a pair of sheep shears.

Nicholas drew back in alarm, but Mr. Furrow had already caught him by the wrist.

"Won't hurt much," Mr. Furrow said, as if this would be reassuring.

The farmer was telling the truth. The shearing didn't hurt *much*. But it did hurt, and Nicholas thought it would go on forever. Eventually, however, he found himself standing in a circle of his own hair, thinking ruefully, *There's my fair hair, so I daresay I'm bare*. And Mr. Furrow pulled back and stood with his arms akimbo, surveying his work with evident satisfaction.

"Um, thank you, Mr. Furrow," Nicholas said without conviction. He rubbed a hand over his bristly head, suddenly conscious of a draft in the barn that he had not noticed before. He could feel it on his scalp.

Mr. Furrow tossed his cigar stub into a pail of water, where a dozen other stubs floated like a tiny armada. "Now, here's the rules, son. When you're on larder duty, you come to my house first thing in the morning. I check the barn before you go in, make sure Rabbit's finished his carrot, and then you can come in for your chores. Got that?"

"Sir?" Nicholas studied Mr. Furrow's face. He seemed serious enough. "I'm sorry, I'm not sure I understand."

Mr. Furrow jerked a thumb toward the mule in the back of the barn. "Rabbit'll kill anything comes near his carrot if he hasn't done with it. And he'll kick you if you make him go too fast in the field. I'd whip him, but he's so old a whipping might kill *him*, and he's our last and only mule. So we just keep away from his carrot and we keep it slow. That's the rules with Rabbit."

"So Rabbit is the mule," Nicholas said, nodding. "I see."

Mr. Furrow tapped a finger against his head. "You got anything up there, boy? Who'd you think Rabbit was, my wife? Of course Rabbit's the mule. Always has been."

"Of course," Nicholas said. "And you call him that because he loves carrots. I get it."

Mr. Furrow looked down at Nicholas as if he were the stupidest creature ever to set foot inside his barn. "Tell me, son, have you ever met a mule that *didn't* like a carrot? Of course he likes carrots. All mules like carrots. You ever met another mule named Rabbit?"

Nicholas decided it was best not to answer.

"His name's Rabbit because he used to be fast," said Mr. Furrow after a pause. "Now he's slow. Unless you go for his carrot, in which case he's fast again—faster than you'd like to believe."

"Why give him a carrot at all, then?" Nicholas wondered. "If he's so dangerous when he has one, I mean."

Mr. Furrow almost crossed his eyes with impatience. "How do you propose we get him to do anything if we don't give him a carrot? Show him a carrot and Rabbit'll follow you anywhere, sweet as a kitten. Don't show him a carrot and he'll stand there doing nothing till he dies. So in the morning you show him a fresh carrot, and at night you give it to him." He looked doubtfully at Nicholas. "Never found it that complicated myself. But if you need me to explain it again..."

Nicholas shook his head. "I believe I've got it all sorted out now, Mr. Furrow, thank you."

"Fine," the farmer muttered. "Now follow me and I'll show you how to do the milk and eggs. Prob'ly take us all day, at this rate."

But Nicholas surprised Mr. Furrow by quickly grasping how to feed chickens, gather eggs, and draw milk into a pail, and before long (though to Nicholas it seemed very long indeed) he was deemed fit for larder duty and sent away.

Nicholas dashed through the hickory trees. Back in the park, the girls were all still dozing. The game of Simon Says was still going on, though the Spiders looked bored and the other boys thoroughly miserable. This time Breaker spotted him, but Nicholas darted through the circle of marbles players (nimbly avoiding the marbles) and slipped through the back door before the Spiders could attempt anything.

At long last Nicholas made it into the library. He had it almost to himself, too. Two girls were seated on the chaise longue with books in their laps, but they had slumped against each other with their eyes closed, each of them drooling on the other one's shoulder. A boy sat in one of the armchairs, paging listlessly through a book on sports. He glanced up when Nicholas came in, saw who it was, and quickly looked down again. There were no staff members in the room, for Mr. Collum was the supervisor on duty, working at his office desk while keeping an eye on the entranceway mirror. Standing at the shelves, looking out through the library door, Nicholas could see the reflection of the director poring over his ledger.

For once Nicholas was glad to see him. With Mr. Collum nearby, he needn't worry about getting cornered by the Spiders. He could just read.

The question now was *what* to read. He had a mere fifteen minutes of free time left and thousands of books to choose from. Nicholas eagerly ran his eyes over the shelves, taking in hundreds of enticing, gold-lettered titles before coming across a thick book called *The Exhaustive Encyclopedia of Sleep*. That settled his decision at once, for though he had been diagnosed with narcolepsy, the doctor who'd examined him hadn't known much about it, and Nicholas had always wanted to learn more.

Snatching the book from the shelf, he scanned its table of contents. Sure enough, it contained several chapters on sleep disorders. Nicholas turned to the first chapter and began to read. He didn't take time to sit in a chair or even on the floor but stood exactly where he was, rapidly flipping pages. The book was tediously written and contained a great deal of extraneous information, but he found it captivating nonetheless.

His first truly surprising discovery was that his most frightening nighttime hallucination—the horrible, cackling woman who often threatened to smother him—had been seen by others as well. Indeed, she had been terrorizing troubled sleepers for ages. In some cultures she'd even been given a name: the Old Hag.

Fascinating, Nicholas thought, and read on.

He learned, much to his relief, that there were no known cases of narcolepsy killing anyone. (Not surprisingly, it had led to some injuries and even a few accidental deaths—the most famous being that of a narcoleptic snake charmer—but no one had died directly from its symptoms.) He also discovered that what sometimes happened to him when he experienced strong emotions was known as *cataplexy*, and that his particular version of it was rare. When others suffered attacks of cataplexy, they were temporarily paralyzed but remained awake. Nicholas always lost consciousness.

So I'm not just different from everyone I know, he mused. *I'm even different from other people with narcolepsy.* It was a melancholy thought, though not as dispiriting as it once might have been. By this point in his life, he was used to feeling like an oddball. He probably would have been surprised to feel otherwise.

When he had finished the book, Nicholas put it back on the shelf and hurried over to the dictionary to look up the words he hadn't recognized. There were seventeen such words in all (he had counted and alphabetized them instinctively), and as he read their definitions he found himself thinking *Oh, of course!* and *Sure, that makes sense!* Definition by definition, the book's more confusing passages all became clear to him, locking into place like the last pieces in a puzzle. By the time he stepped away from the dictionary, Nicholas felt as satisfied as if he'd eaten a delicious meal.

He glanced at the library clock. He had five minutes left! Time for one more book, if he hurried.

Nicholas ran to the bookshelves, his eyes hungrily roaming over the titles. When they fell upon a history of chess, his heart jumped—chess had always intrigued him. But did he risk trying to reach this book? It was on a high shelf. He would have to move the rolling ladder, then climb it, then climb back down to read (he couldn't risk falling asleep at the top of the ladder, which was very high)—and he had precious little time left.

The book was slim, though. He could probably finish it in four minutes.

Nicholas ran to the ladder and began to pull.

What happened next almost startled him to sleep. Evidently, the ladder's wheels and tracks had not been oiled in ages, and the result was awful: The ladder positively shrieked. That really was the best way to describe it—a metallic scream, a scream every bit as loud and piercing as the screams of terrified children. And indeed, the screams of terrified children soon filled the room, for as soon as the ladder began to squeal, both of the girls snapped awake with the conviction that a snake was loose in the library—or perhaps several snakes! or perhaps a ghost!—and began to scream themselves. (The boy, who had not been asleep and was, therefore, perfectly aware that it was the ladder causing the racket, was nevertheless so frightened by the girls' shrieks that he wet his pants and ran from the room.)

Nicholas observed all this with jangling nerves and considerable amusement, but luckily he did not collapse. He did, however, cover his ears until the girls had fled the library, still screaming. Only when they had gone did he realize that Mr. Collum was yelling at him from the entranceway.

"I'm sorry!" Nicholas exclaimed, uncovering his ears as the director stormed into the room. "I only wanted to take down a book!"

Mr. Collum, obviously disconcerted by the shocking tumult, marched across the library with his jeweler's loupe still screwed into his eye. He shook his finger in front of Nicholas's nose. "No! No, no, no!"

Nicholas was dismayed. "No? But aren't we allowed to read the books on the higher shelves?"

Mr. Collum yanked the loupe from his eye and glanced resentfully at the higher shelves. "Absolutely not! You have to choose books from the lower shelves. The ladder is too loud. Surely you can see that."

"I certainly *heard* it," Nicholas said, trying out a smile. Mr. Collum glared in response, and Nicholas quickly moved on. "But couldn't we ask Mr. Pileus to oil it? I'm sure he wouldn't mind—"

"Mr. Pileus is running errands in Pebbleton," Mr. Collum replied gruffly.

"But perhaps when he returns—"

Mr. Collum stomped his foot. "Stop arguing with me, Nicholas! Children are to be silent in the library. Those who aren't silent receive punishments. Are you being silent? Are you?"

Nicholas opened his mouth, then closed it again. He bit his lip.

And then his free time was over.

Good night, Nicholas," Mr. Collum said, locking the door from the outside. Nicholas pressed his ear to the wood. He heard Mr. Collum pause at the candle corner to extinguish the candle. Then his footsteps faded away.

The time was drawing near at last.

Nicholas told himself that he must wait a full two hours before sneaking downstairs. He wanted everyone in the orphanage to be asleep. He had worked too hard to spoil everything by taking unnecessary chances. Yes, he was dying to try his key. But two hours did not seem so long to wait, not after such a long, trying, miserable day, surely the longest day of his life.

With the exception of being screamed at in the library, Nicholas had been enclosed in a bubble of silence ever since lunchtime. None of the children dared speak to him or even go near him for fear the Spiders would find out about it. Nicholas was used to being thought peculiar, and he was used to being bullied, but this new torment was altogether different. He had never been shunned before. In the past, even in his most miserable situations, he had at least exchanged friendly greetings with other children every now and then. He hadn't realized that such small and apparently meaningless interactions could have mattered so much to him. As it turned out, his loneliness had been imperfect then. Now it was finally complete.

He took it all the harder because of John Cole. Their unexpected friendship had made the worst aspects of this place seem almost tolerable. But John was keeping his distance, too. On the few occasions they had crossed paths, he wouldn't even meet Nicholas's eye.

And so, for the first time he could remember, Nicholas had found himself anxious for night to come. He'd still had to get through the rest of his day, though, and the rest of his day had passed with excruciating slowness. In his bubble of silence, he had endured a dull group activity in the parlor, with the Spiders always leering at him. He had sat through another meal with the frightened, snotty-nosed younger children, once again feigning cheerfulness, once again chattering away without answer. And during a seemingly interminable hour of evening chores, Nicholas's only accompaniment had been the tedious clunking of the butter churn.

At the end of this long desert of loneliness, there had been one brief, green oasis: the hour of free time before bed, when Nicholas had returned to the library. This time he'd gone straight to a set of encyclopedias, taken down the *C* volume, and begun reading the entry on chess. He was instantly absorbed—and blessedly so, for the moment his eyes fell on the open pages, all his troubles grew hazy and distant, as if they belonged to another person.

The hour had passed like a dream—a dream of other people, other places. Time seemed to lose meaning. Nicholas was only vaguely aware of his surroundings. Every now and then one of the Spiders glanced in through the doorway—he saw them in his peripheral vision—but they seemed unwilling to enter the library proper, perhaps being afraid they might accidentally read something. At any rate, Mr. Griese was on duty at the desk, and Nicholas paid them no heed. He paid no heed to anything except his reading.

When the hour was over, Nicholas could have sworn it had passed in less than a minute. He found that he had not budged from his spot by the shelves and that his legs and feet ached from having stood still for so long. His mind had been anything but still, though. When he'd finished the entry on chess, he'd pushed on to read the entire *C* volume, after which—having loved it so much—he had gone back to the start of the encyclopedia.

By the time Mr. Collum announced bedtime, Nicholas had read well into the *B*s, and his blood was rushing so fast that his skin seemed to tingle. (At least this was how he described the sensation to himself, perhaps because he had just read the entry titled "Blood.") He had followed the director upstairs in a sort of daze, thinking *flash flood flash blood flash blood flood* over and over, until Mr. Collum asked him if something was wrong.

"Wrong, sir?" Nicholas had repeated, blinking.

Mr. Collum had paused to light the candle at the candle corner. Turning down his lamp flame (evidently to save a few drops of oil), he had frowned and said, "Yes, *wrong*, Nicholas. You have a peculiar expression on your face. Is something the matter?"

Nicholas had shaken his head, as much to clear it as to answer the director's question. On the contrary, he'd thought, for a change something was *right*. But the question made him realize that from now on he would have to work to keep his wits about him. Reading so much so quickly was like having great tubs of information poured into his head all at once. It was bound to knock him off balance, and he couldn't afford to go around wobbly-headed. Not at this place. Not with a treasure to find.

Clearheaded and alone once more, Nicholas sat down on his cot to think over his plan. There were many variables to take into account, and he wanted to be ready for all of them. What would he do if his key didn't work? What would he do if he got caught? What would he do if he felt sleep overcoming him on the stairs? What would he do—this one he could hardly stand to think about—if the ledger wasn't in Mr. Collum's desk drawer? Would he dare to sneak into Mr. Collum's bedroom? No, if that happened, he would just have to wait for another opportunity.

These questions and dozens more Nicholas contemplated, sitting quietly in his candlelit room, gazing with half-focused eyes at the ugly green plaid blanket he'd been given for a bed-cover. As he mulled the many possibilities that lay before him, he let his eyes wander among the multitude of minia-ture rectangles formed by the plaid pattern. He imagined the rectangles as a series of doors that he was passing through—each door a possibility—and as he moved through one after another, leaving them open or closed depending on whether he had settled a question to his satisfaction, he unconsciously counted and categorized them. The entire process was more or less unconscious, in fact; it was only when his period of waiting was over that Nicholas really thought about it. When he did, he was struck by how calm it seemed to have made him. Two hours earlier he had sat down on the cot suspecting he would be too excited to sit still. Instead, he had grown more and more relaxed.

Something to think about, Nicholas told himself.

He rose from his cot, taking the blanket with him. If he was discovered wandering outside his room, he intended to claim that he'd been sleepwalking. He would say that Mr. Collum must have forgotten to lock his door. It was an expla-nation that would work only once. He hoped he wouldn't have to use it.

Nicholas took the key from beneath his pillow. Now, in this moment of truth, it seemed much too crudely made, woefully brittle and thin. He almost hated to try it for fear of being disappointed. But that was nonsense, of course. Nicho-las went to the door. With infinite caution, he inserted the key into the keyhole, willing himself to turn it slowly and gently. Too brisk a motion and he risked snapping it right off inside the lock.

The key turned, caught, turned a bit more—and then, with the most delicious clicking sound he had ever heard, the door unlocked.

Nicholas withdrew the key and kissed it. Then he tucked it inside his matchbox, blew out his candle, and hid the matchbox and the candle in the folds of his blanket. He took a deep breath and nodded to himself. He was ready.

The Manor was quite dark, but Nicholas was able to find his way by memory and moonlight. From the gallery over the entranceway, he looked and listened for some time before creeping down the carpeted staircase. He made a careful circuit of the ground floor, checking for light at the cracks beneath closed doors. Both the boys' dormitory and the ballroom where the girls slept were dark and still. Snores and deep breathing issued from the staff bedrooms.

Finally satisfied that he alone was awake—and not merely satisfied but thrilled, like a cat burglar approaching a safe—Nicholas approached the door to Mr. Collum's office. He had already observed, from a distance, that no light shone from beneath it. A long look through the keyhole revealed only darkness within. A long listen at the keyhole quelled his fears that Mr. Collum had extinguished his lamp and fallen asleep at his desk. The office was unmistakably empty.

Now came the riskiest part. Nicholas couldn't very well claim to have made a skeleton key in his sleep; if he was caught now, he would have no excuse. He tried to move quickly but deliberately. He had foreseen this moment and planned accordingly—he did not risk fumbling with the matchbox while standing up and holding the blanket and candle. Instead, he dropped to his knees and laid everything before him. And it was a good thing he did, for despite his caution he managed to spill a few matches as he took out the key. With straining eyes and probing hands, he searched the area about him until he was certain he had recovered them all. Then he made sure he had a good grip on the key—his hands were sweating—and rose to his feet. He slid the key into the keyhole and tried to turn it.

Nothing happened. It wouldn't budge.

Nicholas took a deep breath and tried again. Still nothing. He took another deep breath, then jiggled the key. He felt it slide the tiniest bit deeper into the keyhole, and this time when he turned the key, it met with no resistance at all. The lock sprang.

He was in.

And the ledger was in the desk drawer.

Nicholas did not read the ledger in Mr. Collum's office. It might take him only a few minutes, but those minutes would be risky indeed. What if Mr. Collum woke up and thought of something he needed from his office? Nicholas took the ledger into the library. He closed the door and stuffed his blanket into the crack beneath it so that no light could escape. He checked the curtains—closed. Only then did he light his candle.

In the candle's flickering light, the library's thousands of books emerged from their shadows, and for a moment Nicholas could not help admiring them again. During free time he had almost never looked up from the pages he was reading, but now he saw the books anew, from without rather than from within, and was reminded of how beautiful they were simply as objects. The geometrical wonder of them all, each book on its own and all the books together, row upon row. The infinite patterns and possibilities they presented. They were truly lovely.

Perhaps one day, Nicholas thought, he would make a book himself. Certainly he would have a library.

But first he must find his treasure.

Fixing his candle in a candlestick and settling on the floor, Nicholas opened the ledger. He saw at once that it had not been used as a ledger at all. There were no figures and sums, no records of expenditures and income. The pages were filled with handwriting that disregarded the printed columns on the paper. Instead it was divided into blocks of text, each of which began with a date. Why, it was a *diary*! And even before Nicholas had turned the first page, he knew that the diary had belonged to none other than Mr. Rothschild.

He kept turning pages, his excitement mounting, and in a matter of minutes he had read them all.

Nicholas closed the diary and sat considering it. Part of him thought he should put it back immediately and return to his room, where he could contemplate in safety what he had learned. Another part resisted this idea, though at present his mind was too busy to identify why. He decided to grant himself a little more time. Crossing his arms, he stared intently at the diary. *What have you told me*, he thought, *and what are you keeping hidden?*

Nicholas thought about what he knew for certain. The diary was eighty-six pages long (not including a few pages torn out and a few left blank at the end), and with the exception of several dark scribbles in the margins (Mr. Rothschild appeared often to have used the margins to blot extra ink from his fountain pens), it was written in a light-handed, elegant script. The entries covered a span of almost forty years, beginning in the first year of the Rothschilds' marriage and ending shortly after Mrs. Rothschild's death. The diary was, in essence, a record of the Rothschilds' life together—a haphazard record, for sometimes months or even years passed between entries—but more particularly it was Mr. Rothschild's admiring record of his wife.

Diana (or "Di," as he usually referred to her) was the only reason the diary existed. After she died, Mr. Rothschild had made only one more entry, in which he stated his intention to establish the orphanage in her honor and declared, in increasingly shaky handwriting, that the best chapter of his life had now closed. It was also the *last* chapter of his life, Nicholas knew—or the next-to-last, anyway, for according to Mrs. Brindle, Mr. Rothschild had only briefly outlived his wife.

One could see why Mr. Rothschild would have been despondent at the loss of Diana. His diary entries painted a portrait of a witty, scholarly woman, always reading, a clever problem-solver. She was warm and affectionate to Mr. Rothschild, kind and generous to others. She had endearing quirks: She was unusually careless in her clothes, always preferring old things to new ones, regardless of fashion; she was afraid of heights and even more so of crowds—indeed, she was amazingly shy and disliked going into town, though according to Mr. Rothschild, she charmed everyone she met. In a word, she was lovely. The diary, with its carelessly torn-out pages, its many gaps in time, and its narrow focus, left much to the imagination, but it did make one thing abundantly clear: Mr. Rothschild adored his wife.

Nicholas, for his part, was entirely skeptical.

The sort of love Mr. Rothschild expressed was the stuff of storybooks, as were the wonderful qualities his wife was said to possess. In real life Nicholas had never seen anything like them. He strongly suspected that such things were fantasies that people desperately wished to believe in, for the truth—that humans were generally a selfish and greedy lot—was so disagreeable. That was why storybook writers invented such admirable qualities for their characters, and Nicholas believed that Mr. Rothschild had written exactly that—a storybook, not a diary. It might be based upon facts (Nicholas certainly hoped it was, for the facts included a treasure), but the virtues and emotions described in it were surely exaggerated. Perhaps the endless admiration Mr. Rothschild expressed made him feel good, not just about his wife but about himself as well. Who wouldn't wish to think himself such a devoted husband?

True, Mr. Rothschild had established the orphanage, which seemed decent enough. But Nicholas would not have been at all surprised to learn that the truth was something more cynical. For example, Mr. Rothschild might have had a poisonous relationship with some distant relative whom he had not wished to inherit his estate. And so rather than be remembered as a vindictive old curmudgeon who had written his only living relative out of his will, he founded the orphanage and directed the remainder of his fortune to charity. After such a remarkable act of generosity, Mr. Rothschild would be remembered as a kindly prince, while the distant relative would be left stewing in private resentment.

It was a possibility, anyway. But Nicholas did not really care about imagined acts of spite any more than imagined virtues. What he really cared about was the treasure—and after reading the diary, he was convinced the treasure existed.

Mr. Rothschild referred to it quite specifically as his wife's treasure, which pointed to the explanation John had offered about Mrs. Rothschild's inheritance. Nicholas did not believe, however, that an actual bundle of money was hidden somewhere in the Manor. His guess was that Diana Rothschild, at her husband's insistence, had used her inheritance to purchase a rare and spectacularly valuable treasure for herself. After all, a single glance at Rothschild's End made clear that Diana never would have needed a penny of those millions, and it would seem characteristic of Mr. Rothschild, with his love of storybook touches, to encourage such an extravagant indulgence.

The exact nature of the treasure remained mysterious. Nicholas had deduced that it consisted of multiple items—it might be precious jewelry, antique gold, a collection of Ming vases, a combination of those things, or something else altogether—and certain details in the diary suggested that it had been obtained in secret. If so, perhaps the stealthy transaction had been arranged to avoid public notice. (The shy Diana would have been horrified at the idea of curious strangers turning up all the time, asking for a look at it.) Or perhaps the treasure had not been acquired in a strictly legal manner— the Rothschilds were rich enough to pay their way through any obstacle. Perhaps both reasons pertained. Regardless, Mr. Rothschild was no more specific about the treasure's contents than he was about its location.

Nicholas did know one important thing for certain: The treasure occupied a room unto itself, a room Mr. Rothschild rather overdramatically called the "treasure chamber." This knowledge alone was enough to make Nicholas want to go knocking on walls and peering behind paintings right away, in search of a hidden door or secret panel. Obviously that was exactly what Mr. Collum had felt upon reading the diary, too.

Unlike Mr. Collum, however, Nicholas could not move freely about the Manor, nor did he have as much time at his disposal. He had to be quiet—no knocking on walls for him—and he had to sleep sometime. He could not go poking about at random, hoping to stumble upon the solution. He needed a plan. He needed to think. And he needed to be careful.

Being careful, Nicholas chastised himself, *probably doesn't include sitting down here with an off-limits diary you've already read and memorized. You ought to have returned it the moment you finished reading it.*

Yet when he moved to pick the diary up, Nicholas was once again aware of a nagging feeling that he had not finished with it. This time he concentrated on the feeling, trying to understand it—and suddenly he did. Had he not, only minutes earlier, been thinking about seeing books differently from within and without? He had read this diary intently focused on the content of its writing, but had he not noticed other things about it that might be important?

Nicholas considered. Yes, he most certainly had.

Without really meaning to, he had formed the opinion that Mr. Rothschild was rather careless with his diary—a surprising attitude, considering its emotional importance, so why had he come to think that? Nicholas thought he knew why. Those dark scribbles in the margins had led him to assume that Mr. Rothschild did not much care about the diary's appearance, a notion strengthened by the fact that some of the diary's pages had obviously and crudely been torn out, each one leaving behind a jagged fringe of paper. Nicholas had suspected that the pages had disclosed the location of the treasure chamber, and that Mr. Rothschild had eventually thought better of leaving such information where it might be discovered. But what if it was not Mr. Rothschild who had torn out the pages? What if it was Mr. Collum? What if those missing pages contained important clues, and Mr. Collum had hidden them in a different place?

There might be other explanations, of course. And of course Mr. Rothschild might be responsible for the missing pages, after all. But if he *wasn't*, then those dark scribbles might not be his doing, either.

Nicholas opened the diary again and fanned the pages until he came to one with scribbles in the margin. Ever so carefully, he moved the book closer to the candle flame, squinting at the scribbles in the improved light. They were not scribbles at all. They were words. Words composed of such tiny, closely printed letters that they were almost completely illegible. They must have been written with a very fine pen and a very careful hand. He put his face as close as he could to the page, but his long nose presented a problem. He turned his head and brought the diary up to his left eye. Now he could make out the letters—that was an *A*, that was an *M*—but it was difficult and uncomfortable, and it would take him forever. He needed a magnifying glass.

Nicholas's mind suddenly conjured an image of Mr. Collum peering through his jeweler's loupe. Of course! These were Mr. Collum's private notes! No doubt he made them so small because he didn't want someone glancing over his shoulder and seeing what he was up to.

Too bad, Mr. Collum, thought Nicholas as he scrambled to his feet. *I'm going to read your notes, and I'm also going to find those missing pages.*

His bravado was short-lived. A thorough search of Mr. Collum's desk drawers turned up neither jeweler's loupe nor loose papers with jagged edges. Were the papers in the filing cabinets? No, Nicholas seriously doubted Mr. Collum would keep them where John might come across them. If he had them at all, he probably kept them on his own person, tucked away in a pocket along with his jeweler's loupe and his skeleton key.

Nicholas found himself hoping that the pages had been hidden away long ago—hidden away or even destroyed. At least then Mr. Collum wouldn't have that advantage over him. In the meantime, he needed something to help him read those notes.

Use your brain, he told himself, and so he did, and by the time he had locked the office door again, he had hit upon his answer.

He headed for the kitchen.

Soon Nicholas had collected what he wanted—a glass filled with water—and returned to the library. He shoved the blanket back into place, lit his candle again, and looked at the diary through the glass. The minuscule letters swelled into view as he passed the glass slowly over them. Nicholas grinned. He ordered his hands to be steady. He was making use of paper's two greatest enemies—fire and water—and an accident would be disastrous. Yes, he would be extremely careful.

Now, if he could just stay awake...

SECRET
PROJECTS

"Look at him!" Nicholas heard Iggy muttering. "He really loves this stuff!"

"Yeah, he thinks it's swell!" Breaker muttered. "Ha!"

It was another dreary afternoon at the Manor. The orphans were all crowded into the hot and stuffy drawing room, enduring another group activity. This time it was a session in papier-mâché led by Miss Candace, the third such session of the week. Most of the children's projects were almost finished, having been shaped and dried over the preceding days. They were now laid out on long makeshift tables, and the children were lined up shoulder to shoulder, painting their creations. The paint fumes and the stifling heat were making Nicholas dizzy. Still, he worked doggedly on.

As usual, no one was speaking to him, but the Spiders had noticed him taking a special interest in his project, and naturally this had earned him special derision. The Spiders believed arts and crafts to be pastimes for girls and toddlers; they were completing their own projects with as much disdain as possible. Besides, as anyone could see, Nicholas had not the least talent for papier-mâché. He had put much painstaking work into a completely nondescript gray block that he claimed (when Miss Candace asked him) to be Plymouth Rock, but which to everyone else resembled a boring chunk of wall.

"He's a dunce!" Nicholas heard Moray say, not for the first time. (Everyone except Miss Candace heard him say it, though he pretended to be whispering.) "What kind of a moron thinks Plymouth Rock was a square?"

Titters and snickers broke out among the group. Nicholas noticed a couple of the haggard older girls looking at him with expressions of pity, though it was difficult to tell whether they pitied him for being mocked or for being so misinformed about Plymouth Rock. He didn't see what John's reaction was. He had purposely stationed himself as far from John as possible, and he tried never to look directly at him. It bothered Nicholas enough when the others averted their eyes; when John did it, he felt even worse.

Nicholas applied more carefully mixed gray paint to his brush and kept working. If everyone truly believed he was hopeless with papier-mâché, that was all the better. They would be even less likely to suspect the true nature of his project. For his part, he was looking forward to being able to open the window in his room without having to disassemble it stone by stone.

The papier-mâché project was not the only sneaky thing Nicholas was up to. Ever since he read Mr. Rothschild's diary (almost a week ago now), he'd been constantly on the lookout for secret passages, hidden panels, trapdoors—anything that might lead to the treasure chamber. At that very moment, though he made a show of concentrating on his project, Nicholas's eyes were once again roving over the drawing-room walls, searching for any odd features. And every single time he had crossed the room to gather more materials, he had studied the floorboards and listened carefully to the sounds they made beneath his shoes. They all appeared to be securely nailed in place, no loose or shifting planks. In fact, they seemed uncommonly solid and well made. The walls seemed perfectly normal, too.

Nicholas looked back down at his work, disappointed. He had thought the drawing room a good place to search. For three days he had imagined how exciting it would be to spot an unusually wide seam in the paneled wainscoting, or hear a certain hollowness beneath the floor, or notice a bookcase that seemed curiously askew. An ill-mortared stone in the fireplace would have made him positively giddy. But he had to accept it: There was nothing unusual about the drawing room; and, with a sigh, Nicholas crossed it off his mental list.

"What's the matter?" whispered Moray, watching him from across the table. "Doesn't your dumb rock look dumb enough for you?"

The other Spiders snorted and elbowed each other.

Nicholas didn't look up. "I wouldn't know," he replied with a shrug. "You're the expert on dumb stuff."

Moray's smug look vanished. "What was that? What did you just say?"

Nicholas smiled sweetly at him—Moray couldn't touch him with Miss Candace around—and went back to his thoughts.

Since he had finally eliminated the drawing room, Nicholas returned once again to Mr. Rothschild's diary. How many times had he gone over those treasure-related entries in his mind, hoping to stir up new insights, to notice something hidden between the lines, something he had previously overlooked? Hundreds? Thousands? And yet this time, as every time, he returned to them with the keenest sense of urgency, for he knew that Mr. Collum was doing exactly the same thing.

Not surprisingly, it was mostly in the margins alongside those particular entries that Mr. Collum had written his tiny notes. Like Nicholas, Mr. Collum had been especially struck by the entry in which Mr. Rothschild wrote, "I honestly think Di could spend hours simply admiring her treasure, simply glorying in its presence. Indeed she *has* spent hours luxuriating in it—countless hours—yet I've seen her go out of her way to visit that treasure chamber just to glance in upon it for a few seconds, such is the pleasure it brings her."

In the margins next to this entry Mr. Collum had written: *Does "go out of her way" merely suggest taking an inefficient path to another room, or does the chamber lie in some far-flung corner?*

Nicholas had wondered the same thing. Perhaps to reach

the treasure, Mrs. Rothschild had needed to pass through a part of the Manor she never would have visited otherwise. The kitchen, for example. The Rothschilds had employed a private cook, whom Mr. Rothschild referred to as Toasty (he had nicknames for almost everyone), and Mrs. Rothschild seldom even boiled an egg. Evidently, she was a cheerful but careless cook—she was always burning her fingers or wounding herself with the grater—and early in their courtship Mr. Rothschild had begged her to stop preparing meals.

The kitchen, therefore, had seemed a promising place to find a hidden entrance to the chamber, and Nicholas, on lunchtime kitchen duty all week, had slyly and methodically searched for secret panels. He had even crawled into the cabinets near the floor, telling Mr. Griese he was in pursuit of a mouse. The only surprising thing he'd found was a mousetrap that snapped closed upon his probing fingers. (He had yelped like a puppy, too. But at least Buford hadn't told anyone about it, and Nicholas counted himself lucky not to have been startled to sleep.)

Eventually it had occurred to him that the Rothschilds probably hosted few dinner parties, for Mrs. Rothschild was too shy to enjoy them. So perhaps "out of her way" referred to a place typically reserved for entertaining guests, such as this drawing room. That would explain why Mr. Collum had been searching it the other morning; he'd probably had the same idea. Nicholas had hoped to prove more observant or even just luckier than Mr. Collum had been, to no avail. The drawing room was out.

But if not the drawing room, then where? If the phrase "out of her way" actually did refer to some far-flung corner, as Mr. Collum had speculated in his notes, then which far-flung corner did it mean? The Manor contained scads of them. One could hardly know where to begin.

Only one other clue gave any hint about the treasure's location. Elsewhere in the diary Mr. Rothschild had written, "Sometimes I wonder if the only thing that prevents Di from setting up residence in her beloved treasure chamber, like those dragons who live among their glittering hoards, is the discomfiting cold. She has never complained, but I have noticed that in chill weather she spends less time reveling in her riches and more time taking tea and meals with me. Thus, I am ashamed to say, I have no great incentive to remedy the problem. I am too selfish and enjoy her company too much."

Discomfiting cold. These words had put Nicholas in mind of chilly subterranean vaults—of trapdoors that opened onto secret stairs. That was why he'd been paying such careful attention to the floorboards, searching for irregularities wherever he walked, not just in the drawing room but everywhere in the Manor.

He was not alone in this. Mr. Collum also suspected that the chamber was underground, for precisely the same reason. He had said as much in his margin notes, right beside the words "discomfiting cold."

Nicholas had read those notes with a grimace. He had read *all* of Mr. Collum's notes with a grimace, in fact, for they had very closely—much too closely—reflected his own thoughts. He did not like it one bit that he and Mr. Collum had drawn the same conclusions. He detested Mr. Collum and did not care to have anything in common with him.

Worse, he hated to see the director making progress toward the mystery's solution. This treasure hunt was a race, the most important race of his life, and Mr. Collum was his only opponent.

Unfortunately, Nicholas did not appear to be making much progress himself. Without an intelligent plan—and so far he'd been maddeningly unable to form one—the best he could do was to keep thinking about those diary entries and keep his eyes open for anything out of the ordinary. Yet even keeping his eyes open was a challenge lately—even more so than usual—for he felt increasingly bleary as a result of his late-night visits to the library.

He could not help creeping downstairs to read each night, though. The temptation was too strong, the books irresistible. He knew how risky it was. What if he fell asleep in the library and didn't wake up before morning? Usually he woke up several times a night (often screaming, alas), but sometimes he slept five or six hours straight. He couldn't afford for that to happen in the library. As a precaution, he'd fixed the broken alarm clock he'd found in his room. It had taken him no time at all. In the library he'd found an excellent book on clock repair, and in the basement he'd found the perfect tools for the job.

The basement itself had been a revelation. Even by candlelight it had dazzled Nicholas with its abundance. Like a curiosity shop, it was crammed full of discarded equipment, furniture, oddments, and artifacts, to say nothing of its marvelous store of tools. It looked as if a troupe of traveling tinkers had dumped their wagons down the stairs. The truth was less bizarre, though, and Nicholas had heard all about it from Mrs. Brindle: The scandalous previous director, Mr. Bottoms, had simply never troubled to have anything repaired. Whenever something broke, he'd had it carried down into the basement. If it was something important, he'd purchased a new item to replace it.

It was a staggering display of wastefulness, the sight of which probably made Mr. Collum sick. But to Nicholas the basement had been a delight. He'd spent a long time examining old radio cabinets, phonographs, lamps and lanterns, stationary bicycles, automobile parts, and boxes and boxes of other things besides, before he remembered the reason he'd come down to the basement in the first place.

Since then Nicholas always carried his alarm clock with him at night, hidden in the blanket with the candle and matchbox. Every hour he set it for the hour ahead. If he went to sleep, the alarm would wake him (and, with luck, *only* him) in time to sneak back up to his room. So far he had managed to stay awake, and he kept close track of the time to make sure the alarm never went off.

And in the meantime Nicholas read.

Oh, how he read! He seemed to read faster with every book, and he was reading books by the dozens. He had long since finished the encyclopedia and moved on to books about physics and mathematics, engines and mechanics, chemistry and biology. The sciences compelled him most, but everything interested him, and he followed his whims from shelf to shelf. Last night, for instance, he had read a book of nonsense poetry (which tickled his fancy) as well as a history of scientific exploration (which inspired him) before diving into a three-volume atlas of the world. When at last he'd ordered himself to bed, his mind was so aglow with new ideas and new knowledge, he almost expected beams of light to shine from his eyes.

So why can't you solve this mystery? Nicholas asked himself now, as he put the final touches on his false section of wall. *What are you missing?* The only good thing about this whole awful place was the library. But the one thing that would get him *out* of this awful place was that treasure.

Stepping back from the table to see what his project looked like from a distance, Nicholas bumped into a girl working at the table behind him. "Pardon me, Gertrude," he said without turning around, and several of the children gasped and began whispering.

Nicholas smiled inwardly. He never missed an opportunity to strengthen his reputation for "seeing things." It worked best with the younger children, who were easy to shock and quick to spread the rumors of his gifts. In this case, it helped that Gertrude McGillicuddy liked to sneak perfume from Mrs. Brindle's bottle—he had smelled it on her before, though she always applied so little of it she must have thought no one could smell it but herself. Nicholas had much too keen a nose to miss the fragrance, though, or to mistake where she'd gotten it.

The children were still whispering about this latest display of clairvoyance, when a distant tapping sound caught Nicholas's ear. Growing louder by the moment, it sounded as if it was coming from the passage outside the drawing room. He turned his eyes to the open doorway, and sure enough, Mr. Collum appeared in it, leaning heavily on a cane.

"Miss Candace," the director called in a breathless voice.

"A word with you, please." He limped into the room, wielding his cane with peculiar violence. Each time it struck the floor, everyone in the drawing room flinched.

Miss Candace happened to be in the middle of a long yawn when she noticed Mr. Collum's cane and attempted to cry out with concern. The result was that she sounded as though she'd been pushed from a height. "Oh, my!" she exclaimed when she'd finished this peculiar bellowing. "Whatever happened? Shall I take a look?"

For someone with such a pronounced limp, Mr. Collum stepped back with surprising nimbleness. "No, no, Miss Candace. I'm fine, I assure you. Merely a twisted ankle. I'll recover soon enough."

"But I'm a nurse!" Miss Candace protested, stooping in an attempt to snatch at Mr. Collum's ankle. "What if you've broken it?"

Again the director retreated quickly. "I'm certain that I haven't," he insisted. "Now, please, Miss Candace—"

Miss Candace yawned again. Mr. Collum waited until she'd finished. He started to speak, and then had to wait again as another ferocious yawn overtook her. Nicholas realized that she must have been the chaperone in the ballroom the night before.

The ballroom, he'd learned, was a terrible place to sleep. The girls' exhaustion was not the result of a single bad night, as he had first thought—they *never* slept well. Mrs. Brindle and Miss Candace suffered, too, though only half as much, for they took turns as the girls' nighttime chaperones. The trouble was noise, and evidently the scoundrel Mr. Bottoms was to blame again. He had directed a mile-long swath of trees to be cut so that electrical power lines might be strung to the Manor, and this empty corridor through the woods now funneled all manner of sounds directly toward the ballroom windows. The bells and whistles of distant trains and riverboats, the howling of wind (the fierce nightly wind was also a result of that corridor), and the rattling of windowpanes all conspired to keep the girls awake. But no other room was large enough to accommodate all of their cots, and the girls suffered their sleepiness with no hope of relief.

Join the club, thought Nicholas, not for the first time. Unlike the girls, he had adjusted to being sleepy. It caused him plenty of problems, but he had learned to disguise it. Except when he was actually asleep, of course. There was no disguising that.

Disguise. Nicholas pursed his lips. Why had that word suddenly struck him so oddly?

"I'm simply concerned about the waste, Miss Candace," Mr. Collum was saying. "Projects are fine, but—"

"Oh, don't worry, Mr. Collum!" Miss Candace interjected. "There were hundreds of old newspapers in the basement, and plenty of wire mesh and wallpaper paste, and gallons and gallons of paint. None of it was being used, you see—" Here she was interrupted by a yawn.

"Yes, yes," Mr. Collum said. "I'm quite aware of all that, Miss Candace. You'll recall that I approved the activity in the first place. My point is not that you wasted *money* but that you've wasted *energy*. Could not the children have made something *useful* out of the papier-mâché?"

"Useful?"

Mr. Collum gestured impatiently toward the tables. "I see

a great variety of false and oversized fruit, Miss Candace. I see what appear to be masks of some kind. I see rather unrealistic-looking barnyard animals—"

Nicholas casually stepped sideways to block Mr. Collum's view of his project.

"—but I see nothing *useful*," the director said again. "Next time, please consider this point. Surely papier-mâché could be put to better use, could it not?"

"I'm sure it could, Mr. Collum," said Miss Candace, though she looked extremely doubtful. "I shall certainly consider it. Now, won't you please let me examine your ankle?"

"Absolutely not," Mr. Collum replied, and turned to go. He limped from the room, again striking the floorboards smartly with his cane and pausing every few steps, as if to rest.

Disguise, Nicholas thought again, and now he knew why. Mr. Collum had not twisted his ankle at all. He was using that cane to sound the floors. His supposed injury was just an excuse to carry the cane around the Manor, rapping floorboards.

He has no more idea where to look than I do, Nicholas thought with relief. *Which means that for the moment, anyway, we're even.*

And so he thought until late that very night, when a brand-new clue fell into his lap.

the Butler's Clues

Nicholas had already stayed in the library longer than he should have. It was quite late. He had been reading intriguing books about electricity and other forms of energy, about light waves and sound waves and radio signals and many other deeply fascinating things, and he had gotten carried away. His mind was so awhirl with ideas that he found himself picturing the Milky Way inside his own head, a spiral galaxy of thoughts tucked inside his cranium. He smiled at the notion as he put away the last book, willing himself to go to bed. But then thinking about galaxies ensnared him, and he decided to allow himself one more book.

He had long ago spied a section of books on astronomy, and selecting the thickest of these, Nicholas settled on the floor. He paged through the book, slowing once or twice to appreciate a particularly lovely illustration, until he came to the final chapter, which explained the process of building an observatory. *Construction instructions*, he was thinking with poetic satisfaction, when to his surprise he came upon a handwritten note in one of the margins. Instantly he recognized the elegant script as Mr. Rothschild's.

Nicholas felt his heart speeding up. He fanned the pages. There were several more handwritten notes, each of which he read with mounting excitement. They were all about amateur observatories—questions about intricacies of construction, placement, maintenance, different kinds of telescopes, and so on. The last one read, "Consult the Butler."

The butler? Why would Mr. Rothschild need to consult his butler about building an amateur observatory?

Nicholas put the book back on the shelf, fixated now on that last note. He scratched his head. *The butler, the butler, the butler.* He froze mid-scratch. He rolled his eyes at himself. Fatigue must be making him dopey. Taking the book from the shelf again, he turned to the final chapter and began flipping pages. He found what he was looking for near the end: a footnote referring to a different book—*The Complete Guide to Amateur Observatories*, written by Brian T. Butler.

Nicholas's eyes darted to the books in the astronomy section. There it was.

He grabbed the other book and sat down with it. When

he fanned its pages in search of more notes, three folded slips of paper fell out and fluttered into his lap. They were yellow and brittle with age. Nicholas unfolded them carefully. The first two, which resembled receipts, appeared to be different companies' estimates for the materials and labor required to construct an amateur observatory. The company names were illegible, far too faded to read, but Nicholas could make out enough to understand what he was looking at. Again he recognized Mr. Rothschild's characteristic hand, with which some figures had been lined through and question marks drawn next to others, and in the margins Mr. Rothschild had scrawled various questions about details and quibbles about cost. And well he might quibble, for the costs were enormous.

The third sheet of paper was a list of telescopes, their features, their manufacturers, the addresses of European companies from which they could be ordered—and their prices, which seemed impossible to believe. With the money necessary to purchase even the least expensive of them, Nicholas could have lived comfortably for years. Had Mr. Rothschild actually *bought* one? That sort of wealth seemed as brilliant, distant, and unreachable as the stars themselves.

Or no, not unreachable. Not unreachable at all.

Mr. Rothschild had been a very rich man. The question was not whether he had actually bought one of those telescopes. The evidence in Nicholas's hands suggested that he had. No, the question—the extremely important question— was where he had *put* the telescope.

If Mr. Rothschild had purchased a telescope, then he had built an observatory to house it. For the first time, it occurred to Nicholas that the treasure might not be inside the Manor.

What if it was hidden inside the observatory? If so, where was the observatory? How large was the estate of Rothschild's End?

Nicholas considered. *Out of her way. Chill weather.* Yes, the observatory could very well be somewhere on the property, somewhere within walking distance, somewhere Diana Rothschild would visit less often in the winter. It would be somewhere high up, somewhere with an unobstructed view of the night sky. Abruptly, Nicholas stood and put the books away. He had just seen, in his mind's eye, the wooded hill at the rear of the park, the one he and John had come to on their walk. What if, at the top of that hill—?

He did not complete this thought, for just at that moment his exhaustion overcame him. It fell on him like a hammer. His eyelids grew heavy, and a cloud drifted over his thoughts. Vaguely it occurred to him that he had put off returning to his room for too long, that he was in danger of losing control of his senses. His eyes briefly widened. Danger? *Yes, danger!* He felt a surge of panic, which helped—it coursed through him like electricity, charging his efforts to gather his things and stagger out of the library. But then it was spent, and he was left foggy, fading, failing. . . .

Halfway up the stairs, Nicholas couldn't remember if he had closed the library door. Too late now. He would be lucky if he reached the top of the stairs without falling backward and breaking his neck. And then somehow he found himself in his cot, with no memory of stumbling into it or even of entering his room. He could not remember whether he had locked his door—or, if he had, whether he had removed his key. None of it could be helped. Nicholas was sliding away, no longer in control of his fate. From somewhere in the darkness, a voice — was it his own? — tried to assure him that any mistakes could be corrected in the morning.

And then the voice changed, and the horrors began.

An hour or so before dawn, Nicholas awoke clearheaded enough to search his pockets. Yes, he had his key. He felt his way to the door. It was locked. *Good enough*, he thought, and tumbled back into his cot. He fell asleep again at once. He couldn't help it, but later he would regret it, for he spent the next hour fleeing one frightening vision after another. They were all so real that when Mrs. Brindle at last unlocked the door and entered the room with her lamp, Nicholas could not believe her bravery. Why did she not scream and run away?

But of course Mrs. Brindle saw nothing to fear, nothing more than a trembling young boy, a boy squeezing himself tightly about the chest as if freezing... and then, after a moment, transforming into something else entirely. A happy boy, polite and cheerful. A strange boy who greeted her with a courtly bow and a wink. An *altogether* strange boy, Mrs. Brindle thought — though certainly not a moper, which she appreciated. Mrs. Brindle disliked mopers.

"Oh!" she cried, rubbing her hip. "Getting an early start, are you? Hate to waste time, do you?"

Nicholas, who knew that she was addressing her wandering pain, nonetheless replied, "I do indeed, Mrs. Brindle! I do indeed, and I'm ever so grateful to you for setting me free. Let the day begin!"

"What?" Mrs. Brindle asked, but Nicholas, whistling brightly, was already off to the bathroom to wash up and change clothes.

"Tell me, Mrs. Brindle," Nicholas said when he returned, "how big is Rothschild's End? The property, I mean."

The housekeeper dug a knuckle into her itchy eye. "How should I know? Might be a thousand acres, might be two thousand. Do I look like a surveyor? Is that what I'm doing when I push a mop up and down these floors—am I measuring?"

Nicholas stepped out of the room so that she could lock the door. "Oh no, of course not. I just wondered what the property boundaries were. I mean, for example, does the estate include all the woods around us?"

" 'For example'? How do you come by these things, boy? *For example.*" Mrs. Brindle shook her head, then winced and grabbed her neck. She sighed. "Yes, yes, of course all the woods are part of 'Child's End. Everyone knows that. The property runs all the way to the river in the south and to the Hopefield farm to the north. To the west I don't know. To the east I don't know. You've asked the wrong person. Now come along," she added, though Nicholas was two steps ahead of her in the passage.

"Why, Mrs. Brindle!" Nicholas said, slowing down to match her pace. "To me it seems you know an awful lot! Although it's true I could ask the other staff members. That's a good suggestion."

Mrs. Brindle frowned. "What suggestion? I didn't make a suggestion. And I doubt anyone else here could tell you more, as none of them's been here long. Mr. Collum had to hire all new staff, you know. And was lucky to get us, for what he pays! Lucky for him Mr. Griese was sick of all that restaurant work and city life and wanted a place where he could keep his own little garden. *You've* seen his herb garden; you know what a wonder it is!"

After that the talk was all about Mr. Griese, and Nicholas let the main part of his attention wander elsewhere. Mrs. Brindle had confirmed his suspicion. The hill behind the park was on the Rothschilds' property.

Nicholas excitedly began to plan his expedition. Indeed, he grew so absorbed in his thoughts that when Mrs. Brindle interrupted herself to wonder aloud who had left trash all over the floor, he almost didn't register the question. Mrs. Brindle was always complaining about trash, and fingerprints on windows and mirrors, and other evidence of human habitation. But then it sank in. They had reached the bottom of the stairs, and Mrs. Brindle was bending to pick up three pieces of paper from the entranceway floor—*three old yellow pieces of paper*. With a gasp, Nicholas sprang forward and snatched them up.

"Who indeed!" he exclaimed indignantly. "Don't worry, Mrs. Brindle—I'll throw these away!"

"Throw what away?" asked Mr. Collum, walking into the entranceway. He was dressed and ready for another day, though he had forgotten his cane. Evidently, he realized this just as Nicholas and Mrs. Brindle turned to look at him, for with a sudden frown he began to feign a limp.

Nicholas swallowed, resisting the urge to hide the papers behind his back.

"Why, trash, Mr. Collum!" said Mrs. Brindle, her voice full of outrage. "Trash on the floor! I don't see how I can be expected to keep this place clean when people throw garbage everywhere they look! It wasn't even there last night! I'm sure of it! They're getting up early just to throw trash on the floor!"

"Calm down, Mrs. Brindle," said Mr. Collum with a tight smile. "I agree that it is unseemly. But my point was to question whether in fact this 'trash' ought to be 'thrown away,' which Nicholas was about to do. Remember, we must waste nothing! Might not that paper be used again? Tell me, Nicholas, what is it you've picked up?"

Nicholas hesitated.

"Nicholas?" Mr. Collum prompted impatiently, and he started to reach for the papers.

"A ball!" Nicholas cried, wadding up the papers. "A ball, Mr. Collum! Right? It isn't trash—it's a toy!" He began tossing the crumpled paper ball into the air and catching it.

Mr. Collum twitched, irritated by the sudden noise and frenzied motion, but then he nodded. "Well, yes, Nicholas, it could be a ball, although a rather sorry one, to be sure. I see you take my point, however. Please remember it in the future." With that, he turned and walked to his office door, remembering, halfway there, to limp.

"Personally, I still say it's trash," Mrs. Brindle muttered when Mr. Collum had closed the door behind him.

"I'll throw it away," Nicholas whispered in reply, and so he did, though not before shredding it into a hundred tiny scraps.

THE EXPEDITION

Midnight, and the full moon was high overhead. A small figure darted from shadow to shadow, traversing the park-like grounds of Rothschild's End. The Manor's windows were dark. No one awake but Nicholas Benedict. He was fully dressed, pajamas and blankets being unsuitable for such an outing, and he carried a large, awkward-looking lantern that he had not yet dared to light. Fortunately the moon was so brilliant, its silvery light so strong even beneath the looming oak trees, that he had no need of a lantern here. On his back he wore an old flour sack with armholes that he'd cut into it, held secure by a strip of fabric that passed across his chest—his *flour-sack backpack*, as he thought of it. Inside the backpack were his box of matches and his alarm clock, with plenty of room for additional items, should any prove necessary. He had come prepared.

Nevertheless, Nicholas was nervous. Never had he taken such a risk—not just of being caught without a good explanation but of wandering into unknown jeopardy. He had never ventured into woods of any kind, and he could not help but think of snakes, scorpions, panthers, bears. Even the thought of stumbling over a sleeping badger was enough to make him anxious. But he would not turn back. Turning back did not even occur to him.

The night was mild and warm, though the moon gave every surface a frosty appearance, and the thin ringing sound of crickets, frogs, cicadas, and other tiny creatures made Nicholas imagine infinitesimal tambourines being jingled behind every leaf and bush. It was cheering in its way, and by the time he reached the woods at the base of the hill, most of his uneasiness had given over to simple, pleasant excitement.

Nicholas knelt to light his lantern. It was a strange conglomeration, this lantern, and looked like none other, for he'd cobbled it together from the parts of several different broken lamps and lanterns he'd found in the basement—a working burner here, an uncracked glass chimney there, and so on until he'd fashioned a veritable Frankenstein's lamp. It was not at all bright, but it lit easily and had a sturdy handle, and Nicholas had scavenged plenty of oil for it.

Even with the lantern, he spent a long time tramping back and forth at the edge of the woods before he spotted anything resembling a path. From a distance he could not be sure, but plunging deeper in among the trees he confirmed his suspicion—it was a path, all right, though long since overgrown. If he hadn't been looking for it, he never would have noticed it. Perhaps it was only a deer trail, but it did lead up the hill, and at the sight of it, Nicholas felt ready to burst with expectation.

You're on the right track, he thought with a grin, and started up at once. He kept a careful eye on the trail, which zigzagged back and forth to make climbing less difficult. It was much darker in these woods than it had been in the park—the leafy branches overhead formed a canopy that completely obscured the sky—and the hill was very high, but then so was Nicholas's enthusiasm. Not even the many spiderwebs he accidentally passed through could diminish it. He merely laughed at himself for being so startled each time, brushed the sticky strands from his face as best he could, and pressed on with a breathless "Sorry, madam spider!" and the hope that his clothes were not accumulating arachnids.

Finally, just as his legs were growing wobbly from climbing, Nicholas reached the summit, where the woods gave way to a broad, open clearing. And there, in the middle of the clearing, stood a curious stone structure—a little building with a dome-shaped roof. Nicholas pressed a fist to his mouth, resisting the urge to shout in triumph.

He had found the observatory.

The structure was almost entirely covered by vines and grown about with weeds. The overgrowth gave it a shaggy appearance that put Nicholas in mind of a giant's head, unshaved and unkempt. Windows would have completed the picture—they would have given it eyes—but there were none. Nor was there an actual door, only a dark, empty doorway visible through the screen of vines, which Nicholas briefly imagined as the giant's gaping maw. The image made him uneasy, however, and he quickly shoved it from his mind. He was about to go in there, after all.

Holding the lantern high, Nicholas approached the black doorway. He spotted rusty, broken hinges still attached to the frame, and a closer inspection convinced him that the door had been knocked down years ago. Not good. With a rising sense of dread, he swept aside the vines, peered into the observatory's dark interior, and saw—nothing much. No telescope, at any rate, and certainly no treasure. Only a large, mostly barren room with a dusty stone floor.

Nicholas ventured two steps through the doorway and stopped, for despite his urgency, he still felt nervous. He swiveled left and right, unsteadily holding out his lantern, which was bright enough to show him everything in the room, if not quite bright enough to dispel all the creepy shadows. The door that used to fit in the doorway lay off to the side, spotted with fungus; a row of old cabinets stood open along the wall to his right, their empty interiors netted with cobwebs; and protruding from the opposite wall were three metal hand cranks. From his reading, Nicholas knew that two of those cranks had been used to open the viewing panels in the observatory roof. The other one, he suspected, had adjusted the position of the telescope (which must have been very large), for on the floor in the center of the room, where the telescope would have stood, was a round metal plate that resembled a giant turntable. The telescope ought to have been firmly secured to it. Instead, broken bolts and bits of rusted metal lay scattered about the floor, evidence of a hasty, forcible removal.

Nicholas's dread was rapidly developing into full-blown despair. The telescope had obviously been stolen, and if someone had taken the telescope . . . He felt his throat tighten, and noticing that his hands were trembling, he put down the lantern, lest he drop it. All day long he had imagined his moment of glorious discovery. Now he imagined someone *else* reveling in that moment ("My, oh, my—not just a telescope to steal, but a treasure, too!")—someone *else* making off with a prize he'd been counting on to change his life.

"Steady now," Nicholas cautioned himself. He took a slow, deep breath, then another, and patted his legs as he might have patted the flank of a nervous horse. "Steady, old boy." If he let himself get too upset, he might go out like a light, and where would he be then? What if his alarm clock failed to wake him? He shuddered at the thought. Removing his flour-sack backpack, he double-checked the alarm clock, taking several more deep breaths as he did so. Soon he began to feel better.

He had yet to begin a proper search, after all. Perhaps the treasure *hadn't* been found by the telescope thieves. It wasn't likely to have been kept out in plain view, was it? If that door could be knocked down so easily, Mr. Rothschild would not have considered it sufficient protection for his wife's precious treasure. No, there surely would have been a hiding place—a secret vault beneath the floor, perhaps even a tunnel leading to a subterranean cave. The observatory itself would not have been the treasure chamber. It would simply have contained the chamber's concealed entrance.

Yes, the more Nicholas thought about it, the better he liked his chances. Any number of people might have known about the Rothschilds' expensive telescope, but there was no reason to assume that anyone knew about the treasure. The crooks who came up here with their crowbars and wagons would have been in a terrific hurry to snatch the telescope and flee. How likely was it that they took time to look around for anything out of the ordinary? Not likely at all.

In a much-improved mood, Nicholas picked up his lantern and went to inspect the old cabinets. He thought they would make a good hiding place for a secret latch or knob. But his search turned up nothing, so he crossed to the opposite wall to take a closer look at the mechanical cranks.

Right away he was impressed by the cranks' design. Whatever system of gears and chains they controlled was contained within the observatory walls and underneath its floor. An ingenious piece of engineering, he thought, although maintaining the hidden mechanisms must have been a pain. If ever they needed to be repaired or serviced, part of the wall would have had to be knocked out and patched up again afterward. Perhaps the design was so perfect that such occasions would have been extremely rare. Or perhaps...

Nicholas ran a finger over the rough mortar between two stones, thinking of the false section of wall in his room. Perhaps some of these stones could be removed just as easily, if only a person knew which ones and the right way to go about it. He looked back at the cranks. What if they operated more than he had thought? What if one of them also moved a stone, or even an entire section of stones, in the wall or floor?

Nicholas eagerly set down his lantern and applied himself

to the lowest of the cranks. It screeched and groaned—it badly needed oiling—and it was exceedingly difficult to turn. Yet turn it did, much to his delight, and as it turned so did the metal plate in the middle of the room, making just the sort of crackling, gravelly noise an actual phonograph would make through its speaker. Nicholas grinned, imagining giant music booming out from a giant record, and he cranked and cranked until he was sure the turntable had gone around at least once. Nothing else happened—no hidden entrances unhid themselves—but he was thoroughly pleased, nonetheless, by this demonstration of mechanical ingenuity. He could easily picture that telescope being rotated so that its lens might be trained on a different section of sky. How he wished he could have seen it in person! How exciting it must have been to *look* through it!

Panting from his exertions, Nicholas mopped his brow with his shirt and gazed up at the domed roof. Even without the telescope, he was excited. For that matter, he would have been excited even without the prospect of treasure. The observatory itself was a grand discovery.

When he'd recovered his breath, Nicholas set to work on the middle crank. He had to use both hands and strain with all his might, and, like the first crank, this one squealed in protest, almost refusing to budge. But then something gave, the crank jerked forward, and Nicholas was rewarded with a popping sound and a shower of dust from above. He paused to look up. Sure enough, one of the rectangular viewing panels had been slightly retracted, leaving a narrow open space near the middle of the dome. A bright shaft of moonbeams and starlight pierced the shadows there, and in that new light hung a spectacular dust cloud, not unlike one of the nebulae he had admired in the astronomy book.

Nicholas laughed with pleasure and went back to work, turning and turning. He could hear the chains rattling inside the walls. Inch by inch, the viewing panel retracted, replaced by a lengthening rectangle of silvery light. Strands of vine dangled in through the opening, and a few passed over it entirely, but there was nonetheless an excellent view of the night sky. Even from where he stood at the cranks, Nicholas could see a slice of the moon and a dozen shining stars.

Pausing only to wipe his sweaty palms on his trousers, Nicholas seized the topmost crank. And he spent the last of his strength on it, but not before the second roof panel was fully retracted. A long, beautiful strip of stars now traversed the dome. Nicholas gasped for breath, wishing he'd thought to bring water, though at the same time he hardly cared about his thirst. Stooping to extinguish his lantern, he waited for all the dust to settle, then went to stand on the turntable and look up at the sky.

He was awestruck. Never had the stars been so bright, the moon so enormous and richly glowing.

This is mine, Nicholas thought, and he meant not just the observatory but the sky, the night, the freedom of the world beyond the orphanage walls. He had not expected to think such a thing. He was merely expressing to himself the feeling, the most delicious feeling, that had arisen in him spontaneously.

A breeze seemed to have arisen, too. Opening the roof panels must have created a draft. It fluttered Nicholas's collar and made his eyes water, blurring the stars. And then the sensation of tears seemed to trigger a sort of emotional reflex, for the next thing he knew, Nicholas was truly crying, which surprised him. He sat down at once, in case he lost consciousness. And then he lay back completely, still gazing up at the blurry, twinkling stars, and for a long time he continued to cry, and for once he did not care, and did not fall asleep.

⌣∴⌣

Just before his alarm clock went off, Nicholas reset it for an hour ahead and returned to sit cross-legged on the turntable. For some time now he had been staring at the cranks. Though he'd finally torn his eyes from the night sky, ideas were streaking through his head like meteors and comets.

The cranks had done their obvious jobs and nothing more. But Nicholas had turned them one at a time, and in a certain order, and only in one direction. What if the sequence mattered? Or the number of turns? What about combinations? Thinking over what he knew about mechanical apparatuses— he had learned a great deal in the last week—Nicholas decided that turning two cranks at the same time might be part of the necessary procedure. Opening a secret entrance might be as simple as that.

Or not simple, exactly, but certainly possible. Nicholas envisioned a system by which both cranks would need to be turned in the right direction until a certain, secret gear engaged, at which point only one should be turned until yet another gear engaged, and so on. Fascinated, he watched it all happening in his mind. Then he reversed the process, contemplating more efficient ways of accomplishing it, and only after several minutes had passed did he realize he'd gotten carried away thinking about mechanical design.

Chiding himself, Nicholas stood up. He needed to focus on the matter at hand. He couldn't stay here all night, after all. He did have to sleep sometime.

For half an hour he worked with the cranks, trying out different combinations, hoping to see a section of the floor rise up to reveal a secret staircase, or a wall stone pop out of place to expose a hidden lever, or simply anything at all out of the ordinary. Unfortunately, he could turn only one stubborn crank at a time—his arms proved too tired to manage two at once—but he was nonetheless able to experiment with the sequence, the direction, the number of turns. Round and round went the cranks; round and round went the turntable. The roof panels opened and closed so many times that clipped, tangled segments of vine were strewn about the floor, and dust no longer fell when the panels retracted. But no secret staircases, no hidden doors appeared.

Nicholas was exhausted and disappointed, but he was not discouraged. Really, he'd hardly begun. With fresher arms, he might be able to turn two cranks simultaneously, which would allow for ever more complex combinations. He could attempt some of those tomorrow night, before fatigue set in, and if those didn't work, he could go back to turning one at a time....Nicholas scratched his head, considering the possibilities.

As it happened, this single, simple physical act brought him abruptly to his senses. He could not ignore his quivering arms, his aching fingers and hands. Was he really going about this the right way? Mr. Rothschild would not have wanted the combination to be too cumbersome, but the number of possibilities for even a very simple one was daunting in the extreme. Nicholas frowned at himself. He *knew* that, yet in his excitement he had thrown himself into the task without thinking it through.

So think it through, Nicholas told himself, and his brain switched tracks.

His first thought was to wonder whether Mr. Rothschild had written the combination in his diary, perhaps on one of those torn-out pages. Finding those would be helpful, to say the least. But what if he couldn't find them? What were his other options?

When a minute of hard thinking turned up no new ideas, Nicholas sighed and shook his head. He would need to ponder all this awhile. He was itchy with impatience, but at least now he was being sensible. Turning things over in his mind, deliberately and carefully, was guaranteed to be more productive than turning these cranks at random. His mind was his strength, and he should use it. In the meantime he should go to bed.

Reluctantly, Nicholas gathered his things, offered the cranks a farewell salute, and went out through the curtain of vines. After so long inside, he felt strangely exposed in the open air, though surely there was no one to see him. He glanced all around. Trees surrounded the clearing, obscuring his view in every direction except upward. *No one is watching but the man in the moon*, he assured himself, *and he will keep your secrets*. He smiled and was about to start downhill when he noticed, near the corner of the observatory, a faint, narrow trail among the weeds.

The trail was so vague that Nicholas had overlooked it earlier. It led away from the observatory, northward through the tall grass and brush that covered the clearing, and down into the far woods—away from the Manor. Nicholas stared wonderingly at it. He had not imagined that there might be more to explore.

Every unfamiliar trail is an invitation, and Nicholas, weary though he was, accepted this one without hesitating. Why, there was no telling what he might find! It might be the key to everything! And so, pausing only to turn up his lantern, Nicholas followed the trail across the clearing and into the trees beyond.

The trail, leading downhill again, did not wind about as the trail on the other side of the hill had done, to make the going easier. Rather, it descended very steeply through the trees, almost in a straight line. Nicholas walked with an awkward, backward-leaning posture, and was often compelled to cling to low branches to keep from stumbling. At the bottom of the hill, the trail vanished into a dry streambed, but Nicholas did not give up on it. Swatting mosquitoes, he made his way across and, with little difficulty, found where the trail continued.

Now it led up—almost straight up—another steep wooded hill, and twice Nicholas had to pause for breath. Once he lost the trail and had to backtrack. But at last, panting and perspiring, he arrived at the top of a wooded ridge, where he sat on a moss-covered boulder to rest. He wondered how far he was prepared to follow this trail. Eventually he would have to retrace every step, and the steps were adding up. Perhaps he should return tomorrow night, when he could set out earlier.

Nicholas hated to quit, however. He decided to press on just a little farther, and heaving himself off the boulder, he followed the trail downward from the ridge. Scarcely had he taken a dozen steps when the trail forked. To the left it continued its steep descent. To the right it ran crosswise to the slope, rather than down. Nicholas's weary legs turned right almost on their own. After another dozen steps, the trail took a sharp turn around an enormous boulder and disappeared. Perhaps it simply headed downhill again on the far side. Nicholas couldn't tell. The boulder was too large, the woods too dark and thick.

Intrigued, Nicholas hurried around the boulder, only to draw up short with a gasp. He very nearly dropped his lantern. Where a moment ago there had been the darkness and closeness of unbroken woods, now there was nothing but empty space and a brilliant night sky. The world seemed to have fallen away completely.

Nicholas had unwittingly blundered onto a bluff. He realized this even as he drew back in alarm. He was not really in danger of falling—or not much, anyway, for the flat ledge of barren stone jutted out several yards—but the open view had appeared so suddenly that its effect was shocking. He was lucky he hadn't collapsed on the spot.

When his heartbeat had settled down, Nicholas ventured onto the bluff again, careful of every step. He made his way out almost to the edge. The bluff overlooked a wide, moonlit valley of rolling farmland. Nicholas gave a low whistle, impressed. Inching forward, he strained his neck to peer over the edge of the bluff. The sheer rock wall plummeted down and down—a very long way down—into more trees below.

The trail must lead to this lonely promontory purely for the sake of the view. And with good reason, Nicholas thought. From here one could gaze down upon the nearest farm as if it were a toy set, its miniature pieces arranged upon a table. The windows of the toy farmhouse reflected the moonlight. Nothing stirred in the toy barnyard. A little lane that might have been made of ribbon led away from the farm, running out across the wide valley, where in the distance Nicholas could see other, even tinier farms.

From his conversation with Mrs. Brindle, Nicholas knew that he was looking down upon the Hopefield farm. It felt strange knowing the name. So it was the Hopefield family who lay asleep in that quiet farmhouse. He wondered what sort of family it was, whether it included any children. He wondered if it had been children who made these trails. If Nicholas had lived down there, he, too, would have ventured into the hills exploring. He, too, would have found this bluff a perfect spot to sit and think. The trails were faint now, though; they appeared seldom, if ever, used. Perhaps the children had grown up and lost interest.

Nicholas settled on the bluff, leaning back on his hands, and let his ankles and feet dangle over the edge. A breeze fluttered in his ears and cooled his bristly scalp. The moon cast the farm fields below in tones of blue and silver. For a long time he gazed out over them, his mind moving more slowly now, more calmly. It was peaceful here. He was in no danger of falling asleep; he no longer felt sleepy in the least. On the contrary, he felt wide awake, alert, and strangely aware of all his emotions, including sadness, including loneliness, though they did not trouble him very much. Eventually

Nicholas stopped looking at the fields and gazed only at the huge, brilliant moon above him.

When the alarm clock rang, its tinny rattling muffled inside his backpack, Nicholas felt startled and disoriented. He fumbled to shut it off, still looking upward. He had the strangest sensation that he was drifting back down to earth, as if he had been up there with the moon all this time. He knew he had to go back. Back to the orphanage, back to the Spiders, back to that prison cell of a room, back to his nightmares. He stood, dusted off his pants, hesitated. And then he set the alarm clock again, and sat down again, and allowed himself just a few minutes more.

Rescues and Reconciliations

The next day was a Friday, which happened to be "special chores" day. After breakfast all the children were told what they would be doing that morning. The older boys were sent off to churn butter, rake out barn stalls, and mend fences with Mr. Furrow at the farm. The older girls were set to washing linens and hanging them on a clothesline in the side yard, with the exception of a few who were to help Mrs. Brindle clean the chandelier. Nicholas and the other children were assigned to yard work.

Under the nervous supervision of Mr. Pileus, who was

working on the Studebaker in the driveway, Nicholas helped trim the azalea bushes, mow the grass, and gather fallen branches from the large front lawn and down the lane. It was a dreary business. The morning was hot and sticky, Nicholas was miserably tired, and as usual the other children were avoiding him. (His only company was a swarm of gnats that followed him everywhere.) Even more tiresome was Mr. Pileus, who kept yelping with alarm and charging over to correct Nicholas's grip on the pruners or to demonstrate how to maintain the proper distance between his feet and the blades of the reel mower.

Nicholas wished Mr. Pileus would leave him alone and stick to the Studebaker, which at this rate would never get fixed. It was plain by now that Mr. Pileus was neither an especially handy handyman nor a mechanically minded mechanic. He did have a knack for noticing problems, but their solutions generally evaded him. Earlier that morning, for instance, he had driven Mr. Collum to the station in Pebbleton (the director had weekend business out of town) and returned in a state of high anxiety. With a fretful scowl, Mr. Pileus had soon scattered tools all around the driveway and porch steps. But though he had started the Studebaker engine numerous times—cringing every time at the squealing sound it produced—that was all the progress he had made.

It didn't help, Nicholas supposed, that the man was so distracted by the children he was supervising. He couldn't take his eyes off them for fear they would suffer grievous injuries. Finally Nicholas couldn't stand it any longer, and when Mr. Pileus ran down the lane to admonish young Buford (whom he'd spotted walking too quickly with a sharp stick), Nicholas drifted over to take a look at the Studebaker's engine.

"I think I have it!" he said when Mr. Pileus came back. "I think I see what you were getting at!"

Mr. Pileus, who had been about to shoo him away, hesitated. He looked confused.

Nicholas hurried on: "It's the fan belt, isn't it? You were testing us, weren't you, to see if anyone would notice the sound! That's an excellent way to teach, if I do say so myself, Mr. Pileus. I *thought* that's what you were up to when you kept starting the engine and shutting it off again. They make such an awful racket, fan belts, and this one obviously needs to be replaced. Would you like me to fetch one from the basement? Did you leave the door unlocked?"

Mr. Pileus blinked. He bent to inspect the fan belt. Then he nodded twice—once for each question—and turned away, his face as red as his hair.

Nicholas saluted him and dashed up the steps. The prospect of working on the Studebaker was infinitely more appealing than pruning shrubberies. It was one thing to read books about engines, quite another to actually lay hands on them. The fan belt would not take long to replace, unfortunately. He wondered if he might suggest other repairs....

His mind full of engine parts, Nicholas charged into the entranceway, flung the door closed behind him—and was brought up short by what he saw. What in the world? A skinny, flaxen-haired girl appeared to be suspended high above the entranceway, her arms extended upward and her legs kicking frantically, as if the air were water and she was trying to swim to the surface.

Nicholas squinted his eyes, which were still adjusting to the indoor gloom. He had experienced so many bizarre hallucinations in his life that for a split second he wondered if he'd been dreaming this entire morning. Was he, in fact, still in his cot upstairs? But in the next instant everything became clear. The girl—it was Gertrude McGillicuddy—was dangling from the chandelier, her eyes wide with terror. Two other girls stood beneath her, shifting anxiously from foot to foot. And in the background, of course, were the Spiders.

Moray and Breaker, holding the tall stepladder that they had yanked from under Gertrude's feet, were laughing silently through their noses. Iggy stood behind them, at the bottom of the staircase, where he could keep an eye on the east and west passages.

"Why, hello, fellows," Nicholas said breezily. "I thought you were supposed to be over at the farm."

"We're taking a break," Breaker said with a sneer. He spoke softly, as if not wishing to be overheard.

"I can see that," said Nicholas. Stepping to his left to peer down the north-running passage, he spied the back of Mrs. Brindle's cleaning apron poking out of a closet. He could just make out her muted muttering as she rummaged around for a missing bottle of polish. "So you slipped away when Mr. Furrow had his back turned."

"There he goes again," Iggy said scornfully, "pretending he can 'see' things."

Nicholas sighed. He hardly needed a crystal ball to see what had happened. The Spiders, sneaking around the Manor, had come upon the girls unattended and decided to have some fun. They were in little danger of being caught. They were out of Mrs. Brindle's line of vision, and thanks to her constant muttering, they would know when she was approaching. She moved so slowly, they would have plenty of time to escape before she reached the entranceway. And of course the girls dared not cry for help.

Nicholas had no such qualms, however. Wasn't he already on the Spiders' enemy list? With an impatient roll of his eyes (as if he were really much too busy always to be spoiling the Spiders' fun), he said, "Well, it's certainly easy enough to see what Mrs. Brindle will think about all this."

"Call her and you'll regret it!" Moray hissed, shooting Nicholas a warning look. "If you can see so much, I guess you can see what I'll do to your face if you tell."

Iggy drew a finger across his throat to make the warning clearer. Above them, Gertrude could be heard panting with effort and fear, her legs bicycling in the empty air beneath her. Her grip was probably weakening, but the Spiders wouldn't have considered that.

Nicholas turned to the mirror near Mr. Collum's office door and pretended to inspect his frayed collar. "Fine," he said casually. "I won't say a word."

Then he grabbed the mirror with both hands and turned it.

He could tell he had achieved the proper angle when the Spiders' mouths fell open. Perhaps they were not the most intelligent creatures, but even they understood that if they could see the back of Mrs. Brindle's apron in the mirror—which was now the case—then Mrs. Brindle had only to turn and glance at the mirror to see *them*.

Moray's face turned a deep shade of crimson. Iggy's face grew so pinched it looked as if it might collapse upon itself like a rotten piece of fruit. Breaker began gesturing wildly toward the east passage, indicating that they should flee before they were spotted.

Moray jabbed a finger in Nicholas's direction. "You're going to pay for this, Fat Nose!" he hissed as they all hurried from the room. "Count on it!"

Nicholas gave him a jaunty salute.

Then the Spiders were gone, and as the girls scrambled to replace the ladder beneath Gertrude, Nicholas returned the mirror to its original angle and headed for the front door. He would have to tell Mr. Pileus he needed help finding the fan belt. He no longer dared to go to the basement alone, not with the Spiders on the prowl.

Even before he reached the door, Nicholas could hear the girls' sighs of relief—Gertrude had safely found her footing again. He did not meet their gazes, however, but opened the door without a word. He knew perfectly well that he was not to be approached, much less thanked, and he did not care to see the girls turn away from him. He would rather do the turning away himself.

So it was that Nicholas left the room in the solitude of his own thoughts, oblivious to the silent looks of gratitude that followed him.

⌣∴⌣

No doubt it was the lack of sleep that led Nicholas to be so careless. He was thinking less clearly than usual, paying less attention to his circumstances, and his mind was taken up with cranks and combinations. But though his circumstances on that particular Friday were uncommonly precarious, Nicholas failed to recognize just how precarious they were.

He knew, of course, that he needed to be extra careful that day. Staff supervision at the Manor was limited even when Mr. Collum was present, much less when he was away on a business trip. What Nicholas did not properly take into account was that the Spiders might also be thinking of this and planning accordingly. He did not think them capable of hatching clever plots.

But clever or not, the Spiders were definitely plotting. The fact was that they had slipped away from the farm with the express purpose of setting a trap for Nicholas. They had simply gotten sidetracked by that business with Gertrude and the ladder, after which—thanks to Nicholas's humiliating interference—they were more determined than ever to punish him. And so they returned to their planning and plotting. And when the moment was right, they sprang.

That moment arrived after lunch, when Nicholas, spending his free time in the library as usual, was compelled to lie down in the midst of reading a book about mechanical engineering. The library supervisor on duty was Miss Candace, who was filing her nails at the desk when Iggy ran in to inform her that young Oliver Crooke was outside in the gazebo complaining of a bitter bellyache.

Miss Candace looked horrified. "Why, then send him inside at once! I'll examine him. He may need a good dosing of castor oil—and perhaps some drops. Did he seem pale at all?"

Iggy said he thought Oliver looked very pale indeed, but that he was crying too hard and would not listen to anyone. Mrs. Brindle had already tried to make him come inside, and he simply wouldn't come. Mr. Pileus and Mr. Griese had been sent for, and they had tried to carry Oliver inside, but he'd clung to the rails of the gazebo with such ferocity—having wound his arms and legs through them—that they feared they might hurt him if they pulled any harder.

"Oh, my!" Miss Candace exclaimed, rising from the desk. "He's having a fit! I'll fetch my bag!"

The nurse hurried out, leaving Iggy alone with Nicholas, asleep on the floor, and one girl who had been drowsily reading an encyclopedia entry on unicorns. At a look from Iggy, the girl also hastened from the library, and moments later Moray and Breaker came into the room, smiling wickedly. They shut the door behind them.

"Finally!" said Moray, rubbing his hands together.

Breaker grunted his agreement. "You can say that again!"

"Finally!" Iggy said.

"Not *you*," Breaker said, shoving him.

Despite their careful planning, it had taken the Spiders much longer than they'd expected to threaten Oliver into feigning his illness, for every child at the Manor feared Miss Candace's treatments almost as much as they feared the Spiders. At last, of course, he had submitted and begun his wailing fit—a fit made all the more authentic by his terror of Miss Candace—and with the Spiders' prompting, all the orphanage staff were eventually gathered around the gazebo, until finally Miss Candace herself had come out.

But all of this had taken time—almost half an hour, in fact—and as a result Nicholas had reached the end of his nap. He awoke to the sound of the Spiders' voices, and he sensed right away the danger he was in. Miss Candace was obviously out of the room, the door was obviously closed, and Nicholas was obviously alone with the Spiders. He felt a horrible tightening in his belly. He would not be talking his way out of this one. He could just tell.

"Breaker, you stay by the door," Moray was saying. "If he wakes up, I don't want him getting out before I'm finished with him."

"But I want to kick him!" Breaker protested. "Why does Iggy get to kick him and I don't?"

"Calm down. We'll all get to kick him. We'll take turns. But I want that door covered, so get over there. Back up, Iggy! I get the first crack at him. Remember, leave the face alone. Old Candy Cane might come back to check on him. We don't want to leave any obvious marks."

Nicholas was trapped against the bookshelves. He knew he could not run. Moray and Iggy would be on him before he even reached his feet. He was going to have to fight them. Fight them and lose badly. He wondered if he could even throw a punch before Moray knocked him down. Maybe he should let Moray kick him once, and then hold on to his leg; maybe that way he could slow down the rest of the attack. His mouth was very dry. His heart was racing. For once he had absolutely no idea what to do.

Then he heard the door open, and a voice said, "Get away from him, Moray."

Nicholas's heart leaped. It was John's voice.

"What are you doing here, Spotty?" Moray asked gruffly. "And what did you just say? Because it sounded like you said—"

"You heard me right," said John. His voice trembled slightly, but his tone was resolute. "Leave him alone. You can't attack him when he's defenseless like this."

Iggy spoke up. "Since when do you tell us what we can't do, Polka Dot?"

"You better scram right now," said Moray. From their voices Nicholas could tell the Spiders were advancing on John. "If you know what's good for you. Get out of here and maybe we won't hunt you down later."

"I'm not leaving," said John.

"I guess you can't count," said Breaker. "Because it's three against one here."

"Actually, it's three against *two*," Nicholas announced, and the Spiders turned to discover him on his feet, a defiant gleam in his eye.

"Are you kidding me?" Moray growled, throwing his hands into the air. "Now he's awake! Can't one thing go right?" In frustration he gave Iggy a one-armed shove. Iggy slunk away from him with big wounded eyes, like a frightened dog kicked by its master, and Breaker took a step back to keep himself out of reach.

Without taking his eyes from the Spiders, John circled around them to stand beside Nicholas. "Better let this one go, Moray. If you have a beef with my friend, you'll need to settle it some other way."

"Your friend?" Moray sneered. "So you're friends with nine-year-olds now? Well, you sure picked a bad one to be your little friend, Spotty. You realize that, right?"

John made no reply. He simply returned Moray's stare with a level gaze and stood on the balls of his feet as if expecting an attack. Nicholas likewise braced himself, but no attack came. Instead, Moray gave John a contemptuous look and said, "Fine. Now we know where we stand. Now we know what we're dealing with. And now *you* can know that you're going to pay."

"Pay big-time," Breaker said, pointing a finger at John.

"Pay a *lot*," Iggy said. "So much that you can't even *afford* it."

"Shut up, Iggy!" said Moray, shoving him again. "You sound like an idiot. Now come on, we'll leave these two sweet little friends alone to think about what we're going to do to them next time."

"Yeah, because next time is going to be bad for them," Breaker said, punching his fist into his palm to demonstrate how bad it would be. He backed out the door after Moray, and Iggy followed, looking more peevish than ever.

"Well," said Nicholas, grinning with relief, "I guess they didn't like their odds."

John went to close the door. "No, three against one is how they like to do it. Otherwise they might get hurt, even though they'll win the fight." He walked back over and extended his hand, looking Nicholas squarely in the eye. "Listen, I'm really sorry about everything, Nick. What do you say?"

Nicholas gladly shook his hand. What little resentment he had felt toward John had vanished at the first sound of his voice in the library. "No hard feelings. And thanks for helping me out. I was kind of in a pickle there. I knew I could beat them up, of course, but I wasn't sure how to do it quietly. This *is* a library, after all."

John laughed and clapped Nicholas on the back. "You really are a fresh one, Nick. You really are." The look of relief was plain on his face. "Anyway, it's swell of you. I don't think I've ever felt so rotten."

"What made you change your mind?" Nicholas asked.

"I didn't change my mind," John said with a grimace. "I made up my mind right away. It just took me this long to find my guts. I won't kid you, Nick, I'm awfully ashamed. It's just—well, I knew taking your side would mean more than a black eye and a fat lip. I knew I'd be making permanent enemies of the Spiders. I guess I wasn't up to it, even though I knew it was right." He made a disgusted sound. "Every day I've been telling myself to do something about it, but like I said, I couldn't find my guts."

"You sure seemed to find them just now," Nicholas said. "You were ready to fight the whole gang."

"It should never have come to that. Honestly, I can't believe this place, Nick. The staff should have seen something was up. I saw it right away. When I noticed Moray and Breaker sneaking back inside during that commotion with Oliver, I knew they were hunting you. And I knew you'd be in the library, of course—everybody knows that's where you spend your free time."

"It's true I've been doing a little reading," Nicholas said

somewhat absently. He bent to pick up the book about engineering. Something had occurred to him, something he probably should take more time to consider. But a powerful impulse overtook him—whether from gratitude or a renewed feeling of friendship or both—and before he could stop himself, he blurted out, "I have a secret!" He looked up at John with his bright, mischievous green eyes. "I have a secret, and you aren't going to believe it!"

CONJURINGS COMBINATIONS, AND CALCULATED RISKS

The two boys met at midnight in the back of the park. Nicholas heard the soft *shush* of John's bare feet in the grass and stepped out from behind the tree where he was hiding. John was prowling several yards away, pausing every few steps to search the shadows. Nicholas whistled like a bobwhite. John froze, peering in his direction (the moon was hidden behind clouds, and it was quite dark beneath the trees) until Nicholas waved with both arms.

"You looked like part of the tree!" John whispered as he

hurried over. He was in his pajamas. "Is it always this dark out here? I don't see how you ever found the path."

"I don't know about 'always.' Last night was my first time out, and there wasn't a cloud in the sky. Here, let's have some light. If you prick your foot on something, you'll have a hard time explaining the blood." Nicholas stooped to light his lantern. "Next time I'll bring some extra shoes for you. There are a lot of rocks out here."

"Extra shoes? How do you expect to find extra shoes? For that matter, how in the world did you come by that lantern?"

"Conjured it," Nicholas replied, turning up the flame. He held the lantern before his face, so that the glass distorted his features, and put on his most mysterious expression.

John narrowed his eyes. "So now you're conjuring things, too? I thought it was just predicting the future."

"Predicting the future helps me conjure things. It's all part of my magic."

"I see," John said drily. "And is that how you're getting out of your room at night? Magic? I have to say, it didn't even occur to me until I was lying in my cot, pretending to be asleep. Suddenly I thought, 'Wait a minute—how does *he* get out?'"

"All shall be revealed in good time," Nicholas said in a wavery fortune-teller voice.

"You aren't going to tell me?"

"I prefer to remain mysterious." Nicholas took his floursack backpack from behind the tree and slipped it on. "Why don't you tell me how *you* got out?" he asked, gesturing for John to follow him. They started up the trail.

Unlike Nicholas, who still had secrets he wanted to keep

to himself, John was happy to discuss the details of his escape. It so happened that Mr. Griese, whose turn it was to chaperone the dormitory, was a frightful snorer. Once everyone was asleep, it had only been a matter of creeping to the door, then timing the opening of the squeaky latch with Mr. Griese's snores.

"We should have that latch oiled," Nicholas said. "What do you think would happen if you were caught?"

"I'd claim a bathroom emergency," John said. "They might go easy on me. You're supposed to tell the chaperone if you need to go — which almost never happens, since the staff hate to be awakened and will treat you like a baby in front of everyone — but I could say I was being quiet out of courtesy. I think they'd believe me. That's one of the benefits of being square, Nick, though I don't suppose it compares with being mysterious."

"I'm sure being square has its merits," Nicholas said, pretending to sound superior. "It's true, however, that mysterious persons such as myself can dispense with bathroom explanations and blame sleepwalking, which everyone knows is more dignified."

"Oh, indeed," John replied. Then in a more serious tone he said, "It really is a good thing you have your own room. I know it's probably scary up there, but in the dormitory, sleepwalking or talking in your sleep would get you punished. You have to wear a dunce cap the whole next day — it's pretty humiliating."

Nicholas was appalled. "But what if you have nightmares?"

"Doesn't matter. Mr. Collum says it's the only way to be sure kids aren't being disruptive just for fun. If you make any noise after bedtime, you get punished, no matter what the reason."

"That's perfectly draconian," Nicholas said.

"I'm sure it is," John agreed. "But listen, Nick, if you're going to keep using words like that, you'll have to start giving the definitions."

The boys continued to talk, lightly and cheerfully, as they wound their way up the path. Once, they noticed the lantern light reflected in the eyes of a small animal crouching in the undergrowth—the eyes appeared as spots of luminescent yellow-green, like fireflies frozen in place—and wondered what it was. Nicholas expressed his hope that it wasn't a bobcat. John expressed his opinion that it was indeed a bobcat and that it wanted to eat Nicholas.

"I think you insulted it," Nicholas said when the creature scampered away. He pressed on up the path.

"No, it's running off to tell its friends. They're going to share you for dinner."

"I'm starting to regret bringing you," Nicholas said, privately reflecting how nervous he would have been if he'd seen those eyes the night before. It made a remarkable difference having a friend along.

When at last they reached the summit, Nicholas made a flourish with his free arm and declared, "Welcome to Giant's Head!" He stepped aside to let John enter the clearing first.

John whistled and hurried forward. "Look at this place! What a find! And you came up here all by yourself—you went in *there* all by yourself? I'm impressed, Nick. Awfully spooky." If he was affected by the spookiness of the place, however, he gave no sign. He brushed aside the dangling vines and plunged into the dark observatory, not even waiting for the lantern.

Nicholas followed him inside. The floor, he saw, was damp and puddled. There had been a thunderstorm that afternoon, and in his weariness he had left the roof panels open last night. John began walking around the room, inspecting everything and exclaiming aloud. The rotten cabinets, the old door, the broken and discarded bits of metal on the floor, and especially those cranks—he was openly admiring of it all. Nicholas felt immensely proud, as if he had not merely discovered the observatory but built it himself.

Standing on tiptoes and gesturing with his hands, he described how large the telescope would have been, to give John a sense of how the room might once have looked. Like Nicholas, John was impressed with the observatory's design, even though at the moment their echoing voices and splashing feet made the place seem more like a primitive cave. He also agreed that if there was a concealed treasure chamber at Giant's Head, the cranks seemed the obvious means of revealing it.

"Let's see if we can turn two at once," he suggested. "Just to try it."

Nicholas agreed, and they each selected a different crank. On a count of three they began to turn. The cranks groaned and squealed, the chains rattled within the walls, and the roof panels slid upward across the dome. The night sky vanished— but that was all that happened. They rested, then reversed direction. The panels began to reopen. The boys glanced around to see if anything else was happening, then quickly looked up again. They found it hard to take their eyes from the retracting panels, which were themselves a curiously appealing sight.

"It's like we're unzipping the roof," John panted.

Soon the panels were fully retracted. The cranks refused to budge further, and nothing else had changed.

"Still, that was swell," John said, wiping his brow. "And now we know we can do it. So what's next? Do you have any ideas about a combination?"

"Not yet," Nicholas admitted. "I was thinking I could tell you what I've read in Mr. Rothschild's diary and see if any details ring a bell. You've been here longer than I have. Maybe you've noticed something or know about something I don't. What do you say?"

"Sure, you tell me what you know, and I'll do my best. It's worth a shot."

"It might take us a while," Nicholas warned. "Several nights, anyway. Quoting from that diary will take a lot longer than it did to read it, and we'll want to discuss everything as we go along. And of course we can't stay up all night, every night, or we'll fall apart."

"No, we need to be careful about that," John agreed. "And we probably shouldn't risk talking about it during the day. It's hard to have private conversations down there. Though, come to think of it, maybe that will change now...."

For a moment John's face took on the familiar melancholy expression that had been absent so far tonight. Nicholas knew he was remembering dinner, when the fact that he had saved a seat for Nicholas had sent ripples of astonishment and confusion throughout the dining hall. Many of the children could be heard asking if Nicholas's exile had ended. But then the Spiders had come in and settled the matter with their hostile glares. The two boys sitting nearest John and Nicholas had scooted as far away as possible, and everyone had stared and stared.

John's cheeks had turned red, and they had stayed that way for the rest of the meal. He hadn't complained, however. And tonight, on the path up to Giant's Head, he'd told Nicholas again how relieved he was to have found his guts. "*You* wouldn't know it, Nick," he'd said, "but it's an awful feeling, being a coward. I'd never tried it before — I'd never had to — and I sure hope I won't ever again."

Nicholas had offered some lighthearted joke in response, but the truth was that he found it awfully nice to be thought brave. No one had ever suggested such a thing to him before.

"I think," he said now, breaking in upon John's unhappy reflections, "we can discuss things if we're sure no one's listening. But only if we're absolutely sure. Otherwise we should save all treasure talk for Giant's Head."

John forced a smile. "Well, it's worth losing a little sleep to find a treasure, isn't it? Besides, I'd be glad to come up here every night, even if all it meant was getting out of that place for a while."

"It's a deal, then," Nicholas said. "If we find the treasure, we share it. And in the meantime we swear ourselves to absolute secrecy."

They shook hands.

"An actual treasure," said John, grinning now. "What do you imagine we'd *do* with it?"

"Escape, of course!" Nicholas said with a laugh. "No more ducking and hiding, always on the lookout for thugs like the

Spiders. No more thickheaded staff running our lives. We'd be independent!"

John shook his head as if he truly couldn't believe it. He went to stand in the center of the turntable and gazed up at the overcast sky. "I don't think my imagination has caught up yet, Nick. I suppose I used to think about the future sometimes, but now—" He shrugged. "Well, for a long time now everything has been as cloudy as that sky." He turned to Nicholas again. "You've got enough imagination for both of us, though, don't you?"

"You bet I do!" Nicholas said, and he began to pace excitedly about the room, gesturing with his hands. "First of all, we'll go to Stonetown. It's the biggest city around, with plenty of shops and antique dealers and all that sort of thing. We'll sell a little of the treasure right away, to get us set up. Then we can take our time figuring out what we want to do next."

"You're not worried it will look fishy?" John asked. "Two kids on their own?"

Nicholas waved him off. "Oh, as for that, I'll make up a story. I can be very persuasive, you know, and everybody seems to trust *you* the moment they meet you. Our parents will always be in a shop around the corner, or in bed with the flu, or in a business meeting—whatever we like—and meanwhile we'll *do* whatever we like!"

"What about school?" John was watching Nicholas pace the floor with a look of growing excitement.

"We can send you to the best private school, if you want," Nicholas replied. "If you pay enough money, nobody asks questions. As for me, though, I'm in no hurry to go to school. School just slows me down."

John laughed. "Sure, let's forget about school for now. So what will we do instead?"

"For one thing, we'll eat like kings! We'll live above a delicatessen, and our icebox will always be crammed full of good things. And I'm going to have about a million books—that much is for sure." He glanced at John. "You'll be welcome to borrow them, as long as you're careful with them."

"Thanks ever so much," John said wryly.

"And we'll live near a park, where we can meet lots of other kids and spend as much time as we want—we can always be the last to go home. And we can walk down to the harbor and watch the ships come in. And we'll never miss a parade—not one!"

"We'll keep busy, then," John said in an approving tone.

"Next to us," Nicholas confirmed, "bees will look lazy." And he went on enumerating other things they would do in the city, from attending baseball games to visiting museums to simply eating ice cream and listening to whatever they pleased on the radio.

The subject was so appealing, and the boys so absorbed in discussing it (with Nicholas doing most of the talking and John encouraging him), that before they knew it almost an hour had passed. They might have kept going even then if John had not succumbed to a yawn, the sight of which brought Nicholas back to the present.

"Of course, we *do* have to find the treasure first," he conceded. "We'll get cracking tomorrow night. Right now I have something else to show you, if you don't think it's already too late. Are you up for a walk?"

John raised his eyebrows. "Well, sure I am. What are you going to show me?"

"It's better as a surprise," said Nicholas.

"I should have known you'd say that." John put his hands on his hips and took a last glance around. "We'd better close the roof before we go, in case it rains again. And listen, Nick, what do you say we get this place cleaned up tomorrow night?"

Nicholas looked at him askance. "Really?"

"You bet! Don't you want to be able to lie on your back and gaze up at the sky? Without lying in a puddle, I mean? We need to sneak a mop and broom up here." He gave Nicholas a sly look. "I don't suppose you could conjure them, could you?"

"Of course," Nicholas said, then pretended to stifle a yawn. "It's hard work conjuring, though. You'll probably have to do most of the cleaning."

Together the boys hiked across the clearing, following the steep trail down into the wooded ravine. The streambed that had been dry the night before was dry no longer—the afternoon thunderstorm had done its own conjuring—but the boys soon found a fallen tree that formed a bridge over the gushing waters.

"Better let me carry the lantern," John said. "I used to do this a lot. There was a big stream in the woods behind our house." Sure enough, he crossed the tree bridge with the natural-looking ease born of experience.

Nicholas, for his part, crawled across on his hands and

feet, like an awkward bear cub. He kept expecting John to tease him, but John stood there quietly, holding the lantern out to light the way. The only sound was the rushing of the water. When at last he had made it safely across, one glance told Nicholas that John's mind had drifted elsewhere—that he was remembering other woods, other tree bridges over other tumbling streams. He'd been about to make a joke, but he kept it to himself.

In silence they climbed the steep trail, up and up to the wooded ridge high above them, where they paused to recover their breath. Then John followed Nicholas down again, turning right at the fork in the trail. Nicholas led the way until the trail made its sharp turn around the huge boulder. There he stopped and turned to John. "Just ahead lies the surprise," he said. "Why don't you walk beside me? It's a bit treacherous, so watch your step."

"You're making me nervous," said John, catching up. "I can't decide if you're about to give me a pony or lead me into a trap."

"Maybe it's both," Nicholas said, grinning impishly. He watched John's face as they rounded the boulder, anticipating his surprised reaction with amusement, and in the next instant was rewarded with an expression of complete startlement and wonder. John even gasped and drew back, which seemed rather dramatic for a boy of his poise. Nicholas assumed John was playing up the surprise for his sake.

But then John said under his breath, "What's going on, Nick? Who is this?"

Now it was Nicholas's turn to be shocked. For when he shifted his gaze away from John's face, he discovered a figure standing on the bluff exactly where he had stood the night before, looking out over the valley. An older girl, or perhaps a young woman, she stood with her hands hanging at her sides, seemingly unaware of the boys' presence. Her long dark hair was drawn back and hung almost to the waist of her plain, ankle-length dress. She stood utterly still.

Heart racing, Nicholas impulsively advanced a couple of steps, holding the lantern before him and intending to speak. Then he checked himself, warned by a terrible premonition. The girl, evidently lost in thought, stood dangerously close to the edge. What if his approach frightened her and she recoiled? He dared not risk it. With a horrible feeling of anxiety, Nicholas began to creep back.

But just then the girl finally seemed to sense she was not alone. She glanced nervously over her shoulder, and then—spying Nicholas—whirled all the way around to face him, her eyes wide with panic. She unconsciously took a step backward.

"No!" Nicholas cried, willing her to be still, to see him for what he was—not a danger, not a threat, just a boy with a lantern—and to his relief she froze in place and did not fall, though she appeared very much alarmed.

She was perhaps thirteen or fourteen years old, with a long, narrow face and pointy chin. Her eyes, very round at the moment, seemed almost too wide for her face. She had put her hands to her cheeks, her fingers fluttering anxiously. Some of them appeared to have black tips, as though she'd been dipping them in inkpots. Her breaths were coming short and quick.

"It's all right," Nicholas said, extending his empty hand toward her in a calming gesture. "Sorry, we didn't mean to scare you."

From behind him John said in a low voice, "You don't know this person, Nick?"

"I didn't conjure her, if that's what you mean," Nicholas muttered, and the girl jerked her head to the side, trying to see who was with him. He smiled encouragingly at her and glanced down at her feet. She was wearing muddy work boots. To his dismay, he saw that the heel of her right boot was mere inches from the edge of the bluff.

"We need to back away," John murmured, then called out, "Don't worry, miss! We're just a couple of boys, and unless you need help we'll go now and leave you in peace. If you need help, say so, and we'll do whatever we can. Otherwise we're leaving straightaway. Just—you're very close to the edge, miss, so please be careful."

John's tone had been soothing, friendly, and above all convincing. Even so, as he'd spoken, the girl had peered intently in his direction with a look of growing suspicion. It was possible she couldn't make out his features in the darkness, Nicholas realized; he was holding the lantern in front of him, and John was behind him. Perhaps she was wondering if they really were just a couple of boys and not scouts for a traveling gang of robbers, ready to take any valuable thing she possessed and finish the job with a push over the edge.

"He's telling the truth," Nicholas said, and he backed slowly away until he stood beside John. "You don't need help, do you?"

The girl was watching him. She gave the slightest shake of her head. No.

"All right," Nicholas said, and together he and John began to withdraw. "That's good. Um…good night, then. I'm Nicholas, by the way. Nicholas Benedict, from the orphanage. The Manor, you know—Rothschild's End."

"Nick!" John whispered. "Are you crazy?"

But Nicholas pressed on. "If you tell on me, I'll be in a world of trouble, and you can be sure I'll never be able to sneak out again. My fate is in your hands, Miss Hopefield. You *are* Miss Hopefield, aren't you?"

The girl's expression changed to bafflement. She made no reply, however, and the boys kept backing away until they were out of sight behind the boulder. Then they turned and hurried up the trail, retracing their steps to the fork and then up to the ridge. Before they had gotten far, they could hear the girl running down the trail below them, hurrying away. Perhaps she was afraid they were trying to deceive her.

"What were you thinking, Nick?" John asked. "Just like that, it's all over! You were right—no way will you be able to sneak out after this, not after she tells on you. And you'll be working double duties for a month!"

"She would have guessed where we came from anyway," Nicholas said. "Where else would we have been from if not the orphanage? I'm sure she knows everyone on the neighboring farms, and the Manor is the only other place for miles."

"I suppose, but why tell her your name?" John persisted. "I guess I should be grateful that you didn't mention mine. And say, how in the world did you know *hers*?"

"All shall be revealed in good time," Nicholas said. He gave John a lopsided grin. "For now you'll just have to trust me."

John shook his head. "I don't suppose there's much else I can do, is there? You and your mysterious ways! Will you at least promise not to rat on me when the time comes?"

"I promise," Nicholas said. "But you already know I wouldn't."

John looked at him, then shrugged. "You're right. I know you wouldn't. Now let's get back," he said wearily. "I'm exhausted. I think I used up all my strength praying for her not to fall over the edge. For a second I thought she was gone for sure. Can you imagine? It would have been the worst thing, the very worst."

As the boys made their way back, they spoke little, each deep in his own thoughts. Nicholas, for his part, was hoping that his instinct had been correct. They had scared the girl badly, had made her feel trapped in that dangerous spot, and he had instantly felt that he should give her something to make up for it. And so he had let her have some power over him, hoping that by doing so he would make her understand—later, anyway, when she was safe at home and had calmed down—that he was friendly, that he could be trusted.

He doubted she would have told anyone about him, regardless. That would require her to explain why *she* was up on that bluff in the middle of the night. Nicholas didn't think she would care to do that, for she had almost certainly sneaked out herself. She had another, more important reason not to tell on him, too: If she told on him, she would never see him again. He was only a boy, a scrawny one at that, and he was much younger. But he was also a potential friend, and Nicholas had a feeling that this girl who went to stand on bluffs alone at night—well, he had a feeling that she could use one.

CHORES and MEMORIES

The Old Hag was in mid-cackle, and Nicholas was cowering, pleading with her not to hurt him, when her laughter turned abruptly into a sort of metallic scraping—or no, it was rather a jingling sound, as if she were coughing up sleigh bells. And then she faded from the room—first her legs, then her torso, then her hideous head—as if scrubbed out of existence by an invisible eraser. Nicholas sat up, drenched in sweat, as the door to his room opened and Mr. Griese entered with a smoky oil lamp and a ring of keys.

"Good morning, Nicholas," croaked Mr. Griese, evidently

having just awakened himself. "Or almost morning, anyway. You're on larder duty today, so you need to wash up quick and hop off to the farm."

Nicholas squinted in the lamplight, trying to collect himself. No matter how many times the horrors visited him in his sleep, they never grew less frightening. Was he truly awake even now, he wondered, or was Mr. Griese going to sprout spider legs and fangs? No, he was awake; he felt sure of it now. That scraping and jingling had been the cook's keys at the keyhole. The Old Hag was gone. The night had passed.

"Why, you're pale as a turnip root," said Mr. Griese, drawing nearer with the lamp, "and your covers are soaked through. Are you ill?"

"Oh, I'm perfectly well, sir, thank you for asking," Nicholas said, and he flung off his covers and sprang up with such energy that the cook drew back, startled. "Only a little hot, but the cold water always takes quick care of that! Please make yourself comfortable. I'll just be a moment. No, don't trouble with the lamp; I can find my way easily enough."

Mr. Griese shrugged and sank onto the cot as Nicholas hurried off to the bathroom. The icy-cold water from the faucet did work wonders. It was painful, but the relief of coming fully awake—of shaking off the last awful vestige of his night—made the pain more than worth it. By the time he had changed out of his pajamas, he was whistling happily, his mind taken up with mysteries and treasure.

When Nicholas returned to his room, Mr. Griese was snoring and had to be awakened, though he grumpily insisted that he had only been resting his eyes. They went down to the kitchen. As Mr. Griese lit the stove, Nicholas gathered up the egg baskets and empty milk jars, which he fitted inside the baskets. He wondered about the Hopefield girl. Was she, too, rising early to do farm chores? Then he thought of John, wondering if it had been difficult to sneak back into the dormitory. If Mr. Griese had been snoring as loudly and steadily as he had been just now, probably not.

A troubling thought suddenly occurred to Nicholas. "Who's the chaperone in the dormitory, Mr. Griese? I suppose it must be Mr. Pileus, since Mr. Collum is out of town?"

Mr. Griese gave him a bleary, sidelong look. "It was me, that's who, and I'm only too happy to be up again. I don't sleep well on a cot. It's a horror on my back."

"But surely the boys aren't left unsupervised until breakfast?"

"Surely they are," Mr. Griese retorted. "Sometimes there just isn't enough staff to go around, Nicholas, and you boys must take care of yourselves. Now off you go. I need my eggs and milk, and snappy, too."

Nicholas left the Manor by the back door, whereupon he immediately set down the baskets and dashed all the way around the building to the porch. It was a long way to dash, and he was panting when he slipped back in through the front door. He made his way, stealthily and quickly, down the east passage to the boys' dormitory.

A modest hall with high ceilings and a single arched window, the dormitory had once served as an extra parlor. Now it was crammed with rows of cots, its walls lined with small wooden lockers. Mr. Griese had left a candle burning in a wall sconce, and by its flickering light Nicholas stole into the room looking for John. He spotted him almost at once. His cot was very near the door.

Nicholas tiptoed over and touched John's shoulder. John opened his eyes with a faraway, dreamy look, but the look rapidly changed to one of bitter disappointment. He'd been dreaming, Nicholas realized, and it was plain that John's dreams were nothing like his own. John's dreams were heartbreaking to leave behind.

"Mr. Griese is in the kitchen," Nicholas whispered. "There's no chaperone in here."

John looked blank for a moment. Then the significance of Nicholas's words settled slowly in his groggy mind, and he sat up. From the direction of his gaze, Nicholas deduced where the Spiders' cots were situated in the next row. The indistinct forms lying on them had not stirred.

"I'm off to the farm. Will you be all right?"

John nodded. "I'll be fine, Nick," he whispered. "Thanks for the warning."

By the time Nicholas had crept out of the dormitory John was already getting dressed.

Though the sky had now begun to lighten, the path through the trees to the farm was still dark. Nicholas fumbled along as best he could, twice almost dropping the baskets when he stumbled over tree roots. He went to the door of the little farmhouse and knocked.

Mr. Furrow came to the door wearing red long johns and tall brown boots. He peered out through the crack at Nicholas, his eyes half open, an unlit cigar stub in his mouth.

Nicholas wondered if he slept that way; if so, it was a miracle he didn't choke. Mr. Furrow cleared his throat. "Early, aren't you? Barney ain't even crowed yet, I'm sure."

"Am I really early?" Nicholas asked, surprised.

"Prob'ly not. Just always feels like it." Mr. Furrow sighed and came outside with a lantern. He looked around. "Where's your wheelbarrow?"

"There's a wheelbarrow?" Nicholas asked. "Well, that makes sense. I wish someone had told me. It would have made carrying these things much easier. I don't suppose you'll let me borrow yours, will you, Mr. Furrow? It will save time."

Mr. Furrow grunted and headed toward the barn. "Why not take my furniture, too? Why not take my house?"

"I'll be sure to return it," Nicholas promised.

At the barn door, Mr. Furrow said, "Stand back, now, and we'll just see if Rabbit's finished his carrot." He unlatched the door and opened it wide enough to look inside with the lantern. The mule, apparently, could not be seen from the door, for Mr. Furrow edged through the gap and craned his neck this way and that. There was a shuffling, thumping sound, and Mr. Furrow cried out and darted nimbly back through the door, slamming it closed. "Finish it, why don't you! Blasted, finicky, slowpoke mule! It ain't tea with the queen, is it?"

Then he leaned against the door and said to Nicholas, without looking at him, "He's got just the tiniest bit more. Shouldn't be but a minute now that I've woke him. He'll be ready for breakfast."

"Did he kick you?" Nicholas asked.

Mr. Furrow looked at him askance. "Am I standing? Did you hear my bones breaking? No, he didn't kick me, boy. Just gave me a charge, is all. Wish he'd move so strong and quick in the field. I think he uses up all he's got guarding that carrot of his. The fool creature." He grunted again—he seemed very fond of grunting—and shifted his cigar stub to the other corner of his mouth. "I just hope he survives another planting season. *You'd* better hope he does, too. How do you feel about pulling a plow, you and your skinny friends?"

"I don't know," Nicholas said. "I doubt we could do it." He saw no point in telling Mr. Furrow that he had only one friend.

"I doubt you could, too," Mr. Furrow said. "Which is why we put up with Rabbit."

Eventually Mr. Furrow deemed they had waited long enough, and a quick glance inside confirmed it. Together they milked the cows and goats, and Nicholas gathered the eggs. As he did so, he found himself thinking about the boys' dormitory. He had never ventured into it before this morning. Having been excluded from it, he had let it grow rather grand in his imagination, with thick mattresses on sturdy beds, and comfortable reading chairs by the windows. In reality it had been quite austere, nothing but cots and lockers. He had known this fact from things he had heard John and Mrs. Brindle say, and yet his emotions, unbeknownst to him, had sneakily transformed his mental image of the place.

This was a good thing to remember, Nicholas thought. He had known that emotions could change a person's perception of facts, but he had never imagined them capable of such slyness. It was important to keep an eye on them—to remain alert to their secret workings. Whenever he came into possession of facts, he must be sure to guard them as vigilantly as Rabbit did his carrots. For how else were mysteries solved if not by the careful analysis of facts?

When at last the milk bottles were brimming and the egg baskets full, Mr. Furrow helped load them all into a rusty wheelbarrow, and Nicholas returned to the Manor. He found John helping Mr. Griese in the kitchen—he had volunteered to do it, even though he was not on the schedule for the morning.

"I do like to keep busy," John said, yawning.

Together they cracked eggs and scrambled them as Mr. Griese prepared biscuits and a thin gravy. In the midst of all this activity, Mrs. Brindle appeared in the doorway, smelling sweetly of perfume, her cleaning apron freshly ironed despite the earliness of the hour. Mr. Griese, instantly red as a boiled lobster, stammered out a polite greeting—and from that moment on, Nicholas and John became invisible. Beneath the grownups' nervous chatter, the boys were able to hold a muttered, private conversation.

"No trouble, then?" Nicholas asked.

"Iggy woke up just as I was about to leave. When he saw what was happening, he tried to block the door and called for the others to wake up. They were too sleepy to catch on, though, and I was able to get by him. He knocked me down, but I jumped up and kept going."

Nicholas peppered the eggs. "You all right?"

"Banged my knee. I've had worse. And it would have been worse this time if you hadn't warned me."

"We need to find what we want to find," Nicholas said significantly, "and get out of this place as quick as we can."

John nodded his agreement. "I'm just hoping Mr. Collum doesn't get a telephone call about you-know-what today."

"Mr. Collum is away on business. Anyway, no one will call, because she isn't going to tell."

"He's due back at noon. And I hope you're right."

Nicholas was right. There was no telephone call. Nor were there any visits from concerned parents or sheriff's deputies. And though Mr. Collum came home from the station looking deeply vexed, his mood evidently had nothing to do with Nicholas, who was not summoned to his office or even looked at askance.

Nicholas liked to think that Mr. Collum had reached another dead end in his search for the treasure, that this was why he seemed so cross. He definitely had not given up, however. This became clear that afternoon, when Miss Candace and Mrs. Brindle took all the orphans to the parlor for a group activity.

Miss Candace, in the lead, was about to unlock the parlor door, when she saw that it had already been unlocked and stood slightly ajar. When she pushed it open, several of the children, including Nicholas, saw Mr. Collum standing near the parlor fireplace, blinking at them in surprise. He had just taken a small painting from over the mantel, and he hastily replaced it as though he'd been caught trying to steal it. Nicholas felt sure he had been searching for hidden levers or loose stones in the fireplace chimney.

Flustered, Mr. Collum pretended to busy himself with the

painting as the group filed into the parlor. When Mrs. Brindle shuffled in, he seized upon his excuse. "Mrs. Brindle," he said sternly, "the paintings in this room have been sorely neglected. They need a good dusting. Please assign someone to the task at once." Without another word, he strode from the parlor.

Mrs. Brindle sighed, then winced, then cast her eye over the group in search of a candidate. Nicholas jumped forward to volunteer, just beating out John, who had been about to do the same. Dusting sounded infinitely preferable to the group activity, which was to involve paper cutouts and thimbles and promised to be shockingly dull. Besides, as he dusted, Nicholas hoped to thoroughly examine the area around the fireplace, just in case Mr. Collum had been onto something.

The activity did prove to be a miserable affair. Several girls fell asleep where they sat and drooled on themselves, and several boys got thumped by thimbles that the Spiders kept surreptitiously flicking at them. John, who was watchful, avoided one thimble that unfortunately struck young Oliver in the eye. (Oliver foolishly claimed his tears were caused by a dust allergy; as Miss Candace led him away for a good dose of drops, he was crying all the harder.) But a couple of the thimbles hit John smartly on the back of his head, and he could only wince and say nothing.

Throughout all of this, Nicholas dusted (and secretly inspected) the paintings, the fireplace, the mantel, the baseboards—everything that reasonably could be dusted. If the parlor concealed any secret panels, he did not detect them. He found this encouraging, for it strengthened his growing conviction that Mr. Collum had no advantages over him in the treasure hunt. Mr. Collum appeared to have been nosing about the parlor entirely at random, not following clues but simply hoping to get lucky.

Nicholas had another reason to feel encouraged: He didn't think Mr. Collum had the missing diary pages. Last night, while Mr. Collum was still out of town, he had let himself into Mr. Collum's bedroom and searched it. The room had been the most simple and spartan imaginable, with almost no furniture—a bed, a wardrobe, a desk—and not even a rug on the floor. It was easy to determine that nothing was hidden in there. And then this morning Nicholas had asked John about it, and John could not remember ever having seen Mr. Collum studying any torn-out pages.

It seemed likely, therefore, that those pages had been removed by Mr. Rothschild. Perhaps they'd been destroyed long ago. That would be unfortunate if a secret combination had been written on them, but at least in that case Mr. Collum wouldn't have it himself. And perhaps the pages had not been destroyed at all but were tucked away somewhere, and Nicholas and John, working together, would figure out the hiding place.

Either way, it appeared that Mr. Collum had nothing to go on but hopes and hunches, whereas Nicholas had the observatory, a brilliant mind, a plan, and a partner....

"Careful with that duster!" Mrs. Brindle called from across the parlor. "Dear heavens, I've never seen anyone attack anything so fiercely—you'll take the paint right off that picture!"

"Sorry, Mrs. Brindle," Nicholas returned with a grin. "I suppose I'm just...just excited."

His back was to the room, but he heard the Spiders snickering at this and Moray whispering loudly, "Get a load of Pickle Nose—he gets excited about *dusting*!"

A few children laughed, but Mrs. Brindle huffed angrily and told Moray that further name-calling would result in double duties for the remainder of the weekend. She clearly meant business, and Moray hushed.

Nicholas turned to catch the bully's eye and give him a wink. *You wait*, he thought, turning away again before Moray could react. *Just you wait and see.*

That night the boys cleaned the observatory with a broom and mop that Nicholas, true to his word, had conjured. Then they retracted the viewing panels, and Nicholas stood on John's shoulders to clear away the roof vines that dangled in. He had to stretch to reach them. Luckily the thick heels of John's dilapidated old boots provided an extra two inches of height.

"That's why I conjured those boots instead of sneakers," Nicholas said.

"Naturally," John said, gritting his teeth as he held tight to Nicholas's ankles. "I'm sure it had nothing to do with what you could find in—well, wherever it is you're getting these things. Your secret treasure trove."

"I'm hurt by your disbelief," Nicholas grunted, yanking down the last of the vines. "Anyway, *this* place is the treasure trove, remember? At least we hope it is. There, it's all clear—you can let me down."

They dragged all the vines out of the observatory, after which John insisted on sweeping the floor again. When at last their work was accomplished, Nicholas turned the lantern down low, and they lay beneath the opened dome, their hands behind their heads, gazing up at a completely cloud-covered sky.

"It's beautiful," John said drily, and both of them giggled.

"I'm glad you're cheering up," Nicholas said. "You've seemed awfully serious today."

"Well, I was a *bit* concerned about that telephone call!" said John indignantly. "I guess you were right, after all, but I think it was reasonable for me to feel worried. Not everyone can predict the future, you know, or conjure things out of thin air."

Nicholas chuckled. "Sure, it isn't your fault, and of course you're a very serious person to begin with. You almost never laugh—or even smile, for that matter." He regretted the words the instant he uttered them. He had spoken without thinking. He had a pretty clear idea about John's solemn moods and had never intended to mention them.

For a time John was silent. Then he said, somewhat stiffly, "You lost your parents when you were a baby, didn't you, Nick?"

Nicholas closed his eyes, wishing he could start over. "Yes," he said, miserable but resigned. "They died in a laboratory accident. They were scientists of some sort. I was sent to live with my aunt, but then she died, too. I don't remember any of them. It's been orphanages all my life."

After another pause, John said, "I'm sorry about all that,

Nick. Honestly I am. But you know, for some of us it hasn't been so long."

"Sorry." Nicholas tried to think of a more fitting response, but nothing came to him. "Sorry, I do know that."

In a rather shaky voice John went on. "I lost my parents exactly fourteen months and five days ago. I miss them every day. What really gets me is I never realized how lucky I was before. Just normal things, like doing chores around the house—I had no idea how much I could miss that. But it was my home, and I was helping people who actually cared about me. Everything was different then. Everything."

John was quiet again after this. His breathing sounded irregular, and Nicholas thought he might be crying.

Nicholas lay with his hands on his chest, thinking how hollow it felt, like an empty gourd. He had never missed having a family, though he had wanted one all his life. Yearned for one, even. Indeed, he used to like to imagine that he had a long-lost brother who would find him one day—it was perfectly possible, he would tell himself. Maybe his aunt could only afford to take in one child, and so the other had been sent elsewhere. At any rate, this brother would find him, and together they would fight off all the bullies and outsmart all the nasty adults. The fantasy had sustained him through many a hard time at Littleview.

"Look, you've had plenty of your own problems, Nick," said John in a strained voice. "And you may be smart, but you're only nine. I don't expect you to understand how I feel."

Nicholas considered this. "Well, I know it must be awfully

hard, anyway. It's why you like to keep so busy, right? To keep your mind occupied."

John rubbed at his eyes and gave a little sigh. "Sure, but then I always did like to keep busy, even before. I guess you do what you're good at. I wish I could read like you, but the truth is I'm a slow reader. It takes me forever to get through a book, and if I sit still too long, my mind drifts. *Anyway*," he said abruptly, sitting up, "I think that's quite enough of that. Don't we want to get started on the diary?"

"Absolutely," Nicholas agreed, and of course he really did want to. But it also occurred to him that, despite their uncomfortable conversation, he'd been enjoying himself, and part of him would have been content to keep on talking about other things. *Well*, he told himself, sitting up, *when you're both rich, you'll have plenty of time for conversations, and you can talk about whatever you please.*

"Fine, then," John said, rubbing his hands together. "I suppose we should start with the first entry that mentions the treasure, then go from there. You have a pretty good idea of the order, right?"

Nicholas raised his eyebrows. "Of course I do. I told you, I have the whole thing memorized."

"What, all of it? I thought…" John's look of surprise was plain enough, even in the gloom. "When you said you remembered it, I thought you meant—you know, *more or less*. Do you mean to say you remember the whole diary word for word?"

"Sure!"

John was growing excited. "Like that morning at breakfast? You know, on your first day, when you repeated everything I'd told you?"

Nicholas nodded. "Exactly like that. Here, I'll show you." And without hesitating, he launched into another word-for-word repetition of the things John had said the first morning. He didn't get far before John leaped to his feet in amazement.

"I can't believe this! You *still* remember all that? I mean, I knew you could—but I didn't know you could—" He began to pace excitedly back and forth. "Do you mean to tell me, Nick, that you remember absolutely *everything*?"

"As far as I know," Nicholas replied with a shrug. "I thought you knew this already."

John wagged his head almost violently. "No, I didn't! Sure, I knew you were smart as a whip, smarter than me, anyhow, and probably smarter than anyone I know—but this! I had no idea! Why, you're like Einstein! Or...or Leonardo da Vinci! Or Galileo or Mozart!"

Nicholas grinned. "I've never even touched a piano, so maybe not Mozart."

Abruptly John came to kneel beside Nicholas, the better to see his eyes in the dim light of the lantern. The older boy stared with almost unnerving intensity. "What did you read during your free time today?"

"Oh, several things! First I read *The Emergence of Electricity*, then—"

John hastily interrupted. "Fine, take that one. Let's say I asked you what the second line on page forty-three was, could you tell me?"

Nicholas thought a moment, then quoted: "'And he was

thrown against the wall with such force that his boots were knocked free of his feet. Miraculously, however, he survived his electrical encounter with little more than…'" He nodded. "That's it. That's the second line."

John clapped his hands to his head. "I can hardly stand it!" he cried, laughing. "But wait, he survived with 'little more than' what? Now I'm curious. You have to tell me!"

By this time Nicholas was laughing, too, although in his usual restrained way (so that what would have been a guffaw came out as a sort of stuttering squeal). He was enjoying John's amazement—which seemed so good-humored and generous, not like the jealous, bitter reactions he had so often experienced—and it was difficult not to laugh at least a little. But he soon checked himself, and he was about to tell John what had happened to the man in the book, when he noticed that something was different in the room.

What it was exactly Nicholas could not say, but the observatory had definitely changed somehow. Was it the echoes of their voices? The draft in the air? He felt a prickling along the back of his neck, and with a frown he reached for the lantern. John, noticing his troubled expression, had likewise fallen silent, and he watched uneasily as Nicholas turned up the lantern flame and dispelled the shadows.

In the stronger light, both boys saw the figure in the doorway.

Both of them screamed.

What happened next took only a moment, but the moment was full of smaller moments, each of them imprinted on Nicholas's swiftly slipping consciousness. He felt himself losing his grip on the lantern. He felt John catching at his shoulder as he slumped sideways. He saw that the figure in the doorway—it was the girl, he saw that now—did not even flinch at their screams. Nor did she speak. But she smiled and raised an eyebrow, and it was perfectly clear what she was thinking: *Now we're even.*

And then she was gone.

And Nicholas was out.

THE BOY ON THE BLUFF

Nicholas was so exhausted the next morning, he almost drowned. Sunday mornings were bath mornings for the orphans. Four bathrooms with tubs were attended by four of the orphanage staff, who sentenced each child to four minutes in the cold water with a scrub brush and soap. The entire business was accomplished in an hour, but it was a very early hour. A chaplain came to Rothschild's End on Sunday mornings to lead a brief service before returning to his own church in Pebbleton, and all the orphans were to be seated in the schoolhouse, clean and well dressed, when he arrived at seven o'clock.

It was six-thirty when Nicholas, the last in his group of boys, stumbled blearily past Mr. Pileus into the appointed bathroom. He had already been awake for over an hour—he was still on larder duty and had been dispatched early to the farm—and he had slept precious little before that, for after he and John had gotten back last night, he had returned the mop and broom to the utility closet and headed straight for the library. He had guessed something about the Hopefield girl (something he hadn't yet shared with John) and felt a powerful impulse to do some research in anticipation of meeting her again. Two hours later he had emerged from the library, barely conscious, and dragged himself upstairs just in time.

Nicholas closed the bathroom door, undressed hurriedly and miserably, and plunged into the tub. The water was not cold anymore, but neither was it altogether clean, for a dozen boys had gone before him, and the water had been changed only once. Naturally, there was to be no wasting of water at the Manor. The soap was strong, though, and Nicholas scrubbed furiously. Before long he had rendered himself pink and squeaky clean, and he was about to climb out of the tub when he remembered that as the last bather, it was his duty to pull the plug.

This was where the trouble began. The tub was unusually deep, and though he tried his best, Nicholas could not pull the plug with his toes. He was compelled to hold his breath and go under the murky water. He didn't want to, but he had to. *Down you go*, he told himself. *Glub glub glub and nothing for it.*

Down he went. *Glub glub*, he thought again, suddenly drowsier than he had been an instant before—in fact, very much drowsier, so drowsy that he was scarcely aware of it. He fumbled around the drain with clumsy fingers. *Glub tug on the tub plug*, he thought. *A most humbling fumbling…*

The next thing he knew, Nicholas was lying on the bathroom floor, coughing and spitting, with a terrible taste of soapy water in his mouth and a terrible realization that he had swallowed a fair quantity of it. A rough towel had been thrown over him, and, opening his eyes, he saw a horrified Mr. Pileus, who, after banging repeatedly on the door, had entered to find Nicholas unconscious under the water.

"Thank you, Mr. Pileus," Nicholas said feebly. "I was only examining the bottom of the tub, but I understand your concern."

Mr. Pileus stared at him bleakly. He was trembling, and his shirt was soaked through from having hauled Nicholas out of the water. Without a word, he turned and left the bathroom. Nicholas sat up, trembling himself. It *was* rather upsetting to think he had almost drowned in a bathtub—upsetting and humiliating. He was glad Mr. Pileus was so quiet. At least the incident would not be broadcast.

Covered from head to toe with goose bumps, Nicholas got up quickly and began to dry off. The towel was stiff and coarse as a floor mat, and it did not absorb water so much as move it around. Nicholas shook his head in disgust. What a way to start the day. And to think he'd disliked taking baths *before*.

The morning did not improve. The late-summer heat was at its peak, and the schoolhouse was already warm by seven

o'clock. By eight o'clock, when the chaplain's service concluded, the schoolhouse was sweltering, and the children
staggered out through the old stable doors as dazed as if they
had been clubbed about the ears. Then followed morning
chores, of which there was an extra helping on Sundays.

But there was also extra free time on Sunday afternoons,
and for once Nicholas joined the two or three girls in the
library in blissful sleep. John had agreed to keep an eye on
him, though it hardly proved necessary, for Mr. Collum was
supervising from his office by means of the entranceway mirror, and the Spiders never even peeked in. Nicholas slept the
entire time with his face behind a book, just out of Mr. Collum's view, and despite the unusual length of his nap, it was
perfectly dreamless and blissful. He awoke feeling refreshed
and eager. He couldn't wait for the night.

Wait he must, however, for many long hours. And when midnight finally arrived, Nicholas found himself waiting yet
again, this time for John. It was another cloudy night; the
park was immersed in inky blackness. The oak branches
overhead tossed in a strong wind. Nicholas, in his impatience,
seemed to be mimicking their frenetic motions—he paced
and waved his arms about and bounced on the balls of his
feet. The wait was made all the more maddening by the
knowledge that it might be for nothing. John might not even
come. He had warned Nicholas that he might not manage to
escape, for Mr. Collum was on duty in the dormitory, and
Mr. Collum—despite those enormous nostrils—did not
snore.

A quarter of an hour had passed, and Nicholas was on the

verge of giving up, when at last John came creeping up, his footsteps masked by the sounds of the branches and the wind. The boys greeted each other in silence, a relieved handshake and an excited clasping of shoulders, and John pulled on the boots Nicholas had brought him. Then, still under cover of darkness, they found their way through the undergrowth to the path, where Nicholas lit his lantern with some difficulty—the wind was problematic—before starting up the hill.

Giant's Head looked the same as it had the night before. But Nicholas knew at once that someone had been there. He was not sure how he knew, but he did. He held his lantern before him and stalked toward the door, with John following silently behind him. The observatory was empty. There was no sign of anything having been altered. So why did Nicholas think someone had been there? He moved further into the room, his senses on high alert.

"What's the matter, Nick?" John whispered. "You've got me spooked."

Suddenly Nicholas knew. "There was a candle in here," he said. "It smells different. I almost couldn't make it out over the lantern oil and the smoke."

John sniffed the air. "I *can't* make it out. You've got quite a nose." He grimaced. "Sorry, I didn't mean—"

Nicholas waved him off. "I know what you meant. You really can't smell it? To me, it's…Wait. Something else is different now."

John, who had noticed nothing, moved away from the door just the same. Tense and silent, the boys watched it.

A shadow appeared. Then the shadow became a form, and the form took on features. Work boots, a long, plain dress, pale hands—one gripping a heavy stick—a canvas bag thrown over a shoulder, and two wary eyes reflecting the lantern light. The girl hesitated in the doorway. She looked fierce and grim, and there could be no doubt that the stick was a warning. But presumably she had come to make friends, not enemies, and Nicholas, with a cry of delight, set down the lantern to welcome her.

"I'm so glad you've come!" he exclaimed. "I wanted to ask you something!" And he began moving his hands and his fingers in a deliberate manner in the air before him.

The girl's jaw dropped. The stick fell from her hand and struck the ground with a thud.

John could scarcely have been more surprised himself. "You know *sign language*, Nick?"

"I found a great thick book on it in the library last night," Nicholas said matter-of-factly, still moving his hands, "but I'm not very good at it yet." His facial expressions, which shifted rapidly as he signed, did not match the words he'd spoken aloud, and for a moment or two, John was bewildered.

"Wait a minute, are you talking to both of us at the same time?"

"Sure I am," Nicholas said, now motionless as he awaited the girl's reply. He was watching her intently. "Is there any reason I shouldn't?"

"But how did you even know she was deaf?" asked John, looking excitedly back and forth between Nicholas and the girl, who, having recovered from her shock, was now positively beaming. Her hands and fingers flew, and her expressions shifted rapidly as she shaped her responses to Nicholas's words.

"It was a few different things," Nicholas said, speaking slowly as he concentrated on the girl's movements. "The fact that she didn't hear us coming on the bluff. The way she looked at us when we spoke—she was trying to read our lips, see, but it was hard to do in the dark. The fact that she didn't even flinch when we screamed last night. And, of course, she never spoke. My guess is that—sorry, hang on a minute. She's asking you to face her so that she can see your lips when you talk."

John obeyed with an apologetic look, and the girl gave him such a smile that John could not help but respond in kind. "I'm John," he said, with a friendly nod. "It's nice to meet you."

"Her name's Violet." Nicholas was watching the girl's hands. "She's glad to meet you, too. Both of us, actually…" He snickered and flicked a glance at John. "She wants to know what we thought we were doing, going out onto her bluff without permission." He paused, concentrating. "And she wants to know where I learned sign language. She says I'm awfully clumsy."

As Nicholas moved his hands and changed his expressions in reply, the girl scowled and shook her head disapprovingly.

"She doesn't believe me," Nicholas explained. "I told her the truth. I figured there's no point in hiding it if we're going to be friends—and surely we're going to be friends, right, Violet?"

Violet raised an eyebrow and looked at John. She had been watching Nicholas's lips.

"It's true," John said to her. He jerked his thumb at

Nicholas. "He's a genius. Ask him something you wouldn't expect him to know—I'll bet you anything he'll know it."

Violet pursed her lips and regarded John doubtfully, as if she suspected a trick. Then she turned back to Nicholas and addressed him in sign language.

"She's asking me the name of the British artist who painted *The Hay Wain*." Nicholas grinned and shrugged. "That's easy—John Constable! He was a famous landscape painter. I'll bet you thought of him because he painted places that are a lot like where we are right now—you know, wooded places and farm scenes—and maybe also because you've just met someone named John. Am I right?"

Violet gaped at him. Her hands, poised in the air before her, remained motionless.

"See what I mean?" John said to her. "Believe me, I was just as surprised as you are. What do you say, do you believe us now?"

Slowly Violet nodded. And then she smiled, delighted. And her hands and fingers began to fly again.

For the next hour the three of them talked at a furious pace, with Nicholas translating Violet's words to John. Except for a few occasions when the boys' spoken words needed clarification, Nicholas did not speak in sign language himself, for Violet was an excellent lip-reader and he was still quite awkward with his hands. He also had much to learn, but he deduced the meaning of a great many unfamiliar signs from context, and the rest Violet explained to him as soon as she saw the questioning look in his eyes. Within thirty minutes Nicholas's vocabulary had grown so dramatically (his questioning looks coming less and less frequently) that Violet grew skeptical again and had to be reassured that he was not playing some elaborate ruse.

Do you promise you didn't already know sign language? she signed. *You aren't just pretending to learn as we speak?*

By this point Nicholas was already in the habit of translating everything instantaneously for John, and as he did so now John laughed and told Violet he knew exactly how she felt.

"Quote everything back to her," he suggested to Nicholas. "Like you did to me over breakfast that time."

But Violet stopped Nicholas before he had gotten properly under way.

No, I believe you. Some of the signs I've used are signs my mother and I made up, signs no one else knows. But you obviously learned them instantly, because I've used them several times and you only needed them explained once. I'm just amazed, I suppose.

"It takes some getting used to," John said upon hearing Nicholas's translation. "To tell you the truth, I'm still not used to it myself."

Without further ado, but with an eagerness they all held in common, the three of them launched back into their involved conversation. The boys told Violet a little about themselves, but mostly they peppered her with questions, and she was perfectly willing to give them elaborate and detailed responses.

Like her mother, Violet had lost all of her hearing when she was a young girl. Starting at an early age, therefore, she had learned English from her father and sign language from her mother, who as a girl had attended a school for deaf children in Stonetown. Violet herself had not attended such a school, as the circumstances of her life had prevented it, but her mother had kept all of her old school materials and proved an excellent teacher.

And Violet, for her part, was a quick and ready learner. She had excelled at the grade school in Pebbleton, from which she had graduated the year before with an eighth-grade diploma. In the Pebbleton area, such a diploma represented the pinnacle of educational achievement, for the nearest public high school was in the next county, and there was no bus service. Few local children attended high school. Most simply continued to work on their family farms or else found jobs in Pebbleton or elsewhere.

Violet was one of those who continued to reside on the family farm. She could communicate easily with her family—though only with her family. To express herself to anyone else in the area, she required pencil and paper. This was one reason she felt so excited to make friends with Nicholas and John.

Another reason, Violet signed—more tentatively, with an expression of great seriousness—*is that my older brother died in the war.*

Nicholas hesitated, taken aback by the solemn turn in the conversation. He was at a loss what to do or say.

Violet frowned. *Tell him*, she signed.

Nicholas collected himself and related what she had said. John's expression grew troubled. He nodded and asked Violet to go on.

She and her brother had been very close, Violet said, and she missed him desperately. She grew tearful as she began to describe how it felt, then quickly broke off what she had begun to say. *But you're both orphans*, she signed. *So you know.*

Nicholas, of course, did *not* know—not exactly, anyway. John did, though, and he responded to Violet's words with a brief, halting, equally emotional account of losing his parents. It was clear to Nicholas, observing and translating, that a current of understanding and sympathy had passed almost instantly between Violet and John; and strangely, though he had suffered no such painful loss, his role in expressing their sadness somehow made Nicholas feel it himself, and much more keenly than he would have thought. As he translated and clarified their words, he was compelled to steel himself against the emotion, to shove it down in his mind, for fear it would send him off to sleep.

To his relief, they soon moved on to other, less somber topics. And yet the entire conversation remained strangely intense, for reasons as complicated as Nicholas's unexpected emotions. For it is a curious fact about secret meetings that a bond almost always forms among the participants, a bond that can feel both mysterious and powerful. What is more, when the participants' personalities and experiences fit together well, this bond of secrecy can transform quite naturally into real friendship. Such was the case with the boys and Violet, and all of them knew it. They could all feel it.

"You used to come up here often, didn't you?" Nicholas asked Violet. "Just to look around, I guess? It was you who made that old track."

Yes, Violet signed. *My brother and I would come together.* She paused. *But I haven't come at all since he went away.*

Nicholas asked Violet if she knew when the telescope had been stolen. She nodded and told him that it had happened just before her brother went off to war. One day they had arrived to find the door broken down and the place empty. The observatory had not been used in years, she said—she had always known it to be overgrown with vines and weeds— but finding it in such a state had upset them, regardless. They had begun to think of it as their own, even though they had never entered it, and they were outraged by its shocking mistreatment.

Violet looked around the room in approval. She was glad, she said, to see that they had cleaned up the place. In her view it revealed a lot about their character.

"*My* character, at any rate," John remarked wryly. "Nicholas only cleaned because I made him."

"I resent that!" Nicholas cried, crossing his arms. "I was *going* to clean...or, that is, I probably would have, anyway. I mean, I might have. Eventually." He grinned. "But I did help, after all. Once you suggested it."

Violet was laughing. Her laughter was mostly silent, but her shoulders shook, and her breath came out in audible bursts, and her face—not an especially lovely face, by most measures—took on a wonderful radiance, the likes of which Nicholas had never seen. It lifted his spirits amazingly.

I think I know something about your *character, too,* Violet signed. And reaching into her shoulder bag, she produced a tightly rolled sheet of paper and handed it to Nicholas, who unrolled it with no small curiosity.

It was a drawing—an exceedingly skillful drawing—of a boy on a bluff.

Nicholas looked up with a start. "Why, this is...*me!*"

Violet was grinning. *Finally it's your turn to be surprised,* she signed. *I saw you from my window. I spend a lot of time at my window when I can't sleep. The moon was beautiful that night.*

The boy on the bluff sat with his legs dangling over the edge, gazing up at the sky. He was rendered in fine detail, as if well lit—and indeed he had been, by that enormous moon, although Violet had not included the moon in the drawing. *She must have terrific eyesight*, Nicholas thought absently, but a greater part of his mind was considering the implications of the drawing and what Violet had said about his character.

Like Nicholas, she had been awake late at night, almost certainly alone as she gazed out at the moonlit world. Had she felt a kinship with him before they ever met? Who had she thought him to be? What kind of boy was that boy on the bluff?

Staring at the drawing, Nicholas became aware of a curious feeling welling up in him—curious and very powerful. He found that he did not want to disappoint this girl, to disillusion her. He wanted to be whoever Violet had thought he was, sitting on that rock in the night.

The Bundle at the End of the Tunnel

After breakfast the next morning, the boys went out behind the Manor in hopes of speaking in private. Nicholas was more ebullient than ever, and as they passed through the clusters of children playing marbles and jumping rope, he chattered happily about everything that crossed his mind—everything but the most important things, which required secrecy—and saluted everyone who met his eye, greeting the other children by name even as they anxiously turned away. John, however, though he had been cheerful enough over breakfast, grew steadily less so at the sight of the other children recoiling. He was still not used to being shunned. The constantly averted eyes and retreating steps depressed his spirits horribly.

Nicholas noticed his gloomy expression and guessed the cause. "It helps to be at a distance," he said, tossing his head back toward the children. "When you're not right in among them, you don't feel quite so *avoided*."

John looked glumly at him. "I know you're already an old hand at this. Last week must have been awful for you. You didn't have anyone."

"Sure, it was bad," Nicholas said lightly, "but it was only a few days, and now I have you and"—he glanced back to be sure they had drawn out of earshot—"and Violet."

"I'm glad you do," John said. "I'm glad we both do." And brightening a little—in fact, almost smiling—he said, "I still can't believe you learned sign language in one night!"

"Well, as much as I could learn from one book, anyway," said Nicholas. "It was a good book, though. Excellent illustrations. Definitely worth the risk."

John frowned. "What risk?"

"Oh, I had a devil of a time reaching it. I had to climb halfway up the ladder and then lean out as far as I could, hoping I wouldn't fall. It was even harder putting it back on the shelf."

"For Pete's sake, Nick, why don't you oil that ladder? Then you can just move it and reach any book you like."

"Why, that never occurred to me!" said Nicholas with a look of amazement.

John began to reply, then checked himself. His eyes narrowed. "Okay, you're putting me on. I suppose you've already tried it?"

Nicholas shrugged. "I have, and it didn't work. The wheels and the tracks are in terrible shape. Badly rusted, almost falling apart. I could fix them easily enough with tools and some new parts—or even some scrap parts—but not quietly, so I can't risk doing it at night."

They walked past the schoolhouse lot, where two boys were kicking a heavy rock back and forth. The Spiders were leaning against the wooden fence, urging them to kick harder and harder, and the boys did not appear to be enjoying themselves. Nicholas and John veered away, giving the Spiders a wide berth and keeping in clear view of the gazebo, where Mr. Pileus was standing on duty. Moray spied them and yelled something insulting that neither boy could make out.

"So is your face!" Nicholas called back, hoping it applied.

They kept walking.

Presently John said, "Well, let's get to it, Nick. Have you made a decision?"

"I think so," Nicholas replied, kneeling to tie his shoe. The laces had broken and were so short that tying them was like performing surgery on an insect. "Actually, I'm pretty certain. How about you?"

"I think we're in agreement," said John.

Indeed, the boys had felt the agreement forming between them the night before. It might almost have formed the moment Violet made her first appearance. In reality, it had required no serious or prolonged consideration. If they were going to be friends with Violet, they had to let her in on their secret. Still, it had seemed only right to sleep on the matter before making the agreement official.

"We'll tell her tonight, then," Nicholas said. "And we'll get to work."

The plan was to meet Violet at Giant's Head at ten-thirty. John had assured Nicholas that there was no need to wait until midnight. Everyone was asleep by ten o'clock, he said, and Violet had confirmed that her parents and her two little sisters were also asleep by then. And so at precisely ten o'clock that night, Nicholas was waiting for John at their usual meeting place, behind the largest oak tree at the far end of the park. Half an hour later he was still waiting. John had not shown up. Finally he left the boots, a candle, and some matches at the base of the oak tree, just in case John came along later, and he hurried up the hill alone.

Violet was already waiting in the observatory. Nicholas knew this before he saw her, for the flickering light of a candle shone from the doorway. He found her studying the cranks, her hands on her hips, her back to the door. But something alerted her to his presence, and she turned to greet him with a smile.

Where is John? she signed.

"He didn't make it out," Nicholas replied. "Maybe he'll come along later."

Do you think he got caught? Should we be worried?

"I don't think so. John's awfully careful. More likely something just kept him from sneaking out."

Too bad. I brought enough for three. Violet took a thin blanket from her canvas bag and spread it on the floor. Then she opened a small bundle and laid out corn bread, a wedge of cheese, a jar of jam, and a bottle of milk. *There's nothing like a late-night picnic. Are you hungry?*

Nicholas laughed with delight. "I'm always hungry!" he exclaimed, and rubbed his hands together in anticipation. But then he hesitated. "Are you sure you can spare it? Won't your parents miss the food?"

Violet winked. *Not a bit. We have plenty of food, if not much else. And since I'm always the one who cooks supper and cleans up afterward, it's easy for me to tuck away a few things for later while my parents tend to my sisters.*

Nicholas needed no further convincing. Eagerly he sat down to eat, and for a time they spoke of rather ordinary things, such as how they had spent their days and whether cheese could properly be eaten with jam. Nicholas thought it could, but Violet insisted he eat them separately. Her little sisters ate them together, she said, and her sisters—though she loved them—were extremely silly. She did not like to think that Nicholas was as silly as they were.

"Oh, never!" Nicholas cried, putting on his most serious expression. "I avoid silliness at all costs!"

Violet nodded her serious approval, and then both of them laughed.

When at last they had eaten their fill, Nicholas told Violet he had a secret—that both he and John did, and that they had agreed to share it with her. The only condition was that she promise not to tell a soul. None of them could tell anyone, he said, without first asking permission of the others. Would Violet agree to that condition?

Looking somewhat puzzled, Violet nevertheless crossed her heart and promised.

And so Nicholas told her about the treasure. He started slowly, laying out the details before hinting where they might lead—the recently discovered diary, Mr. Collum's strange behavior, Mrs. Rothschild's missing inheritance....

At this point Violet interrupted him. *Yes, everyone around here knows about that. Some say that the money was buried with her—that Mr. Rothschild disliked his father-in-law and so never let his wife touch the inheritance during her lifetime. The rumor got around so much that the cemetery in Pebbleton hired a guard. They were afraid of thieves digging up her coffin. Isn't that horrible?*

Nicholas agreed that it was quite shocking. And then he told Violet what he had read in the diary.

Violet watched his lips intently, her eyes growing rounder and rounder. And then, when Nicholas had finished explaining his theory about the treasure—including his suspicion that it was hidden in or around Giant's Head—Violet looked excitedly about her, as if she might spy the treasure in plain sight. Finally looking back at Nicholas, she made several false starts, raising her hands only to drop them again in bewilderment, before finally signing, *Do you honestly think it's real?*

"I'm sure of it!" Nicholas replied, quite exuberantly, for Violet's excitement had renewed his own, and once again he felt thrilled by the prospect of riches.

If you're sure of it, then it must be true. With a mind like yours... Violet faltered again, unable to express her wonderment. After a pause, she signed, *And we'll share it? The three of us? Is that what you're saying?*

"Of course!" Nicholas said. "Three minds are better than one, right? We'll figure out how to find it, and then we'll share it. There'll be plenty for all of us." He explained his plan to relate key passages from the diary. "One of you might notice something I've overlooked—a coded combination for the cranks, or some hint about where to search, or something that hasn't even occurred to me. Or perhaps something *will* occur to me once I start talking about it. That happens to me a lot. The important thing is that we pay attention and think it all through...."

Nicholas had detected, over the course of this speech, that Violet's excitement was shading into something else, some emotion altogether more profound. He could see it in her eyes, which, though trained attentively on his lips, nonetheless reflected a kind of deep musing, as if, like Nicholas, she could listen carefully and ponder other things at the same time.

"What is it, Violet?" Nicholas asked, interrupting himself midstream. "What are you thinking of?"

Violet considered before answering. Then, locking eyes with him, she signed, *You have no idea what this means to me.*

"It means a lot to all of us," Nicholas agreed. "It's going to change our lives."

Violet nodded slowly. *It seems fated,* she signed. *The timing is too perfect. That we should all meet one another now, in this way, with a mystery to be solved and a treasure to be gained. Does it not seem as if it were meant to be?*

Nicholas had to admit that it did feel unusual, and he was about to say as much when Violet rose abruptly, as if she had just decided something. Or perhaps something had just occurred to her. Whichever it was, she looked at Nicholas with a troubled expression, the reason for which he could not guess, and told him that she needed to show him something.

Nicholas felt a shiver of excitement. "Does it have to do with the treasure?"

But Violet had already taken up his lantern and was headed for the door. Nicholas leaped up to follow her. They headed north, along the now-familiar trail. Violet was in the lead, which left Nicholas unable to ask her questions. As they entered the trees beyond the clearing, his mind darted from possibility to possibility. Were they headed to the bluff? To her home? Was it possible she knew of something that would shed light on the treasure's location? A clue in the woods that she had never realized was a clue?

Down into the ravine they went, clinging to trees on the steep descent, then crossing the streambed (whose waters had mostly receded now) by means of stepping-stones. Beyond the next ridge, at the fork in the trail, Violet turned left, away from the bluff.

A dozen paces took them to still another fork. Again Violet turned left. The path they followed now led westward and slightly uphill—not down to the farm, then. Nicholas felt his excitement increase. This path was wider than the others and appeared once to have been well cleared and maintained, though it was now fairly overgrown, in obvious disuse. Before long, it led out of the trees into a strange landscape of rocks— enormous boulders and slabs and scattered piles of rubble— running all the way up to the ridge.

Tromping through gravel and weeds, Violet headed for an impressive mound of rubble surrounded by boulders; and walking around the largest of these, she knelt and positioned the lantern so that Nicholas could see, in among the rubble, the mouth of a narrow tunnel or cave scarcely larger than the lantern itself.

Violet beckoned for Nicholas to kneel beside her and peer into the opening. It was small enough that he doubted a bear could pass through it, but he was less certain about mountain lions, and as he moved to join her, Nicholas ardently hoped that Violet knew what she was doing.

At first he saw nothing. The lantern revealed a long, cramped tunnel, quite empty save for spiderwebs and loose rocks. But Violet had seemed convinced he would see something significant, so Nicholas strained his eyes until, at last, he did. Just at the outer limit of the lantern's light, he could make out a sort of bundle, something wrapped in burlap or other heavy cloth. Or part of a bundle, anyway—he could tell that the tunnel opened up into a rocky chamber and that the bundle lay mostly out of sight, with just its nearer part visible. His heart was beating faster now. Was it possible that *this* was the treasure chamber? Had there been some sort of secret entrance here in the woods? Perhaps a tunnel—even an entire series of tunnels—that led between Giant's Head and this subterranean cave?

One glance at Violet's face answered his questions. This was not the treasure. It was something else entirely, something very troubling to her. Nicholas felt that it must have to do with her brother, and beating down his disappointment, he waited for her to explain. She gave no sign of doing so, however, but only gazed with sad eyes at the mysterious bundle at the end of the tunnel.

He gestured to catch her attention. "What is it, Violet? What is that thing?"

And Violet told him.

It did not have to do with her brother, after all, at least not directly. But it did have to do with Violet's family, and in particular Violet herself. The bundle at the end of the tunnel was the symbol of a crushed dream.

Violet was an artist. Even before she could read and write, she had drawn pictures to express herself, and her talent, which was immediately apparent to everyone, had been supported and expanded through constant practice. Over the years she had acquired a great many art supplies and art books as birthday and Christmas presents, and had purchased even more with her own modest savings. Her family's farmhouse was a veritable art gallery. Once, when Violet was nine, a distant aunt had visited and, seeing Violet's paintings and drawings, had suggested that Violet might benefit from art school. The aunt knew of a reputable one in Stonetown to which anyone with an eighth-grade degree might apply.

"It's expensive, certainly," the aunt had said. "But it's the only one in the region."

At the time, Violet had five years left until she graduated from eighth grade at the school in Pebbleton. As soon as the aunt had gone, she asked her parents if five years was enough time to save the money she would need to pay the art school's tuition. Her parents, wretched at the prospect of disappointing her, nevertheless had to inform Violet that it was extremely unlikely she could attend. Even if the farm grew more productive than it had been in recent years, even if they scrimped and saved, the Hopefields probably couldn't afford to send her.

This was just before the war, Violet signed. *Crops had been terrible for a long time. I could hardly argue. I knew better than that. It was hard, though. I cried myself to sleep for a week.*

And then, it seemed, a miracle had occurred. The very next week a scout for a mining company in Stonetown had knocked on their door. Evidently, he believed his company had a good chance of finding a rare mineral—an exceedingly valuable mineral—in the hills behind their farm. The Hopefield property extended all the way to the nearest ridge, which happened to be exactly the best place for an exploratory mine, and the scout had come to see if Mr. Hopefield would sign a contract allowing the company to drill there.

The family stood to make a great deal of money, the scout had explained, and at no risk. The contract would be for five years, during which time the Hopefields would receive a percentage of the value of any rare minerals discovered, and after which, if the mining operation continued to be successful, a new, even more profitable contract could be negotiated. If no minerals were found and the company ceased its operations before the contract expired, the Hopefields would still receive a handsome sum at that time—a "withdrawal award," as it was called in the contract.

There had been little need for discussion. Mr. Hopefield had signed the contract. And suddenly it seemed almost certain that Violet could attend the art school, after all. The company came and cleared a lane up the hill. A team of mules, straining and puffing, had pulled a wagon bearing the state-of-the-art drill up to this spot. An engineer and his assistant unloaded the drill, positioned it, and set to work. The hills rang with the tremendous noise. Violet could not hear it, but she could feel the vibrations in her feet even from a distance.

A dozen men streamed in and out of the lengthening tunnel, carting and sorting through rubble.

It went on for weeks, and Violet and her brother often stole up the hill to watch the work progress. They were so full of hope—so excited to think that at any moment the miners would strike a vein—they hated to be anywhere else, even though the work was dull and tedious to watch. Indeed, the only thing more dull and tedious was when the work stopped. And often it did stop, sometimes because the foreman had a safety concern, other times because the drill broke down.

At the times when the drill broke down, Violet and her brother would watch with bleak impatience as the engineer and his assistant carted the machine back out into the open, where, in the better light, they would spread out tools and blueprints and make their repairs. Hideous, tiresome hours would pass as the men tried one thing after another. Sometimes they were forced to dismantle the drill entirely, in which case the other workers would retire to their camp, done for the day, and Violet and her brother would trudge back down to the farm. For two children anxious to be rich, such interruptions were an agony.

But it was the final interruption that destroyed their hopes altogether. Violet and her brother happened to be there when it occurred. In fact, it was Violet who first understood it was coming. She was watching the activity with glazed eyes when suddenly she became aware of a rumbling, much different from the usual vibrations, issuing from the hillside beneath their feet. For several seconds no one else seemed to notice it. Then, just when Violet realized what the rumbling might be, men came streaming out of the mine, waving their arms and shouting, "Get back, get back!" The last to emerge were the engineer and his assistant—and they barely made it out. A billowing cloud of dust followed them out into the daylight, and just like that, the tunnel vanished—taking art school with it.

The hill was too unstable for more drilling, Violet signed. *That's what the foreman said. He was extremely upset. He said that the deeper they had drilled, the greater his concerns had been, and that he had warned the company to shut down its operations. The company executives had not listened to him, but that would change now, he said. The conditions were much too risky. It would be too dangerous even to try to get the drill out.*

But the very next day the foreman's boss came to my father and told him that the foreman had been badly mistaken. The drilling conditions in the hill were perfectly fine, he said, perfectly normal. Cave-ins were always a risk, even in the safest of operations, he said. The only problem was that this expensive drill was now temporarily out of reach, and trying to tunnel through the rubble to reach it might cause more rocks to fall on the drill and destroy it. Once the company had figured out how to solve these problems, they would continue their work. Officially, he said, the company had not ended its mining operations. The operations were definitely ongoing—the work was just interrupted.

Nicholas was appalled. "Wait a minute! Do you mean they don't intend to pay your family any money? But that's outrageous!"

Yes, but they have the law on their side. As long as that drill remains on our property, they can insist that the operations are ongoing. There can be no "withdrawal award" if there has been no official withdrawal. I have wished, so many times, that the cave-in had destroyed the drill completely. But everyone could see it, as plain as day, at the end of this little tunnel. It's back there. There's just no way for them to get to it. They can pretend to be working on the problem until the contract expires, and then they never have to think about it again.

Nicholas spat in the dirt. "It's just pure wickedness," he muttered. "Pure, gross wickedness."

For a long time, Violet signed, *I crawled back in there every day to look at it. I was small enough then—I'm not anymore.*

"You crawled in *there*?" Nicholas said. He peered into the little tunnel again, imagining spiders, scorpions, snakes—even another cave-in. If that tunnel had collapsed while Violet was crawling through it...He shuddered.

My parents didn't know, of course. We were all forbidden to go anywhere near this place. It was too dangerous. But I crept up here and crawled down the tunnel to see the drill. Everything had collapsed around it, but that one pocket remained, as if it were protected by magic. Oh, I hated that drill. I despised it. But I took care of it like gold. When I was your age, I was more naive than you are. I thought there must be some mistake. At least I wanted to believe it. And so I greased everything and wrapped the whole drill in cloth, like a mummy, so that when the company finally got it out, they could go right back to work. I was so stupid then.

"You weren't stupid, you were just decent!" Nicholas said angrily. "You just didn't realize that grownups are so selfish. But they are! If you aren't in their family, you might as well not be a person! They don't—" He broke off. Violet wasn't looking at him. She was crying silently, looking down that long, narrow tunnel.

After a time she turned to him. *My parents have worked so hard, trying to save enough money, trying to make it up to me. But they couldn't save enough. There just isn't any way. And now that five-year contract is due to expire in weeks—can you believe it? This is what I mean about the timing. After all these years, it's suddenly as if one ruined dream is finally ending and a better one is opening, right at the same time.*

Violet smiled at Nicholas through her tears. *That's what I mean when I say this all seems fated. It's too perfect, isn't it? I have you now, you and John, and we're going to find that treasure, aren't we?*

Nicholas smiled back at her. "Count on it," he said, and he threw her a salute. "Art school, here you come."

MISSING TREASURES, MISSING PEOPLE, and THE MYSTERIOUS MR. BOOKER

At breakfast the next morning, an owlish, bespectacled boy named Vern was wearing a dunce cap. The Spiders insisted that Vern sit with them, so that they might more easily mock him and enjoy themselves. There was a great deal of laughter in the dining room, and a certain amount of crying on Vern's part, that Mr. Pileus did nothing about, for it was he who had been on duty when Vern woke up screaming, and he was evidently resentful and weary. He sat drinking coffee and staring at nothing with reddened eyes.

"He seemed to think Vern was dying," John told Nicholas over their oatmeal and scrambled eggs. "He was pale and shaking, not very much comfort to poor Vern. It was only a nightmare, of course."

Nicholas leaned over the table. In a low voice he said, "Is that what happened, then?"

John nodded. They spoke no more about it until they were outside walking around, at which time John explained that his hand had actually been on the door handle—this after two long minutes of creeping from cot to door—when Vern screamed. Luckily, a full-blown commotion ensued, and by the time Mr. Pileus had gotten his lamp lit, John was only one of several boys who appeared to have leaped groggily to their feet. John had rubbed his eyes and acted confused and got back into his cot as Mr. Pileus shushed them all and put out the light again.

"That's an awfully close call," Nicholas said. "What if Vern had waited a few more minutes to have his nightmare? You would have been gone. Someone would surely have noticed."

"You don't have to tell me," John said. "That's all I could think about as I lay there waiting for everyone to go to sleep again." He looked sheepishly at Nicholas. "It took them a long time, though—Mr. Pileus was shaken up, I think, and couldn't get back to sleep—he kept tossing and turning. And I...well, listening to everyone's breathing..."

"It's okay," Nicholas said. "I can't decently complain about you falling asleep when you didn't mean to, can I? But say, does one of the other men sleep in Mr. Pileus's room when he's in the dormitory?"

"Not that I know of. Why?"

Nicholas rolled his eyes. "That butler's rope in my room is supposed to sound a bell in Mr. Pileus's room if I have an emergency. Clearly, Mr. Collum didn't think everything through when he made my 'special arrangement.' I'm glad I have my own way out."

"How *do* you get out, anyway?" John asked, trying to sound nonchalant.

Nicholas only shook his head. "Nice try."

They spent the rest of their walk discussing what Nicholas had learned from Violet the night before. John was every bit as disgusted with the mining company as Nicholas had been, and he seemed deeply moved at the thought of Violet's broken dreams. He grew quiet and somber when Nicholas told him about Violet's parents, how they had worked extra hard to save up their money, only to fail in the end.

"I'm sure she could go *eventually*," Nicholas said, "after she found a job and was able to pay for school herself. But that might take years. Much better to find treasure than a job, don't you think? It's quicker, anyway."

John gave Nicholas a puzzled look. "You seem awfully certain she could find a job, Nick. What sort of job do you think she can find? Jobs are scarce, and Violet's deaf and mute. Sure, she's talented, but you can bet a lot of people wouldn't give her any chance to prove it. I don't think it would be as easy as you think. Did Violet say something about getting a job?"

"Sure, she said she hoped to take on some sewing work for a lady in Pebbleton this year." Nicholas frowned. "She did say it wouldn't be for very much money, though. Just a little extra to help her parents out."

John said nothing further. Neither did Nicholas, whose mood had gone sour. He disliked being wrong, disliked it intensely. The truth was, he should have known better, indeed *would* have known better if he had taken a moment to think. But he had been caught up thinking about other things. Treasure, mostly, and the glory of finding it.

Nicholas was not, however, especially saddened by this new perspective on Violet's problems. For one thing, he felt certain that the treasure was going to solve them. For another (though one day he would be ashamed to remember it), in some strange way he was actually pleased to know of her misfortune, to be on the inside of her miserable story. He felt the same way about John. Nicholas was thrilled to have friends who, like him, felt set apart from everyone else. For together they were *not* set apart—or rather, they were, but they were set apart together. The feeling was so unfamiliar, and so pleasant, that even in his downcast mood Nicholas found himself thinking it would almost be nice if he never solved the mystery, never found the treasure, but instead went on like this indefinitely, with his two outcast friends, meeting in secret, with all their problems to discuss and an enormous mystery to solve.

But Nicholas still had to get through his days at the Manor, and the days were tricky at best, awful at worst. Later that morning, for example, he awoke from a nap to find himself locked inside a pitch-black basement.

It had happened like this: During Crafts and Skills, Mr. Pileus had sent Nicholas and Vern to the basement to fetch paint thinner and varnish. Nicholas suspected that Mr. Pileus was still upset with both of them—they had both given him a good scare in the past couple of days—and wanted them out of his sight as much as possible. That would also explain why he didn't check on Nicholas but simply accepted Vern's explanation (a truthful one, as it happened) that he had succumbed to a nap. Mr. Pileus had only grunted and sent Vern back for the remainder of the varnish.

Unfortunately, Moray, seeing an opportunity, had gripped Vern's elbow before he left and whispered for him to turn off the light and lock the basement door. Vern understood, of course, that the humiliating dunce cap on his head would be the least of his problems if he disobeyed. And so as he exited the basement for the second time, he turned Mr. Pileus's key, which had been left in the lock, and scurried guiltily away.

Nicholas remained in the basement for two hours. No one came to check on him. John told him later that he had asked Mr. Pileus if he might do so, but Mr. Pileus had grumpily refused. As soon as Crafts and Skills ended, the Spiders hurried inside, so that they might be the ones to unlock the door and witness the pleasingly sad spectacle of Nicholas huddled alone at the bottom of the stairs.

The light had been turned back on, but that was no surprise. Any frightened fool could have groped his way up the stairs and fumbled around until he found the switch. What surprised the Spiders was the music. And as they descended the stairs to discover their so-called victim riding on a stationary bicycle, grinning hugely and singing along to a phonograph—*a phonograph somehow powered by the bicycle he was pedaling*—their surprise turned to confusion, and finally to fury. While they had been stripping and varnishing furniture in the morning heat, Nicholas Benedict had been *enjoying* himself?

"Hello there, fellows!" Nicholas called, somewhat breathlessly, as they came down. "How was Crafts and Skills?"

"What...is...this?" Moray seethed, and Iggy and Breaker glowered intensely.

"Why, it's music!" Nicholas cried. "I suppose the phonograph was considered broken—this bicycle, too, for that matter—but things are rarely broken for good, you know, if only you have proper tools and know how to use them." He waved a hand around him, still pedaling. "Luckily, the basement is *full* of tools, so I've just been tinkering around."

Moray stalked forward with the obvious intention of yanking Nicholas off the bicycle, but just then Mr. Pileus entered the basement, followed by several of the other boys. Nicholas quickly explained that, as the basement door had been locked—"accidentally, I'm sure"—and no one had answered his shouts for help, he had naturally felt a need to occupy himself.

Mr. Pileus studied the bicycle and the phonograph in silence. Then he grunted. And then he smiled. And then he selected a different record from the box of records Nicholas had found, and he took a turn on the bicycle.

It had turned out to be an enjoyable morning, therefore, and Nicholas was feeling more than a little triumphant. Yet at the same time, somewhere in the shadows of his mind, a voice was asking "What next?" The incident reminded him that he could never let his guard down, not even for a moment. As long as he lived at the Manor, he could never relax, and he would never be completely safe.

It would have been bad enough even without the Spiders. Look at poor Vern, for instance. Not only was he forced to wear the dunce cap because of his nightmare, he'd been given extra chores for the day. And then, because he'd "accidentally" locked Nicholas in the basement, he was given extra chores for the entire week. The punishment was awfully harsh, Nicholas thought. For him, losing so much free time would have been torture. All that lost reading time!

Reading was exactly what Nicholas was doing that afternoon when Vern came into the library with a feather duster. The pitiful boy puttered miserably about without meeting anyone's eye, his dunce cap giving his head the ridiculous look of an upside-down ice-cream cone. From time to time Vern glanced out through the open doorway, and each time he did, he saw Mr. Collum's stern face looking back at him through the entranceway mirror, and in evident terror he redoubled his efforts with the duster.

Nicholas observed all this with a mixture of pity and amusement, though only with part of his attention, for as usual he was deeply engrossed in his reading. As he stood at the shelves, however, he slowly became aware of the fact that Vern was sidling toward him, dusting the books nearer and nearer to Nicholas. He felt vaguely irritated—surely Vern could have picked other places to dust just then—and in fact was about to suggest as much, when he saw Vern slip a small, folded piece of paper into the empty space on the shelf from which Nicholas had taken his current book. He saw Vern cast a frightened glance at him before quickly sidling away again.

Nicholas sighed. No doubt it was a threat from the Spiders, or some sort of warning or ultimatum. He was tempted not even to look at it, but as always curiosity got the better of him. He unfolded the slip of paper and read: *I am relly sorry for locking that door I had no choise.* And with a start, he realized that the note was from Vern himself. Turning around, he saw Vern scurrying out of the library without looking back.

What do you know, he thought. *Someone around here actually has a conscience.*

On an impulse, Nicholas put away his book and hurried out into the entranceway, thinking that if no one else was around, he might persuade Vern to talk to him. He could use another ally, even if it had to be a secret one.

He met with no such luck, however. The entranceway was already empty, and Nicholas saw no one in the east or west passage. He went to check the kitchen, but there was no sign of Vern there, either. *Well, it was a long shot, anyway,* he thought, and started back toward the library. He stopped to poke his head into the butler's pantry, just in case. It was empty, too, and Nicholas was about to withdraw, when he heard agitated voices coming from the anteroom beyond it.

The Spiders' voices.

Nicholas considered. The door to the anteroom was slightly ajar, and it was dark in the butler's pantry. The conditions for eavesdropping were perfect. Could this be a trap? Had Vern been sent to him as bait? He glanced around. He sniffed the air. He hesitated a moment longer. Then he slipped into the butler's pantry and crept toward the ante-room door, poised to flee at the first hint of trouble.

"It's embarrassing!" Breaker was grumbling. "He goes around like he doesn't have a care in the world! Like he's *enjoying* himself!"

"What if people start to think he's smarter than us or something?" Iggy put in. "I mean, he—he *isn't*, right? I mean, you don't think he can really, you know—"

"Shut up, Iggy," Moray snapped. "Now listen, both of you, we're going to get him, all right. I don't care if we have to take a punishment for it. We're going to get him good—so good that everyone will see it. There won't be any doubt."

"I don't want to get *punished*, though," Breaker protested.

"Me, neither," Iggy whined. "Can't we get him some other way?"

"We'll keep our eyes open, sure. But if we don't get a safe crack at him soon, we're going to have to take our chances. Otherwise, we look like fools."

"Well, if we're going to get punished for it," Breaker muttered, "we'd better make it good."

"By *good* you mean *bad*, right?" Iggy said.

"What do you think?" Breaker snarled.

"It will be bad, all right," Moray said. His tone was harsh and determined. "You can count on it."

After this dismaying pronouncement, the Spiders went out the back door, and Nicholas heard nothing further. He had heard enough, in any case, to fill his belly with dread. If the Spiders were willing to take punishment, there was no limit to what they might do to him, and very little he could do to protect himself.

Nicholas trudged back to the library. Which was the worse fate? he wondered. To be surprised by an unavoidable vicious attack, or to know it was coming?

The answer made little difference, he knew.

He was going to have to suffer both.

⌣∴⌢

Midnight at Giant's Head. Three youthful figures were huddled around a lantern with its flame turned low. They were indoors, and yet a slice of starry sky shone down upon their circle. They had been together in the observatory for more than an hour. Already, in the interest of thoroughness, they had once again scoured the room in hopes of teasing out its secrets. But the secrets had remained secrets for the time being, and afterward they had dined on biscuits and honey, washed down with milk. Now two of them were concentrating earnestly as the third, with uncanny accuracy, recited key passages from the diary on which their hopes of fortune rested. For dramatic purposes, he was making his voice as deep as he could (which was not very deep), in order to sound at least a little like the grown man who had written the diary.

"'I have heard from Mr. Booker,'" Nicholas intoned huskily, "'and naturally he requires advance payment. Must be careful in handling this. Beanie is a fine and formidable accountant but has little notion of privacy within the household. If I do not record the payment, Beanie will note the large difference in the accounts and ask me about it. If he does so in Di's presence, I will undoubtedly stammer and arouse her suspicions. She has that effect on me. Likewise, she will be suspicious if Beanie asks *her* about it, for I am usually quite meticulous in matters of money. And yet I am determined to surprise her.'"

Here the strain of trying to speak deeply sent Nicholas into a coughing fit.

"Just use your regular voice, Nick," John suggested when at last the coughing subsided and Nicholas, with watering eyes, prepared to speak again. "I doubt Mr. Rothschild sounded quite so much like a frog, anyway. And we'll never get anywhere if you keep coughing."

Violet nodded her agreement.

"Well, if you insist," Nicholas said. "The next entry is from the following day. Ready?" Again he recited from memory:

"'The solution has occurred to me. Cash will suffice. Beanie has not the least interest in how I spend my money. Even such a sizable bank withdrawal will not trouble him. His only concern is that every penny be accounted for.

"'On Wednesday we take our train to Stonetown, where on some pretext I shall go out alone to conclude arrangements with Mr. Booker. He is, by all accounts, the best in his profession, so I am hopeful for success. On Thursday we sail for Europe—twelve weeks of travel, and with fair wind and good luck, we shall return from an enjoyable holiday to an even finer surprise.'"

Nicholas paused to interject, "My best guess is that this Mr. Booker was a detective or some kind of hired gun. Either he was good at tracking things down, or he was good at dealing with criminals."

What was Mr. Rothschild hiring him to do? Violet signed.

"Either to locate his wife's treasure or to get it back from someone," Nicholas replied, after translating her question for John. "Apparently, it had gone missing, or at least part of it had. Maybe stolen, maybe lost in transit—the diary never makes clear which. This is what I mean when I say Mr. Rothschild is kind of shady about some things. Up to this point he hasn't even mentioned the treasure."

"What about the inheritance?" John asked.

Nicholas shook his head. "He never mentions it anywhere. Not once. That's another reason I think there's something fishy about how they got the treasure. At any rate, they got it, but there was some kind of problem. My guess is that they acquired it through some sort of foreign dealer, or maybe several dealers, and that some of the crates got mislaid or misrouted, possibly on purpose, and Mr. Rothschild hired Mr. Booker to find them."

And Mr. Booker did find them? Violet signed.

"Evidently," Nicholas said. "I'm pretty sure Mr. Rothschild left his diary at home while they traveled, because the next entry is dated just over twelve weeks later. Are you ready?" The other two nodded eagerly, and Nicholas recited:

"'Sailed into Stonetown on Friday, after a lovely holiday. Could not wait to meet privately with Mr. Booker, who, for obvious reasons, was unable to communicate with me as we traveled. He had succeeded! And so last night, after months of secrecy and subterfuge, I was at last able to reveal to Di the great surprise—her treasure completely recovered! She was stunned, amazed, overjoyed. Rarely have I seen her so delighted! (And, I must confess, rarely have I felt so pleased with myself.)'"

What's next? Violet signed. *What else does he say about it?*

Nicholas shrugged. "That's it, unfortunately. After that he writes a few lines about their holiday—lots of museums and bookshops and cafés—and goes to bed."

John rubbed his head. "So there's never any mention of how many pieces the treasure contained? Or how big they were? Or whether they're all the same kind of thing or lots of different things?"

Nicholas shook his head.

Violet gestured toward the cranks on the wall. *I've been thinking about your combination idea*, she signed, and Nicholas translated for John as she did so. Already the three of them had developed such a rhythm that there was scarcely any pause in their conversations. *Are the diary pages numbered?*

"No," Nicholas replied. "The entries are dated. I've studied the dates carefully, too. Everything seems to line up, as far as I can tell. No suspicious patterns. But maybe one of you would notice something I didn't. I should write them down for you."

Violet got out an oversized tablet and began flipping through it in search of a blank page. Every page she turned contained a detailed drawing.

"Wait!" said John. "Can we see those drawings? They look amazing."

They're studies for paintings, mostly, Violet signed. She handed over the tablet, and Nicholas, turning up the lantern, scooted closer to John to look at the drawings. He whistled in admiration.

"I know," John said. "These are really swell."

The first drawing depicted the main street in Pebbleton, which Nicholas recognized at once. Several figures populated the scene, moving among the market vendors and businesses, but something seemed strangely amiss. After a moment both boys realized what it was. The day had been rendered bright and sunny, but everyone in the drawing appeared to be drenched, with wet hair and soggy clothes. Some carried dripping umbrellas folded under their arms. And yet the streets were dry—there were no puddles, and no water dripped from the awnings over the market stalls.

The next few drawings were also familiar scenes. At first glance they appeared to be copies of famous magazine covers, illustrations that had been reproduced and framed and hung on the walls of thousands of homes. Both Nicholas and John recognized them at once: There was the one of boys sledding down a hill, there was the one of a grandfather and grandson going fishing, there was the one of a family playing cards at the kitchen table. The scenes had been copied in extraordinary detail; there was no mistaking them. They looked exactly the same as the originals in all but one important respect—the people were missing.

The snow-covered hill was devoid of life. No one stood at the edge of the fishpond. The playing cards were laid out on a table in an empty kitchen. The effect was altogether unsettling. The boys looked at each other, deeply impressed.

"These are incredible, Violet," Nicholas said.

"I can't get over how they look so strange," John said. "I mean, they don't *look* strange. Everything looks all normal and familiar, but you definitely feel like something is wrong."

"Because something is missing," Nicholas said. "And you'd never know it if you hadn't seen the originals. I mean, if you didn't know the people were supposed to be there."

Violet thanked them somewhat solemnly and took the tablet back. *I'm doing a series,* she signed. *I'm calling it* Absence.

"They're good," John said in a slightly choked voice. He cleared his throat. "They're really good. They're perfect." Violet looked at him and nodded.

Only then did Nicholas understand that the drawings were about Violet's brother. He felt suddenly foolish. How had he not realized that at once? Violet, meanwhile, had found a blank page, and she handed the tablet and a pencil to Nicholas, who accepted them gratefully. He was glad to have something to do. His friends' sadness made him uncomfortable. He felt as if he should say something meaningful, but he could think of nothing, and even if he did, it would surely seem less meaningful coming from him.

As Nicholas wrote down all the dates from the diary entries, John told Violet that he thought she could be a famous artist. "Like Picasso or someone," he said wonderingly. "I mean, you really have talent!"

Violet looked at Nicholas expectantly. She wanted to reply to John but needed Nicholas to translate.

"Oh!" Nicholas said, still writing. "Go ahead, Violet. I can do this and interpret at the same time." He took his eyes from the page but continued to write, and as Violet signed he said to John, "She doesn't care to be a famous artist. She'd be perfectly happy if she could just find steady work as an illustrator. She loves to think about people's stories and re-create them in pictures."

Nicholas finished writing the dates and handed the paper to Violet. She and John studied them carefully, but, like Nicholas, they found nothing unusual in them, no hidden codes or patterns. They were only days in another person's life, a life long since ended, a life that had been lived on that very property.

A life full of secrets, as all lives are.

For a long time the three of them pondered the diary's entry dates, speculating on one thing and another, but never with any definite notions about them. At last Nicholas suggested they take a break to clear their heads. "Here," he said, going to the cranks, "you two look up at the stars while I give you a spin."

So John and Violet lay back on the turntable, both of them grinning, as Nicholas cranked and the sky slowly wheeled above them. Afterward they all took turns at the crank as the others spun. For such a simple form of entertainment, it certainly lifted their spirits.

"You never run out of ideas, do you, Nick?" John said. "Say, that reminds me! Violet, wait till you hear what he was up to in the basement this morning...."

Violet was amused by John's account of the basement incident and impressed by his descriptions of Nicholas's bicycle-powered phonograph. But she was also somewhat taken aback. This was the first she had heard about Nicholas's narcolepsy, and she asked him to explain it to her.

"Don't worry, it isn't contagious," Nicholas said, when Violet yawned during his (admittedly very lengthy) explanation. He grinned. "I mean, I'm pretty sure it isn't my fault that you're sleepy."

Violet grinned back and argued that it most certainly *was* his fault, for if not for him she would have gone to bed hours ago. In fact, she said, she sincerely hoped that they found this treasure before the harvest season, which would soon be upon them. She doubted that she could give her father all the extra help he would need and still keep such late hours. She would be too tired to think straight.

"It's going to be hard for us, too, Nick," said John. "School's going to be starting, you know. We'll have hours of schoolwork every day, and at the same time we'll have to work extra hours on the farm, helping Mr. Furrow with the harvest and trying not to get bitten or kicked by Rabbit."

Kicked by a rabbit? Violet signed, looking puzzled, and soon the boys had her silently laughing with their anecdotes about the dangerous old mule and his precious carrots. She knew how it was with mules, she said. She had been around them all her life.

We're down to just one old mule ourselves, she signed, shaking her head. *What my father really needs is a tractor. Without my brother to help, he's had to work himself to the bone. But my parents have been saving up all their money, hoping to send me to art school.*

"Well, after we find the treasure," Nicholas said, "your father can buy a tractor *and* you can go to art school. We can all do whatever we want! Come on, let's get back to work."

John was rubbing his eyes. "Sorry, you two," he said through a yawn. "I don't think I can look at any more numbers tonight. I'm so tired I can hardly see straight." He stood up and stretched. "But if you don't mind, I'd like to have a look at that collapsed mine before we go back. I've been curious to see it ever since Nick told me about it."

The others agreed. They closed up the roof panels, and minutes later John was kneeling before the narrow tunnel entrance, lantern in hand. He let out a low whistle and looked over his shoulder at Violet. "You really crawled in there? Did you even have room to be up on your hands and knees?"

Violet shook her head. *I had to worm my way back there on my belly. It was too hard to carry my candle, so I put it into my pocket with a matchbox and lit it when I reached the little cave.*

Nicholas looked horrified as he translated this, and John whistled again. "In the dark, no less!"

There was a little sunlight from the opening here, but, yes, it was really dark. Of course, that first time I was hoping I might be able to tie a rope around the drill. I thought they could use a team of mules to drag it out. I'd be in awful trouble for crawling back in there, but I didn't care. The drill was much too large, though. It wouldn't fit through the tunnel.

"So instead you just started taking care of it?" John asked. "That's what Nick told me."

Yes.

"What about your brother? Did he help you?"

My brother had more sense than I did. He would never have let me do something so dangerous, so I never told him.

They sat quietly for a while. The insects buzzed in the trees. Somewhere in the distance an owl hooted. All three of them were sleepy, and all three were reluctant to go to bed, to leave one another's company.

"Oh, well," John said at last. "I suppose it's time to hit the sack. We didn't find the treasure tonight, but at least we got to know each other a little better." Then he grimaced, for he had forgotten to face Violet when he spoke, and could see her look of uncertainty. He apologized and repeated himself, looking painfully embarrassed.

Violet patted his shoulder. *You're right, we have gotten to know each other. And I already know you're kind, so don't worry.* She paused, her hands still in the air before her. Something had occurred to her. *You know, I think that's what we need to be doing. Not just getting to know each other better but getting to know the Rothschilds better. Knowing what kind of people they were will help us make better guesses, don't you think?*

"Say, that's a great idea!" John said, and to Nicholas he added, "Do you hear that? Tomorrow night you have to fill us in on how rich people think."

"It does seem like a good idea for you to know more about them," Nicholas admitted, "but just because they're rich, don't expect them to have very rich thoughts. They *were* grownups, after all."

I happen to know some very good and loving grownups, Violet signed.

Nicholas rolled his eyes. "Parents don't count."

And he turned away before she could make a reply.

Sleight of Hand

The next two days were maddening. Constant rain and no chance for a meeting at Giant's Head, nor any opportunities for John and Nicholas to speak in private. Despite the nasty weather, the orphans still had to fetch eggs and milk from the farm and herbs from Mr. Griese's herb garden, and as a result the Manor floors were always muddy or wet, and someone was always pushing a mop around. Someone suggested to Mr. Collum that the phonograph Nicholas had repaired be brought upstairs so that the children might listen to music and have a dance, but he refused on the grounds that the children were being too noisy as it was. And on the second day, John showed up at breakfast with a fat lip.

"What happened to you?" Nicholas asked, though he felt sure he knew the answer and glanced instinctively toward the other table, where the Spiders sat. Sure enough, they all looked especially pleased with themselves.

"I let my guard down," John muttered, staring miserably at his oatmeal. "When Mr. Collum stepped out of the dormitory for a minute, Iggy and Breaker jumped me. They grabbed my arms, and before I could fight back, Moray socked me in the face. Then they ran back to their cots just as Mr. Collum was coming back in. He didn't see a thing. And of course none of the other boys would dare rat on the Spiders."

"But they can't get away with that!"

"They already did, Nick. If I told on them, Mr. Collum would probably believe me, but he couldn't punish them—there's no proof that they did it. It's my word against theirs. Anyway, I need to remember to take care of myself. I just hope Miss Candace doesn't notice."

Nicholas fumed, but when he started to complain further, John asked him to drop it. He said he didn't want to talk about it—or anything else, for that matter. He was in a foul mood and just wanted to be left alone. And so Nicholas fell silent. Although as usual the two of them stuck together as much as possible—for company's sake, as well as protection—they spoke very little.

The rain let up the following evening. The air outside smelled fresh and fertile, and the clearing sky was a vast

palette of blues and greens, with a lovely, glowing streak of
orange at the horizon. Nicholas, dispatched by Mr. Griese to
fetch parsley from his herb garden, was soaking it all in with
a wonderful feeling of gratitude. He was excited about the
prospect of another meeting at Giant's Head that night. But
he was also taken in by the sheer beauty of the evening.
Knowing that the Spiders had been assigned to help Miss
Candace with some task in the West Wing, he allowed himself to dawdle.

He plucked some rosemary and sniffed it. Nicholas liked
rosemary, but he preferred the sweetness of thyme. He was
just crossing the garden to pluck some, when he noticed that
the wooden cover was off the well. Someone had unlocked it
and slid it aside. That was odd, he thought, certainly odd
enough to investigate, for it was not like Mr. Pileus to leave
such a danger unattended.

Nicholas was halfway to the well when he heard a clatter
of stone echo up from inside, followed by a splash, a scrab-
bling sound, and a faint, unmistakably human muttering.
Someone's fallen in! he thought, breaking into a run. How long
had the person been down there? But upon reaching the well
Nicholas saw, just below the rim, the top rungs of a ladder set
into the stone. And when he peered down into the darkness,
he saw none other than Mr. Collum, clinging to the lowest
ladder rungs, his feet submerged in water, the thin metal
handle of a lamp clenched between his teeth.

Nicholas was surprised enough to cry out, and Mr. Collum, startled, looked up at him with guilty—then suddenly
furious—eyes.

"I'm inspecting the well!" the director roared, in the process accidentally releasing the handle of the lamp, which splashed into the water and went out with a hiss.

The roaring increased now, issuing up from nearly perfect blackness, and Mr. Collum ordered him to bring another lamp straightaway. Nicholas turned and dashed into the Manor. Soon Mr. Griese would be barking at him for taking so long to bring the parsley, and before that Mr. Collum would berate him for approaching the open well without permission. But at the moment all Nicholas could think was this: *He's searching outside now! He's catching up! He's catching up!*

꒰‧꒱

That night, John was waiting for Nicholas behind the oak tree, and for the first time in ages, he smiled. "For crying out loud, Nick, I've been waiting here a whole minute. What kept you? Where are my boots? This grass is really wet."

Nicholas took the boots from his flour-sack backpack, along with a clean rag. "Here, you can dry your feet first with this."

John looked with amusement at Nicholas's own feet, which were wrapped in cloths like bandages. "I like your new shoes."

"Just trying to keep my old shoes dry. They're all I've got."

"Couldn't you conjure yourself another pair?"

"Sure, but I'm fond of these."

John snickered. He seemed to be in such a good mood, in fact, that Nicholas decided not to tell him why he was late. The truth was that he had sneaked into Mr. Collum's office with a glass of water to see if there were any new scribblings in the ledger. And sure enough there were, written in Mr. Collum's minuscule print, on one of the blank pages in the back:

Discomfiting cold + out of her way = not in the Manor proper? Consider: The well? The gazebo? The schoolhouse? The farm? Elsewhere on the property?

A line had been drawn through "the well," crossing it off the list.

Nicholas had closed the ledger with sweaty, sticky fingers and put it away. How long did he and his friends have before Mr. Collum had searched all the other places on his list and started to look *elsewhere on the property?*

The thought had been disturbing enough to send him back up to his room, where he sat on his cot and gazed at the plaid pattern of his blanket until he felt reasonably calm again. Afterward, he had come outside with the idea of telling John and Violet what he had learned. But now he realized there was no point in worrying them, no point in spoiling the fun.

It *was* fun, after all. John was in high spirits, and Nicholas's own mood was rapidly improving. Why not? The rain was behind them, they were out in the fresh open air, and they were back on the track of treasure.

The boys climbed the hill in eager anticipation, and to their delight they found that Violet had arrived ahead of them. Already she had set out scrambled-egg sandwiches and a large baked potato, which she had divided into portions. At once the three of them fell to talking and eating, all with a distinct feeling of celebration, as if they had been reunited after a much longer separation than three days. And when at last they had eaten every crumb, and Violet had folded up her blanket and put it away, they got down to business.

"Be warned," Nicholas said, "I don't think we can really trust what Mr. Rothschild says about his wife. He makes her sound like someone from a book—charming, intelligent, generous, and so on and so forth. I know, I know," he said, holding up a hand when the others began to protest. "I'm sure it must be different with parents, or *some* parents, anyway. But I never knew mine, and personally I've never met any grownups who were truly generous and kind to people outside their own family."

"But what about Violet?" John asked.

But what about John? Violet signed at the same time.

With a laugh, Nicholas translated, and John and Violet looked at each other and grinned.

"Do you mean to suggest that you two will turn out differently?" Nicholas pretended to look doubtful. "I suppose it's possible," he grudgingly admitted. "But I think it's more likely that you'll lose all your decent qualities as you get older. I think it's a natural process, like getting wrinkles and gray hair."

Violet and John expressed their indignation, but Nicholas only laughed his curious laugh—with its high-pitched rattling, like a broken mechanical toy—and steered the conversation back on course.

"Let's just consider Diana Rothschild," he said in a conciliatory tone. "Her husband goes on and on about her fine and selfless qualities. But at the same time, she loves her treasure, doesn't she? She likes to 'luxuriate' in it like a dragon, as Mr.

Rothschild says himself. Which to me makes her seem cold and greedy."

"Me, too, actually," said John, and Violet nodded.

"Right, so my point is just that figuring out her character could be tricky. The same goes for Mr. Rothschild."

Why don't we start with simple facts? Violet signed.

"Sure," Nicholas said, "and the facts are simple enough, because there aren't very many. An awful lot of the diary is devoted to—well, to Mr. Rothschild's being *so devoted*. He likes the way the light shines on her glossy hair and all that kind of rubbish. And he's always buying her expensive yarn for her knitting, or fetching her a book, or bringing her coffee with milk."

"So we know she knits," John said. "And reads. And likes coffee with milk."

"Oh yes, she loves those things. She's always knitting or reading. And apparently she was a marvelous conversationalist; at least she was with him. He seemed to believe she knew a lot about everything because she read so much and remembered everything she read—"

Like you, Violet signed.

John laughed. "I was going to say the same thing! She does sound like you, Nick."

"I suppose," Nicholas said with a shrug. "But I'm not so shy. Mrs. Rothschild didn't like speaking with anyone she didn't already know well. She didn't like being the center of attention, not even with Mr. Rothschild, really. There's one entry...Here, let me quote something for you."

Violet and John leaned forward in attitudes of close attention.

"'What a terrible mistake I made this morning!'" Nicholas recited. "'After the Carson wedding in Stonetown, which we could not decently avoid attending, there was of course much mention of Di in the society pages, as there always is whenever she makes her rare appearances. What an effect she has, what a splash she makes! I am always, of course, immensely proud of her and tremendously amused by these gossipy writings, which I always cut from the newspaper and put away—until this morning. For this morning, alas, I foolishly told Di of my little stash, and her intense embarrassment, modesty, and feelings of privacy compelled her to insist that I burn it at once!

"'I meekly bowed to her demands, tearing up and discarding most of the clippings as she watched from her reading chair by the window. However, I am ashamed to admit that because I could not bear to lose those few clippings that included photographs of her (so rare to come by!), I employed sleight of hand to save them. They are now hidden away in a place I know she will never look.'"

John threw out his hands. "Hang on! That sounds like a clue!"

Maybe he hid other things with those clippings, Violet signed excitedly. *A hiding place could be used for anything, after all.*

"I know what you're thinking," Nicholas said. "He might have hidden the torn-out diary pages in the same place. I've considered that. But it's awfully hard to narrow down a clue like that. There must be millions of places where Mrs. Rothschild would never look, right? It could be anywhere, so where would we start?"

John sighed. "I see what you mean. I suppose we could

eliminate where she *would* look, but that doesn't help much. We can rule out her knitting basket and her reading chair, and that's about it."

Is there nothing else to go on? Violet signed. *Was Mrs. Rothschild afraid of spiders, for instance? That might keep her out of the basement.*

"I don't know about spiders," Nicholas said, "but she *was* afraid of heights. Mr. Rothschild mentions it early on, when he says that some organization tried to entice her to attend a social event by pointing out that there would be a hot-air balloon and that she could go up in it if she liked. He said she shuddered when she read the letter, and they had a good laugh about it, because the only thing she feared worse than crowds was heights."

That seems significant, Violet signed, frowning. *Wouldn't that rule out the observatory as a hiding place for the treasure chamber? She wouldn't come up here if she was afraid of heights, would she?*

Nicholas shrugged. "She might. Acrophobia—fear of heights—has varying degrees of severity. Anyway, there's no sort of view of anything except sky up here. It doesn't really *feel* high, if you see what I mean. I doubt you would ever find her on the roof, and she would never set foot out on your bluff, but this is solid ground. I think it's probably different."

"Still," John put in, "her phobia might have had some bearing on where Mr. Rothschild hid those clippings. Nick and I should start thinking about high places around the Manor that would make good hiding spots. It's worth considering, isn't it?"

Nicholas agreed that it was. He had considered it already,

in fact, from dozens of different angles. But he knew that talking about things was different from thinking about them privately—already the clue felt new to him, instead of old and pointless—and he was willing to be hopeful.

I can't help you with that, Violet signed. *Can you tell me anything else about the Rothschilds?*

"Not much," Nicholas admitted. "You know as much about Mrs. Rothschild as I do now. And Mr. Rothschild almost never talks about himself. Let's see, what do I know about him? Well, he has a goofy sense of humor. He tends to call people by nicknames. Toasty and Stubby and Beanie and so on. Toasty's the cook, and Beanie's his accountant. I'm not sure who Stubby was, but I know he worked at the Manor, because Mr. Rothschild says at one point that seeing Stubby work so hard made him tired."

"So maybe Mr. Rothschild is lazy," John suggested. "In which case he probably wouldn't have hidden the clippings in a place it would be hard for him to get to."

Nicholas tapped his nose and pointed at John. "That's a good point! You know how he solved his problem about watching Stubby work so hard? He said he turned his desk to face the wall."

He does have a sense of humor, Violet signed, smiling. *But it is his desk, after all, and not an easy chair. So it seems that he is working himself.*

Once again Nicholas tapped his nose, this time pointing at Violet. "Another good point! So maybe he isn't lazy—he just doesn't like watching other people work too hard. Like you and your father, Violet."

I don't like to see my father working so hard because I care about him, Violet signed. *Do you think Mr. Rothschild really cared about Stubby? Were they friends?*

Nicholas considered this. "I don't think so. Or not exactly. He did seem to respect Stubby, because at one point he mentions Stubby saying he would like more privacy, and Mr. Rothschild says that he intends to see what he can do about it. He says, 'If Di cherishes her privacy so much, I can hardly argue with Stubby's desire for the same.'"

"Sounds like Stubby might actually have *lived* at the Manor," John said. "Was he the butler, do you think?"

"Possibly. He worked hard, and he wanted more privacy. That's all I know. And I think we've covered everything I know about Mr. Rothschild, too. He made a big deal about his wife, he liked to joke around, and, of course"—Nicholas swept his arms around to indicate the observatory—"he was an amateur astronomer who could afford to build a place like this and put a fabulous telescope in it."

Violet looked wistfully up through the opening in the roof. *I wish I could have looked through that telescope,* she signed. *I'll bet the stars were glorious.*

"When we find that treasure," Nicholas said, "you can buy one for yourself."

In the library the following day, Nicholas stared longingly at a book about extrasensory perception. It was a book he had spied long ago, a book he would very much like to read, but it sat on the highest shelf—so high he could barely make out the gold-lettered title on its spine—and there was no way to reach it without moving the ladder. Once again he thought about how to get to the book. The stepladder the girls had used to clean the chandelier was kept in a closet in the ball-room, which made it impossible to obtain. Perhaps John might help him move some of the library furniture during the night—but no, none of it was anywhere near tall enough. Climb the shelves? Very dangerous. For a decent foothold, he would need to remove the books all the way up, a laborious and tricky process in itself. And then, of course, he would have to replace them all again. It would take hours.

Nicholas scowled at the shelves. How frustrating to be so near something he desired, and yet prevented at every turn simply because…Nicholas blinked. He found himself staring at the ladder as if he had never seen anything like it before.

"I'm sure I thought of it because we talked about it!" Nicholas said at Giant's Head that night. "I'll bet it was in the back of my mind all along, but talking about it with you two pushed it to the front. In fact, that was why I was thinking about that book again—I was thinking about the way the brain works, how solutions seem to pop out of nowhere sometimes, depending on any number of factors we may or may not even be thinking about or aware of—"

"Fine, Nick," John said, gesturing for Nicholas to calm down. "That's fine, it really is. I know you love thinking about that stuff, but really, the important thing right now is—"

"But wait!" Nicholas cried. "Do you see? Maybe the reason I was thinking about that book was because it's on the highest shelf! Which suggests that one part of my mind wanted me to look up there, even though the rest of my mind didn't know exactly why, and *that* part of my mind assumed it must be because of the book, which is all about thinking and perception in the first place! So it's like a circle—"

Violet was waving at him to be silent. *It's fascinating, but please, tell us what you're talking about. You said you think you know where the hiding place is? Where is this highest shelf you mentioned?*

"You're talking about the library!" cried John, catching up to Nicholas's meaning at last. The younger boy had been speaking so quickly and excitedly—speaking as much to himself as to either of his friends—that it had been hard to follow him until then. "If Mrs. Rothschild was afraid of heights—"

"Exactly! She would never climb that ladder! That's why Mr. Rothschild sometimes had to fetch a book for her—because it was on one of the higher shelves!"

He could easily have hidden newspaper clippings inside a book, Violet signed. *Most likely one she would never ask him to take down. Otherwise, he might have to sneak the clippings out of it and hide them again.*

"I think we're onto something," John said. "This is definitely worth a shot. Were you able to read all the titles on the top shelves, Nick? Are there any obvious candidates?"

Nicholas nodded. "I had to squint, but I could read them all. I think I've narrowed it down to the most likely candidate. Let's see what you think." He rattled off a long list of titles—there were dozens of them—then stopped, paused, and with a huge grin announced the final title: *Clippings*.

"You're joking!" John exclaimed.

Violet shook her head in disbelief. *There is that sense of humor again. Or maybe he meant it to be like "The Purloined*

Letter." Do you know that story? Nobody finds a stolen letter because it's hidden in plain sight.

"The difference here," Nicholas said, "is that Mrs. Rothschild wouldn't have been looking for the clippings, because she thought they'd been destroyed. My guess is that Mr. Rothschild chose a book with a title that pleased him—either because he thought it was funny or because it would be easy for him to remember—and then put it up on the highest shelf, where she would never look for it. Who knows? She might not even have been able to read the titles up there. It was hard enough for me, and I have good eyesight."

"Does the diary ever mention her wearing spectacles?" John asked.

"No, but that doesn't mean she didn't need them. And even with spectacles she might have had trouble seeing that top shelf."

Why didn't you take the book down? Violet signed. *Was someone watching you?*

Nicholas and John explained about the ladder. Violet suggested that she could bring a large stepladder from her barn, and the boys could sneak it into the Manor.

"Thanks, but I think it's too risky," Nicholas said. "If we get caught—well, it will be hard to claim that I was sleepwalking if I'm carrying a ladder from your farm. Besides—and even worse—it would surely tip off Mr. Collum. You know he'd wonder what was so important that I'd go to such trouble and take such a risk. If he finds out that I can get out of my room, he might actually figure out what we're up to."

The three of them talked for some time about different ways of reaching the book, but no one suggested anything feasible. Nicholas, for his part, had something in mind, but he didn't want to suggest it. He kept hoping that together they might come up with a better solution. No one did, however, and eventually they lapsed into thoughtful silence.

After a while Nicholas saw John brighten, open his mouth to speak, and then instantly close it again, looking much disturbed. For a long time he sat staring at the lantern, his face growing increasingly glum. Then, without looking up, he muttered, "I'll do it, Nick. I can tell you don't want to ask me. But something has occurred to me, and if it's occurred to me, then I'm sure it's already occurred to you. I'll do it."

What is he talking about? Violet signed to Nicholas.

"A distraction," Nicholas said, exchanging grave looks with John. "And a sacrifice."

They wasted no time. Having bidden farewell to Violet until the next clear night, the boys hurried back to the Manor. They did not part ways in the park as usual. Instead, Nicholas accompanied John all the way to the back door, where John handed Nicholas the boots, dried his feet with the rag, and prepared to slip inside. They had already made the arrangements: John would start screaming in exactly ten minutes.

"One...two...three...," Nicholas whispered, establishing the rhythm.

"Four...five...six...," John whispered at the same pace.

They shook hands, and—his lips moving soundlessly as he continued to count—John tiptoed inside.

Nicholas hastened to the side door and up the servants' stairs to his room, avoiding every creaking board without needing to think about it. He had memorized them all long ago. Quickly he stashed his things and changed into his pajamas. *Do not go to sleep*, he ordered himself, for he was beginning to feel very sleepy indeed, despite his hammering heart. *Do. Not. Go. To. Sleep.*

When Nicholas entered the library, his face still damp from the cold water he had splashed on it, eight minutes had passed. He stuffed his blanket into the crack beneath the door, lit the candle stub he'd brought, and held it aloft. There was the book. Top shelf, far right corner. He went to the ladder, gauged how far he would have to pull it along its squealing tracks. Not far. Six feet or so. He should be able to do it quickly, and John had agreed to scream as long as he could without raising suspicion—ten or fifteen seconds, probably. By then Mr. Griese, who was on duty tonight, would surely be shaking him like a maraca, and John would have to pretend to wake up.

Nine minutes.

Nicholas was about to turn from the shelves and put down his candle when he noticed, on the shelf just beneath *Clippings*, a book titled *The Secrets of Marriage*. Every nerve in his body jolted, as if he'd been shocked. What if *that* book was the one? For that matter—Nicholas was pacing now, holding the candle up, reading the titles of the books on the second-highest shelf—what if it was yet another book, a book at the opposite end of the library?

"No, no, no," Nicholas whispered as he read not one, not two, but three different titles that might have been good clues. How had he been so blind? Weren't *any* of the higher shelves possible hiding places? Any shelf that required the ladder to reach? That book on extrasensory perception had drawn his eye to the top shelf, and so it was the top shelf alone that Nicholas had been focused on. And when he'd spied that title, *Clippings*, so perfectly placed in the top corner—well, that had settled it for him. In his excitement, he had turned right away to planning how to get it.

He had thirty seconds to make a decision, assuming John had continued counting at the same pace. Desperately he thought, *Slow down! I need more time, John!* But he had no hope that John would hear his mental plea. He had to figure this out, and he had to do it now, or John was going to suffer for nothing.

Nicholas decided there was no time to consider anything but the top two shelves. Besides *Clippings* and *The Secrets of Marriage*, the other suspicious titles on those shelves were *What Modesty Requires*, *The Hidden Word*, and *Legerdemain* (a word that meant "sleight of hand," which was the way Mr. Rothschild had described sneaking the clippings out of his wife's sight). *The Hidden Word* and *Legerdemain* were very near to each other, in a small section of books about puzzles, codes, magic, and that sort of thing. He couldn't say for sure about Mrs. Rothschild, but Nicholas found such topics fascinating. Perhaps Mr. Rothschild would have thought those books too tempting—his wife might want to read them.

Twenty seconds.

What Modesty Requires was a different matter. If Mrs. Rothschild truly was as shy and modest as Mr. Rothschild claimed, would she not be embarrassed to be seen reading a book about modesty? Especially if she had to ask her husband to bring it to her? It might depend on what kind of book it was, Nicholas thought. It was in a section of...

He blinked. *What Modesty Requires* was surrounded by books about geography. It was clearly out of place! Had Mr. Rothschild put it there on purpose? Had he chosen a book he doubted his wife would ask to read—a book whose title reminded him of its secret contents—and hidden it among other books in which she had no interest? Did Mrs. Rothschild like geography? There was no mention of any such thing in the diary.

Ten seconds. He couldn't think about it any longer. He had to make a choice.

Nicholas set the candle on the floor and grabbed the ladder, ready to move it. He thought, *She was an avid reader, very curious. John and Violet thought she was like me—and I'm interested in everything. Everything. And I notice when books are out of place.*

He looked up into the top corner. It was hard to see. Was it possible, after all, that his first suspicion had been correct? Was it possible that something in his mind—something of which he was not even aware—*knew* which book was the correct one? Might it have known the answer all along?

"I don't know," Nicholas whispered despondently. "I don't know, I don't know!"

And then the screaming began.

SACRIFICES

When John appeared at breakfast the next morning in the dunce cap, he looked so ridiculous that Nicholas felt a fleeting—a very fleeting—impulse to tease him. But though John was doing his best to look defiant, or at least unaffected, it was clear he was miserable. And because all eyes and ears were upon him—the Spiders had already passed the word to watch for crying, or even sniffling, because they wanted to jeer if it happened—he and Nicholas were unable to talk at all. As soon as he sat down, though, Nicholas gave him a significant look, and John managed a weak smile and nodded.

"Hey, Spotty!" Iggy called out. "Spotty the Clown! Did you have a scary, scary dream last night? Did you cry and cry?"

Titters and snorts erupted all over the room, and John's smile faded and did not return, not even when Miss Candace sent Iggy away without his breakfast. He ate his own breakfast in silence, without interest.

So the day went for John. Set apart as usual, but even more than usual an object of scorn. Every time anyone laughed, he assumed they were laughing about him. When, during free time, he was sent to the farm to churn butter, an extra chore that not even John enjoyed, Nicholas knew he must feel relieved. At least at the farm no one was making fun of him.

Nicholas, for his part, was definitely relieved about something: Not a single person had noticed that the ladder had been moved. Nobody mentioned it or even gave it a second glance.

The mission had taken its toll, but it had been a success.

That night Nicholas waited in vain for John to show up. Perhaps the day had been too wearing on him and he'd fallen asleep. Whatever the reason, Nicholas thought, it was a shame. After such a hideous and lonely day, John surely could have used some time with his friends at Giant's Head, and it would have done him good to see the rewards of his sacrifice—to say nothing of how excited Nicholas was to share the information he'd uncovered. Instead, Nicholas spent half an hour pacing under the towering old oak trees, thinking, *I'm in the park marking time in the dark starting rhymes as a lark*, before finally marching up the hill alone.

In the observatory he had to wait still more, for Violet did not arrive for some time, and when she did, Nicholas saw at once that the news he was so eager to break would have to be delayed even longer.

Even in the wan light of the lantern, Violet's eyes were obviously puffy and red. She had been crying, she admitted (when Nicholas inquired), because her parents had sat up late in the kitchen, privately discussing how to tell her the truth about their limited savings. Usually they went to bed much earlier, she said, her father being so exhausted from his day's work; and Violet, noticing a lamp was still lit downstairs, had crept to the top of the stairs and peered down. She could see her mother in the kitchen, signing, and in this way she was able to make out much of their conversation. Her parents didn't realize, she said, that she already knew art school was out of the question. The last time they had discussed the matter was the year before, when Violet's first chance to apply for admission had passed.

At the time, Violet signed, *we were all so upset about my brother, art school seemed the least of my concerns. I told them then not to worry about me, that I would hold out hope for this year and that maybe a miracle would happen in the meantime. They assumed I meant the mining company might still come through for us somehow, and I suppose I did, though I didn't truly believe it. Now that the contract is about to expire, they expect me to ask about it. They so dread breaking my heart.*

"That's why you got upset?" Nicholas asked. "Because they're so worried about you?"

Of course. Tomorrow I intend to tell them that I don't care to go to art school anymore. I can't bear how sad it makes them to disappoint me. And who knows? Maybe a miracle will happen, after all. Just not the one anyone expected.

"If you mean the treasure," Nicholas said, no longer able to resist talking about it, "we're one step closer to your miracle!" With an impish grin, he withdrew a handful of papers from his flour-sack backpack and waved them with a flourish. "I got the clippings! And I found a clue! No missing diary pages, unfortunately, but still, we have something new to go on!"

Violet brightened at this news, her face taking on its familiar radiance, and she grew very intent as Nicholas told her all about the night before, how he had been forced to make a last-second decision with so little to go on, how in the end he had stuck with the original plan.

"I also snagged *The Secrets of Marriage*," he said, "since it was in easy reach, too. But it turned out to be an awfully dull set of rules about working hard to accommodate each other, being respectful, and so on, and of course it contained no real secrets at all. *Clippings*, on the other hand, was the jackpot! It was a collection of barbershop stories, by the way—meant to be amusing but actually quite dreary. If you ask me, I'll bet Mrs. Rothschild had already read it and found it just as dreary as I do, and Mr. Rothschild knew she would never want to read it again."

As he spoke Nicholas was laying out the clippings on the floor for Violet to read, and she was rapidly and somewhat anxiously glancing back and forth between his lips and the clippings. Nicholas quit chattering and let her devote her attention to the papers, which naturally she was eager to read for herself. There were seven in all, five of them being gossip columns, one being an engagement announcement, and the last being an obituary of Mr. Rodney Rexal, the rich shipping merchant who had been Mrs. Rothschild's father. Violet bent over the engagement announcement for a closer look at the photograph.

She's quite plain, Violet signed. *Her dress is beautiful, but Mrs. Rothschild — or, I suppose, Miss Rexal at that time — is not pretty at all. From what you told me, I had expected her to be lovely.*

"Well, remember," Nicholas said, "Mr. Rothschild's diary might have given you that impression, but we know his opinions can't exactly be trusted."

Violet frowned. She pointed out that some of what Mr. Rothschild had written about his wife had to be true, after all. Had Nicholas not made his decision about which book to fetch based upon what he knew of Mrs. Rothschild from the diary? *You told me you thought she was too intelligent and perceptive not to have noticed that book being in the wrong section. That Mr. Rothschild wouldn't have taken such a chance, and that someone must simply have mis-shelved the book since then. And were you not correct?*

"That's true," Nicholas admitted. "But when I made my decision, I was really just considering Mr. Rothschild's high opinion of his wife — not Mrs. Rothschild herself." He gestured toward the clippings from the gossip columns. "Still, other people did seem to share his opinion of her wit."

Violet returned to her reading. Nicholas, of course, already knew it all by heart: paragraph after paragraph about the charming, the dazzling, the gracious and funny Mrs. Rothschild — always followed by a paragraph of complaint that Mrs. Rothschild, as a rule, chose to keep these entertaining gifts of hers hidden away on Mr. Rothschild's elegant country estate, instead of making regular appearances in Stonetown's high society. The tone was always chiding, even wounded, as if Stonetown's high society was deeply saddened and offended that Mrs. Rothschild did not care very much about it.

The longest of the columns described indignantly how Mrs. Rothschild had "so far attended only a single event" during one lengthy visit to the city—a "literary ladies luncheon, ever since which, citing other 'important obligations,' her elusive ladyship has declined all further invitations!" The column was accompanied by a photograph of Mrs. Rothschild at the luncheon, laughing with another woman, both of them carrying a sizable armload of books. The photograph caption read: "Overbooked!"

Violet had moved on to Mr. Rexal's obituary, then back to the other clippings. *The dates all match up*, she signed. *She got married, her father died soon after, and at least two of these columns mention the fortune she must have inherited.* She looked up at Nicholas. *But where is the clue?*

Nicholas picked up the column about the literary luncheon. "Did you read this one?"

Rather quickly, but yes. Why?

"Well, think carefully about the last paragraph." And without looking at the paper itself, Nicholas began to quote from it: "'Readers of yesterday's column know exactly where and with whom Mrs. Rothschild has spent her days thus far, and how dull and dry these days must have passed for the lady! Could it be that Mr. Rothschild insists that his wife accompany him to such business meetings, to such horrid appointments with agents and accountants and others of their ilk, because he is jealous of her company? If so, for shame, Mr. Rothschild! Allow the lady livelier days! Meanwhile, curious readers may rest assured that tomorrow's column shall be a continuing chronicle of her lady Rothschild's oh-so-important obligations!' "

Wait, Violet signed, rummaging among the other clippings. *But these are all from other months, even other years! Not one of them is from that week!*

Nicholas tapped his nose and pointed at her. "Exactly! There should be at least two other columns from that week talking about where Mrs. Rothschild was spending her time. She was being elusive, this one says, and spending all her time with Mr. Rothschild at meetings. What if they were making private arrangements to purchase the treasure? The timing is right—it's the same year as that obituary—and Stonetown is the perfect place to arrange for shipments of valuable goods, clandestine or otherwise. It's the biggest city in the region and has the biggest port!"

Violet looked excited. *So if we knew more about what the Rothschilds were doing that week, we might have a clue about the treasure.*

"The business districts they visited," Nicholas said, ticking off on his fingers, "the names of the agents they met with, whether or not they spent time with art dealers, or gold merchants, or purveyors of Oriental rugs—"

Purveyors? Violet signed.

"Another word for suppliers or merchants," Nicholas said rather impatiently. "The point is that if we can figure out what the treasure *is*, we might be able to narrow down where it's *hidden*. Or, even better," he added with a gleam in his eye, "if we can learn who Mr. Rothschild hired to construct this observatory, we might be able to find out if there really is a secret to the cranks!"

Do you really think so? It was a long time ago.

"If it's a family business," Nicholas said, "there might be a child or even a grandchild who knows the secret. Honestly, if you were an architect or builder, and you were asked to install a secret mechanism in an amateur observatory—and maybe some sort of secret panel leading to a secret room—don't you think you would pass on that little tidbit to your children, and they to theirs? It's a great story, after all."

This is really exciting, Violet signed, and her shining face confirmed her words. *But where do you think we can find out these things? The other clippings must have been among those Mr. Rothschild burned. Do you think someone else saved them?*

"Not necessarily a person," Nicholas said grinning, "but a place."

A library!

"Yes. Stonetown Library, to be specific. I've read that it has a repository of newspapers from all over the country. You can bet it has all the old Stonetown papers. I just need an excuse to go there. Once I learn the names of the people the Rothschilds met with that week, I can track down information about them. I can find out all sorts of things."

How in the world would you manage that? Violet wondered. *Do you think Mr. Collum would let you go?*

"Not yet," Nicholas confessed. "But I can be very persuasive. I'll find a way."

I can't believe it. This is really happening! We're really making progress!

"I know!" Nicholas said. "I only wish John were here—this would surely cheer him up."

Violet's expression changed abruptly. *What's the matter? What happened?*

Nicholas told her about John's terrible day. Nor did he stop there, but for some reason went on about how miserable John usually was during the days, even when he was not being compelled to wear the dunce cap. He explained that the John whom Violet knew at Giant's Head and the John who lived doggedly and grimly as an outcast at Rothschild's End were two different boys entirely. He said he had rarely seen John smile even before his Spider-induced exile began, and that since then John's smiles were scarcer still.

"You wouldn't believe the difference," Nicholas said emphatically (in the course of his speech, he had grown quite animated), "between that John and the one *you* know. You couldn't! Why—"

And then, abruptly, Nicholas fell silent. As he'd been speaking, Violet's face had grown longer and longer, and the sight of her sad expression had distressed him extremely, yet some strange impulse had propelled him forward, causing him to speak with even greater fervor and emphasis, until at last he'd seen her eyes fill with tears, and Violet had covered her face with her hands and begun to cry. Only then, when there seemed to be no point in continuing to speak, was Nicholas able to shut off his flow of words, and in doing so he was brought to wonder what had motivated him to go on so.

It was possible, he supposed, that he had been trying to make these nighttime meetings at Giant's Head seem as important and special as he could, because he had wanted to make sure that Violet felt exactly as he did. He wanted all of them to feel that way, all three of them, and talking about the positive effect these secret meetings had on John had been one way to heighten that feeling. He had wanted to feel even more intensely the thrill of their unique, secret friendship— but he had been too persuasive, had focused too much on John's misery and too little on these brief, happy respites. And so Violet, who was already in a sensitive emotional state, could take no pleasure in his words at all but had plunged into a profound sadness.

Nicholas was disappointed. He felt sorry for making Violet so sad, and even sorrier that she seemed unable to recover. She eventually stopped crying, but the mood of their meeting had been significantly dampened. They spoke matter-of-factly rather than excitedly about their plans, and Nicholas's few attempts at humor were met with faint, polite smiles. It was not long before Violet said she was exhausted and should go to bed.

Can you make it back all right on your own? she signed as they parted. *What if you fall asleep? Do you need me to walk with you?*

"Oh, of course not!" Nicholas replied carelessly, though the truth was that a new feeling of loneliness in his belly made him wish very much for her company, for someone to walk back with him in the dark. "You're tired, Violet. You go to bed. I'll be fine, I promise."

Violet nodded, and they clasped hands and said goodbye. Nicholas watched her walk across the clearing and into the trees, making no use of the candle and matches she always carried with her. She knew the trail, and these woods, as well as she knew her own room, and she seemed to be afraid of nothing. Perhaps she still felt as though she had nothing to lose, and so had nothing to fear.

"But you do," Nicholas whispered. "We all do."

And though he was not entirely sure what he meant by that, he found that he did not wish to think about it.

The Rothschild Report

The next day, John did not make an appearance at breakfast. Nicholas, straining his ears, heard some of the boys talking about Miss Candace and her infamous medicines, and he felt a rush of alarm. Scarfing down his food, he slipped out of the dining hall and sneaked down the long east passageway to the boys' dormitory. It was a risk, but one he felt he had to take.

The dormitory was empty, and Nicholas was about to go searching for John elsewhere, when he heard a groan from behind a closed door at the other end of the room. The bathroom. Running down the long row of cots, Nicholas came to the door and cried, "John! Is that you in there? Are you all right?"

There was a long pause, and then: "Nick?" The voice was feeble, strained.

"Yes, it's me! Open up!"

The door opened to reveal John, pale and trembling, in his pajamas. Against the pasty whiteness of his face, his chicken pox scars stood out even more pronouncedly than usual. His eyelids seemed to be tinged with blue, and they drooped horribly.

"John! What's the matter? You look terrible!"

"Thanks," John muttered. He smacked his dry lips. "You shouldn't be in here, Nick. The Spiders—"

"Forget the Spiders!" Nicholas cried. "Tell me what's wrong with you!"

John leaned against the doorframe. His legs were wobbly. "Miss Candace made me drink some hideous thing. I don't know. Something called 'distillation of chuck-root.'"

"Chuck-root? But that's an emetic—a very powerful one. Why would she want to make you throw up?"

John shook his head, then groaned. "I need to remember not to shake my head. I have to keep still or it's worse. Anyway, I don't know why it's supposed to help. Miss Candace thought it would, so she forced me to take it. She said she thought I was suffering from a severe case of melancholy and some other things, maybe some kind of worm. I forget what she called it."

Nicholas put his hands to his head. "But that's outrageous! Did she not notice that you were forced to wear a dunce cap all day yesterday? And work extra chores? Of course you were feeling down in the dumps! Who wouldn't be?"

"Beats me," John said. "Now, listen, Nick, thanks for checking on me, but you need to get out of here. I'll be fine eventually, right?"

"What about the Spiders?" Nicholas asked. "What if they come in here?"

"They want nothing to do with me. They don't know that it's the medicine making me throw up. They think I might be contagious. Don't worry. Now go. If I'm better at all, I'll see you tonight." He started to close the door, then opened it again. "And it had better be worth it, Nick. Tell me it's going to be worth it."

Nicholas grinned and threw him a salute. "It's going to be worth it, sir!"

John, rather pathetically, tried to smile, then closed the door.

John still looked terrible when he showed up in the park that night, but at least he showed up. "I'm much better," he said. "Just weak. Let's get moving." And so they moved, though very slowly, with John trudging along behind Nicholas and pausing often to rest.

John's arduous climb was rewarded with a shower of concerned attention from Violet, who made quite a fuss about his sufferings of the day before, even before she'd learned of his sufferings from that same day. She patted his shoulder and asked him questions and in general made a great show of appreciating his sacrifices. To top it all off, she had brought the boys thick slices of chocolate cake, along with plenty of milk, and John had recovered sufficiently from the effects of the chuck-root to enjoy his cake very much. By the third bite he was smiling a little, and once they had shown him the clippings and told him everything they'd discussed the night before, he was grinning from ear to ear.

"One of the staff goes into Stonetown every month or two," John said excitedly. "So you wouldn't have to ask for a special chaperone, which ought to make it easier." He snapped his fingers. "You know what? I'm pretty sure I heard Mr. Collum talking to Mr. Pileus about needing to make a trip soon. They need to find some cheap parts for the Studebaker."

"That's perfect!" Nicholas cried. "I'll just convince Mr. Collum to let me ride along with Mr. Pileus."

"How do you propose to do that, Nick?"

Nicholas widened his eyes and wiggled his fingers in the air. "*Mysteriously*," he said. "That's how."

John snorted and rolled his eyes. He was in a fine mood now. He was still weak, though, and by the time they had thoroughly discussed their plans, he was thoroughly worn out. "I hate to say it, but we should probably go to bed soon. Tomorrow's the first day of school," he reminded Nicholas. "Things are about to change."

It was true. The headmaster, Mr. Cypher, had arrived that morning and had already taken up residence in the comfortable loft over the schoolhouse. Nicholas had seen him talking with the other staff members, laughing outrageously at everything anyone said. Each time, he would take his hat off and slap it against his leg, then put it on again. It was quite a dilapidated hat.

Nicholas had also observed Mr. Collum offer to help Mr.

Cypher "get settled" in the schoolhouse—then proceed to spend an entire hour inside the building on the pretext of knocking down cobwebs and shifting furniture while the headmaster puttered about, bemused by this "help" that seemed to accomplish nothing. Nicholas, though, was not bemused in the least. Mr. Collum had been searching for the treasure chamber, which meant he was one step closer to searching *elsewhere on the property*.

Nicholas knew he had better get that trip to Stonetown soon. He had better not fail in his attempt to convince Mr. Collum. He was going to get one chance, and he had better make the most of it.

He just needed to figure out how.

"The headmaster can't teach worth a flip," John was saying, "but he's harmless enough. He's not severe, I mean. He was here last year, too."

"Why doesn't he get a room in the Manor, like the other staff members?"

"He likes the schoolhouse. He says it's nice out there at night."

"Is that so?" Nicholas was surprised. "During the day it's stuffy and hot," he explained to Violet. "Just last Sunday five kids staggered out of the chaplain's service because they couldn't stand the heat anymore. They knew they'd be punished—they just couldn't help themselves."

Very hot, then, Violet signed. She shook her head sympathetically. *Perfect for school.*

"Apparently the breeze shifts at night or something," John said with a shrug. "It gets so pleasant out there, Mr. Cypher hates taking his turn as chaperone in the boys' dormitory.

But of course he has to. The other men insist on it. That way they get more nights in their own rooms, where they sleep better.... But, say, sorry, Violet. This can't be very interesting for you. You don't know any of these people."

Don't be silly, Violet signed, though it was obvious her mind was elsewhere. After a pause she signed, *It is strange for me to think of school, though, and another year starting without me.*

Suddenly Nicholas remembered that Violet had been planning to tell her parents that she no longer wished to go to art school. It must have been a difficult thing to do; her evening must have been very trying, and here he was going on about a stuffy schoolhouse. "How... er, how did it go with your parents, Violet?" He quickly explained to John what Violet had intended to do.

Violet, though she seemed subdued, told them that it had gone well. She said that she'd made the chocolate cake that evening on the pretense of "celebrating a new beginning"— these were the words she had used with her parents. She had insisted that art school may have been the dream of her childhood but that now she intended to find a new dream.

They were confused, Violet signed, *but I could see the relief in their faces. I was very convincing, if I say so myself. I didn't appear the least bit disappointed or sad.* She smiled. *It helped that I have a secret hope.*

"I think it helps all of us, doesn't it?" John said after a silence. "It makes a lot of the bad stuff bearable."

"I don't understand," said Nicholas, looking blank. "What is this secret hope that you two are talking about?"

The others, startled, were both about to reply when they noticed the corners of Nicholas's lips twitching.

You're impossible, Violet signed. *Absolutely impossible.*

"That's it," John said, climbing to his feet. He grabbed Nicholas's arm and hauled him up. "It's back to the loony bin for you."

Nicholas clapped his hands to his cheeks. "Oh! *That* secret hope!"

Too late, Violet signed. *Off you go.*

Violet's secret hope was indeed one they all shared, a hope Nicholas carried with him that Saturday when he stepped into Mr. Collum's office during afternoon free time. Mr. Collum was on library duty—supervising by means of the entranceway mirror, as usual—and so he was aware of Nicholas's approach. Through the mirror Nicholas had watched Mr. Collum's face grow annoyed and had seen him close the ledger (the all-important ledger) and remove his jeweler's loupe.

Nicholas took a deep breath. He wasn't off to the best start.

"Yes, what is it, Nicholas?" Mr. Collum demanded. The impression of the loupe had left a ring of pink skin around his eye. "I'm very busy."

Nicholas ducked his head humbly. "Oh! I know you are, Mr. Collum, and I hate to interrupt you, but I have a very important request. As you know, sir, school started this week—"

"I am perfectly aware of that, Nicholas. I am the director of this orphanage."

"Yes, sir! Which is exactly why you're the person I have to speak with about my project. I need your permission, you see.

Mr. Cypher—I know you're aware of this, of course—Mr. Cypher has announced that everyone my age and older will complete a research project this year, and I have something in mind, but it's rather ambitious."

Mr. Collum sighed heavily and drummed his fingers on the desk. "Get to the point, Nicholas."

"Yes, sir. Well, Mr. Collum, since I arrived here some weeks ago, I've heard all sorts of interesting rumors about the missing inheritance of Mrs. Rothschild—of the Rothschilds for whom the Manor is named, as I'm sure you know—and I'm just fascinated by it. I thought it would be really interesting to learn all I could about the case and make a thorough report about it."

Nicholas could not have missed the change in Mr. Collum's expression, even if he had not been looking for it. From deep impatience to sharp interest—interest tinged with anxiety—in the space of a heartbeat.

"It's such a mystery!" Nicholas hurried on. "Of course, I could never hope to solve it, not when so many others have failed to do so. But wouldn't it be keen to have all the pertinent information about the case gathered together? Like a list of clues, I mean."

"And where," Mr. Collum said slowly, adopting an air of professorial interest, "do you mean to find all this 'pertinent information'?"

"Well," Nicholas said eagerly, "it occurred to me that Stonetown Library keeps all sorts of old newspapers on file. They go back years and years. I thought I might dig around and find every little thing I could...." Nicholas cocked his head to the side. "Have you ever read gossip columns, sir? Or the society pages in general?"

Mr. Collum looked almost stricken at these words, and Nicholas knew at once that Mr. Collum had wondered about those hidden clippings mentioned in Mr. Rothschild's diary—had wondered and yet had never considered their potential significance. "No," Mr. Collum replied coldly, though with a strong hint of uncertainty. "Gossip columns are not the sort of thing to which a man of my position devotes his attention."

"I should say not," Nicholas agreed. "As for myself, though, whenever I come across a newspaper, I always read everything, front to back. The gossip columns are full of interesting details, very particular details, about the comings and goings of important people. I should think any detective worth his salt could find enough information in those pages to solve a dozen mysteries every day, if he cared to."

Nicholas had chosen his words carefully, and they had produced the exact effect intended. Mr. Collum had been listening with marked attention. And now that Nicholas had lapsed into a waiting silence, the director drew back in his chair and gazed thoughtfully at the ceiling for a long time before saying, more to himself than to Nicholas, "Very interesting indeed. Not a boy's work, however. No, I think not." He lowered his eyes until they rested on Nicholas's hopeful face.

"It seems a worthy topic for research, Nicholas, I grant you. But I do not see that it merits a half day's journey into the largest city in the region. You'd have to be accompanied by a chaperone, for one thing, and as you know, we cannot spare the staff."

"Oh, I wouldn't need to make a special trip, Mr. Collum! Couldn't I just go along with one of the staff on the next essential trip?"

Mr. Collum shook his head. A frown was beginning to form. "It makes little sense for me to take you with me, Nicholas. Train fare is costly, even for children."

"So you're planning a trip yourself, Mr. Collum?" Nicholas asked.

The director's frown now took full shape. "My travel plans are none of your business, Nicholas—but yes, I may accompany Mr. Pileus on a forthcoming trip. To attend to matters..."

It was uncharacteristic of Mr. Collum to answer such a question directly, and Nicholas knew that he was torn between competing obligations and newfound hopes. No doubt he had not intended to go to Stonetown on the next trip, but Nicholas's idea had prompted him to consider it.

The critical moment had arrived. It was now or never. Nicholas secretly crossed his fingers and moved into the second phase of his plan.

"I'd be happy to attend to any errands for you, Mr. Collum," he said quickly. "Train fare is less expensive for children, you know. It would save money if I went in your place. And meanwhile I could go to the library—"

Mr. Collum thumped his desk. The prospect of saving money had powerful appeal, and resisting it irked him extremely. "You could scarcely begin your work before you would need to return, Nicholas! It would be a waste of time *and* money. Now let us drop the subject once and for all!"

Nicholas braced himself. "Yes, sir. If you'll forgive me, I

have just one last thing to tell you. Some important information of which you've not yet been made aware."

Mr. Collum had been about to jab his finger at the doorway and order Nicholas to leave. His hand was already up, his finger extended, his mouth open to speak. He hesitated. Then he lowered his hand. "Very well, Nicholas. What is it? Make it snappy."

Nicholas set a large book on the desk. "I just read that book yesterday, Mr. Collum."

Mr. Collum snatched up the book. "A collection of mysteries? What of it?"

"The book itself isn't important, sir. The important thing is that I read it in ten minutes and remember every word. Open the book to any page, Mr. Collum, and I'll prove it to you."

Mr. Collum dropped the book in disgust. "I haven't time for your parlor tricks, Nicholas! How do I know you haven't been studying this book from the moment you arrived at the Manor? For that matter, how do I know you hadn't already memorized this book before you came here? How do I know you aren't up to some sort of mischief? What do you hope to gain by convincing me of such a thing?"

"I only wish to make myself useful," Nicholas said meekly, "just as you encouraged me to do on my first night here. I haven't made many friends—only John Cole, on your recommendation—and would like to spend my time in some meaningful way. It doesn't have to be that book of mysteries, Mr. Collum. Choose any book you like. I'll read it and memorize it right away."

Mr. Collum, now in a highly agitated state, leaped from

his desk and stormed out of the office. He returned with a fat volume of travel tales, which he shoved into Nicholas's hands. "There! Read it if you must! I'll time you!" He took out his pocket watch.

Nicholas grinned. "That won't be necessary, Mr. Collum. I've already read this book. Would you like me to quote from it? Or would you prefer to see me read something? If so, I recommend you select a book from a higher shelf, one that I'm unable to reach. That way you'll be more likely to find a book I haven't read."

Mr. Collum grabbed the book back from Nicholas with a huff, flung it open, and said, "I shall read a sentence, Nicholas. If you can tell me the sentence that follows it, we shall have more to discuss. If you fail, you will leave my office immediately and report to Mrs. Brindle. You will tell her that she is to assign you a week's worth of extra duties as punishment for wasting my time. Do you understand?"

"Yes, sir!" Nicholas cried, and he saluted.

Mr. Collum scowled, turned his eyes to the open book, and read, "'The anxiety of the mariner may take forms as infinite and various as the ocean upon which he travels.'"

Nicholas did not hesitate an instant. "'Superstition and routine,'" he recited, "'gossip and drink, hobby and horseplay—and of course, that most dread manifestation of all: *mutiny*.'"

Mr. Collum was staring at the page. He blinked several times. Then, glancing up at Nicholas, he quickly fanned the pages to arrive at a different passage, whose opening words he read aloud. Nicholas quoted the remainder of the passage word for word.

Without comment, Mr. Collum left the study and returned with a different book, this time one from a higher shelf. He bade Nicholas read it, and Nicholas did. It was a thin volume, scarcely more than a pamphlet, and Nicholas finished reading it in less than three minutes. He handed it to Mr. Collum, who followed along with his eyes as Nicholas quoted from it.

Mr. Collum took a seat at his desk. His lips pursed, he gazed at Nicholas in silence for almost a full minute, during which time Nicholas returned his gaze frankly, and not without pride, but with any hint of insolence carefully absent in his expression. It was critical that Mr. Collum reach the conclusion that he was useful—useful, but not a threat.

At length Mr. Collum, in a slow, deliberate, musing tone, said, "So your Mrs. Ferrier was correct, after all. At least in part. You have an eidetic memory. I once knew a man with a similar gift, a street performer who would ask passersby for the titles of their favorite books, then quote extensively from the books in question. His eyes were a camera, he said, that recorded whole pages in a moment. Clearly, it is the same with you."

Nicholas waited. Mr. Collum was working something out in his own mind, and it would not do to prompt or interrupt him.

"And yet," Mr. Collum continued, "when by chance I had occasion to dine with this man, I discovered, in the course of our conversation, that he had less sense than an intelligent dog. He could not speak meaningfully of anything he had read, though he remembered every word. He had a flimsy understanding of basic principles of science and mathematics.

He could do nothing practical at all, nothing in the least. It was for this reason that he had become a performer—for any real work of intelligence he was entirely unsuited, despite his gift."

Nicholas knew what Mr. Collum was getting at and understood why it was important to him. Mr. Collum did not wish to believe he had been entirely incorrect in his original assumptions about Nicholas. Nor did he care to entrust Nicholas with a task whose deeper purpose Mr. Collum wished to keep secret, a purpose that Nicholas—if he were truly intelligent and clever—might be able to guess. And yet it was obvious that Nicholas could, indeed, be exceedingly useful to him, and in his desperate state, Mr. Collum was eager to convince himself that he might safely take advantage of Nicholas's abilities.

The director had fallen into another considering silence. Presently he nodded. "I am glad you came to me, Nicholas. You may well be of some assistance to me, and I applaud your interest in making yourself useful. I shall have to think on this, however. You have proved to me that you have a gift. What you have not yet shown me is whether you are responsible or mature enough to be allowed to take such a trip. Let us see how you behave in the coming days, while I consider the matter. Perhaps you may go, after all."

"Oh, thank you, Mr. Collum! I won't let you down, sir!"

"We shall see, Nicholas. In the meantime, you are strictly forbidden to discuss this matter with anyone. I cannot have every child in the Manor begging for special trips to the Stonetown Library. Do I make myself clear?"

"Perfectly clear, Mr. Collum! Not a word, not a peep!"

"Very well, Nicholas. You are dismissed."

"Yes, sir!"

"We are not in the Army, Nicholas. There is no need to salute."

"Yes, sir, Mr. Collum!" Nicholas replied, and bowed.

RESTLESS GHOSTS

Almost a week had passed since Nicholas approached Mr.
Collum with his request, a week of rising expectation. Though
he had yet to be granted permission to go to Stonetown, he
felt sure that he would be. Mr. Collum only wished to seem
to have given the matter real thought. He did not like to
think that a boy could march into his office and change his
mind about anything so quickly.

In the meantime, Nicholas, John, and Violet continued to
hold their meetings at Giant's Head. Night after night they
discussed the clippings, after which Nicholas would recount

diary entries (even the seemingly unimportant ones about buying flowers or special yarn for Mrs. Rothschild's knitting) in hopes of some odd detail catching their attention—some suggestion of a combination for the cranks, some previously unnoticed hint about the treasure's location. But Nicholas seemed to have overlooked nothing; no further clues emerged, and more and more their hopes were pinned to Mr. Collum's decision.

At times they grew weary of their futile efforts, and their conversation would turn to less mysterious matters. Their favorite subject was their future life in Stonetown—when Violet would be residing at the art school (which had elegant dormitories) and the boys would live somewhere nearby, so that they could visit easily. But as often as not, they simply talked about whatever occurred to them, and watched the crescent moon fattening into a half moon, and appreciated one another's company.

And yet a change had been taking place in John that prevented him from truly enjoying himself. More and more, the dreariness of his days seemed to follow him up to Giant's Head like a shadow. Less and less did he find himself able to laugh or even smile. When at last Violet expressed concern, John admitted that his outcast status at the Manor was taking a toll on him.

"At first," he said, "it was such a great relief to be with you two at night, the rotten stuff just faded away." He shrugged sadly. It was hardly even a shrug; it was more of a sad twitch. "And it's still good to see you—it's the only good thing, really—but the fading away has stopped. I guess I never realized how hard it would be." John frowned at his own words, and with an apologetic glance at Nicholas, he said, "I'm not saying I regret it, Nick. It was the right thing to do. I just don't think I expected it to last so long."

There was little Nicholas could say to argue with this, little he could do to make it seem better than it was. Their exile certainly had lasted a long time, and it most certainly would continue. It had become a matter of routine. The other children spoke to them only when circumstances required it, and even then the interactions were awkward and unpleasant. Otherwise the boys lived in a strange silence, broken only by the occasional taunt or insult slung at them from one of the Spiders. And, of course, they always had to be on guard against possible attacks.

"You just have to hang in there," Nicholas said, for lack of more encouraging words. "You know things will be better soon."

John grimaced. "But I don't know that, Nick! I don't know anything of the sort. How can I?"

Nicholas was taken aback. "But the treasure—"

"Oh, the treasure, the treasure!" John snapped. "What if we can't find it? We don't have forever, you know! What do you think happens if we don't find it soon? Why do you think Mr. Collum is so desperate to find it himself? There's no money, Nick! He'll have to close the orphanage! Believe me, I've heard him muttering as he goes over the books. There's no way he can keep the orphanage running much longer, not without more money."

Nicholas was stunned by this news and stung by John's harsh tone. He looked at Violet, who seemed equally upset.

I never realized, she signed, her eyes filling with tears. *I've been telling myself that if we didn't find the treasure, at least now I have some friends. But you're telling me that if we don't find it, you'll go. Isn't that what John's saying? Nicholas, you aren't translating. Ask him, please.*

Nicholas, collecting himself, translated what Violet had said.

John was staring at his hands. He looked extremely downcast. "I'm...sorry, Nick. I'm sorry I jumped on you like that. But yes, that's exactly what I'm saying. If the orphanage runs out of money, they'll have to send us to other places, and there's no telling where. We're sure to be split up, though. Mr. Collum has been making visits to other orphanages—that's why he took that weekend trip recently—to look into possible arrangements. It doesn't look good."

Violet wiped at her eyes with the heels of her hands. *It isn't fair*, she signed. *Not when we were so close.*

"Listen," Nicholas said to them, "maybe it doesn't look good, but everything is going to be fine. I promise! I'll be going to Stonetown—you know I will—and I'm going to figure this out if it's the last thing I do. All right? Let's not give up hope yet! We still have time!"

Violet sniffed and nodded. Then she smiled, and it was a small but genuine smile, with much of its usual warmth. *Of course. It's fate, right? We agreed that it was fate.*

"We're going to make our own fate!" Nicholas cried, his voice ringing with determination.

John, shaking his head as if coming awake from a bad dream, reached out and shook Nicholas's hand. In a slightly more upbeat voice he said, "Like I've always said, Nick. You're a fresh one."

Maybe it's just that the timing has to be perfect, Violet signed. *The mining company contract expires a week from Friday. Maybe we're meant to find the treasure on that very day. It would be a way of showing that for every evil thing, there is a good thing.*

"We can show that," Nicholas said with a laugh, "even if we're early."

After this exchange, the friends began to speak of other things. But the truth was, despite his show of bravado, Nicholas felt as if he'd been punched in the gut. He tried, as they talked, to shake the terrible sense of foreboding that John's words had caused in him — tried and failed. And then, as if to give dramatic voice to his uneasiness, thunder began to rumble over the hills.

Quickly they all clasped hands and said goodbye, hurrying back to their beds to beat the storm. As the boys picked their way down the dark path to the Manor, with wind tossing the branches overhead and the woods groaning and rushing all around them, Nicholas found himself wondering if, after this night, things would ever be the same again. He could not say exactly why, but he had an awful premonition that they would not be.

And in this case, as in so many others, Nicholas turned out to be right.

For three days and three nights the rain never stopped or slackened. At its gentlest, it took the form of a hard downpour. At its most fierce, it was a lashing, crashing storm. Once again the Manor passageways were muddied, mopped, and muddied again in a ceaseless, hopeless routine. Once again the orphans grew irritable and restless, the staff snappish and gloomy. Once again Nicholas and John were prevented any sort of private discussion that mattered to them. For Nicholas the only consolation was that the bad weather must surely have been delaying Mr. Collum's search outside the Manor. It was thin comfort, though, and when at last he was summoned to Mr. Collum's office on a Sunday afternoon, he was in such low spirits that he feared the worst.

Mr. Collum's manner instantly encouraged him. There was an air of expectation, as well as a certain craftiness, in the way he greeted Nicholas, both of which Nicholas attributed to the director's hope of taking advantage of him. Sure enough, no sooner had the office door closed than Mr. Collum granted Nicholas permission to accompany Mr. Pileus to Stonetown.

"Oh, thank you, sir!" Nicholas cried.

Mr. Collum held up a warning finger and reminded Nicholas not to discuss the trip with anyone. "If asked," he said sternly, "you may say only that you have an appointment and that you do not wish to elaborate." He also instructed Nicholas to bring the report directly to him before showing it to Mr. Cypher. As orphanage director, Mr. Collum said, he naturally took a special interest in the details of the case.

"Of course, Mr. Collum!" said Nicholas, who had no intention of including any significant details in his report, anyway. Nor would he be keeping quiet about the trip—at least not with his friends. But his tone and expression conveyed the utmost sincerity, and shortly afterward he skipped out of the office on the lightest of feet.

"Tomorrow morning," he told John over supper, as soon as the boys nearest them had left the table.

"Finally," said John, with a look of relief. "That's something, anyway." He shooed a fly away from his plate. "Funny, though, yesterday I felt sure I heard them planning the trip for next week. I wonder why he changed the day."

"He's excited," Nicholas guessed. "He expects me to bring him a thorough report, and the sooner the better, right?"

"Excited or desperate," John said grimly. "I think the hammer's about to fall. After the service this morning, Mr. Collum said he needed me to do some filing. But when I went by his office later, he was on the telephone and sent me away. He said he'd finish the filing himself. He's never done *that* before. Something really serious must be going on."

The dining hall was emptying out, the buzz of conversation dying down. Outside, the storm raged on unabated, making it all but certain there would be no meeting at Giant's Head that night. This would likely be their last chance to speak for some time. John, glancing around, suddenly leaned forward with a very sober, very earnest expression. "Listen, Nick—"

But Nicholas began speaking at the same time. "Can you believe Mr. Cypher gave me two days' worth of schoolwork to do on the train? Sure, I finished it already, but what if I had been someone else? It seems rather severe to assign—"

"Nick!" John interrupted. "I want to talk to you about something serious. I've been thinking. Don't you suppose—?"

Nicholas shook his head. "Not here, John," he muttered. "I think they're listening."

John glanced around again. Mrs. Brindle stood in the kitchen doorway, talking to Mr. Griese, so Nicholas had not been referring to her. The few remaining children in the dining hall avoided his eye. Perhaps they had been trying to hear him, perhaps not. But Nicholas was already pushing back his chair.

"We'll have to talk about it when I get back," he said mysteriously, for he had a strong suspicion about what John wanted to tell him—and an even stronger unwillingness to hear it. "In the meantime, wish me luck."

John rose to shake his hand. "Good luck, Nick. Go save the day."

Nicholas laughed, saluted, and told John that luck would not be required.

⌒∴∾

When Nicholas awoke for the third time in as many hours, he sat up in his cot, took the matchbox from beneath his pillow, and lit a candle with trembling fingers. He braced himself for whatever the light might reveal. Often and often had he believed himself entirely awake, only to be greeted by nightmare hallucinations. This time an empty room confronted him—either that or an unusually dull nightmare. He went to wash his face and returned to sit on his cot. Yes, he was fully awake, but still full of that familiar dread.

Ever since the last meeting at Giant's Head, Nicholas had felt a terrible urgency, and sitting here waiting for morning, he felt it all the more keenly. He had hours to go and nothing to do. An idea crept into his mind, as it had done many times before without finding a comfortable seat. This time Nicholas welcomed it. He got up again, taking his blanket with him, and gathered his alarm clock, his candle, his matches. He was going to explore the rest of the upstairs.

At the candle corner Nicholas paused to light the candle in the sconce, using the flame from the candle he carried. He listened awhile, cautious as ever, before moving on. Cautious and, yes, nervous. The second floor of the Manor, in the middle of the night, was almost as creepy as a nightmare. Shadowy passages stretching away in all directions, wind and rain rattling and ticking against the windows, and doorway after doorway. No wonder he had resisted exploring for so long. He had to admit to himself that one reason he'd decided he needed a plan before searching the Manor—a reason he hadn't set out searching at random—was simple fear. Finding the clues that led him to the observatory had been exciting, but also a relief. They had suggested there was nothing to be found upstairs, anyway.

But that wasn't necessarily true, and on some level Nicholas had known this. It surprised him, and bothered him more than a little, that he was able to trick himself so easily into not thinking about things that he did not care to think about. He had always been good at persuading people—evidently, this included himself.

For an hour Nicholas moved along the passages, poking his head into all the rooms and sometimes entering them. Most were entirely empty. A few contained extremely dusty antique furniture, including a grand piano. The doors to these rooms were locked, and Nicholas had to make use of his key. Really, he thought, it seemed absurd to lock the rooms with furniture in them, however fine the furniture might once have been. Was Mr. Collum afraid that some delinquent orphan would make off with a *piano*?

Not expecting to find anything, Nicholas nonetheless

took a close look at all the furniture he came upon. A canopy bed, nothing beneath it. The piano, nothing inside it but hammers and wires. A grandfather clock, nothing in its cabinet. A few chests and end tables and armoires, all empty. A handsome mahogany desk with empty drawers.

On his way out of the room with the desk in it, Nicholas stopped and looked back. The desk was facing the wall. He glanced around. The far wall contained a built-in bookcase, empty of books. An armchair stood in the corner. With some surprise, Nicholas realized that this room had quite possibly been Mr. Rothschild's study. He had always imagined Mr. Collum's office to have been Mr. Rothschild's — but without good reason; he saw that now. It made more sense for that office in the entranceway to have belonged to some member of the Manor staff, most likely the butler.

Nicholas wondered about that butler. Was he the one Mr. Rothschild called Stubby — the man who had worked so hard that Mr. Rothschild felt compelled to move his desk? Nicholas walked about the study, keeping his eye on the door. He had envisioned another room opposite this one, some sort of workroom or office, which, if the door was open, Mr. Rothschild might have seen from his desk. But no matter where he stood, he could see nothing beyond the doorway except the empty passage.

Nicholas went to the window and drew back the curtain, releasing a shower of dust. He coughed, covered his nose and mouth, and looked out. The window overlooked the park. The schoolhouse — which once had been a stable — was plainly visible among the trees. Had Stubby been a stable groom? Possibly. There was nothing else to see. The woods to the east. The wooded hill to the north, its summit (and the observatory) well out of view. To the west, the stand of hickories that separated the farm from the park. From this vantage point, the rooftop of Mr. Furrow's barn could just be seen behind the hickories, as well as a broad swath of fenced pasture beyond it.

A picture of Mr. Furrow swam up in Nicholas's mind. The gruff old man with his leathery skin, his constant cigar. Not always a lit cigar, either. Often merely the stump of one. The stub.

Stubby.

Nicholas stared at those hickory trees, which were noticeably younger than the park's towering oaks. How old were they, exactly? How long ago had they been planted? Stubby had asked for privacy. Mr. Rothschild had intended to do something about it. He had planted those trees.

Nicholas couldn't believe it. He had imagined Mr. Rothschild's "Stubby" to be a man with very short, stubby legs — a man long since departed from the estate. Hadn't Mrs. Brindle said that all of the original Manor staff had been replaced? Either she had been wrong, or else she did not think of Mr. Furrow, set apart on his farm, as a true member of the orphanage staff.

Nicholas laughed aloud. He couldn't help himself. He was delighted by his discovery — delighted, amused, and excited. So Mr. Furrow had known the Rothschilds! What might he be able to tell about them? What had he seen? All this time, and a personal acquaintance of the Rothschilds had been *right here*. Why —

Nicholas blinked, staggered, and realized — too late — that

his excitement had brought him perilously close to the edge of sleep. He dropped to his knees, fumbled around for the blanket beneath his arm, tried to remember what he had done with his candle. The fact was that he had left it standing on Mr. Rothschild's old desk, but before Nicholas could remember this, a flash of horror, an imagined picture of the curtains going up in flames, finished the job that his excitement had begun, and sent him straight to sleep.

Nicholas awoke to the final, gasping *cling*s and *clang*s of his alarm clock's bell. It fell silent, having fully unwound, even as he opened his eyes and sat up. So it had been ringing and ringing. He was lucky he had brought it with him, lucky it had awakened him. He remembered that he had left it set for half an hour before sunrise. He had wanted to be dressed and ready when Mr. Pileus came up to fetch him. That meant he had been asleep in this room for a few hours. His fatigue had gotten the better of him.

Nicholas rubbed his eyes and yawned. He felt good, even somewhat rested. And even in his sleep, which had been blessedly free of nightmares, he had retained a sense of excitement, of expectation. Nicholas bundled his matchbox and alarm clock into the blanket and got to his feet. It was time to be moving. The candle on Mr. Rothschild's desk was smoky and sputtering, close to guttering out.

Nicholas smiled to himself. *"I enjoy muttering 'sputtering' and 'guttering,'"* he muttered (he made a special point of muttering it) and was wondering whether smoke might accurately be described as *fluttering*—he thought it might—when the candle went out for good, leaving him in darkness.

Nicholas remained calm. His memory and sense of bearings were such that he could find his way back to his room even in total blackness, but he wouldn't have to do that. He had his matches, and the larger candle back at his candle corner was probably still burning; its glow would lead him down the last passage or two.

He was kneeling to unbundle his blanket when he heard a floorboard creak. He froze, listening. Had it been his imagination? No, it had not. The sound had come from somewhere down the passageway, and—much to his alarm—his eyes now confirmed what his ears had suggested: A telltale flicker of candlelight shone in the passage beyond the open door. Shadows moved across the passage walls. Nicholas's good feeling guttered out as completely as his candle had. Should he risk movement, try to hide behind the armchair? Oh, why had he left the study door open? It would be the only open doorway along the entire passage. He knelt there, petrified, his heart galloping.

Then he heard whispers. His hair rose on the back of his neck. He experienced a flash of déjà vu—the eeriness of the scene, the rising sense of dread, was very much like what he had experienced in many a nightmare, and Nicholas found himself almost hoping that this was a hallucination, that he hadn't truly, fully awoken after all.

But it wasn't the Old Hag who appeared in the doorway. It was the Spiders. Smiling a three-headed smile.

Nicholas rose shakily to his feet, searching for a clever word of greeting as the other boys stepped into the room, taking care not to leave open a path to the door. He had not prepared for such a meeting in such a place. "Why, howdy, strangers," he managed. "What brings you to these parts?" He offered a welcoming smile, though inwardly he grimaced, for his greeting had been anything but clever.

"Well, well, well," Moray said, grinning back. And Iggy and Breaker, flanking him, grinned and repeated his words: "Well, well, well. Well, well, well." They were all in their pajamas, which might have made them seem less threatening if their expressions had not been so full of menace. "We came looking for *you*, Fat Nose. We wanted a private word with you. Wanted to give you a special farewell before your special *trip*."

"Yeah, because you're so *special*," sneered Iggy, who was holding the candle. Nicholas recognized it as the one from his candle corner. "And *you* get to go on special—"

"Shut up, Iggy!" Moray snapped, and Iggy shut up. "You've been doing a good job avoiding us, Benedict. We decided we needed to take extra trouble to get you alone. So we stayed awake all night—"

"All night," Breaker growled.

"—waiting for Mr. Collum to go to sleep so we could get this." Moray held up Mr. Collum's skeleton key, dangling on its familiar black ribbon. "He tossed and turned forever, and I was starting to get worried we wouldn't have a chance to visit you, but then the thunder finally stopped, and he went to sleep, and we got our chance, after all."

"But you weren't in your room, Stupid Nose!" Breaker grumbled.

"No, you weren't," Moray said, giving Nicholas a suspicious look. "I wonder how you managed that."

"Oh, you know me, Moray," Nicholas said lightly, wondering if the Spiders had locked his door again. His own key was in his pocket. "I'm full of magic, remember? I knew you were coming, so I took special measures."

"Is that a fact?" Moray said. "If you knew we were coming, why did you make all that racket, then? We were all set to go back down. We thought you and old Pileus must have left early. But then what did we hear?"

"It sounded like an alarm clock," Iggy said. "That's what it sounded like, Moray."

Moray rolled his eyes. "I know what it sounded like, Iggy! I was talking to Dumb Nose here. But I don't see no alarm clock. What *was* that sound, Dumb Nose? Was it your teeth chattering? Did you know we were coming to find you, after all?"

"Yeah, were your teeth chattering because you were so *scared*?" Iggy said with a laugh. "Were you—" He checked himself, feeling the heat of Moray's glare on him.

"Put that candle on that desk," Moray said to Iggy. "Then you and Breaker hold his arms." To Nicholas he said, "Here's how it will be. If you run around or fight back, I'm going to sock you in the face ten times. If you don't, I'm only going to sock you in the face five times. You have my word on that, so now you know where we stand."

Nicholas clutched his blanket firmly against his chest. "Because you're so honorable? Because of your code?"

"Exactly," Moray said as Iggy and Breaker took up their positions. Nicholas stood where he was, hugging his blanket tightly, and the bullies grinned at each other as they clenched his arms with powerful, two-handed grips.

Nicholas's heart raced even faster than before. "I'll report this, you know," he ventured, though he knew that the Spiders must have considered that. "You're going to be in huge trouble."

"Report what?" Moray asked. "You're going to fall out of bed, that's all. A lot. And we're going to lock you back in your room and put Mr. Collum's key back inside his suit coat on the chair, and if you say anything, it'll be your word against ours, and where's your evidence?"

Iggy and Breaker laughed.

"So tell me," Moray said, squaring off to throw his first punch. "Did you see *this* coming?"

"See what?" Nicholas asked, somehow managing to keep the tremble out of his voice. "You mean, that you're going to try to hit me on the left side of my cheek with your right fist? Yes, I saw it, Moray. Really, it wasn't difficult, because you're so predictable."

Iggy and Breaker stopped laughing. Moray's smile faded, then slowly returned as he made up his mind about something. Nicholas watched it happen. And he saw Moray's muscles tense. And when, a split second later, Moray lashed out as hard as he could with his *left* hand, Nicholas was already moving. He had been ready for it.

Breaker and Iggy, however, were not ready at all. They had not had time to consider that Moray, who always socked his victims with his right hand, would hate to prove Nicholas correct and so would switch to the left. Nor had they expected Nicholas to duck, and at the same time to lift his feet from the floor, so that suddenly they were supporting the entire weight of his body, and as a result were pulled off balance—

were pulled toward each other, in fact, and into the path of Moray's wild swing.

Moray, too, was surprised, as his fist glanced off the tip of Iggy's chin before smacking into Breaker's ear. And as all three boys cried out in pain and confusion, Nicholas broke free and ran from the room, pausing only to blow out the candle on the desk.

The darkness would buy him some time, he thought, and so would locking his door. But not much. Already he could hear the Spiders cursing and hurrying after him, following the sound of his footsteps. He ran as softly as he could, and he might have gotten a better lead if he had not stumbled, almost falling and causing enough noise to keep the Spiders on his trail. By memory he made his desperate way through the darkness, turning corner after corner. Right, then right again, then left—and then he was at his door, which, to his relief, the Spiders had left unlocked. He darted inside, locked the door behind him, and considered what to do next.

The Spiders had Mr. Collum's key and a whole lot of fury.

Nicholas had a few seconds and very few options.

He was going to have to make a sacrifice. But he was going to make it worth it.

When the Spiders unlocked Nicholas's door and stormed into the room, they were expecting to fumble around blindly in the dark until they laid hands on him, at which point they intended to wreak a terrible vengeance. They could scarcely contain their rage. Moray was hissing, "Not this time! Not *this* time!" and Iggy and Breaker were almost foaming at the mouth. And so they had no idea what to do with themselves when they perceived the room to be empty.

For empty it clearly was. Three walls were lined with boxes. The fourth, bizarrely, had a square hole in it—a window without glass—and through this hole the weak gray light of dawn shone into the room. Just below the hole an empty cot trembled and jerked like a thing alive. It squeaked and groaned noisily as it moved, and the Spiders all had the fleeting, frightening impression that it was occupied by a restless ghost. Then it sank into their spinning minds that a rope had been tied around one of the cot's legs, and that the other end of the rope had been tossed out the window—and that Nicholas Benedict must be climbing down the rope even as they stood there gawking.

In unison they jumped and ran to the window, climbing onto the cot to look out. Sure enough, Nicholas had just reached the ground below.

"He's getting away!" Iggy shouted, quite forgetting to whisper.

"Let's follow him!" Breaker cried, doing the same.

Moray looked dubiously at the rope. It was made out of strips of old sheets that had been knotted together. "I don't know if this would hold us," he muttered. And then as an afterthought he said, "Must have taken a while to make this. He must've already done it...." And Moray shivered at the possibility that Nicholas Benedict truly *had* foreseen all the events of this morning and had prepared his escape ahead of time.

Meanwhile, in the side yard below, Nicholas was looking up at them, grinning so widely that even in the dim light they could see his teeth. "I left a present for you!" he called up.

"Or at any rate, it's on its way!" And throwing the Spiders a carefree salute, he ran off through the wet grass, disappearing around the corner of the Manor.

"What did he say?" Breaker asked as they stepped down from the cot. "Did he say something about a present?"

Iggy brightened. "Really? An actual present? Why would he have done that?"

Moray shoved him. "Of *course* not an actual present, you dimwit! He probably meant...well, I don't know what he meant. He said it was on its way, didn't he?" He hesitated, considering, then punched his fists together. "Forget it! He was just trying to distract us! He still has to sneak back inside, doesn't he? So let's go find him!"

But even as the Spiders turned to make their hasty exit, they heard the thumping, heavy steps of a man running up the servants' stairs. And not knowing what else to do, they stood there, horrified, as an equally horrified Mr. Pileus burst through the door. He was wearing a knee-length nightgown, and curly strands of red hair poked out from beneath his nightcap. The lamp in his hand burned brightly, illuminating his anxious face from below. He looked quite stricken.

"What on earth?" Mr. Pileus cried, turning this way and that with his lamp. "What are you boys doing in here? Where's Nicholas? He pulled the emergency rope! And what—the window? What happened? My word, what's going on!" These words, taken together, were more than Mr. Pileus had spoken in several days, and as his eyes moved back to the boys, and his expression shifted slowly from fright to outrage, he added to them one final, fateful question: "And you, Moray—what are you hiding behind your back?"

AN UNEXPECTED COMPLICATION

Not one egg! Not one decent egg in weeks!"

The stationmaster was complaining to the train conductor again. They stood on the platform just outside Nicholas's open compartment window.

"The word's gotten out! Every egg thief in the county makes special trips out to my place now! They know what a heavy sleeper I am! They know I don't have a dog!"

"Why not get a dog?" the train conductor asked, checking his watch.

"My wife hates dogs! She's terrified of them! A dog bit her on the bottom when she was a baby or something!"

"Well, get your own chickens, then."

"She hates chickens, too! I think a chicken pecked her on the bottom, too! I told her, I said, 'Why not be afraid of cats instead? Why not snakes? Snakes are terrifying!' But no, it's only dogs and chickens with her! Nothing else scares her! She loves animals! Just not dogs or chickens!"

"Well, there are worse problems to have," said the train conductor.

"For you, maybe! I can't do without my eggs! Eggs are almost all I eat! I haven't even been able to buy them here in Pebbleton! Nancy Ovum used to sell 'em in the market every morning—she had a brisk business, too!—but last month she moved away and took her chickens with her! You know what I think? I think that's why these people have been stealing my eggs! Because they can't buy them from Nancy Ovum anymore!"

"Nice work, Detective," the train conductor said, putting away his watch. "Now I have to go. Good luck with your eggs."

"I don't *have* any eggs!" cried the stationmaster, now red in the face. "This is my point!"

Nicholas smiled as he listened to all this. *Nice work, Detective.* Couldn't those same words be said to him? He hadn't solved his mystery yet, but at least he was still on the trail of clues, which was an achievement in itself. And now the train was whistling, pulling away from the station, and Nicholas was headed for Stonetown. The sun still hung low in the east, yet what a morning it had been already!

Mr. Pileus opened a sack of egg sandwiches that Mr. Griese had prepared for them and handed one to Nicholas. He did not take one for himself but put a hand on his belly and looked nervously out the window.

Happily munching his own sandwich, Nicholas also gazed out the window, watching the farm country slide past as he reflected on his morning's tricky accomplishments. Mere hours ago, he'd had every reason to fear that Mr. Collum would change his mind and forbid him to go on this trip. That papier-mâché window was a serious violation, after all, and Nicholas had been forced to reveal it. But he had handled the situation perfectly by summoning Mr. Pileus. In doing so, he'd proved that he had a good excuse for using that window—he was being attacked!—and had gotten the Spiders punished besides.

True, Mr. Collum had been anything but pleased. "A blatant disregard for property and rules!" he'd said angrily as Nicholas stood trembling before him. "To say nothing of your own safety! Why, when Mr. Pileus found out what you'd done, he had to take a seltzer and lie down! Do you realize that you could have slipped and broken your neck?"

"Oh yes, sir!" Nicholas cried emphatically. "And I didn't want to climb down at all, only when I heard those boys outside my door—they were taunting me, telling me they had your key and were about to come in and knock me around— why, I just panicked! I know I was wrong to have opened up that window again, and I'm really sorry about that. I was just worried about what would happen if I had an emergency and Mr. Pileus wasn't in his room—when he's on duty in the dormitory, for instance—and so I made arrangements for escape, just in case. But I hoped never to use them, and I *hadn't*, either, until this morning."

Mr. Collum listened to this speech, some of which was true and some of which wasn't, with an uncharacteristic degree of patience. He seemed to want to believe Nicholas — and Nicholas thought it likely that he did. Mr. Collum wanted to let him go on this trip. Because he needed the information Nicholas would bring him, and he needed it soon.

"Be that as it may," Mr. Collum said at length, "rules were broken, and for that you must be punished. The other three boys are certainly going to be punished, and punished extremely, for stealing my key and entering your room. As for you —" Mr. Collum cleared his throat. "Well. I agree that these were unusual circumstances, and I do dislike interfering with school projects. Therefore I shall let you accompany Mr. Pileus, and you may serve out your punishment when you return."

"Oh, thank you, Mr. Collum!" Nicholas cried, even though he was slightly dismayed. (He had cherished a small hope that he might avoid punishment altogether.) "Thank you, sir! You won't be disappointed!"

Mr. Collum arched an eyebrow. "I am already disappointed, Nicholas. It is now for you to make amends. Your report had better be thorough and well organized. Dismissed!"

Nicholas had flown from his office before he could change his mind, and out in the entranceway (much to his delight) he had come upon a sleepy Mrs. Brindle informing the dejected and sullen Spiders of the extra chores they must do before breakfast. Already each boy held a mop or broom.

Their eyes popped in disbelief as Nicholas sauntered past them, grinning.

"Good morning, Mrs. Brindle!" he said, tipping an imaginary hat to her. "And a good hard day of work to you, fellows! I'm off on my *special* trip to Stonetown!" And with a wink, he'd skipped upstairs to fetch his suitcase.

Most of the half day's journey to Stonetown followed the same tracks that had carried Nicholas to Pebbleton in the first place. (His previous residence, Littleview Orphanage, had been located in one of Stonetown's suburbs.) The farmland and small towns passing by were all familiar to him, therefore, and yet they seemed remarkably changed. For Nicholas had read so many books in the last weeks, had learned so much about so many things, that he felt as though he were looking out through entirely new eyes.

He recognized, for instance, the different styles of architecture in the buildings, and understood the workings of the tractors and farm equipment in the fields, and knew what sort of crops were being readied for harvest. In fact, Nicholas knew a great deal about almost everything that he saw, and he stared out the window as if spellbound. He felt as if he'd been given X-ray vision, or something rather like X-ray vision yet even greater, for he could see all the hidden details of everything. The effect was quite thrilling.

He spent no time talking to Mr. Pileus, who was furious with him for having behaved so recklessly. (Not that Mr. Pileus would have been talking, anyway.) And so much of the journey passed this way, with Nicholas gazing out at a changed world, while at the same time he gazed inward, thinking over the most significant event of his eventful morning: After he had climbed down from his room, he had headed straight for the farm to have a conversation with Mr. Furrow.

The extremely groggy Mr. Furrow had been surprised to see him, of course, standing in pajamas outside the farmhouse door, upon which Nicholas had been knocking most energetically. Scratching his chest through his long johns, the farmer had squinted down at him and asked if he was lost. Because the man was still so sleepy and was, as usual, speaking around a dead cigar stub, his question sounded like this: "Woss a madder, you loss?" Nicholas knew what Mr. Furrow had meant to say, however, even though it was a silly question, considering that he had seen Nicholas many times by now.

"Oh no, Mr. Furrow—it's me, Nicholas Benedict, the new boy at the Manor. Why, just last week you were showing me how gentle and obedient Rabbit gets after you've shown him a fresh carrot. Does that ring a bell?"

Mr. Furrow shook his head, though only to indicate his bemusement. With some difficulty, he muttered, "Yes. Maybe. I don't care. Why are you here? Why are you standing there in the mud in your bare feet?"

"It's sort of an emergency," Nicholas said quickly, and relying on the fact that he had never seen the farmer speaking with Mr. Collum (or with any of the orphanage staff, for that matter), he went on. "You see, Mr. Furrow, I'm leaving this morning on a trip to Stonetown. I'm working on a very important project about the Rothschilds for Mr. Collum. And I only just discovered that you *knew* the Rothschilds! I wondered what you could tell me about them—anything you say would be useful for my report, and I'd be ever so grateful!"

Mr. Furrow stared at Nicholas for several seconds. Then, with a groan, he sat down in the doorway, rubbing his face with his hands. "Tell me again," he said, "why this is an emergency." He blinked at Nicholas with bloodshot eyes.

"Oh, it's a long story, and I don't want to bore you, but I thought I could make it up to you by doing some extra chores around your house. When I get back from Stonetown, I mean. After I finish my report—the one I'm doing for *Mr. Collum*," Nicholas stressed again, hoping it would make a difference.

"Isn't much to tell," Mr. Furrow mumbled. "Rothschild was a good man, hired me when I was young, kept me up with a good team of mules, Rabbit being the last of which. We didn't talk much. He gave me what I needed and left me alone, which is how I like it, and I kept his larder good and supplied."

"What about Mrs. Rothschild, then?" Nicholas pressed. "I suppose you know about her missing inheritance. Any ideas about that?"

"Not a one," Mr. Furrow said with a frown, "and I don't much care. She didn't need an inheritance any more than a mule needs extra stubbornness. They had more than plenty." He coughed, took the cigar stub from his mouth, and studied it, as if perhaps he could see the past in it. "Nice lady, though. Very generous, always asking me over for dinner. I went once or twice, just to be polite, and they treated me like a prince. But I hate socializing; I just like my animals and my fields, and I think Rothschild understood that. I think he finally got her to quit asking, which I appreciated. Still, she was most kind. Brought me gifts on my birthday, that sort of business."

Nicholas heard all this without much surprise. It made sense for the Rothschilds to treat Mr. Furrow well, contented employees being much more productive and easy to work with than discontented ones.

"Didn't you want to write down some notes or something?" Mr. Furrow asked suspiciously.

"I have an excellent memory," Nicholas said. "You were just saying that Mrs. Rothschild brought you gifts on your birthday."

"Nothing unusual in that," Mr. Furrow grunted. "Never wanted anything for herself, always giving things away. Ask any of the staff, they could tell you. Mr. Rothschild often had to put his foot down, as well he should—else they might've had nothing left for themselves." He turned his cigar stub left and right between his fingers, still examining it thoughtfully. "To tell the truth, I think she was as shy as me. That's what the staff said, anyhow. She didn't like socializing any more than I do. I reckon it might've been hard on her just asking me to dinner. I don't know. Didn't show it, though. Very friendly, funny lady when she was around you. You could just ask the staff."

"You keep saying to ask the staff, Mr. Furrow," Nicholas observed, "but aren't they all gone now?"

Mr. Furrow sighed. "Oh, I suppose they are. Very true. It's just gotten worse and worse over there," he muttered, with a nod in the direction of the Manor. "Stayed pretty good for a while after the Rothschilds died, may they rest in peace.

Still had good staff at the place, and the director was a solid fellow, an old friend of Rothschild's. But after he left and that Mr. Bottoms came, oh, it all went downhill fast. That fellow was about as inclined to work as Rabbit is, and not half so smart."

"So I've heard," Nicholas said, and he cleared his throat. He had another question for Mr. Furrow, one he'd had to work up nerve to ask, as he was somewhat afraid of the answer. "But to get back to the Rothschilds—which of them was the amateur astronomer? Or was it both?"

Mr. Furrow looked up from his cigar stub. "Now, how do you know about that?"

"Oh, various sources," Nicholas said vaguely.

Mr. Furrow shrugged. "Well, it was both. They were both brainy types, both of them interested in everything. Rothschild even had a place built up on that hilltop behind the Manor, one of those little buildings with a telescope in it—"

"An observatory?" Nicholas prompted.

"I think that's what they called it, yes."

"And did they both go up there? I've heard Mrs. Rothschild was afraid of heights."

"If she was, I didn't know anything about it," Mr. Furrow said. He stuck the cigar stub back into his mouth. "And I would have been in bed anytime they used it. You have to use them at night, you know, or you can't see anything."

"I've heard that," Nicholas said. "So you never saw Mrs. Rothschild herself going up that hill?"

"Oh, as for that, I'm sure I did. She loved horses, you know. Never rode them, just liked having them. She used to lead them around all over the place. I never understood why she didn't get up in the saddle. Thought maybe she didn't want to make a spectacle of herself." Mr. Furrow barked a raspy laugh. "Fear of heights, you say? Well, that would explain it, then. Funny to learn something like that after all these years."

Nicholas agreed that it surely was, then prodded Mr. Furrow to tell him what horses had to do with the observatory.

"Only that I'd see her lead the horses up into the hills sometimes. She walked everywhere with them. She'd walk all the way to the river and back."

The morning was getting brighter, and Nicholas knew it was time to return to the Manor. He had already worked out what he would say, and was hopeful that Mr. Collum would still let him go on the trip. He was nervous, though, and ready to see what his fate would be. And his most important question had been answered—Mrs. Rothschild had not been afraid to go up that hill. So the observatory was not ruled out as a possible entrance to the treasure chamber.

All in all, Nicholas believed it had been a productive conversation, and thanking Mr. Furrow, he left the farmer sitting pensively on his own doorstep, reflecting on times long since past.

Nicholas awoke from his third nap of the day to the sounds of hissing steam, booming voices on loudspeakers, and the great, echoing clatter of trains moving in and out of a grand terminal. Mr. Pileus stood silently before him, holding their suitcases. They had arrived at Stonetown's central station.

They disembarked, and together they mounted the stairs to the main exit, shoulder to shoulder with other travelers,

Mr. Pileus with a protective, almost painful grip on Nicholas's arm. They emerged into the incredible bustle and energy of the city, with the blaring of automobile horns, the clanging of streetcars, and hurrying pedestrians everywhere. Mr. Pileus hailed a taxicab, then gritted his teeth and closed his eyes as their driver wove in and out among the street traffic. Every time they came to a sudden stop—which was often—Mr. Pileus (quite unnecessarily) threw out an arm to prevent Nicholas from tumbling to the floorboard.

And on the steps of Stonetown Library, with the taxicab waiting at the curb, Mr. Pileus beseeched Nicholas in a strained voice to do exactly as he had been told. Nicholas was tempted to make a joke by asking Mr. Pileus to repeat the instructions, for what Nicholas had been told was to be waiting on these very steps at exactly six o'clock, to not leave the library premises for even an instant before then, to speak to no strangers (except, insofar as it was necessary, to the librarians), to always hold the handrails when taking stairs, to inform the head librarian of his special condition (Mr. Collum had sent along a note), and in general to exercise good common sense in regard to his safety. These lengthy instructions had left the man so utterly exhausted and breathless that Nicholas had pity on him, resisting the joke and assuring Mr. Pileus that he would follow them to the letter. Then he turned and dashed up the stone steps with such reckless abandon that Mr. Pileus almost fainted.

The library was a massive structure every bit as impressive to Nicholas as the train terminal had been. Towering columns rose up in front of the building, and its front entrance gave onto a glorious main lobby, a huge tiled area with handsome card catalogs ringing it all the way around. The lobby was overlooked by a second-floor gallery, in rather the same manner as the entranceway and gallery at Roth-schild's End, though on a dramatically larger scale, and was lit by a stupendous chandelier. Its marbled walls gleamed invitingly in the strong light. Nicholas was quite stirred at the sight of it all.

As he made his way across the lobby to the front desk, where a number of people stood waiting to check out books, Nicholas passed over a beautiful engraved plaque that had been set into the tiled floor. He read it at a glance, as he read everything, and was already two steps beyond it before he realized the significance of what he had read. Startled, he ran backward, almost tripping, to take another look, hoping he had mistaken the dates on the plaque.

He had not. He read the plaque slowly, carefully, three times, and each time it said the same thing. *Construction of this Free and Public Library of Stonetown, designed by the eminent architects Mason & Mason, funded by the Alexandria Foundation, and open to all citizens of our great republic . . .*

It was at exactly this point each time that Nicholas groaned and shook his head, each time with more intensity. For here the plaque listed the year construction had begun and the year it had been completed—and according to these dates, *the library had not even existed yet* when the Rothschilds had spent their mysterious week in Stonetown. Thus the library's collection would include no newspapers from that time. How could it? There had been no place to keep them, no librarians to collect them! Construction had not even begun until later that year! Nicholas clapped his hands to his head. This whole trip had been for nothing! And those news-papers had been his only lead!

When he noticed a couple of the library patrons giving him curious looks, Nicholas made an effort to calm himself. He had no wish to collapse in the middle of the lobby. Perhaps, he thought, some old newspapers had been donated to the library after it was built. That was possible, wasn't it? Or perhaps the library had obtained older newspapers by some other means. There was only one way to find out, and Nicholas, bracing himself for disappointment, got in line at the desk.

He had not braced himself well enough, unfortunately.

A short while later, Nicholas awoke on the cold tile floor behind the desk. Leaning over him was the librarian who had disappointed him, an ancient woman with wispy white hair. Her skin was so wrinkled, she might have been a thousand years old; she might once have shelved books in the ancient library at Alexandria. In one trembling hand she held the note from Mr. Collum, which Nicholas had been carrying when he collapsed. Luckily she had spied the paper and read it. She had not sent for a doctor, therefore, but had simply asked a younger librarian to drag the sleeping boy out of the way.

When Nicholas had assured her that he was absolutely fine, he began asking other questions. Though the library possessed no newspapers from the years he had specified—that much he had to accept—he still hoped to learn what he could, and the old librarian was most helpful. Before long he was seated at a reading table, poring over old directories and indexes.

But though the librarian was helpful, the directories were not. In a city the size of Stonetown, there were countless architects and builders who might have been hired to design and construct the Rothschilds' observatory. After flipping page after page in hopes of finding a clue, something obvious that would leap out at him, Nicholas turned to a new strategy. He got the most recent directory and compared its entries with much older ones, trying to find currently existing businesses that had been around years ago, when the Rothschilds were in town. There were dozens, however, and they were spread out all over the city and in the suburbs. Making inquiries at all of them could take weeks, even months. And there was no guarantee that any of them had a connection to the Rothschilds.

Nicholas found that his mouth had grown pasty and developed a sour taste. He went for a drink of water, his mind churning. When he got back to his seat, he searched for the name Booker in listings for private detectives, without success. Among the other listings he found plenty of Bookers, but none that would seem to have had anything to do with the Rothschilds' treasure. No shipping merchants or antique dealers or any such thing. Was there any point in trying to contact anyone at all? His original, focused plan had dissolved into a wild-goose chase.

Nicholas shoved his chair back from the table. He needed to clear his head, which was starting to throb. He went to a window that overlooked the busy street. He imagined himself going out into the city in search of answers. If he had more time...

But he didn't have more time. He had a few hours. And as he looked out upon the crowded, noisy sidewalks, he felt a rising despair. Did he really think he could go investigating even if he had more time? A nine-year-old boy with narco-lepsy, alone in the city? What would he do when naps over-came him? What would happen if a car horn startled him to sleep? Whom could he trust to help him?

No one. He could trust no one. How many people walk-ing down the sidewalk right now had been just like Moray, Breaker, or Iggy when they were young? How many had been like all the other orphans, the ones who lived in fear and treated Nicholas badly because of it? How foolish would he be to think they were any different now?

Nicholas turned from the window. The prospect of escap-ing from the Manor suddenly seemed much less appealing—even with the treasure, even with John. Would they really come live by themselves in this huge, daunting city full of strangers? The notion seemed almost preposterous now. He supposed they would need to come to Stonetown to sell the treasure for money—a tricky business in itself, and possibly a dangerous one—but after that, he would want to get far away from here, far away from other people.

You're forgetting, Nicholas thought, rubbing his temples. *You have no idea where the treasure might be. No idea. No clue. And almost no time left to find any.* Indeed, it was beginning to seem horribly likely that he would never find the treasure—that the orphanage would be shut down before he found it, that he would be sent away, and worst of all, that he would be alone again, separated from John and Violet.

With that hopeless thought, Nicholas looked around him, wondering what in the world to do now.

All of these books, books in the tens of thousands, and for the first time in his life, he didn't even feel like reading.

Nicholas had expected to return to 'Child's End in the morning, but Mr. Pileus had purchased tickets for the afternoon train. Perhaps the overly cautious handyman had thought they would need more time to conclude their tasks in Stonetown, or perhaps he'd worried about oversleeping, for the morning train departed very early. In any case, he and Nicholas spent several dreary hours sitting on their luggage at the station, then several more on the train, before arriving at Pebbleton station just as a thunderstorm broke loose.

Rain pummeled the Studebaker as it made its way up the

orphanage lane. Lightning fractured the sky. Muddy rivulets streamed across the lane, just visible in the light from the headlamps. Mr. Pileus, when at last he had parked near the Manor's porch steps, looked ready to collapse with relief.

And yet as he and Nicholas mounted the steps—they were both thoroughly soaked—Mr. Pileus's anxiety seemed to return. He kept casting sidelong glances at Nicholas, as if worried he had brought the wrong boy back from Stonetown. And no sooner had they stepped inside than he hurried off to his room, taking his new hat from beneath his jacket and dripping water on the floors.

Perhaps he had an urgent need to use the bathroom, thought Nicholas, likewise dripping. It was the hour before bedtime, and he could hear loud voices and movement coming from the direction of the drawing room. From the sound of it—the tromping of innumerable feet, the discordant laughter and cries of boys and girls alike—Nicholas deduced that the entire group of orphans had been gathered for some activity or game. He could hear Miss Candace calling out instructions.

He decided to go straight in. This might be his only chance to see John, and he wanted to tell him to meet in the library that night, so that they could talk. They had deemed inside meetings too risky in the past, but time was pressing, and Nicholas refused to wait for better weather. He just hoped they could manage a quick private word now, among all the commotion.

Suitcase in hand, Nicholas was crossing the entranceway when Mr. Collum's office door opened.

"Ah, Nicholas," said Mr. Collum, looking him up and

down. "I see you've arrived as expected, though perhaps not as dry as one might wish. Come along, I'll let you into your room. You can change out of those wet clothes, and meanwhile you can tell me what you learned at the library. I trust you are writing a lengthy and detailed report, but for now you can give me a brief accounting."

"I'll be delighted to do so, Mr. Collum," Nicholas said, trying hard to sound sincere. "But if you please, I was hoping to join the others in the drawing room. It sounds like they're having tremendous fun. May I just duck in there for the rest of the activity? I'll come straight to your office afterward."

Mr. Collum frowned. "I'm afraid you can't join the activity in such a state, Nicholas. You're a sodden mess. You might catch a chill. Come now, change your clothes and let us talk. There will be other activities." He dropped a heavy hand on Nicholas's shoulder to guide him toward the stairs.

Nicholas wriggled away. "Please, Mr. Collum! It's been such a dreary trip. Can't I go in there even for a minute? I'd like to say hello to John."

"Nicholas!" said Mr. Collum sharply. He took a deep breath, composing himself, and continued in an even tone. "It is disrespectful to wheedle and argue, Nicholas. Please refrain from doing so." He hesitated, looking at the stairs, then shook his head. "Come into my office a minute."

Biting his lip, Nicholas followed the director into his office. Mr. Collum had said "a minute," after all, so perhaps he did not intend to keep Nicholas long. What was more, he seemed troubled, and Nicholas suddenly realized that something was going on—something had happened—and he would probably be wise to find out what it was.

"Have a seat, Nicholas."

Nicholas frowned and sat down. Mr. Collum had never invited him to sit before.

"I have some happy news," said Mr. Collum in a tone of false cheer. Seating himself behind the desk, he reached into a drawer and took out his pipe, which he inspected as if searching for flaws. He cleared his throat, and without looking up, he said, "John Cole has been adopted."

Nicholas stopped breathing. The walls of the office began to pulse in his vision like the chambers of a heart. "What... what did you say?" He whispered the question so faintly he did not even hear it himself.

Mr. Collum glanced at him and quickly looked back at his pipe. "It is the very best news for John, I'm sure you will agree. Of course, we are all extremely sorry to lose him. You know how highly I thought of John, and you told me yourself that he was your... only friend." He coughed, stood, and began rummaging among the papers on his desk, as if looking for something.

"But how—?" Nicholas looked down at his hands, which had begun to tremble, and he clasped them tightly together to still them. "How did this happen?"

Mr. Collum, obviously agitated, continued to riffle through the papers. "This is an orphanage, after all, Nicholas. I was contacted by a couple hoping to adopt a responsible boy of John's age, a hard worker and a good boy, preferably one who had lost his parents only recently, so that he understood from experience how to get along in a family household. John was the clear choice—indeed, the only choice—and so I invited the couple to meet him. They did, and they liked him at once, and as I had already drawn up the necessary papers, the adoption was managed efficiently and quickly."

Realization hit Nicholas like a slap. Suddenly he was on his feet. "And you sent me away! You knew this was going to happen, and you made sure I was out of town! Why would you do that? Did you think I'd ruin his chances? He was my *friend*, Mr. Collum! My friend! And I didn't even get to tell him goodbye!"

Mr. Collum looked at Nicholas with a mixed expression of warning and concern. "Calm yourself, Nicholas. Do not do something that you'll regret. I arranged matters this way for your own good. I knew that John was your friend and that parting would be painful. It was better this way. A clean break."

Nicholas gripped the edge of Mr. Collum's desk, trying to steady himself. If he had been strong enough, he would have picked it up and thrown it at Mr. Collum. Instead, he stood there shaking, telling himself to breathe slowly, breathe slowly, breathe slowly. His eyes stung with tears.

"You should try to be happy for him," Mr. Collum said quietly. "He's been taken into a good family. Not wealthy, by any means, but he will be secure, and I know he will be appreciated."

Something about Mr. Collum's condescending tone made Nicholas lose what little control he'd gained, and banging his hands on the desk, he shouted, "*I* appreciated him as my *friend*! And you didn't even let me say goodbye! It wasn't better this way, Mr. Collum—it was the worst possible thing you could do!" His tears were flowing freely now; he tasted them as they streamed into his mouth. "You know nothing about children, Mr. Collum! Nothing! Children aren't numbers! You can't just add them and subtract them and expect everything to come out right!"

Mr. Collum, shocked, took a step backward. Nicholas could see his jaw clenching and unclenching, and his right hand was squeezing his pipe as if to crush it. "I—I hardly know what to say, Nicholas. You must realize that you are in serious trouble for speaking to me in this way. You will have to be punished. I understand that you are upset, but that does not excuse you."

Nicholas, recovering from his outburst, had fallen back into his chair and covered his face with his hands. He was trying his hardest not to break into uncontrollable sobs.

There was a silence, and then Mr. Collum said, "You may take the night to get hold of yourself. Tomorrow morning we shall discuss your library trip. No doubt you will feel better after a good night's sleep. Also," he muttered, again looking at the papers on his desk, "you may be comforted to know that John wrote you a letter. He pressed it on me before he left, and begged me to give it to you."

Nicholas was staring at Mr. Collum through his fingers. "A letter? He left me a letter?" He lowered his hands, then thrust one of them forward demandingly. "Well, where is it? Give it to me!"

Mr. Collum scowled at him. "Manners, young man! You are only making things worse for yourself with such impudent behavior." He looked back down at his desk, still scowling. "The letter is yours, however, and you shall receive it as soon as I locate it. I cannot fathom what's happened. I was exceedingly careful to leave it right here"—he tapped the desk before him—"right on top of these papers, where I could find it easily. Look beneath my desk, Nicholas. Do you see a sealed envelope with your name on it?"

Nicholas dropped to the floor. There was nothing. He leaped to his feet. "When did you leave that letter there? Are you sure you left it there?"

"Of course I'm sure!" Mr. Collum snapped. "You are not to interrogate me, Nicholas! I placed the letter there this very afternoon, right after we had all gathered in the entranceway to see John off." He was speaking to himself now, not to Nicholas, as he tried to remember exactly what had occurred. "Yes, that's when John gave me the letter, and I sent the other children off to their chores, and I came in here and set it down."

Nicholas felt his stomach turn. "You mean, the other children saw John give you the letter? And they heard him tell you to give it to me?"

This time it was Mr. Collum who banged the desk. "I said that is enough, Nicholas! Enough with the questions! Enough with your impertinence! Be silent and let me think a moment!"

But Nicholas had had enough, too, and rising once more to his feet, he cried, "You can think all you want! I already know what happened! You left the letter out where anyone could find it! And then at some point you left your office unlocked—maybe you thought you could just step over to the bathroom for a minute without troubling to lock the door. Maybe you had your precious ledger with you, so you weren't worried about losing anything *important*."

Mr. Collum, shocked yet again, gaped at Nicholas. "My . . . *precious ledger*?"

"But that ledger isn't everything, Mr. Collum!" Nicholas yelled, jabbing his finger at the director. "I can tell you that much! And for all your talk of Mr. Bottoms being so reckless and irresponsible, take a look at yourself! You sure go to a lot of trouble to lock a little boy into his room each night, and to lock all the rooms with valuable things in them, but you left your own office door unlocked today, didn't you? Didn't you!"

Nicholas could see from Mr. Collum's expression that his words had struck home. Not waiting for the director to collect himself—he was pale and quivering with anger—Nicholas wiped his eyes, grabbed his suitcase, and turned on his heel. He paused at the doorway. "You can forget any report on the Rothschilds," he said without looking back. "You're never going to get it. Never." And then he hurried out, slamming the door behind him.

In the drawing room he found all the orphans standing in disorderly rows, wheeling their arms about like windmills. Miss Candace stood before them, demonstrating the maneuver and talking about the virtues of daily calisthenics. She seemed completely unaware, though Nicholas saw it plainly enough from the doorway, that the Spiders kept "accidentally" slapping the children nearest them as they circled their arms, then winking at one another and snickering.

"Moray!" Nicholas screamed, so loudly that it hurt his throat.

Fifty faces turned in unison to stare at him. The arms froze. Miss Candace stopped talking and blinked at Nicholas in surprise. Clearly, she thought something was wrong with him, barging into the drawing room with wet clothes and puffy, red eyes, his teeth beginning to chatter.

"Who has the letter?" Nicholas demanded, his voice cracking. He wove through the other children to get to Moray, near the middle of the room. He stopped inches away from the sneering bully and dropped his suitcase, narrowly missing Moray's oversized feet. "Is it you? Or is it one of your leeches?" He shot angry looks at Iggy and Breaker, standing nearby. They both seemed impressed by Nicholas's audacity—but they were also smirking with evident satisfaction.

Moray crossed his arms and stood looking down at Nicholas like a Rottweiler pestered by a yipping terrier. "No idea what you're talking about. You're in my space, though."

"Nicholas," Miss Candace said. "Come here and let me look at you. What's the matter?"

"Leave me alone!" Nicholas shouted at her. "Nothing's the matter with me except I want my letter back!"

Miss Candace, looking frightened, hurried from the room to find help. Nicholas did not appear to notice. He stood with his chest heaving and teeth chattering, his hand extended as if he truly expected Moray to comply with his demands. He could hardly see straight, could hardly think of anything except getting back John's letter.

Moray watched Miss Candace leave, then broke into a grin, feigning a look of sudden understanding. "Oh, *that* letter! The letter from John! Sure, I remember now!"

"So give it back, Moray! Give it back or you'll be sorry!"

Moray pretended to look troubled. "But we *can't* give you that letter back, Big Nose. I mean, golly, I'd love to, but we sort of burned it, didn't we, boys?"

Iggy and Breaker chuckled.

Nicholas's eyes were stinging again. Slowly he lowered his

hand. He could see that Moray was telling the truth. He bit his lip, trying not to cry. He had no idea what to do.

"Naturally, we read it first," Moray said with a shrug. "Lots of interesting stuff. Too bad you'll never know any of it. *We* know, but you don't. Get it?"

Moray's words seemed to come from the end of a tunnel, for Nicholas had given up, he'd lost control, and now he was crying, weeping, sinking to his knees. Moray put a foot against Nicholas's shoulder and gave a slight push. Nicholas had no strength in him to resist. He toppled over onto his side, curled up, and continued to sob and sob.

"Everyone look at the big future-teller!" Moray shouted triumphantly. "I guess he didn't see this coming, after all!"

Nicholas, rocking back and forth in an agony of humiliation and despair, wished, for the first time in his life, that his emotions would send him to sleep. He didn't think he could bear them any longer.

And then, in the next moment, he didn't have to.

⌣∶∾

When Nicholas awoke, he was alone in the drawing room except for one other child, the younger boy named Oliver, who stood in the doorway watching him with wide eyes. Nicholas sat up, his head aching and his throat raw from crying. He looked bleakly at Oliver. "Well? What are you doing here? Where did everybody go?"

"To get ready for bed," Oliver said. "Mr. Collum said I'm to watch you and let him know when you wake up."

Nicholas got shakily to his feet. He felt as if he had been taken apart and put back together again with all his parts in the wrong places. Everything seemed to hurt. Nothing seemed right.

Oliver lingered in the doorway. He seemed to want to say something else, but Nicholas, in his misery, was only vaguely aware of the boy's presence. At any rate, he didn't care about anything that anyone said. He was leaving. He picked up his suitcase, considering his next step.

"They were lying," Oliver whispered, and Nicholas looked at him. "The Spiders, I mean. They didn't read that letter."

Nicholas thought about this. Yes, that seemed right. He dimly remembered Moray's tone, and it had been noticeably false. He shrugged. "I know," he said. "I mean, I realize that now. Doesn't matter."

Oliver glanced nervously up and down the passageway and edged further into the room. "It doesn't? I...well, I just thought that it might. So I wanted you to know, in case it did. They—they made me get the envelope for them. I'm sorry. I didn't know what else to do. I didn't know they were going to burn it. They made a lot of us watch. They were saying that this is what happens if you try to cross them. And then they made Caroline dump the ashes out behind the gardening shed, even though it was raining."

Nicholas shrugged again to show his lack of interest. He didn't want to think about the Spiders anymore. He wanted Oliver to leave him alone. But Oliver stayed, looking at him expectantly. And even in his desolate mood, Nicholas could not quite suppress his urge to understand things, to understand and explain.

"It makes sense," he said finally. "Moray probably didn't think of reading the letter until after they'd already burned it. He hates to read, you know, and he was excited. By the time it occurred to him that he could have known something I didn't, it was too late. So he lied. He wanted me to at least *think* that he did. He wanted to make me feel as bad as possible."

"Right!" Oliver said. "Which is why I wanted you to know the truth. But please, don't say anything about this to the Spiders. They'll kill me if they know I told you. I'm...well, I'm really sorry about everything. I'm sorry you lost your friend."

Nicholas sighed. "Thanks, Oliver," he said wearily. "Don't worry, I'm never going to talk to the Spiders again. Now you'd better go make your report to Mr. Collum. You can tell him I'm heading upstairs now."

Oliver seemed disappointed somehow, but he said nothing, only turned and hurried out. Nicholas trudged upstairs and leaned against his door, waiting. It was not Mr. Collum who showed up to unlock his door, however, but Mr. Pileus, now wearing his nightgown, nightcap, and slippers. He looked almost sheepish as he let Nicholas into his room, and Nicholas suddenly understood what those anxious glances on the Manor steps had been about. Mr. Pileus had known about John's adoption, had known what Nicholas was about to learn. Everybody seemed to know everything but Nicholas.

In his absence, a tarpaulin had been hung over the hole in his wall, and several boxes stacked in front of it. His cot had been moved into the empty space the boxes had occupied. Nicholas washed up and changed into his pajamas while Mr. Pileus waited. Then, seeing that Mr. Pileus was reluctantly beginning to speak, he said, "Don't worry, Mr. Pileus; only a fool would sneak out that window on a night like tonight. I'm not going to do anything of the sort."

Mr. Pileus nodded and went out, locking the door behind him.

For two hours Nicholas lay on his cot, gazing at the plaid pattern on his blanket. Then he rose, changed into his one set of dry clothes, and packed everything he possessed into his suitcase, including the blanket, including his shoes. Though the boxes had been moved around, he quickly located the one in which he had stashed the old, oversized boots, the ones he had always brought for John. He grimaced, remembering the way the two of them had joked about his conjuring the boots. No more jokes with John. No more anything.

The boots were stowed inside his flour-sack backpack. Nicholas put the backpack on, unlocked his door, and returned for his suitcase. Then he blew out his candle, and in stocking feet he made his way down the servants' stairs in the darkness. In the basement he found another tarpaulin, and by cutting it to length, with a small hole in the center, he fashioned a sort of rain cloak. With effort he squeezed his head through the hole. His head would get wet, the old boots would be muddy, but his clothes and his bags would remain dry, or mostly so. He paused at the side door to put on the boots, then left the Manor in the same way he had entered it the very first time. Skulking like a thief.

It was a miserable walk to Pebbleton in the driving rain, and it took Nicholas several hours. Mud sucked at his boots, inside which his feet were wet and aching. His suitcase, though light, seemed heavier than a bag of stones after the first mile; after the second it felt heavier than an anvil. Nicholas slogged along with his eyes almost closed against the rain. One wretched step after the other.

He had not gone far from the Manor before it occurred to him that he would not be able to tell Violet goodbye, either. He briefly considered crossing the hills to Violet's farm, but he did not want her to see him like this, so downcast and defeated. He could never think of Violet without thinking of the drawing she had made of him—of that defiant, illuminated boy on the bluff. Now he began to wonder if the moon had spotlighted him only to call attention to his isolation, his insignificance. There he had sat, a lonely little boy on a huge, high rock as old as the world. What could his life possibly matter?

No, Nicholas did not wish Violet to see this version of the boy in her drawing. He would try to write her a letter and explain how he could not stay at the Manor another day—not after what had happened. John had gone away to a new life, and Nicholas had been publicly humiliated, his secret exposed. Even if not for the Spiders, how could he stand to live under the authority of Mr. Collum, who had so cruelly mistreated him? In his letter, Nicholas would explain how he doubted they could have found the treasure, anyway. He'd found nothing useful in Stonetown. There were no more clues. The orphanage would have closed, and he would have been sent away soon.

Nicholas shivered inside his cloak. It would not be a pleasant letter to write. Violet was going to be miserable, too. Her only friends would suddenly be gone. She'd no longer have any hope of finding the treasure. And like a mean-spirited symbol of all her losses, her old dream of mining-company money, already insubstantial as smoke, would finally drift away when that contract expired the day after tomorrow — and her dream of art school would be over for good. Nicholas could hardly bear to think of it.

He would tell Violet not to worry about *him*, anyway. He would not tell her how frightened he was. He would not tell her that he had no idea what to do. He had a vague notion of hiding in the Stonetown Library, reading books by night, until he figured something out. But it would be hard to find food, harder still to keep from being discovered. He couldn't trust himself to stay awake, and when he was asleep, his screams would give him away. Perhaps he was destined to live like a wild animal in the woods. That idea frightened him, too. All he knew for certain was that right now he needed to get away — to escape from everyone and everything that had caused him such anguish.

In Pebbleton, in the hours before dawn, he found a dry space beneath the porch of the general store, and there he slept until his alarm clock awakened him from hideous dreams. He had been crying out in fear, but no one was around to hear him. It was for this reason that he had chosen the porch of an empty building on an empty street in town.

Still wrapped in his rain cloak, Nicholas emerged from beneath the porch into a misty dawn. In the distance he saw the electric lamps of the train station glistening in the mist, and the light and the weather reminded him eerily of his arrival in Pebbleton, when he had been hopeful of making a new start in a new home. He wondered where that hope had come from. He couldn't imagine being hopeful anymore.

Like many a vagrant before him, Nicholas made his way to the train tracks. He knew the train schedule, of course—he'd memorized it without trying—and he intended to hop the first train of the day, which was due to arrive any minute. A short distance up the tracks was a little patch of woods, and there Nicholas hid, waiting, knowing that every minute that passed brought him closer to the moment his absence at the Manor would be discovered. If Mr. Collum telephoned the county sheriff, and the word got around that an orphan had run away, someone might think to search the train. So once again Nicholas was in a race with Mr. Collum—but this time Nicholas's only hope was to escape, penniless and scared, into the larger world. That was how far his dreams had tumbled.

Before long Nicholas heard the whistle in the distance, followed by the chugging of the train. Then he saw a light, and the engine appeared out of the gloom. The train was slowing down for its approach to the station, growing louder as it grew nearer, until the cars began clattering and screeching past, filling his vision. The noise was quite deafening. Nicholas clenched his teeth, trying to steel his nerves. He knew it was dangerous to hop a train, but he could not afford to let anyone see him boarding.

As soon as he judged the train cars to be moving slowly enough, Nicholas darted out from his hiding place and began running awkwardly alongside the tracks. He stumbled, recovered, took hold of a ladder at the rear of a car, and with great difficulty—almost losing his grip, almost falling—he pulled himself up. His pulse, pounding in his ears, muted the sound of the train's bells. He was so hot and shaky he might have just run a mile. But he had made it.

By the time the train had pulled into the station, Nicholas was in a washroom. He changed into his dry shoes, stowed the boots and his crude rain cloak inside his suitcase, and groomed himself with the aid of a mirror. He needed to appear as respectable as possible.

Casually he made his way through the train cars, which had yet to acquire many passengers. Few of them even appeared to notice him. Only one, a sleepy-looking man with thick, bushy hair and a bedraggled suit, glanced at Nicholas for longer than a second. This man gazed at him, in fact, for several seconds, with a look of mild curiosity, and Nicholas was glad to leave him behind. He passed through a dining car, where the smell of food being cooked made his mouth water and his empty stomach growl. But a man was working behind the counter, and there was no chance of sneaking anything to eat. Nicholas moved on, searching for places to hide, in case hiding should prove necessary.

At last he came to a dark, empty car near the front of the train. This seemed to be a good bet, and Nicholas was looking it over when he heard a familiar voice discussing a familiar problem.

"I'm going to have to build a fence!" the stationmaster was saying. "That's all there is to it!"

"Big place you have out there, though," said another voice. "A fence will cost you a pretty penny."

The stationmaster was speaking with the train conductor on the station platform, just outside the windows. Nicholas peered out. He didn't recognize this conductor. The stationmaster must talk about his stolen eggs to anyone who would listen.

"I know it's going to cost me a pretty penny! But what else am I supposed to do? Go the rest of my life without eating another egg?"

"Well, let me know how it turns out," said the conductor, yawning. He turned to mount the steps of the very train car Nicholas was standing in.

Nicholas dropped to his belly and crawled under a row of seats. There he lay, still and quiet, until the conductor had walked past him and the train had pulled away from the station. He had won the race with Mr. Collum. Now he had only to avoid the conductor.

Avoiding the conductor did not prove to be easy, however. After a few more stops, the train began to fill up. There were passengers in every car now, and Nicholas could no longer hide beneath the seats when the conductor passed through collecting tickets. After the next stop he would be in a real pickle, so he worked his way through the train, studying all the passengers and formulating a plan. It was a good thing he did, too, for it wasn't long before he found himself caught between passengers crowding the aisle behind him and the conductor approaching him from the front.

The conductor, sweating and harried, nonetheless noticed Nicholas trying to brush past him, and he put out his arm. Nicholas was ready for this, though. Looking up with his most winning smile, he explained that he was part of a large family whose tickets had already been collected. He described the family, seated at the back of the train, in great detail, and claimed that he had boarded with them and been seated with them and that the conductor had taken his own ticket, as well. Didn't the conductor remember?

He spoke so earnestly and with such accurate detail that he almost convinced himself, and the conductor, for his part, was entirely persuaded. He trusted Nicholas's account better than his own memory. "Of course, of course, young man," he said, and patting Nicholas on the head, he moved on.

Nicholas was safe.

Or rather, he believed he was safe.

After speaking with the conductor, Nicholas quickly took the nearest available seat in the crowded car, sitting with his arms folded protectively over his suitcase, not making eye contact with anyone around him. And so he sat for the next few minutes, weary and uncomfortable but extremely relieved—until he felt a tap on his shoulder, and everything changed forever.

THE
KINDNESS
OF
STRANGERS

Nicholas looked up. It was the man in the bedraggled suit, the one with bushy hair who had looked at him right after he'd hopped the train.

"Come with me to the dining car," the man said quietly. "Let's get a bite to eat and have a little talk." His brown eyes, rimmed with red, did not express suspicion or displeasure. Nor was his voice unkind, but it was quite firm, and Nicholas sensed that trying to argue would only make matters worse. For the moment, anyway, it was best to play the part of the obedient boy, respectful of adults who wished to speak with him.

"Sure," Nicholas said lightly, and bringing his suitcase, he followed the man out of the car, his heart beating triple-time. Was the man some sort of railway official? Did he keep track of the tickets? Had he heard Nicholas lying to the conductor? Were they really going to the dining car, or had that just been an excuse to keep Nicholas from trying to get away?

They really were going to the dining car. The man told Nicholas to order whatever he liked, and ordered coffee for himself, and paid for it all. They sat at a small, round table in the corner. All around them dishes clinked, and people ate and talked as if this were a regular day, a regular train journey. But Nicholas had a feeling he was sitting down to the most fateful meal of his life.

"You look hungry," the man said. He gestured at the eggs and biscuits and gravy Nicholas had ordered. "Please, tuck in."

Nicholas didn't have to be told twice. Whatever was going to happen next, he might as well meet it with a full stomach. The eggs didn't taste as good as Mr. Griese's, but he hardly cared. He shoveled them into his mouth and washed them down with great gulps of lukewarm milk.

The man sipped his coffee and looked casually about the car, giving Nicholas time to eat. He looked even more tired up close. He needed a shave, and his bushy brown hair, though carefully combed, bore the imprint of a hat worn at a strange angle. *Down and forward*, Nicholas thought, and instantly knew that the man had slept with his hat on, tilted down to cover his eyes.

The man seemed to read his thoughts, or perhaps he had

followed Nicholas's gaze. He reached up and felt his hair, then looked about beneath his chair. "Now, where did I leave my hat?" he muttered. "Tell me, was I wearing it when you boarded at Pebbleton?" His eyes met Nicholas's. They were not accusatory, nor even challenging, but they conveyed absolute certainty. They made it clear to Nicholas that there was no point lying to him.

"No," Nicholas said. "Maybe you took it off in your sleep."

"Maybe I did," the man acknowledged. "Or maybe it fell off. I'll need to check under my seat. I'm so tired I can hardly keep track of my own feet, much less hats and bags." He sipped his coffee thoughtfully. After a pause he said, "How did you know I slept with my hat on?"

"The mark in your hair," Nicholas said through a mouthful of biscuit. He swallowed. "The angle."

The man looked at him, then shook his head wonderingly. "I thought perhaps I'd been wrong about Pebbleton. I thought you might have boarded much earlier and passed by me while I was asleep. Instead, it simply turns out that you are even more clever than I suspected."

"What makes you think I'm clever?" Nicholas asked. He was genuinely curious, for this man had struck him as being very clever himself.

"First of all, the story you told the conductor was most impressive," the man said with a smile. "If I hadn't known better, I might have believed you myself. But I saw that family board—the family you claimed to be with—and they didn't get on the train when you did. And yet you described them perfectly, as if you'd spent your whole life with them. Do you want something else to eat?"

Nicholas had cleaned his plate. "No, thank you. I'm quite full." This happened to be the truth, but it was also true that his stomach was clenching and unclenching like a fist. He was caught in his lie. He had suspected as much, but now he knew it for sure.

"You're welcome," the man said. He extended his hand. "My name's Harinton, by the way. Sam Harinton. Pleased to meet you...." He lifted his eyebrows inquiringly.

"Matthews," Nicholas replied, giving the man's hand a firm shake. "James Matthews. Pleased to meet you, too."

Mr. Harinton nodded and sat back in his chair. "To continue, James—or shall I call you Jim? Yes? To continue, Jim, another reason I know you're clever is that you remembered whether or not I was wearing my hat when you first saw me. And then, just now, you deduced that I'd slept with it on, merely by looking at my hair. Now, if I hadn't been traveling for three days without benefit of a shower, you wouldn't have been able to tell that, I promise. When my hair is clean, it's actually quite springy and healthy-looking."

Mr. Harinton winked, and Nicholas smiled. He saw that the man was trying to be jovial and friendly. But why? What did he want?

"Finally, Jim," said Mr. Harinton, "you are clever enough not to give your real name to a stranger whose purposes are unclear to you. Yes, I know that Jim is not your real name. We needn't argue about it. Jim will do fine for now. More important, Jim, is that you are clever enough to see that I can tell when a person's lying. I have a feeling that *you* can tell when someone is lying, too. Am I right?"

"Usually," Nicholas said. "At least, I think so."

Mr. Harinton nodded. "Some people just have a gift. As for me, I've had lots of training. I'm an attorney for the government. I've spent my career figuring out when people are lying and when they aren't, and I've gotten pretty good at it, if I do say so myself."

"For the government?" Nicholas asked. "That sounds like an important job."

Mr. Harinton arched an eyebrow. He finished his coffee with a gulp. "Another thing I've gotten pretty good at, Jim, is knowing when people are trying to change the subject. Also when they're trying to flatter you, to get you on their side. But listen, I'm already on your side, all right?"

Nicholas shrugged. He did not know what to say.

"All right," said Mr. Harinton, as if answering himself. "Yes, I work for the government. I was stationed overseas during the war, but now my station is wherever I am—I mean, wherever they send me. I've been down in Chesterton for the last month. Now I'm heading overseas again. Am I telling the truth?"

Nicholas regarded him warily. He nodded.

"Swell, now we're getting somewhere." Mr. Harinton asked for more coffee, and when he had a fresh cup, he said, "My question to you, Jim, is what are you running from?"

Nicholas made no reply.

Mr. Harinton waited a minute, then resumed talking about himself. "It's true, I haven't had a proper home in years. My life feels awfully wearisome sometimes, but I like what I do. It's important work, good work. I do hope someday to have a wife and family, though. Family is important, too, right?"

Nicholas could tell that Mr. Harinton was trying to put him at ease by talking about himself. At the same time, he was gauging Nicholas's reactions to what he was saying. Nicholas kept his face entirely blank.

After a long, expectant pause, Mr. Harinton sighed. He leaned over the table, lacing his fingers together, and speaking very softly, he said, "Look, let me make you a deal. If you're coming out of some bad situation, I won't force you to go back. I'll just try to help you. You have to understand my position, Jim. I can't see a kid like you, a kid all on his own, and go on about my business and pretend that I didn't. It wouldn't be decent. You can see that, right? But you have to trust me with the truth. How else can I know what your situation is? How else can I help you?"

Nicholas carefully considered Mr. Harinton's words. He was reminded of when he first met John, of how he had been forced to tell the truth, to take a chance on John's decency. In fact, he suddenly realized that Mr. Harinton reminded him very much of John himself, if only John had been a grownup. The moment he realized this, his resistance began to soften.

He met Mr. Harinton's gaze. "What will you do if I don't tell you anything? Turn me in?"

Mr. Harinton's brow wrinkled. "Well, I'll have to do *something*, son. I'm to leave the country in a couple of days, and where I'm going, I can't take you with me. It wouldn't be safe, and anyway, it's against policy. So, yes, I'll probably have to tell someone."

"Who? The police?"

Mr. Harinton scratched his head. "I'm wondering why

this matters to you. Let me think. No, I don't suppose I would call the police, at least not right away. You aren't a notorious criminal, are you?" He narrowed his eyes in mock suspicion.

"Would I tell you if I were?" Nicholas said.

"No, I suppose not. You aren't making this easy for me, are you?" Mr. Harinton shifted in his chair. After a considering pause, and in a tone of great seriousness, he said, "Jim, I promise that I'm not going to let anything bad happen to you. No matter what you tell me, I'm going to help you. I give you my word."

Nicholas felt his cheeks flush, and he looked down at the table in an agony of confusion. He was still weighing what to say—what to do—when he felt the heavy shawl of sleep falling over him. *Oh no*, he thought. *Oh no, oh no.* All of a sudden his decision was made for him.

"I have a sleeping problem," he said quickly. "I have to take a nap. If I can trust you, Mr. Harinton, if I really can trust you…"

Nicholas couldn't finish. Blackness overtook him. He slumped forward, knocking his plate off the table, and was asleep before it struck the floor.

The train rattled along its tracks. There was the murmur of conversation, the *clink* of dishes. Nicholas was still in the dining car. But he was lying down on a hard surface. The floor. And he was covered with something—a blanket, perhaps. Or no, it smelled like aftershave and perspiration. A man's suit coat. He opened his eyes. He was wedged into the corner, beneath the table. He saw Mr. Harinton's legs, crossed at the knee, and heard the telltale crinkle and snap of newspaper pages being turned and folded. He lay there for several minutes, assessing the situation.

He was safe.

He could feel it in his bones—a lightening, as if an enormous weight had been taken from him. He would not have to fend for himself in the city. He would not have to live in the woods like a wild animal. This man, Mr. Harinton, could be trusted. He was perhaps the first truly trustworthy man Nicholas had ever known—trustworthy and decent, as John had been.

When Nicholas got up from under the table, Mr. Harinton smiled and folded the newspaper he'd been reading. "So it really was just a nap," he said, with evident relief. "I'm very glad. I thought I understood you, but you were mumbling. I worried I might be making a mistake not calling for a doctor."

Nicholas handed him the suit coat. "Thank you."

"That's fine," said Mr. Harinton, slipping the suit coat on again. "I thought you might get cold on the floor."

"I don't mean just for covering me up," Nicholas said. "I mean for everything."

"You are entirely welcome," Mr. Harinton said. "Would you like a lemonade? I know I'm always thirsty after a nap." Nicholas said that he would, and when he had drunk the lemonade down, Mr. Harinton ordered him another and set it on the table before him.

Nicholas took a deep breath. "I'll tell you everything, Mr. Harinton. I'll tell you the truth."

Mr. Harinton looked even more relieved than before. Nicholas saw his shoulders relax. "I can't tell you how glad I am to hear that, son."

Nicholas extended his hand. "It's Nicholas, Mr. Harinton—Nicholas Benedict."

Mr. Harinton took his hand and shook it warmly. "That's a fine name, Nicholas. And I am honored to know it."

For the next hour Nicholas told Mr. Harinton the truth—the truth about his narcolepsy, about the many orphanages he had known, about the Spiders, about his locked room at Rothschild's End, about losing his only friend there and the cruel way Mr. Collum had arranged it, about his final humiliation before all the other children, about running away. He left out only the parts about Violet and the treasure.

Through it all, Mr. Harinton listened intently, with alternating looks of surprise and sympathy. Occasionally he asked a question, but for the most part questions were unnecessary. Nicholas was an excellent storyteller, and Mr. Harinton could tell that he was speaking truthfully.

Nicholas was nearing the end of his tale when the conductor passed through the dining car, announcing that Stonetown station was the next stop. He had passed through a few times before, each time with a disapproving glance in their direction. Nicholas had assumed the conductor thought he should be sitting with his family, not pestering a stranger in the dining car. Now the man was approaching their table. He cleared his throat, and Nicholas stopped talking.

Mr. Harinton looked up. "Yes?"

"Maybe it's none of my business," the conductor said. "But it seems to me the boy ought to be made to apologize. Kids don't learn right from wrong otherwise."

Mr. Harinton said, "I see your point, although I don't quite agree that *making* someone apologize accomplishes much." He turned to Nicholas. "What do you think? Do you believe you should apologize for lying?"

The conductor frowned. "And not just for lying—for hopping the train!"

Nicholas was taken aback. Clearly, the conductor and Mr. Harinton had spoken while he was asleep. "I'm very sorry," he said to the conductor, without missing a beat. "It wasn't right of me, and I do beg your pardon."

"Well, now," the conductor said, only slightly satisfied. "I hope you've learned your lesson." With a polite nod at Mr. Harinton, he left the car.

Mr. Harinton was studying Nicholas's face with some amusement. "Why, Nicholas. I don't believe your apology was entirely sincere."

Nicholas grinned. "I guess you really are good at telling these things," he admitted. "What happened while I was asleep? I take it he saw me and spoke to you."

"He grew suspicious. He didn't know what connection you had to me, or why you were sleeping beneath my table. I was compelled to tell him a white lie. I said that you were my nephew from Chesterton, that you had begged me to take you with me to Stonetown, and that when I refused, you must have hopped the train. I told him that I would take full responsibility for you."

"And he believed all that?"

"Not everyone shares our gift for sniffing out falsehoods," said Mr. Harinton. "And at any rate, I believe he was more concerned about your ticket."

"Oh no! Did you have to buy one for me?"

Mr. Harinton pretended to look distressed. "And from

Chesterton, no less! Even though you didn't board until Pebbleton!" He winked. "The price we pay for deceit, I suppose.
Never worry, Nicholas. Consider it a loan, if you like. One
day you can pay me back. Now let's return to more important
matters. Namely, what to do next."

Nicholas sat up straighter in his chair.

"I have a cousin who lives in Stonetown," Mr. Harinton
said. "A kind, trustworthy woman. We've been friends since
childhood. I'd like for you to meet her. She's one of the very
few people I would trust with your well-being. When she
hears what you've been through, she's going to want to take
you under her wing—she's that kind of person. I know that
she can help find a home for you. A good home, son."

Nicholas hesitated. It seemed a big decision, though he
saw no better alternatives.

"Before you answer," Mr. Harinton hastened to say, "I
want to promise you something. I'll be returning in a month
for another brief stay in Stonetown, and I'll check on you as
soon as I'm back. I don't expect there to be any problems, but
if there are, you won't be left to deal with them on your own.
I'm not just abandoning you to the wind. What do you say?"

All hesitation had flown. Nicholas nodded emphatically.
He could scarcely believe his good fortune.

Immediately upon their arrival at the station in Stonetown,
Mr. Harinton telephoned the sheriff in Pebbleton to inform
him that young Nicholas Benedict was safe. He asked the
sheriff to pass the news to Rothschild's End and to tell Mr.
Collum that he would be phoning that evening to discuss
Nicholas's return.

"I said to *discuss* it," he assured Nicholas, hanging up the telephone. "Not to arrange it."

Nicholas needed no reassurance. He had no more doubts about Mr. Harinton. Not one. He trusted the man completely, and doing so gave him a tremendous feeling of lightness and relief. He had never experienced anything like it.

The next few hours were a whirl of activity. Mr. Harinton had his own matters to attend to, as well as dealing with the arrangements for Nicholas, and they left the station at a gallop, lugging their baggage with them. They made several stops around Stonetown, at a variety of government offices, before finally, late that afternoon, settling into a hotel room near the station. Nicholas, his belly full of soup and French bread, rested drowsily on the sofa as Mr. Harinton made one telephone call after another.

Despite his curiosity, Nicholas could not keep from closing his eyes. Now Mr. Harinton was speaking to his cousin for the second time; they had already agreed to meet the following morning, but then the cousin had called back, wanting to know if Nicholas liked waffles.

"I believe he's asleep now," Mr. Harinton said in a low voice, "but I imagine waffles are a safe bet."

Nicholas smiled to himself and tumbled off to sleep. When he awoke half an hour later, Mr. Harinton was still on the telephone, though now he seemed to be speaking with an associate. Nicholas listened without opening his eyes.

"Yes," Mr. Harinton said wearily, "I'm fully aware of when I'm expected to arrive. What can I tell you? Something important has come up. Yes, believe it or not, something as important as the job. Listen, I can take the overnight

tomorrow and still be there in plenty of time. Yes, I understand perfectly well that I'll have to make the arrangements
myself. And pay for the ticket changes myself—yes, I know.
Don't do me any favors, Weber." He sighed, listened to the
person on the line, and said, "Calm down, Weber. I figured
as much. I know it isn't your fault. Yes, policy is policy. Tell
them I'll be there when they expect me, all right? I won't be
fresh as a daisy, but I'll be there. Yes, good night to you, too."

Nicholas cracked open one eye. He saw Mr. Harinton
hang up the telephone and rub his face. He was leaning
against the wall in obvious exhaustion, his eyelids drooping
heavily. He seemed to be lost in thought. Then he seemed to
be going to sleep. Then he started, shook his head, and shuffled into the bathroom. Nicholas heard bathwater running.

He rose and went to the window. The room was on the
fourth floor, overlooking an alley. Far below, two cats were
yowling at each other, and street sounds drifted up through
the alley to his window. The rush of traffic and honking of
horns. To Nicholas it all sounded as pleasant as the ebb and
flow of ocean waves, of seabirds and laughter. He had been
happy before, at least briefly so, on several occasions, and
what he was feeling now was rather like that, only deeper and
stranger. It was happiness amplified by hope—not just for
himself, but for people in general—and anchored by something else, something he had yet to put his finger on.

Mr. Harinton was real. There were adults in the world
who would actually make sacrifices for the sake of others—
not just for their own families but for anyone who needed
help. Nicholas had always had the impression that families
looked after one another, and he had come to understand

that, on rare occasions, children would do the same. Had not John made a sacrifice for his sake? But this was different. What Mr. Harinton was doing certainly helped Nicholas — but it also simply felt *right* to Nicholas. It made him want to be exactly like Mr. Harinton himself.

No sooner had he thought this than he realized what was anchoring his happiness. It was purpose. He knew what he wanted to do. He knew the way he thought things should be, and Mr. Harinton was proving that other people — even adults — could feel the same way. Nicholas had something to aim for now. He might not know what he wanted to be when he grew up, but he knew with absolute certainty *how* he wanted to be.

He felt so excited, he found himself wishing he could get started right away.

And then he sat down, shaken by the thought.

For having thought this, Nicholas suddenly saw with horrible clarity something that he should have seen long ago. It was awful to see it all — and even worse to realize what he was going to have to do. In his mind's eye, he saw his dream of a new life drifting away like a lost balloon. And for some time he sat there, hating to see it go.

But then it was gone, and he began to invent a new dream, and he began to feel better.

By the time Mr. Harinton had finished his bath, Nicholas knew everything that he wanted to do — and almost everything that he *needed* to do. At the very least, he knew where to begin.

Mr. Harinton opened the bathroom door. He was freshly scrubbed and shaved, and he was wearing clean clothes, but he still looked exhausted. Seeing Nicholas awake, he smiled wearily and said, "What do you say to some dinner, Nicholas?"

"That would be very nice, thank you, Mr. Harinton," Nicholas said, standing. "And perhaps over dinner we could discuss a few things. I've made a decision, you see."

Mr. Harinton looked perplexed. "Is that right? A decision about what?"

"I can't tell you how much I appreciate what you've done, Mr. Harinton. But I hope to show you. And with your help, I think I can do it."

"Do what, Nicholas? What are you talking about?"

Nicholas braced himself. He knew that once he said it, he would do it.

And then he said it.

"I want to go back, Mr. Harinton. Back to 'Child's End.'"

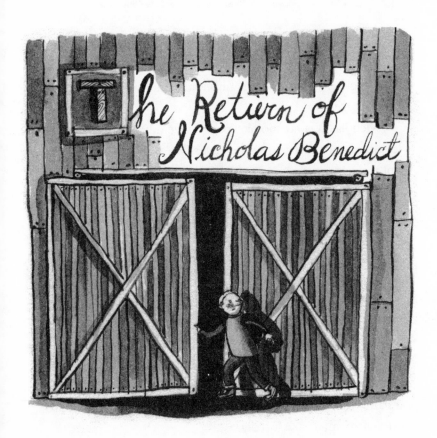

The Return of Nicholas Benedict

Once again Nicholas watched Pebbleton station approach from the window of a train. This time, however, he was the only passenger to disembark, and he did not see the Studebaker anywhere. He waited, nervously, on the empty platform. The late-summer evening was soft with twilight, the air warm and dry. The pungent odors of coal smoke and creosote that usually hung about the train tracks were carried off by a mild breeze, replaced by the more pleasant, earthy scents carried in from the town's surrounding farm fields. Nicholas's keen nose detected these traveling fragrances as if they were visible flotsam and jetsam borne along a stream. And in the distance he heard the agreeable sound of cowbells clanking, all the area cows ambling home from their day in the pastures.

Nicholas was far too nervous to give much thought to the loveliness of the evening, however. He was only glad it was not raining.

The stationmaster was saying goodbye to the train conductor, who was wishing him luck with his egg dilemma. Then the train whistle was blowing, and then Nicholas was alone. He sat down on his suitcase to wait.

Immediately he stood up again and began to pace.

So much depended on what he accomplished in the coming hours; so many lives would be affected by his success or failure; and Nicholas felt more nervous than he ever had. (He also knew that he faced a harsh scolding and punishment, which was enough on its own to make any child antsy and fretful.) But there was nothing to be done except wait, and so Nicholas waited. Nervously.

He had been pacing almost an hour when the Studebaker appeared, coming along the main street. He squinted to get a better look at it and was disappointed to see Mr. Collum in the passenger seat. His terrible scolding would begin right away, then. He had rather hoped it would wait until he'd arrived at the Manor.

Nicholas picked up his suitcase, squared his shoulders, and marched reluctantly but resolutely to the street curb.

The hour-long ride to Rothschild's End passed just as he would have predicted, with Mr. Collum constantly, endlessly, angrily reprimanding him for his irresponsible, inconsiderate, and mischievous behavior. "I say *mischievous*, Nicholas, for did I not, on your very first night at the Manor, point out that unsupervised children could be much tempted to mischief? And did you not assure me that you were never so inclined? Yet you appear to have gone to great lengths—great lengths!—to prove exactly the opposite!"

At the deserted crossroads, where Mr. Pileus got out of the Studebaker to scout for traffic, Mr. Collum mopped his brow and muttered, "And I hope you're aware of what you've done to that poor man. So racked with worry he almost suffered a breakdown. Miss Candace could do nothing for him. Indeed, I fear she made things worse. I understand he spent all of last night in the bathroom."

It was true that Mr. Pileus looked sorely exhausted, and Nicholas began to worry that he would fall asleep behind the wheel. But by pinching his ears and slapping his cheeks, Mr. Pileus kept himself awake until they had arrived safely, at which point he mumbled something about bed and staggered away.

Mr. Collum let Nicholas into his room. Mr. Pileus had diligently filled in the hole in the wall. This time he'd used the proper amount of water, and the mortar had had sufficient time to dry. Nicholas looked with resignation at the place where his window had been. So much for that. He took his pajamas from his suitcase, along with his toothbrush and toothpaste, and slid the suitcase back under the cot. How familiar the routine felt, yet how strange. Having been away from it, even for one night, made Nicholas feel anew the harshness of his nightly imprisonment.

He got ready for bed as quickly as possible. Then he took

a deep breath, gazed into the bathroom mirror, and steeled himself for the next difficult task. Mr. Collum had already made clear what his punishments would be—weeks of extra chores, no time in the library, early bedtimes each night. All that remained was for Nicholas to make his apology.

He went back to his room, where Mr. Collum stood in the doorway, yawning and waiting expectantly. Clasping his hands together, Nicholas looked the director in the eye. "I'm truly sorry for the worry I've caused, Mr. Collum, and for all the trouble, too. I won't offer any excuses. In fact, I'd like to speak with you tomorrow to discuss other ways of making amends. I don't mean instead of my punishments," he said quickly, seeing Mr. Collum's color rising, "but in addition to them. For instance, I would like to deliver my Rothschild report, after all."

Mr. Collum's expression changed. He straightened, cleared his throat, and said, "As for that, young man, perhaps you should do as I originally requested and give me a brief overview."

"I will if you like, Mr. Collum, although there isn't—" Nicholas blinked heavily. He shook his head. "Oh, I'm very sorry, Mr. Collum, but I...I..." He stumbled over to his cot.

"You don't mean it!" Mr. Collum cried. "For heaven's sake, Nicholas! Now? Again?"

"Tomorrow...tomorrow..." Nicholas was mumbling now, sinking onto his side. He closed his eyes.

Mr. Collum cursed under his breath, stomped his foot, and closed the door. He locked it and stomped away.

Nicholas sat up. He listened. Then he leaped from his cot and began unpacking his suitcase in the dark, not even taking time to light a candle. He had a lot of work to do, and to have any hope of success, he needed to get started right away.

Fully dressed, with his suitcase in one hand and his key in the other, Nicholas let himself out of his room. Silently he slipped down the servants' stairs and listened at Mr. Pileus's door. Sounds of heavy breathing issued from within. Through the keyhole he saw that the room was dark. Satisfied, he tiptoed across the passage, unlocked the basement door, and disappeared down the steps.

A short while later Nicholas sneaked out the Manor's side door, staggering under the weight of his burdens. By the light of a newly risen moon, he made his way to the back of the garden shed—the nearest decent hiding spot. There he deposited his heavy suitcase, his heavy flour-sack backpack, and a heavy bag he had fashioned from his tarpaulin rain cloak. Wheezing from his efforts, he looked up at the round yellow moon, hanging low over the trees. Had it really been only a month since he'd sat alone on that bluff, gazing up at the full moon? That night seemed like ages ago. It might almost have happened to someone else. Almost.

Nicholas lit a match and knelt to study the ground. Sure enough, he detected the last faint traces of a minuscule ash pile, the remains of John's letter. It couldn't have been much to begin with, and now it was scarcely more than a gray smudge, most of the ashes having been blown away by wind or blended into the earth by rain. He looked mournfully at the spot until he felt the match starting to burn his fingers. *Good luck, John*, he thought. He shook out the match.

As soon as his wheezing had subsided, he went back inside

the Manor for his lantern and an extra supply of candles. He also paid a visit to the pantry. Then, leaving the heavy bags where he had hidden them, he hurried across the park, through the hickories, and over to the orphanage farm.

The farmhouse windows were dark, the barnyard still and quiet. Nicholas set his shoulders. He squared his jaw. He took a deep breath. Now was the time for patience and courage. He had to move with infinite stealth. He had to remain calm.

With almost agonizing slowness, Nicholas unlatched the barn door. He handled the latch as if it were explosive. He moved as slowly as a sloth on a vine. Never had he been so silent, so stealthy. Minutes passed as he opened the door just wide enough to slip through. Slowly he retreated a safe distance from the barn to light a small candle, which he carefully shaded with his hand. Then he tiptoed back to the door, slipped through the narrow crack, and began stalking toward the rear of the barn.

He moved now like a heron on the prowl for fish. One slow step, freeze. Wait. Another slow step, freeze. Wait. Always with his eyes searching, searching the ground before him.

And then he saw it. The half-finished carrot. It lay between the large, dangerous front hooves of Rabbit. The mule was asleep on his feet, yet even in his sleep he radiated hostility, or so it seemed to Nicholas. Sweat trickled down his face. If he made the least noise or misstep...

Now came the decisive moment. He could not risk Rabbit's seeing him do what he had to do next. And so, memorizing the exact position of the half-eaten carrot, Nicholas blew out his candle. The little flame made a very faint, very soft flicking sound as it was extinguished. In the sudden darkness that followed, Nicholas held his breath.

Nothing happened. All the animals remained asleep. Still holding his breath, Nicholas inched forward. Quietly. Carefully. Steadily. If he gauged wrong, he might very well touch a hoof instead of a carrot.

Don't gauge wrong, he told himself.

In one smooth motion Nicholas stooped, reached out a hand—and took hold of the carrot. He slipped it into his pocket. Still stooping, he backed away, took out his matchbox, and struck a match. There is no way to strike a match silently, and even as it flared to life, Nicholas heard the mule's breathing change, heard a shifting of hooves. With trembling fingers, he lit his candle, and in its stronger light he suddenly saw Rabbit's glossy black eyes fixed upon him. Nicholas stood rooted in place.

The mule looked down at the spot where the carrot stub had been. He put his nose to the ground, his nostrils flaring and contracting as he snuffled around in the dust and straw. Then he looked up at Nicholas with murderous eyes. His ears drew back flat against his head. His rubbery lips curled up to reveal two rows of hard yellow teeth. He brayed a horrible mule curse, so loud and frightening that Nicholas almost dropped his candle, and every powerful muscle in the creature's body tensed as he prepared to charge.

"Oh, please!" Nicholas whispered, digging frantically in his pocket. "Please, just one second! Look what I have for you!" His fingers closed around what he was digging for— the fresh carrot, the largest carrot he'd been able to find in the pantry—and he whipped it from his pocket and held it up for Rabbit to see.

Instantly the mule's ears straightened and rotated forward. He made a pleasant grumbling sound, and stepping closer, he pressed his head against Nicholas, almost knocking him down. His huge nostrils flared and flared as he sniffed, but Nicholas had already tucked the carrot back into his pocket.

"Not yet, old fellow," he said, scratching Rabbit gratefully between the ears. "First we have a job to do. Now come on, we have to hurry!"

Rabbit, as docile as a lamb, followed Nicholas out into the night.

⌣∴⌣

In the hour before dawn, a boy crept wearily and stealthily onto the Hopefield farm. He was the same boy rendered in Violet Hopefield's drawing—the boy on the bluff—yet in the month since that drawing had been made, he had learned so much, had come to feel and think so differently than before, that Nicholas Benedict looked upon that boy in his memory as something like a friendly stranger. He almost expected Violet not to recognize him.

She did, of course, and at the sight of him her face lit up. Nicholas saw the familiar radiance of her expression even in the darkness of her room—her relief and delight as brilliant as a sunrise. Indeed, no sooner had her eyes opened than she was leaping from her bed to embrace him, lifting him right off his feet and swinging him back and forth so vigorously that his boots almost fell off.

In her grogginess Violet was somewhat confused, however, and when at last she released Nicholas, she looked around wonderingly, perhaps searching for John, perhaps puzzled by how he had gotten in.

Nicholas drew her over to the open window and showed her the tall stepladder he had taken from her barn. *I need to show you something,* he signed. *Come with me. I'll explain everything soon. Hurry, please. We don't have much time.*

Violet quickly pulled on her boots and buttoned a jacket over her nightgown. *What about John?*

Nicholas shook his head. *Not tonight,* he signed, not wanting to tell her the sad news just yet. Sad for the two of them, anyway, if not for John. He turned away before she could ask more questions.

Only when they had descended the stepladder and stood in the moonlit farmyard did Violet notice Nicholas's rough appearance. His clothes were filthy, his face streaked with grime, his hands scraped and bloodied to the last knuckle. She stepped back, shocked. *What happened to you?*

Nicholas grinned. *I know, I look like I've been fighting a bear all night. I feel like it, too. Come on, I'll explain as we go, but we really need to hurry. If I don't get back before sunrise, I'll be in huge trouble.*

When they had reached the hill path and were under the cover of trees, Nicholas lit the lantern that he'd left there and led the way up. Now that he was no longer worried about Violet's parents overhearing him, he let loose a great torrent of words, his head turned toward Violet so that she might read his lips, interrupting himself every few seconds to look where he was going.

"Something's happened to me, Violet—a lot of things, actually—but the most important thing is that I've realized how selfish I've been. No, don't argue, it's true! I don't mean I've been wicked, exactly, but I've always been worried about myself more than anyone else. I suppose it's natural enough— you have to learn how to take care of yourself in orphanages, especially when the grownups aren't looking out for you— but it's simply no way to live! There's no joy in it!

"Can you believe that yesterday it occurred to me, for the first time, that I should try to help protect the other kids from the Spiders? For the first time, Violet! It amazes me to think of it. Sure I'm only nine, but I'm supposed to be smarter than all of them put together, am I not? And yet I've just gone about my business, resenting the way everyone treats me and dealing with the Spiders whenever I have to. But everyone is scared! No one knows what to do! And who's going to show them if not me? Why, over and over again in my mind, I've been seeing poor little Vern, frightened out of his wits, sneaking up to me to give me a note saying he's sorry. And Oliver taking a risk to tell me something important, simply to be decent. Sure, I said thanks, but I hardly even looked at him! And I left without once considering how scared he might have been, how much courage it might have taken just to speak to me. I was too preoccupied with my own problems!"

Nicholas stumbled over a rock, regained his footing, and kept going. Violet followed him up the path, trying to watch his lips and her step at the same time. He never slowed down.

"And this treasure! This ridiculous treasure!" Nicholas rolled his eyes. "I've put all this thought into finding the treasure and having it solve all my problems. But what about *your* problems, Violet? What about John's? What about all the other kids? Do you know what happened the other morning, just before I left for Stonetown? John was about to suggest that we tell Mr. Collum what we've learned. I'm sure of it. And I'm also sure I know why. John wasn't just thinking about himself, see. He was thinking about all the other orphans. What happens to them if the Manor gets closed down? Sure, maybe they'll get sent to a better place. But maybe it will be worse. Who can say? And what about the staff? What happens to old Mrs. Brindle if the Manor closes? What are the chances anyone else will hire her? What will *she* do?

"Do you see, Violet? John was thinking we should share information with Mr. Collum, even if we got in trouble, because maybe Mr. Collum knew something we didn't, and if we all worked together, we might find a solution. But do you know what I did? I cut him off. I didn't want to hear it! The last thing I wanted to do was share anything with Mr. Collum—and probably get punished in the bargain. No, thanks!"

Violet tried to catch Nicholas's arm. She wanted to stop him, wanted to say something, but Nicholas shook his head. "Please let me finish, Violet. I promise I'll answer all your questions and tell you whatever you want to know soon. And I'll listen to whatever you have to say, too. Is that all right?"

Violet put her hands on her hips and regarded him. She must have seen that he felt ready to burst with emotion. Perhaps she understood that if he tried to hold it in now, he'd simply collapse. She nodded. *All right. Go on.*

Nicholas smiled with relief and gratitude. "Thank you,

Violet. Really, I mean it." He started on up the path. "And really, I want to thank you for a lot of other things besides. That drawing of yours—well, I won't get into that now— but that drawing, and all the picnics, and your friendship most of all. I'm ashamed when I think of the sacrifices you've made, like telling your parents you don't really want to go to art school anymore, even though it's killing you not to go— you do these things because you care about them. Well, I care about you, but until recently it never occurred to me to make a sacrifice for you."

He gave Violet a rueful look. "I didn't want you to go, see. Something in me—well, I wouldn't even let myself think about what I could do for you. Not if it meant losing you. And isn't that what art school would mean? You would leave!"

Violet couldn't help herself. *Sorry, I'm confused. If we found the treasure—*

"But what if we never did?" Nicholas interrupted. "If we didn't find the treasure, I wouldn't want you to go to art school any more than I'd want John to be adopted. Sure, I wanted you both to be happy—but not if it meant losing you! Oh, it's very mixed up, Violet. I never thought about any of this, really, not the way I'm telling you about it. I avoided any thoughts of the kind. I didn't want to see the truth, I guess.

"But I see it now. I see that some things are hard to do but that you can't live with yourself if you don't do them. I see that the best way to help myself is to help the people I care about. The rest will sort itself out—it *has* to, right?" Nicholas stopped and looked at Violet searchingly, as if he doubted his own words and only needed her agreement to believe them. She nodded and squeezed his arm.

I think so, Violet signed. *I hope so.* She offered him a slight smile. *I still want to think we have a chance of finding the treasure, though. Am I wrong? Have you learned something? Is that what this is about?*

"The treasure?" said Nicholas, as if he'd forgotten it. "Oh! Sorry, I've just been so focused on this other thing—" He laughed and shook his head. "No, I don't know. I do have something new I'm going to try, but I haven't had a chance yet. This other business had to come first, and it took longer than I expected. You see—well, come on, a few more steps and you *will* see."

Nicholas took Violet's hand, and together they hurried on up the path. So intently focused had Violet been on reading Nicholas's lips—it was extremely hard to do as they stumbled up the path, with the lantern moving, and so often having to check her footing—that she had not paid attention to where they were heading until now. But here they were, coming out of the trees and into the boulder field, the site of the collapsed mine, of her collapsed dreams.

And there, gleaming in the moonlight, was the drill.

Mysteries and Revelations

Violet's hands flew to her mouth, her eyes grew wide, and she burst into tears. She threw her arms around Nicholas, squeezing him tightly. Nicholas squeezed back, trying hard not to be overly affected by her emotion. He had expected her to be thrilled, but her rush of tears had caught him off guard. He took deep breaths and imagined an infinite field of green plaid. Given his current state of exhaustion, if he fell asleep now, he might not wake for hours.

Violet drew back from him, her face shining with tears. She ran over to the drill, walking around and around it, inspecting it. Shaking her head, she looked at Nicholas. *How did you do this?* she signed. *It's perfect. It's just as it always was, only*—she glanced in the direction of the collapsed mine, the too-narrow tunnel, then back at Nicholas in amazement—*only now it's out here! How is this possible?*

"We did it together, Violet," Nicholas said, grinning. "If you hadn't mummified it so well, greasing the parts and wrapping it all up the way you did, I doubt I could have taken it apart."

Violet stared. *You…took it apart? And put it back together again the way it was?*

Nicholas shrugged. "You told me that the engineer and his assistant used to have to dismantle it sometimes. It should have occurred to me right then that I could do the same thing."

But they had blueprints! And tools!

"Oh, I had plenty of tools myself!" Nicholas said, and he gestured up toward the ridge. Violet looked and saw a powerful mule tethered to a tree, asleep on its feet. Strapped to its back was a set of makeshift saddlebags, including a battered suitcase. "Rabbit carried them up here for me. As for the blueprints, well, once I had taken the drill apart, I knew where everything was supposed to go, didn't I? It's actually a pretty simple machine. The hardest thing was getting the parts out through the tunnel. I had to take the larger pieces out one at a time, and the rest in small bundles. It made for a lot of crawling. Good thing I'm still so small, right?"

I can't believe it, Violet signed. *I don't know what to say.*

Nicholas drew an envelope from beneath his shirt. "I know the contract expires today—but not before the mining company has to officially cease its operations. That drill is in perfect condition and perfectly retrievable. A friend of mine has assured me the company will have to honor its agreement and pay your family what it owes." He handed the envelope to Violet. "Here are the names and telephone numbers of a few high officials, as well as a powerful attorney—all friends of my friend, all of them aware of the situation now. He contacted them this morning—or, I suppose I should say, yesterday morning."

Violet was turning the envelope over and over in her hands. She seemed to be in a state of shock.

Nicholas glanced at the moon, now disconcertingly low in the sky. He waved to get her attention. "I really need to hurry, Violet. I can't stay much longer."

Violet nodded slowly, as if it were taking some time for his words to sink in. Then she slipped the envelope into her jacket pocket and signed, *How do we explain to the company what you've done without getting you in trouble at the orphanage?*

"You don't owe them any explanations," Nicholas replied. "Let it be a miracle. The drill is worth a lot of money—it only makes sense for them to take it back and pay you. Anyway, my friend's friends will make sure that they do."

But who is this friend?

"A very fine person. You'd like him, Violet. But I'll have to tell you more about him tomorrow, or whenever we can meet next." Again Nicholas glanced anxiously at the sky. "I wish we could talk more, but this took me longer than I hoped it would."

Violet nodded, understanding the need for haste, but her face expressed her frustration. *I'm sorry, I just have so many questions! Surely I can tell my parents what you've done, right? They'll be so grateful! They'll—*

Nicholas shook his head, interrupting, "You know me, Violet. I prefer to remain mysterious." He grinned. "Honestly, you're the only one who needs to know. That's more than enough for me."

Violet frowned. *We can argue about this later. But of course we will tell John, right? He needs to see what you've done here. He'll be amazed! And he'll be so proud of you, Nicholas. I know he will!*

There was no longer any avoiding it. Nicholas had to explain what had happened with John. He didn't even want to think about it himself, but of course he had to, and so fighting back the tears that had suddenly started to fill his eyes, Nicholas told Violet he had something difficult to say and begged her not to interrupt him. Then, speaking quickly (both to get it over with and because he was in such a hurry), he began to explain. As he did, he saw, through the watery haze in his eyes, Violet's worried look turn to one of astonishment, then confusion, and then, finally, sympathy.

That must have been so terrible for you, Violet signed when Nicholas had finished, and she hugged him, gently patting his back as she might have done with a much smaller child.

Nicholas thought of Violet's little sisters. No doubt she'd had practice comforting them many a time. She was quite good at it; he could feel her sympathy through and through. Somehow, though, it made him want to cry even harder, to let all his feelings come pouring out—a dangerous impulse under the circumstances. He bit his lip, fighting back the urge.

"I know it's hard for you, too, Violet," Nicholas said

finally, stepping away and wiping the tears from his eyes. "I know you've lost a friend, too. I'm really sorry."

Violet smiled. She, too, wiped away tears, and she started to sign something, but Nicholas grabbed her hands.

"We'll talk more tonight! I promise! Tonight I'll listen to everything you have to say! I know we have lots to talk about. For now let me just give you something before I go." He reached into his pockets and took out several nuts and bolts, as well as two or three small, unidentifiable mechanical parts, and dumped them into Violet's open hands. "You should keep these as souvenirs. I'm pretty sure the drill will run more efficiently without them."

Violet's eyebrows shot up. Quickly she set the pieces down so that she could sign, *You mean you* improved *the* drill?

Nicholas winked. "Don't tell anyone," he said.

Violet was still trying to sign to Nicholas as he hurried away, but he dared not pay her any more attention. Both her sympathy and her tearful expressions of gratitude had already come close to undoing him. He was in a race against the sunrise, and he still had more work ahead of him. He couldn't risk falling asleep. Not yet. Not now. Not when he was so close.

Up the trail, over the ridge, and down again Nicholas led Rabbit. So long as he had the promise of a carrot before him, the old mule was remarkably tolerant, and Nicholas felt guilty knowing he would not get his fresh carrot. Giving it to him now would throw the morning schedule into chaos, though, and make life harder for Mr. Furrow. "I'll make it up to you soon," Nicholas murmured, patting Rabbit's side. "I promise. Pretty soon there will be no more hard days for you."

Nicholas had had an extraordinarily hard day himself—*days*, actually, and nights, too—and was fairly amazed he had not collapsed. True, he had fallen asleep twice during his night's labor, both times while crawling through that spooky, narrow tunnel, but both times his alarm clock had awakened him. (And both times, unfortunately, he had sat up in a panic, knocking his skull painfully against the tunnel ceiling. Now he had two knots on his head, both throbbing, and with his long nose and these new, knobby horns, he suspected he looked like a giraffe.) Now he had one last thing to do before returning the tools to the basement and Rabbit to the barn. He was pressing his luck, he knew. But he thought he had just enough time.

Tethering the mule to a tree at the edge of the clearing, Nicholas took a hammer and chisel from one of the saddle-bags and trotted toward Giant's Head with a curious mixture of satisfaction, bafflement, and dread.

On the one hand, he was pleased that it had finally occurred to him that he could simply break into the walls. But on the other, why hadn't he thought of it sooner? He had tools enough. A few well-placed holes should be all it took to show him if there were any special, secret gears at work in the observatory. Was it because some stubborn part of him had wanted to solve the mystery with his wits rather than a chisel? Or had he been too afraid that he would find nothing behind the wall? He had to admit, he was afraid of that possibility even now.

Nicholas shuffled through the high grass, wondering at himself. The biggest mystery of all had to be the contra-dictory workings of his own mind. Why, he'd even been tempted to reject this idea when it occurred to him yesterday! He'd told himself he might damage some hidden mechanism by accident. But if he damaged something, could he not repair it? Could he not repair anything under the sun? And why would he not wish to know the truth?

There could be no more shying away from truth, he told himself. Never again, no matter what. He must always seek it out.

Inside the observatory, Nicholas carried his lantern over to the cranks. For a long minute he stood there, considering the best place to start chiseling. Then he shook himself with a laugh. *You've got a lot of work to do*, he thought, for even now he was delaying the moment of truth. Putting down his lantern, Nicholas positioned the chisel between two stones, took a deep breath, and set to hammering.

Five minutes later the wall had several small holes in it. All of them revealed the same thing: nothing. Nothing more than the gears and chains that moved the viewing panels and the turntable. There were no hidden mechanisms. There was no entrance to any treasure chamber in the observatory.

Nicholas sighed and rubbed the tender bumps on his head. He was both surprised and not surprised. That is, he was surprised by the fact that he was *not* surprised to find nothing. For only now that he had forced himself to look inside the walls did he realize that he hadn't really expected to find anything there. Had some part of him *always* known this would be the case? If so, it was amazing how long he had put off the inevitable.

Nicholas gathered his tools, took up his lantern, and hurried out. He could marvel at his own thickheadedness later.

Right now he was still in a race against the dawn. And he still had to figure out what to do next.

The fact was, Nicholas's mind had been in a whirl since yesterday, and he had yet to think everything through. Part of his plan had involved the treasure, or at least some knowledge of its whereabouts. But that was as far as he'd gotten, and now even that much was lost to him. Time was short, and he was no closer to finding the treasure than he ever had been. Had he been foolish to believe it even existed?

No, he reminded himself as he ran back over to Rabbit. He might have been overly optimistic, but he had not been utterly foolish. There *was* the matter of the missing inheritance, after all. There was Mr. Rothschild's diary and its mentions of treasure. And there was Mr. Collum, who clearly believed that the treasure existed, that it was hidden somewhere on the Rothschild estate.

So what had he missed? Nicholas put his things back into the saddlebags, awakened Rabbit again, and set off on the final leg of his long night's journey. The moon had sunk beyond a distant hill, birds were beginning to rustle and chirp in the trees, and Nicholas's thoughts were dashing hither and thither. Was there some evidence hidden in plain sight that he had overlooked, like that purloined letter in the story Violet had mentioned? If so, what?

Think, Nicholas commanded himself. He tried to marshal his scattered notions.

The first thing that occurred to him was that he had been aware of certain evidence all along but that his experience had led him to be suspicious of it. Namely, the truth about Mrs. Rothschild's character. Both Mr. Rothschild and Mr. Furrow seemed to believe that she really had been kind, generous, and selfless, and now that Nicholas had met Mr. Harinton—now that he'd finally met a living example of such a person—he was prepared to believe it. But then how to make sense of Diana Rothschild reveling in her treasure like a greedy dragon? And how to make sense of that missing inheritance?

Nicholas wished he could visit a different library, one older than the library in Stonetown, and read all the newspapers from that very important year. It was remarkable, really, the significance of that single year in this mystery: Mrs. Rothschild's rich father, Mr. Rexal, had died, after which she had presumably received the inheritance, after which the Rothschilds had made that unusual trip into Stonetown...to do what? In all those business meetings and appointments with various kinds of agents, what had they been up to if not securing the treasure? Had they not been making secretive arrangements at all? Had Nicholas imagined everything?

Something told him otherwise. They did go to Stonetown, after all, despite Mrs. Rothschild's reluctance to appear in high society. Nicholas recalled the photograph of Mrs. Rothschild at that literary luncheon, her arms full of books; that luncheon had been the only invitation she had accepted. Next, for some reason not immediately clear to him, Nicholas imagined Mrs. Rothschild visiting the Stonetown Library. He pictured her wandering around the lobby. Why was that? Was it because she had loved books so much?

But it was impossible for Mrs. Rothschild to have visited the Stonetown Library. Construction on the library would not begin until later that year. Wasn't that right? Nicholas's mind summoned the image of the plaque set into the floor of that beautiful lobby:

Construction of this Free and Public Library of Stonetown, designed by the eminent architects Mason & Mason, funded by the Alexandria Foundation, and open to all citizens of our great republic...

For the first time it occurred to him how appropriate those names were—a mason was a builder, after all, and Alexandria had been the site of the greatest library in the ancient world. Nicholas found himself smiling with relief, for ever since he had looked at that plaque, there had been a sort of itch in his brain, and now at last he seemed to have scratched it. No wonder he'd kept seeing those words in his mind.

Nicholas took a few more paces down the trail, then stopped so abruptly that Rabbit's nose bumped him between the shoulder blades and nearly sent him tumbling. He had just realized that the itch was not entirely gone. In fact, all of a sudden it seemed stronger than ever. Why was that?

He took another look at the plaque in his mind. Then he gasped. He staggered sideways, laying a hand against Rabbit to steady himself. It was as if every thought in his mind had suddenly gone luminescent—as if his head were the observatory on the hill, and Nicholas had cranked open the roof, and the moonlight had flooded in.

He had solved the mystery.

⌣∴∼

"You see? I can't wake him," a sleepy, half-stupefied Nicholas heard Mrs. Brindle saying. He kept his eyes closed. He was in his cot. "He's been this way all morning."

"Let him sleep, then," said Mr. Collum, his voice testy but resigned. "I'll have Mr. Pileus check on him again in an hour."

"But what do you suppose happened to him? Why, look at those bumps! Do you think those boys knocked him about?"

"It's impossible. I was in the dormitory all night and did not sleep a wink. No, perhaps he fell out of bed during one of his nightmares. I understand he often flails about quite violently."

"Must've fallen out multiple times if that's true," Mrs. Brindle murmured. "Shall I fetch Miss Pretty Pills?"

"No name-calling, please, Mrs. Brindle. And no, let us leave Miss Candace out of this. He seems to be resting peacefully. No doubt his ridiculous escapades have simply left him over-tired. Come, let's return to our duties."

The adults returned to their duties, and Nicholas returned to dreaming. As sometimes happened in his dreams, he relived recent events as if for the first time. With an extraordinary sense of reality, his dream self staggered out of the woods with Rabbit, successfully returned the tools to the basement, put the mule safely away in the barn. He caught a fleeting glimpse of the Old Hag on the trail through the hickory trees, but luck smiled upon him, and she passed without seeing him. Shivering from the awful sight of her, Nicholas made his way back to the Manor, washed up, changed into his pajamas, hid his filthy clothes, and collapsed into the cot.

Now the Old Hag was back. He couldn't move, couldn't breathe. She had passed through the solid stone wall and floated hideously over his bed. Then she was standing on his chest.

Nicholas screamed, and the fearsome creature disappeared in a puff of smoke. Suddenly standing over the cot where the Old Hag had been was Mr. Pileus, looking most fretful.

Nicholas, panting and trembling, broke into a grin. "How do you do, Mr. Pileus? I trust you slept well." He sat up in the cot and stretched. "Do you by any chance know what time it is?"

Mr. Pileus showed Nicholas his pocket watch.

It was after lunchtime. He had slept through the morning. Mr. Pileus had brought up a plate of food—freshly picked beans and tomatoes, a rough chunk of brown bread, a glass of cool milk. Nicholas wolfed it all down with tremendous satisfaction as Mr. Pileus inspected his wall, casting increasingly nervous glances at Nicholas.

At last Mr. Pileus frowned and said, "Slow down or you might choke."

Nicholas saluted and slowed down, but only a little. The exertions of last night had left him ravenous, and indeed he was still hungry when he'd finished. He hoped his extra chores would include pantry and kitchen work. Perhaps he could sneak an extra bite or two. First, however—and far more important than food—he needed to meet with Mr. Collum.

"Is everyone over at the school, Mr. Pileus? And is Mr. Collum expecting me?"

Mr. Pileus nodded. Paused. Nodded again. So yes on both counts.

"I'll be ready in no time, then!" Nicholas cried, and dashed to the bathroom with his things.

Mr. Collum was in his office. He looked to be in a sad state of exhaustion. Dark circles beneath his eyes, his face drawn, his tie loosened. He sat staring bemusedly at the ledger on his desk. The ledger was closed. The jeweler's loupe rested upon it. He was only thinking. Or trying not to think. When he became aware of Nicholas standing in his doorway, he straightened, cleared his throat, and absently tightened his tie as if preparing to go out. He was reviving himself, gathering his wits.

"Come in, Nicholas!" Mr. Collum said. "Please close the door behind you. Have a seat. Let us waste no time."

Nicholas did not sit, however, but launched at once into his speech. "I agree entirely, Mr. Collum. And in the interest of not wasting time, allow me to tell you right off that I have not been entirely forthcoming with you. The fact is, I know about the treasure you're looking for. Mrs. Rothschild's treasure. You know how quickly I read, Mr. Collum, so you'll believe me when I tell you that I've read Mr. Rothschild's diary. I sneaked a glance at it once, in an unguarded moment. And I have solved the mystery, and I am prepared to share with you what I know."

Mr. Collum, who had started from his chair at the mention of the treasure, slowly sank down into it again. He laid his palms flat on his desk, his eyes swiveling left and right in confused agitation. He seemed to be having trouble absorbing Nicholas's words. His eyes came to rest again on Nicholas's face. "You...you *know*? About...everything?"

"I do. And as I say, I will reveal it all to you." Only now did Nicholas take a seat. He drew his legs up so that he was sitting cross-legged in the chair, and lacing his fingers together and leaning forward, he said earnestly, "I do have a few conditions, however. Things you must agree to first."

Mr. Collum's face, which had begun to show excitement, colored. His hands trembled on the desk. "Conditions," he said flatly. "You have *conditions*?"

Nicholas smiled. "Yes, but I think you'll find them acceptable. If you'll just agree to them, I'll take you to the treasure. You have only to give me your word."

Mr. Collum's nostrils flared. He stared at Nicholas, obviously trying to master his anger. He seemed unable to speak.

"Shall I list them for you?" Nicholas prompted. "Or is now not a good time? Would you prefer that I write them down and bring you the list later?"

Mr. Collum opened his mouth as if to speak, but no sound came out. A glass of water stood on his desk, and with a sudden movement he grabbed it and drank all the water in a gulp. Then he banged the glass down and stared at Nicholas again. He looked as though he were bracing himself for a blow.

In a conciliatory tone, Nicholas suggested that perhaps he could quickly rattle off the conditions now—in the interest of saving time. Mr. Collum only stared, his lips drawn together in a tight line. And so Nicholas listed the conditions.

Mr. Hopefield, he said, the owner of the farm just to the north of the Manor, was soon to acquire a tractor. Nicholas wanted Mr. Collum to approach Mr. Hopefield and suggest a cooperative arrangement. The orphanage farm could borrow Mr. Hopefield's tractor, and in exchange Mr. Hopefield, during the busy harvest season, would receive help in his fields from a rotating group of older children.

"I'm confident we can arrange it so that everyone benefits, and no one is overworked—especially not any of the children. We'll be able to produce more crops and sell the excess in town."

Mr. Collum blinked, confused. "This—this is your condition?" he asked, finding his voice.

"The first one," Nicholas said, and hurried on.

Mr. Collum must also purchase additional chickens for the orphanage farm. The surplus eggs could likewise be sold in Pebbleton, where there happened to be a great demand for them, and yet a scarce supply. Cream, too, for that matter. Nicholas was certain that a daily trip into Pebbleton with eggs, cream, and vegetables to sell would be most profitable.

"We won't get rich, mind you," Nicholas said, "but you know how to manage money wisely, Mr. Collum, and I'm positive that with a few adjustments, we can keep the orphanage running."

Mr. Collum was leaning forward now, turning his head first to one side and then to the other, as if he were not hearing Nicholas properly.

"Of course," Nicholas continued, still speaking rapidly, "we won't be needing our old mule anymore, but I happen to know of a man who is in urgent need of a watchdog for his barn, only he can't *have* a watchdog—his wife is afraid of dogs, you see—and I feel quite certain that he'd be willing to pay good money for a watch *mule*." He allowed himself a quick, nickering laugh, and Mr. Collum's eyebrows rose in surprise. He had never heard Nicholas laugh before.

"We can explain to the man," Nicholas went on, "that all he needs to do is put Rabbit in his barn with a carrot each night. Rabbit will take care of the rest. And we can use the proceeds from the sale to buy the extra chickens. Do you see how neatly that works?"

Mr. Collum's eyes darted left and right as he weighed these suggestions. "But where do *you* come in?" he muttered. His eyes settled on Nicholas's face again. "What about *you*?"

"Oh, I'm glad you asked!" Nicholas cried. "What I would like to do, you see, is repair all that extra equipment in the basement so that we can sell it—or, even better, rent it out, which would provide a small but steady income for the Manor. None of that stuff is being used, anyway, and I'm quite handy with tools."

"But...but...but these are all *excellent* ideas!" Mr. Collum cried, suddenly animated. He leaped to his feet, thumping his fists on his desk and almost upsetting the empty glass. He wasn't looking at Nicholas—his eyes were fixed on some point above Nicholas's head. "Why, they really might work! We don't need much! Only a little bit more, and I'm sure we can make a go of it! No humiliations! My reputation—" Mr. Collum caught himself. He closed his mouth and looked about the office, plainly disconcerted. He was still avoiding Nicholas's eye.

Nicholas raised a finger. "To be clear on one thing, though, we must keep the bicycle-powered phonograph and records, to be used for socials and rainy-day activities. We can take turns on the bicycle, which is excellent exercise, and the others can dance, which is also excellent exercise. I'm sure you'll agree, Mr. Collum, that exercise promotes good health. True, it can be noisy, which I believe was your reason for prohibiting the use of the phonograph. But my conditions provide for that, too. We'll clean up Mr. Rothschild's old study upstairs, which you may then use as a second study, or even as your main one—whichever you like. When you're up *there*, you'll be protected from any noise down *here*. It's the same principle that has you locking me into my room each night, isn't it? So that my screams won't disturb anyone on the other floor? But unlike me, Mr. Collum, you will have a choice."

This was the only part in Nicholas's speech in which his tone grew icy and accusing. He quickly shook it off, however, and went on cheerfully to explain his last few conditions. The girls' dormitory would be relocated to the schoolhouse, which was mild, quiet, and pleasant at night and would offer the girls better sleep. School would be held in the ballroom, which during the daytime was more comfortable than the hot and stuffy schoolhouse. Nicholas named one or two other ways in which the Manor could be made to run more efficiently, then drew to a close.

"I believe that's all for now, Mr. Collum," he said. "Though I hope you'll allow me to consult with you in the future about other possible improvements. I'm sure more will occur to me as we move forward with these changes."

By this time the director had retaken his seat and was listening intently to every word. When at last Nicholas lapsed into a waiting silence, Mr. Collum was plainly baffled. Cocking his head to the side, he said, "But I repeat, Nicholas, what about you? Don't you wish to be released from your punishments? Or to be moved into a different room? Or to receive some reward? What is it that you want for *yourself*?"

"Oh, as for that," Nicholas said, waving off the question, "all of this *is* for me—for me as much as anyone. As you've said yourself, the Manor is going to be my home for a while. Why wouldn't I want it to be as pleasant a home as possible?" His face took on a sly expression, and with a subtle shrug, he added, "Naturally, I also wish to partake of the treasure."

Mr. Collum suddenly looked extremely serious. "Ah," he said, narrowing his eyes. "So now we come to the truth at last."

"No," Nicholas said, and he looked Mr. Collum directly in the eye. "We arrived at the truth the moment I walked into this room. You've already admitted that with the changes I'm suggesting, we can probably save the orphanage. There is no reason for you to keep all the treasure for yourself, Mr. Collum. None whatsoever."

Mr. Collum pursed his lips, obviously weighing his response.

"However," said Nicholas in a much lighter tone, "we can negotiate those details later." He jumped up. "If you'll just agree to these conditions, I'll take you to the treasure right away."

Mr. Collum likewise jumped up—in surprise. "You can't be serious!"

Nicholas frowned in mock confusion. "I can't?" He knew Mr. Collum had no idea how to handle him. Mr. Collum could not understand why Nicholas would take him to the treasure without arriving at some agreement first. Why would the boy throw away his only bargaining chip?

Mr. Collum quickly recovered, and seizing the opportunity, he cried, "But of course I'll agree to the conditions! They're very fine recommendations, Nicholas, and I'll be delighted to implement the changes you suggest. I give you my word."

And with that, Mr. Collum extended his hand to Nicholas for the first time. And Nicholas shook it.

"I take you at your word, then," Nicholas said with a smile. "And now you had better prepare yourself."

Mr. Collum swallowed, took a sharp breath, nodded. "Lead the way, young man."

Nicholas did. With Mr. Collum at his heels, he marched out of the office, across the entranceway, and into the library, where, with a delighted look, he threw out his arms and turned in a slow circle. "Welcome," he exclaimed triumphantly, "to the treasure chamber!"

I don't understand," Mr. Collum said, glancing about the library. "You don't mean the library itself, surely. Do you mean there is a secret panel that leads to the chamber? Where is it?"

Nicholas gestured at the shelves. "The books are the treasure, Mr. Collum. The books! Mrs. Rothschild spent hour upon hour luxuriating in *books*. She loved them so much she often looked in on them even when she didn't intend to read. She'd go out of her way to do so. And why shouldn't she? They're beautiful, aren't they?"

Mr. Collum was bewildered. Slowly he sat down in one of the chairs. "But he called it her treasure. He specifically called it...called it..."

"But it *is* a treasure, Mr. Collum," insisted Nicholas. "Think of the wealth of knowledge in this room! Think of the riches! It's easy to see why Mr. Rothschild would call the books her treasure. They were a treasure even before he had them re-covered so beautifully."

Mr. Collum stiffened. His eyes gained focus as he looked at Nicholas. "Re-covered? But I thought..." His voice trailed off as understanding dawned on him.

"You thought that the treasure had gone missing? Or been stolen?" Nicholas chuckled and shook his head. "I was misled by that, too. But of course he was only referring to the new covers on all the books—those lovely leather covers with the golden lettering. That was his big surprise for Diana. I can't believe I didn't see it! He had nicknames for almost everybody, didn't he? So when he referred to 'Mr. Booker,' why didn't I realize that the man had something to do with *books*? But it's clear enough now, isn't it? Mr. Rothschild hired him to 'recover' this entire library while he and Diana were out of the country!"

"It's possible," Mr. Collum muttered dejectedly. He rubbed his face. "It's possible, yes. But it isn't certain. I'm sure it isn't certain."

"I'm afraid it is," Nicholas said gently. "All the clues point to it. Just think, Mr. Rothschild referred to the 'discomfiting cold,' didn't he? Well, look around, Mr. Collum. There's no fireplace in this library. It's one of the very few rooms in the Manor not to have one. Neither of us has been in here during the winter, you know. You arrived in the spring, and I came in the summer. I'll bet in the winter, we'll find out that this room gets awfully chilly."

Mr. Collum was not listening. Something had occurred to him. He'd risen to his feet again and gone to a window to look out, deep in thought. Suddenly snapping his fingers, he whirled to face Nicholas. "You're forgetting something, Nicholas! The missing inheritance! If these books are the treasure, then where did those millions go? Hmm? Tell me *that*!"

"I hate to disappoint you, Mr. Collum," said Nicholas (though this was not entirely true), "but those missing millions went to the construction of the Stonetown Library, the first free and public library in the entire region. Mrs. Rothschild donated the money anonymously, of course, because she wouldn't have wanted all the attention. But neither did she need that money, and it was just like her to give it away. I know that now, though I didn't used to. I didn't believe people like Mrs. Rothschild existed. But some do. Not many, maybe, but some."

"But how…" Mr. Collum's voice faltered. And once again he sat down, this time on the window seat behind him, and he sat more heavily than before. He put his head into his hands. At long last, he had come to accept that Nicholas possessed a most extraordinary mind, which was an unnerving fact on its own, but one made still worse by his understanding that if Nicholas truly was a genius, then he was probably right about the missing inheritance.

"I…I don't understand yet, Nicholas," Mr. Collum said quietly, from behind his hands. "Please explain to me how you know all this."

Nicholas came to sit beside Mr. Collum on the window seat. He looked out across the library at all the beautiful books, and speaking softly, he said, "Construction on the Stonetown Library began the same year Mrs. Rothschild received her inheritance, not long after she and Mr. Rothschild went into Stonetown to have a lot of meetings. I'm certain she was making arrangements for the library to be built. She formed a charitable foundation as a cover, so that she might remain anonymous. She called it the Alexandria Foundation, which seems a perfect choice, when you think about it. Alexandria was the site of the greatest library in the ancient world. Awfully clever of her, don't you think?"

Mr. Collum shrugged. "I wouldn't know," he muttered. "It appears that I'm no fair judge of cleverness."

"Well, you can take my word for it," Nicholas said. "It was awfully clever of her, and I'll tell you why. The reason behind the name 'Alexandria' seemed so obvious that nobody ever wondered if there were other reasons, too. Sly reasons. In all these years, no one appears ever to have considered that 'Alexandria' might also be an anagram for the anonymous donor—the person behind the foundation. Do you remember Mrs. Rothschild's maiden name, Mr. Collum?"

"Rexal, wasn't it?"

"Exactly. Her maiden name was *Diana Rexal*. Rearrange the letters, Mr. Collum, and you have *Alexandria*." Nicholas grinned. "Diana was smart. I'll bet she already knew about that anagram when she was *my* age—and I'll bet she loved it. When the time came to name the foundation, I'm sure the choice was plain to her."

"And you have proof of all this?" Mr. Collum asked, lowering his hands.

"Why, do you still have your doubts?"

Mr. Collum considered, then shook his head. "I only wondered."

Nicholas shrugged. "So far it's all circumstantial evidence, but everything seems to fit, doesn't it? We might never be able to get actual proof. You know Mrs. Rothschild would have arranged it so that no one could ever find out for sure. Otherwise someone *would* have figured it out, and she would have been in all the newspapers, which is the last thing she would have wanted. Her privacy was so important to her. And Mr. Rothschild was careful to protect it, too — he never mentions the inheritance anywhere in his diary. He wouldn't have wanted anyone to come across it accidentally and discover the truth."

The two former treasure hunters sat for some time in silence.

"I can't believe it," Mr. Collum said at last. "All this time, and the answer was right here in plain sight."

"Isn't that the way?" Nicholas agreed. "Those Rothschilds really had us going. But as for me, I'm glad it turned out this way. It seems more decent, somehow. I think I feel richer than any amount of money could have made me feel."

Mr. Collum looked at him askance. "Are you joking, son?"

Nicholas shook his head. "Of course, I might be wrong about that. I've been wrong about a lot of things."

Mr. Collum smiled at him then. It seemed a rather grudging smile, but it was a smile, nonetheless. "Well, you did solve a mystery. A mystery that has thwarted curious minds for decades. I suppose that would make anyone feel rich."

Again the two of them sat in silence for some time.

Then, as if by unspoken agreement, they stood up and shook hands. They went their separate ways, each to his duties.

Giant's Head was vacant when Nicholas arrived that night—a windy, starry night, with strips of clouds racing across the face of the moon. He had arrived earlier than usual, and he had brought a broom. Putting down his lantern, he set about sweeping the observatory floor, clearing away the dust and bits of rubble left behind by his chiseling. The whole time he thought of John. He wondered what his friend was doing now, whether he was happy with his new family. Now that Nicholas was on somewhat better terms with Mr. Collum, he intended to get the family's address and write John a letter. He would explain everything that had happened. He would say that he planned to keep Giant's Head clean in John's honor. And he would wish John all the happiness in the world. And mean it.

Even so, and despite his general state of excitement, by the time Violet arrived, Nicholas had grown rather melancholy, and the sight of her in the doorway lifted his spirits. Her hair was flying all about her head—the wind was really howling around the observatory now—and Nicholas even laughed and told her she looked like a witch.

"A good witch, though," he said as she came in. "My favorite, in fact."

Violet smiled affectionately at him and rubbed his head. (Nicholas cringed, but by some miracle she missed both of his painful knots.) *You will need another haircut soon*, she signed. *Your hair has gotten so long I can actually see it.*

They sat down to talk. Violet, to Nicholas's delight, had brought an entire blackberry pie and an entire bottle of milk, and she cut big slices for each of them. As Nicholas ate, Violet told him about her day. Everything had gone wonderfully well, she said. Everyone was amazed and excited. After a brief telephone conversation, the mining-company officials had sent a representative to confirm that the drill was indeed retrievable. Shocked though they were, they understood their position and agreed to fulfill their obligations at once. And no sooner had this been arranged than Mr. Collum had telephoned her father to discuss ways they might cooperate to help each other.

Mr. Collum had somehow gotten the impression that my father intended to purchase a tractor, Violet signed, *which surprised my father very much, as he hadn't actually decided that yet but was considering it.*

Nicholas grinned and wiped milk from his mouth. "Well, it only makes sense, doesn't it? Now that you're getting the money from the mining company, those savings can be spent on a tractor, and you can still go to art school next year."

We'll see about that, Violet signed. *There are a lot of things to consider.*

Nicholas was amazed. "Like what? You aren't serious, are you? It's your dream!"

Violet did not seem concerned. *We can discuss this later. Don't worry, I'm fine. We're all happier than we have been in ages.*

No matter what, everything is going to be all right. Now, I know you have things to tell me, too. So tell me, please. There is plenty of pie. You don't have to eat it all at once.

Nicholas told Violet about everything—about his first disappointing trip to Stonetown, about running away after he found out about John, about meeting Mr. Harinton. She knew about the drill, of course, so he passed over this to tell her about the night before, about the realizations that had come to him.

"You can see I paid a visit on my way back to the Manor," Nicholas said, indicating the holes in the wall.

Yes, I noticed those. I figured you must have found nothing or you would have told me immediately.

"I don't want to get your hopes up," Nicholas said, "so let me tell you right off—there isn't going to be any money coming from the treasure."

Violet nodded. She did not seem particularly disappointed. On the contrary, she seemed excited, perhaps because it was clear that Nicholas had solved the mystery and was about to tell her. She had yet to even touch her pie, and her hands kept going to her mouth as if to cover a smile. She actually seemed almost giddy.

Nicholas wrinkled his brow. "Are you okay, Violet? You're behaving kind of oddly."

Violet rolled her eyes. *Quit stalling and tell me what you figured out. Please hurry. You must know the anticipation is killing me.*

And so Nicholas told her. He explained about the two libraries, one of them Mrs. Rothschild's treasure, the other her secret gift to the public at large. Violet, awed, slowly shook her head as Nicholas spoke. He went on to tell her about his conversation with Mr. Collum and how they had seemed to come to an understanding.

What about those missing pages? Violet wanted to know. *The ones from the diary. Did Mr. Collum not tear them out, after all?*

"He never mentioned them," Nicholas said, "and I didn't bring them up. I'm glad that you did, though, because I think I have an answer for that, too. I think the last orphanage director, Mr. Bottoms, is the one who tore them out. I think they were all pages that referred to the observatory."

Please explain, and please hurry, Violet signed. She still seemed oddly eager, even though Nicholas had explained the most exciting parts.

"It's just a guess," Nicholas admitted, "but I think it makes sense. Mr. Rothschild wouldn't have torn the pages out so carelessly, and it seems strange that he never mentions the observatory anywhere in the diary. No, I think Mr. Bottoms found the diary, and I think *he* searched for the treasure, too, and he kept the diary hidden in that secret bureau drawer, where he could consult it whenever he wished. He kept searching until right before he was arrested, and he tore out those pages in case anyone found the diary."

Why? Violet signed with evident impatience.

"Because Mr. Bottoms stole the telescope and sold it! He needed the money, see, because he had managed things so badly. He probably hoped no one would find out that the observatory even existed."

Nicholas paused, reflecting. Violet was about to start signing, when he said, "Do you know what else? I'll bet Mr. Bottoms discovered the diary right after he became director, and he actually convinced himself that he could find the treasure. That's what made him so careless and irresponsible with the orphanage funds. He thought he was going to discover riches any day, and the riches would take care of all the problems. But one thing led to another, the situation got worse and worse, he didn't solve the mystery, and he turned desperate. It's just like something John said to me on my very first morning at the Manor. He said Mr. Bottoms started out foolish and lazy and ended up foolish and crooked."

Thinking of John again, Nicholas lapsed into silence. He had at last become one of those orphans with someone to miss. He had a great deal more sympathy for them now.

You miss him, Violet signed, reading his mind. She reached forward to fiddle with the lantern, turning the flame low and then up again.

Nicholas sighed. "Of course I miss him. I sure wish I had that letter he wrote me. But I'm going to write to him soon. I guess you'll want to write to him, too, won't you? After I find out his address, I'll give it to you."

Violet didn't answer. Nicholas wasn't even sure she had been watching his lips. She seemed fixated on the lantern, once again turning the flame down and then up again. He gestured to get her attention. "What are you doing, Violet? Do you see something wrong with it?"

Violet shook her head. *Finally it's my turn to be mysterious*, she signed.

Nicholas frowned. "You're up to something."

Yes. I have a surprise for you.

Nicholas looked at the lantern, and the answer came to him. "You were signaling someone! But who—?" He turned to the doorway in time to see a figure stepping in from the windy darkness.

"Who do you think, Nick? She was signaling *me*!"

It was John.

Nicholas cried out in astonishment.

And then he fell asleep.

When Nicholas opened his eyes, John was still there. It hadn't been a hallucination, then. He hadn't been dreaming this whole time. There sat John, eating a slice of blackberry pie, his eyes twinkling in the lantern light. There sat Violet, beaming, tossing her head toward Nicholas to alert John that he'd awakened. Nicholas sat up, and John put down his pie, and the friends embraced.

"I can't believe it!" Nicholas said. "How is this possible, John? How are you here?"

John laughed. "You're the genius, Nick. You tell me."

Frowning, Nicholas considered. John and Violet looked at each other, clearly amused. And suddenly he knew. Wide-eyed, he turned to Violet. "You! You...you asked your parents to adopt John? *You're* the family that adopted him?"

At exactly the same time, John and Violet tapped their noses with their fingers, then pointed them at Nicholas. They were grinning, immensely pleased with themselves. It was obvious that they had planned this response ahead of time.

Nicholas was so excited he leaped to his feet. "But how did you do that, Violet? How did you convince them? How did you explain how you even knew about John? Surely you didn't...wait a minute. You did, didn't you? You had to! You told them about our secret meetings!"

Yes, Violet signed. *I had to. I knew they'd be upset that I'd been sneaking out. But I also knew they'd understand. I told them everything, and they agreed with me that we should adopt John. He needed a family, and he was already my good friend. Why not a brother, too?*

Nicholas laughed with pleasure. "Of course! It's perfect!" He clapped his hands.

"That's what Mr. Collum was being so odd about, Nick." John grinned and began helping himself to more pie. "Remember our last conversation, when I told you he'd asked me to do some filing, but then when I got to his office, he was on the telephone and sent me away? Remember how I thought they had changed the day of your trip to Stonetown? They were secretly arranging for the Hopefields to visit. Mr. Collum didn't want you to know about it."

"I know he didn't!" Nicholas cried, bridling at the memory.

"And he didn't want *me* to know about it, either," John said, "because he knew I'd tell you. He sure is dense when it comes to these things. I couldn't believe it when Violet told me he'd arranged it that way on purpose. At the time I thought it was just a bad coincidence. I hated not being able to tell you goodbye. I knew I was going to see you again soon, but still, I hated leaving you alone at the Manor."

"You wrote me that letter," Nicholas said. "I appreciated that, even though I didn't get it."

"I know," John said, shaking his head. "We realized you must not have gotten it after you told Violet that I was gone. From what you told her, you clearly didn't know what had happened."

I kept trying to tell you, Violet signed with a look of exasperation. *But you wouldn't listen!*

Nicholas slapped his forehead. "Back in your bedroom, when you said, 'What about John?'—I thought you were asking where he was! But you were asking if you should go *get* him!"

Violet nodded. *He was sleeping just down the hallway. And I thought you knew it.*

"So, what happened to my letter, Nick? Did the Spiders get their hands on it?" John asked. When Nicholas confirmed this, he groaned and said, "I wish Mr. Collum had been more careful with it. If it's any consolation, you didn't miss much. I thought he'd tell you who had adopted me, so I just wrote, 'See you soon, Giant Head.' I knew you'd understand."

"I would have, if only I'd had a chance to read it," Nicholas said. "For that matter, if Mr. Collum had told me it was the Hopefields who'd adopted you, I'd have known I would see you again, anyway." He looked wonderingly at Violet. "Obviously, he doesn't know that we're friends, and he doesn't know about our meetings. So you must have convinced your parents to keep all of this a secret. How did you manage that?"

I begged them, Violet signed. *I told them how Mr. Collum has been locking you in a room at night, and about the dunce caps and so on, and they agreed to keep quiet until they learned more. They thought you might not be telling the truth, but for the time being, they trusted my opinion that you were honest and that Mr. Collum is not a very wise man. They understood that you might be punished horribly if he learned about your sneaking out.*

"I've backed up everything Violet told them, of course," John said. "They're pretty shocked about how things are at the Manor. They're wondering what they can do about it."

"As for that," Nicholas said, "things are already starting to improve. It's true Mr. Collum isn't a wise man, but I'm beginning to think there's hope for him." He quickly moved on to his next question—he had so many, he'd have asked them all at the same time if he could. "But Violet, do your parents know that you came here tonight? Did they actually give you permission?"

Violet shrugged. *It really isn't dangerous, you know. We just had to promise to stick together, to be careful, and to be back before midnight.*

"And we can't come every night, Nick," said John with an apologetic look. "Only two or three times a week."

But it only has to be this way for a while, Violet signed. *Because we're also going to try to adopt you.*

Nicholas started. "What?"

We have to straighten out the finances, but we want to do it.

The trouble is just that they won't let an orphan be adopted unless the family has a certain amount of money. It's a silly rule, but the lawmakers in Stonetown seem to think you can't be properly cared for otherwise. My parents have some savings, as you know—that's how they were able to adopt John—but it isn't enough money to adopt two children, not on its own. If I don't go to art school, though—

"Wait, wait, wait," Nicholas interrupted, waving his hands. "That's what you were talking about earlier? No, no, that's not an option. I appreciate it, Violet, but it simply isn't an option. Art school is your dream! I didn't crawl through that filthy, scary tunnel a dozen times so I could come live on the farm with you. I did it so you could go to art school next year."

But you can't stay in that awful place. I asked my parents to adopt John as soon as they could because he was so miserable—you told me that yourself—but once we've figured out—

Nicholas interrupted her again. "Please don't feel bad, Violet. You did exactly what you should have done. And now you absolutely have to go to art school. It's what I want! Sure, I'd love to be in your family, but Rothschild's End is where I belong right now. I have a lot of work to do there, work that I want to do. Honestly! I don't have to live with you to see you, right? The fact that we can all still meet up here makes everything perfect."

"What did I tell you, Violet?" John said.

You said he would insist that I go, Violet signed with a rueful look.

Nicholas made a bow to John. "I see some of my powers rubbed off on you."

But are you sure? Violet signed. *Are you absolutely sure?*

"Absolutely, positively," said Nicholas, and he said it with such conviction and such a reassuring smile that Violet relented.

It was the most convincing lie he'd ever told. The thought of being in an actual family with Violet and John, with parents who sounded like the best parents imaginable, with silly little sisters to make him laugh—it was almost irresistible. But Nicholas had thought of Violet, how for her parents' sake she'd insisted that she had a new dream, and her own example shored up his resolve.

He knew he could be happy at Rothschild's End if he worked hard enough. He knew many things now that he had not known only a short time earlier. He knew that despite all the good things happening now, John would still miss his parents, and Violet and her family would still miss her brother, and Nicholas would miss having John at the Manor, and when Violet went away to art school, he would miss her, too. And in a year or two, when he had finished all the books in the library and gone away to a university (for this was his plan), Nicholas suspected that he would miss not only John and Violet but some of the other children as well.

Nothing's easy, Nicholas thought, sneaking glances at his friends, who were serving themselves more pie. *But some things help.*

Grinning with blackberry-stained teeth, John said, "Well, come on, Nick! Aren't you going to fill me in on the treasure hunt? I see you knocked some holes in the walls. So what's next?"

Nicholas and Violet exchanged glances.

"Treasure?" Nicholas asked with a blank expression. "Oh, yes—the *treasure*!"

Don't toy with him, Violet signed, giving Nicholas a stern look. *Tell him.*

"She says to tell you," Nicholas said. He saluted Violet and sat down. He did not begin right away, however, but savored this last moment before the mystery of the treasure was finally put to rest for all of them. Here they were once again, the three of them sharing secrets in the night, and once again Nicholas felt as if he were on the edge of everything. He knew that he would never forget this moment—that he wouldn't have forgotten it even if his memory had been less than perfect—and he wished he could stretch it out forever.

"Well?" John said, and laughed. "Are you going to tell me or not? What are those looks about? Wait, don't tell me you've found it! Have you, Nick? Have you actually found it?"

Nicholas looked at John. He looked at Violet. And then he grinned, tapped his nose, and pointed.

An End at the Beginning

Nicholas stepped back from the radio cabinet to look it over. Streaked with grime and draped with cobwebs, it would still need a good cleaning, but it should work—he felt sure he'd fixed the problem. Setting down his tools, he plugged the radio into his bicycle-powered generator, then climbed onto the bicycle and began to pedal furiously. Soon music was streaming out of the cabinet speakers, and Nicholas, satisfied and pleased, whistled along until he was out of breath.

He would need help moving the cabinet into his "repaired items" corner of the basement (which was already becoming crowded), so for now he left it where it stood and turned his attention to a couple of smaller, portable radios in need of repair. He was in the middle of disassembling the first one when Vern appeared at the top of the stairs. The poor boy looked frightened, as always.

"Hello there, Vern," Nicholas called up. When Vern didn't reply, he sighed and put down his screwdriver. "I assume you have a message for me?"

Vern cast an anxious glance down the passageway.

Nicholas could tell that something was afoot. "You're allowed to speak to me if one of the staff tells you to, remember? The Spiders won't punish you for that."

Vern nodded. In a squeaky voice he said, "Mr. Collum wants you to go and help Mr. Furrow with the…the…I can't remember what you call it. Your seesaw with the two butter churns."

"My teeter-totter butter churner? What, is there a problem with the chain?"

"I don't know. It just stopped working right before me and Caroline were about to get our turn on it. I didn't get a turn on it yesterday, either. And now it's getting late, and—"

"Sure, I'll be right over," Nicholas said. "Just let me grab some tools. Don't worry, you'll get your churn turn, Vern!"

Vern started to smile but caught himself. He nodded anxiously and turned as if to go.

"Oh, say, Vern!" Nicholas called up as he began gathering tools. "Have you given any thought to my suggestion?"

Vern gulped and shook his head. "I don't think I can do that, Nicholas."

"Well, think about it, will you? Tonight's the perfect

night! Mr. Griese is on duty in the dormitory, and you know how he snores. It'll be easy for you to sneak out."

Vern shook his head more vigorously.

"All right, suit yourself. But if you change your mind, come on up. I'll be leaving my room around midnight."

Vern nodded. Then shook his head. Then ran off.

Nicholas smiled to himself. He had been setting up tonight's project ever since he'd come back from Stonetown two weeks earlier. Two weeks! It was hard to believe so much time had passed. He had been extremely busy helping Mr. Collum put his suggested changes into effect, not to mention serving out his punishments. Luckily, Mr. Collum had seen that the most efficient course was to make Nicholas's "extra duties" be this repair work in the basement, which he enjoyed tremendously. At any rate, the Spiders had all been doing double duties for their own violations, so there were scarcely any extra chores to be done.

But Nicholas had not been content with repair work alone. He had cooked up several other projects, too, including the bicycle-powered generator and the teeter-totter butter churner (which had doubled butter production and which everyone enjoyed using), and almost all of them had been a success. He had even managed to help Miss Candace discover "on her own" that she needed spectacles. (She was delighted, though she did find it ironic that although she could see remarkably better now, she couldn't find her medicine drops anywhere. Her entire supply seemed to have gone missing on the very day she made her trip to the optometrist.)

The one tricky thing—the only project on which Nicholas had made no noticeable progress—had been the situation with Mrs. Brindle and Mr. Griese. Though he felt quite sure that Mrs. Brindle would be a better supervisor if only she and Mr. Griese could overcome their confusion, the mechanics of love seemed far more complex than any engine, and Nicholas hesitated to intervene for fear of breaking something. Perhaps in this case the solution was time, and time alone. Anyway, if all went according to plan tonight, spotty supervision might be less of a problem.

Having filled his flour-sack backpack with the necessary tools, Nicholas came up from the basement and knocked on Mr. Pileus's door. "I'm heading over to work on the butter churners," he said as Mr. Pileus locked the basement door. "Want to come along? I know you're on break, but if you're interested..."

Mr. Pileus nodded. Nothing interested him more than these projects of Nicholas's. He was learning all sorts of things. He cleared his throat. "I need to replace the alternator in the Studebaker later," he said as they went out the side door, "if you'd like to join me. I've already asked Mr. Collum."

"I'd love to," said Nicholas, thinking *alternator later, Studebaker later*—he was pleased by how the words' sounds mimicked that of an engine being cranked—before quickly shifting his own mental gears. "But say, are you sure the alternator is the problem? I've been thinking..."

They headed off for the farm. Neither of them appeared to have glimpsed the two boys ducking behind the gardening shed to avoid being seen. Or rather, one of the boys ducked, and the other boy was yanked. The yanked one, Vern, was now quaking with fear as the yanker, Moray, towered threateningly over him.

"I'm going to ask you one more time," Moray said, tapping his belt buckle, "and then I start swinging the belt."

"But that's it, I promise!" Vern squeaked. "That's exactly what he said. He'll be leaving his room at midnight."

Moray spat into the grass. "Yes, but *how*, exactly? You never told me that."

Vern gulped. "He said Mr. Collum has started leaving his door unlocked at night, in case he needs to use the bathroom or something."

"Is that so? He and old Collum sure are acting like old buddies now. Still, that's pretty interesting, what you say about the door being unlocked. Why would he tell *you* that?"

"Because he wants to be my friend. That's what he said yesterday. I told him no way, I don't want any trouble with the Spiders! And he said he was working on a special secret project that's awfully fascinating, and he'd let me in on it if I'd just be his friend and talk to him sometimes when no one's looking. He said he gets lonely."

Moray guffawed. "Sure he gets lonely! That's the whole point, isn't it?"

"Sure," Vern said, laughing feebly. "Anyhow, that's what he was talking about just now. He said tonight would be perfect for me to sneak out, because Mr. Griese is on duty and he snores a lot."

"Mr. Griese does snore a lot," Moray said, frowning. "I wonder where little Dumb Nose heard about that?"

Vern retreated a step. "Not me! Maybe it was John Cole! I mean, I'm sure it was, right? It had to be! It sure wasn't me, Moray!"

But Moray, lost in thought, was no longer interested in

461

Vern. Without a word, he walked away, in search of the other Spiders. Vern, mopping his brow with his shirt, sank back against the shed in relief. Then, when he was sure Moray had gone, he ran off to the farm. He meant to have his turn on that teeter-totter. After a day like today, he felt that he deserved it.

A few minutes before midnight, the Spiders made their way up the Manor stairs in almost perfect blackness. There was no moon that night, and it was overcast as well, with not even a hint of starlight through uncurtained windows to help guide the way. Clinging to one another, following the walls, the boys crept in the general direction of Nicholas Benedict's room. They were soon disoriented, however, for this time there was no candle lit at the candle corner, and they were caught up in a hushed argument about which direction to turn when they suddenly spied a candle flame in the distance. It drifted into view at the far northern end of the passage, near the rear of the Manor. Then it vanished, but they had seen the direction it was moving.

"He's already out of his room," Iggy whispered.

"Shut up, Iggy," Moray whispered, and Breaker elbowed Iggy to emphasize the point, and then the three of them hurried down the long passage, moving as silently as they could. They were, in fact, quite silent, for with this hunt in mind they had all gone to bed in their stocking feet.

When they reached the end of the passage, they spotted the candle flame again, and once again it drifted out of view.

"He's moving fast," Breaker whispered. "What's his big hurry?"

"Maybe he heard us," Moray whispered. "Come on!"

The boys rushed through the darkness, arms outstretched, until they reached the end of the passage. Once again the distant candle flame floated out of sight; once again they pursued it. They were panting now, and growing heated from exertion, and when, after rounding the next corner, they saw no candle flame at all, they were exasperated. But then, after a moment's jostling, they all realized that they were not entirely immersed in darkness. The door to one of the rooms stood partly ajar, and from within the room issued the faintest glow.

They stalked to the doorway and looked in. It was a windowless room with a few odd pieces of furniture in it. A bureau, a trunk, a chifforobe—all just visible. The boys' straining eyes soon detected the source of light. A candle flickered from behind the bureau, its light so dim that it seemed obvious someone was trying to conceal its flame. Someone hiding behind the bureau. Moray nudged the others, and together they stepped into the room, no longer bothering to be quiet.

"Close the door, Iggy," Moray said.

Iggy closed the door. Instantly they heard the telltale hiss of a candle being extinguished, and everything went dark.

"It's too late for that, Dumb Nose," Moray called into the darkness. "You should've put it out sooner. Breaker, you and Iggy track him down while I guard the door."

There followed a good deal of shuffling and muttering, the knock of someone's head against the bureau, an odd splashing sound, and cursing.

"Moray," Breaker said. "I think we have a problem."

"A big problem," Iggy said. "Plus my socks are wet."

Both of them had found the candle at the same time. It was floating in a large bowl of water, and a string had been tied to it. Breaker explained this to Moray, who, realizing that something fishy was afoot, fumbled for the doorknob behind him. His hand came upon the string, and suddenly he understood. The candle had been tied to the doorknob. When Iggy closed the door, the candle had been pulled over into the water and its flame extinguished.

Moray tried to open the door. It was locked.

The Spiders spent the next several minutes arguing furiously with one another. When at last they had grown quiet, trying to think their way out of the predicament, a voice sounded in the darkness. It was Nicholas Benedict's voice.

"Hello there, fellows," Nicholas said. "What are you doing in there in the dark? Why don't you light the candle?"

"Because we don't have any matches!" Iggy said.

"Shut up, Iggy," Moray said. He had followed the sound of Nicholas's voice and come up against the door.

"Can you hear me all right?" Nicholas asked. "Perhaps you should all gather around the keyhole."

"I don't know how you did this, Dumb Nose," said Moray, "but if you don't let us out of here—"

"If I don't let you out of there," Nicholas interrupted calmly, "then you will spend the night in complete darkness, in a room without windows. You could be in there even longer than that, actually. You're going to have to scream really loudly for anyone to hear you. Of course, Mr. Collum's going to assume that you stole his key again, and that you locked yourselves in there for some reason, and that you either lost his key or else you're trying to keep it hidden from him. Either way you're going to be in huge trouble. Again."

"He must have Mr. Collum's key!" Iggy cried.

"You're a genius," Breaker muttered. "Of course he does. How else could he lock us in here?"

"We'll tell him you did it, Benedict!" Moray growled.

"And I'll tell him that I didn't," Nicholas said. "It'll be your word against mine. You know how that works, don't you? Anyway, it's going to be hard to explain how I managed to drag all three of you up here, isn't it?"

The Spiders were silent.

"Tell me," Nicholas said, "how have you enjoyed all your extra chores? Are you looking forward to more of them?"

Again, silence.

"I think it should be clear by now," Nicholas said, "that you're never going to win. Sure, maybe every now and then you'll manage to hurt me somehow, like you did with John's letter—which, by the way, I know that you didn't read—but I am always, *always* going to make life harder for you when you do. Can you understand that? Is it really worth it? Wouldn't it be easier to call a truce?"

"What do you want?" Moray said gruffly, after another long silence.

"That's an excellent question, Moray," said Nicholas. "What do I want? I'll tell you. I want you to stop bullying everyone. Not just me. Everyone. You leave the other kids alone. If they want to talk to me, they can talk to me. And you don't stuff people in trash cans. You don't hurt them. You don't make fun of them. If you do any of those things, I will make you pay for it. It's as simple as that. If you leave people alone, nothing happens to you. Who knows? You might even make new friends. It's actually a pretty good deal."

Moray muttered something.

"What's that?" Nicholas said. "I couldn't hear you. Do you need more time to consider? I'll be glad to come back in an hour, if you like. If I don't fall asleep, that is."

"We'll do it," Moray said.

"Do I have your word?" Nicholas asked. "Your word of honor? You'll stick to your code?"

"Yes."

"Wait a minute, please. I need all three of you to say it. I have witnesses here, as well." Nicholas struck a match and relit his candle. Then he lit the candles carried by Gertrude, Buford, Oliver, and Vern. Their faces glowed, and not just from the candlelight. Nicholas returned their smiles with one of his own. He could have lured the Spiders into his trap without them, but he had thought it important to give them an opportunity to participate. All four had leaped at the chance.

"All right," Nicholas said. "We're ready."

One by one, the Spiders approached the keyhole, peeked out incredulously at the children gathered in the passageway, and promised to be good.

Nicholas unlocked the door, quickly pocketing his key, and the Spiders filed out into the passageway. Moray looked furious, and the other two looked confused. None of them spoke. Everyone seemed at a loss for what to do next. Everyone but Nicholas.

"Well," he said cheerfully, "I sure am glad that's settled. By the way, Moray, let me know if you'd like some help with your arithmetic. I've noticed you're having a hard time with it."

Moray glowered at him. "I don't want your stupid help."

"Suit yourself," Nicholas said with a shrug. "But if you change your mind, the offer stands."

Iggy coughed. He raised his hand. "Uh, do you think you could help me with my spelling?"

"Don't tell him to shut up," Nicholas said when Moray opened his mouth, and Moray, startled, quickly closed it. "I'll be glad to help you with anything, Iggy. The same goes for you, Breaker. Just think about it and let me know. There's no hurry. Only I suppose you really should hurry back to your beds. All of you should," he added, looking around at the younger children.

Nicholas started down the passage, beckoning for the others to join him. "Let's go down as a group. All of the boys should sneak back into the dormitory at the same time, so you don't have to risk opening the door more than once. Remember to keep quiet, everyone."

By candlelight the group shuffled along the passageway. No one spoke, although many a perplexed look passed from neighbor to neighbor. For the first time ever, the Spiders and the other children were in something together—they were on the same side—and everyone felt the strangeness of the situation. Some of them even enjoyed it.

When they reached the gallery, all but Nicholas blew out their candles, which Nicholas put inside his flour-sack backpack. Then, shading his own candle to minimize the glow, he led them all downstairs.

At the door to the dormitory, Nicholas gave the boys a goodbye salute. The younger ones waved at him. So did Iggy. Breaker offered Nicholas a slight upward jerk of his chin, which might or might not be interpreted as a farewell gesture. Moray made a face. Nicholas winked at him and turned away. The boys waited for Nicholas and Gertrude to leave so that there would be no light, and then they all slipped into the dormitory together.

Nicholas walked Gertrude to the door of the ballroom. It would be her last night to sleep in there—or *not* sleep in there, as had been so often the case. Tomorrow, the girls' cots were finally to be relocated into the more comfortable, renovated stable building, and the school desks would be moved into the ballroom, according to Nicholas's plan. Every girl in the orphanage was excited, and Nicholas, for his part, looked forward to seeing what they were like when they'd had a good night's sleep.

He patted Gertrude's arm and turned to go, but before he could take a step, Gertrude flung her arms about him and hugged him tightly. He had to lift the candle high to keep her hair from catching fire. He grinned as she released him, and blew out the candle, and waited for her to slip safely into the ballroom before tiptoeing away in darkness.

Alone again, Nicholas made his slow, silent way upstairs. For the first time all night, his shoulders relaxed. He couldn't quite believe he'd pulled it off. He knew that the Spiders were not going to change overnight, of course. There would still be problems. It would often be a struggle. Indeed, he thought it likely that he would continue to face one difficult challenge after another. But when had that not been the case?

Nicholas crept across the dark gallery, reflecting on the turns his life had taken since his arrival at 'Child's End. Had it really been only six weeks? He had started out friendless, and now he had two of the best friends imaginable. He had started out as a prisoner in his own room, the very room he was now unlocking with his own secret key, and now he had the run of the Manor, not to mention his beloved Giant's Head.

Inside the room, Nicholas relit his candle and settled onto his cot.

You also couldn't see past your own nose when you got here, he told himself. *Though to be fair, it's an awfully long nose.*

He giggled sleepily. Then yawned. Then shook his head, trying to clear it.

If Nicholas Benedict truly had been able to see the future, his own would have startled him to sleep at once, for he would have seen that he was destined to do things far greater than he ever could have imagined—that wonderful and amazing people would one day be drawn to him like metal to a magnet; that together with Nicholas they would form a most unusual kind of family; and that together, during one of the world's darkest, most dangerous hours, they would change the course of history.

But Nicholas Benedict saw none of this. For now he was simply a little boy on a cot, trying to fight off sleep as he had done countless times before—although this time he resisted not out of fear but for a different reason entirely.

Gazing at his blanket, Nicholas tried to focus his mind. He began to contemplate the different ways the Spiders might try to wriggle out of their agreement. He imagined the cat-and-mouse games he would have to play to keep one step ahead of them. He would need to prepare for every possibility.

He shifted his candle so that it cast better light on his blanket. With one finger he began tracing rectangles in the plaid pattern, once again imagining them as doors and thinking his way through them. His eyes grew heavier and heavier, but still he resisted sleep.

Changing direction, Nicholas began to consider the various projects he was cooking up, and to speculate about those that had not even occurred to him yet but that were sure to do so eventually. He yawned again, and again he shook his head.

He was terribly sleepy, so much so that he would soon be forced to give in and lie down. But he did not want to go to sleep. At the moment he did not even want to rest. After all he had accomplished, and considering how much he had learned and how far he had come, it is a curious fact—indeed, a remarkable one—that what Nicholas wanted now, more than anything, was to get started.